BLOOD IN THE CANE FIELD

by ANNE L. SIMON

Sewanee Tennessee

Enjoy!
Anne L. Simon

Copyright © 2014 Anne L. Simon
Border Press
PO Box 3124
Sewanee TN 37375

www.borderpressbooks.com

Blood in the Cane Field is a work of fiction. Although the story is set in a real place, the characters, situations, and location details are the product of the author's imagination. Similarity to actual persons and events is accidental.

Library of Congress Control Number: 2014936988

ISBN-13: 978-0-9898641-3-8

Cover art by Nan M. Landry

Dedicated to everyone who works in the American system of justice—a flawed system, but the best as yet devised by man.

PROLOGUE

Skree-eee. Skree-eee. Skree-eee. Sixty miles offshore in the Gulf of Mexico, a Mayday alarm screamed out over the grinding of compressors on the platform of the well-site known as the Weeks Island Number Three. High in the rigging, the failure of a critical chain cut loose a ten-ton load of drilling pipe. A bundle of deadly missiles hurtled down through the scaffolding, dead-on to crush whatever and whoever lay below. Bob Duplantis stood directly in the path, paralyzed by fear, exposed and helpless, a split second away from the excruciating pain of being crushed to a grisly death.

Skree-eee. Skree-eee. Skree-eee. A second ear-splitting shriek followed the first.

Emerging from sleep, Bob's thick forearm flung toward the source of the sound that had triggered this reactive nightmare. His own alarm clock. He swatted the buzzer to silence and quiet returned. No more May-day. He lay still, waiting for his pulse to slow.

Bob stretched out his other arm, slowly this time, to let the fingers of his hand trail gently across his wife's broad back. Marie Angelle moaned and nestled deeper into her covers, a rejection of the invitation for an encore of last night's long program. OK. OK. Be content, Bob told himself. The first and last of his fourteen days onshore were always the best, and yesterday was no exception. The Gumbo Festival up the road in New Iberia had provided a convenient opportunity to dance, drink, and indulge in warm cracklings and Tabasco-spiced shrimp and sausage jambalaya. Let Marie Angelle sleep off the extra beers that fueled their farewell fling. She wouldn't report to the hospital for her shift until eleven. He had to get up and get moving, but he could catch up on his sleep with a few winks on the chopper ride back out to the drilling platform of the Weeks Island Number Three.

Bob shuffled to the kitchen, plugged in the coffeemaker, gaped his mouth in a monstrous yawn, and opened the back door.

"Get up, Praline," he croaked in his morning voice to the golden brown lab who lay curled up on a well-chewed scrap of carpet that served as her bed. His first words of the day were always scratchy, but Praline understood her master's command. The dog unfolded from her coil and stretched her back legs to execute a perfect yoga downward-facing-dog. Five seconds later she straightened to stand on all fours, rippling her body as she shook off sleep, and loped through the doorway into the dark. Praline was entitled to a good morning run out across the cane field. For the next two weeks, while Bob worked offshore and Marie Angelle pulled long shifts at the hospital, Praline would spend all her days confined behind a chain link fence in the run along the side of the house.

Eyes crusted with sleep, Bob staggered back down the hall to the shower. On the way he stopped to check on his son. Not in his bed. Damn kid. Where do they go all night? Just eighteen and in his senior year in high school, it was time for Dad and Mom to let him run his own life. But that was hard to do, knowing what dangers lurked out there. Marie Angelle would have to deal with Bob Junior for the next two weeks. Summer school over now; got to get that boy a part-time job, Bob thought. Then he'd have to get up in the morning, and maybe, just maybe, he'd get home to bed before midnight.

Bob showered and returned to the kitchen a half hour later, now dressed in a gray jumpsuit with red and black letters spelling TEXACO across his back. He opened the back door and stuck two fingers in his mouth to whistle for his dog to return.

"Praline! Here, Praline! Come on, girl," Bob called into the first light. No response. He stepped down into the yard and got more insistent. "Damn dog, get your big ass in here."

Usually after her morning run Praline tore back into the house for breakfast. When the dog did not appear, Bob picked up the dog's leash from a counter beneath the telephone, walked to the rear property line, and stepped out onto the rough of the cane field. His heavy steel-toed boots crunched the dry stubble. A month of pitiless summer sun, without a drop of rain, had browned the sprouting weeds and opened a honeycomb of cracks in the earth. Bob moved briskly now, impatiently calling out, "Damn it, Praline. Get yourself in here! You're gonna make me miss my ride."

Past the rear of the yard, well into the fallow cane field that lay beyond, Bob barely made out Praline's silhouette at the rear of the apartment complex that faced the side street to the right. The dog's nose rooted into the sugarcane stubble. Her wide head perked up at her master's voice but swiftly dropped back to the business at hand.

"Damn dog," Bob muttered. "Probably got her snout into somebody's garbage."

Bob took long strides now, springing from the crest of one fallow sugarcane row to the next, calling out all the while, "Goddammit, girl. You're making me late, for sure."

Praline still did not respond; the dog stayed hard on task, her wide tongue lapping now at the furrow between two rows. Twitching with irritation, Bob stomped ever more quickly toward his disobedient animal.

Before reaching Praline, Bob stumbled on something in his path. He staggered, dropped to one knee, and reached out a hand to break his fall. Righting himself, his breath cut off at what he felt beneath his fingers. He yanked his hand back and waited for the return of enough breath to propel another step. He had clutched a bare arm, a dark-skinned bare arm. Cold.

A small person lay across his path, face down on the ground, head propped up awkwardly on a cane row, his feet barely reaching another.

"What the...?"

The kick of Bob's boot had not roused a twitch or a stir. A dark puddle splayed from the inert body of the small boy into the furrow between the resting place for his head and the one for his feet.

A slow slurping sound pulled Bob's eyes away from the boy's body and forward to the object of his dog's fixation. Praline's wide red tongue lapped at the chest of another body, a man stretched out on his side one cane row away, just this side of the concrete apron at the rear of the apartments. A shudder rippled through Bob's frame, from his wobbly knees to the top of his head, and he shut his eyes momentarily to block out the sight. Oh, God! Another one? Dead also? A white man. Blood oozing from this body pooled in the furrow, mixing with that from the boy.

Bob stepped over the cane row to reach Praline and her quarry. "Come here, Praline," he commanded.

The dog's nose spun in the direction of the intrusion, and a growl rumbled deep in her throat. Defiantly she planted her big paws wide apart, in position to hold her ground. Shiny brown lips curled back to expose two sharp incisors, each heading a necklace of white pebble teeth that marched back to the source of the sound. Barely congealed blood is better than the best Cajun boudin for an animal. Praline would not relinquish her delicacy without a fight.

A gargle deep in Bob's throat matched that from his dog. "Oh my God!" he whispered.

With his right hand, he reached forward to snap the leash on Praline's collar. The dog's head instantly spun to the intrusion. Bob's scream of pain pierced the early morning quiet as Praline sank her teeth deep into the soft flesh on the back of her master's hand. Blood spurting out from the wound mingled with that from the two bodies on the ground.

* * *

The EMTs who responded to Marie Angelle's 911 call put a pressure bandage on the deep gash in Bob's hand, but they couldn't complete the treatment. Bob ended up stuck in the emergency room for two hours. Paper work, waiting for the doc, more paper work, then eight stitches on the base of his thumb and instructions to use the hand as little as possible for the next two weeks. Bob had to give a detailed statement to City Policewoman Sgt. Theresa Wiltz. He didn't make the van ride to Houma. At noon, the chopper left for the rig without him.

Bob missed his shift. Two week's pay lost.

Bob Junior walked into the house about noon. "So what's all the commotion going on around here, Dad?" He tossed the comment over his shoulder with teenage self concern, not breaking his pace toward his bedroom.

"June. If you'd come home at a decent hour..."

Bob cut short the lecture he had on the tip of his tongue. What's the point? At least Junior wasn't across the field at the Pecan Gardens Apartments. Bob had banned the pick-up basketball game over there when tipped off about the other activities of the residents.

Bob headed to the fridge and pulled out a beer, popped the top, and walked out into the backyard. All the emergency vehicles had left, but four uniformed cops patrolled a rectangular portion of the field. They had cordoned it off with yellow crime-scene tape after they had finished the job of the first responders to preserve the evidence, document the scene, and collect the dead. The detectives would come later to do a thorough investigation.

Figures moved back and forth on the concrete apron behind the apartments, no doubt buzzing with conjecture about the most exciting event ever to happen at the Pecan Gardens Apartments.

again to walk up the concrete path that bisected the front lawn. Trustee labor kept the grounds in tip-top condition. To the right of the walk, in a bed of colorful impatiens, a feather-crowned Indian raised stone eyes in gratitude for the arrival of European enlightenment. To the left of the walk, in an identical flowerbed, stood a twenty-foot statue of a haughty explorer who claimed these lands for France. Farther forward, occupying a bulge in the center of the walk, a young Confederate soldier leaned on his musket. The inscription in the concrete base encircling the pedestal proclaimed: *Nobly they stood the test. Richly they earned their rest.*

I remember my grandfather pointing to these statues with pride. Yes, they made an altogether impressive display —provided one remained totally insensitive to the hubris of it all and ignored the diverse ethnic strands that truly formed the rich heritage of St. Mary Parish.

Just before I reached the front steps of the courthouse, a sleek black Camaro swept into the parking lot and docked in a corner spot. There, low hanging branches of an old oak tree provided a merciful shield from the southern sun. Only the black Camaro used this choice parking spot. An unwritten rule: this space is reserved for Tony Blendera, the assistant district attorney assigned to prosecute serious felonies in St. Mary Parish.

Tony unfolded his compact frame from the low-slung seat and greeted me with an affectionate whack on the shoulder. Tony likes to get close and touch.

"I hear tell we had a double homicide Saturday night," he said. "But you must know that already, to be coming in for jail-call this morning."

"I actually heard the commotion, Tony. Right across the highway from my house. Warden Dandy called me early this morning to tell me a double murderer had checked into his hotel, and he was bringing him down for first appearance. Of course, I corrected him. Maybe charged with a double murder, but I'd be seeing about that."

"Is this the sixth capital crime we've had this year?" Tony asked.

"Yeah. But we haven't had to try but one. Let's hope we can plead this case out and get back out to the Gulf for our weekend pleasures. Weekends are made for house projects and fishing, not baby-sitting a sequestered capital jury."

When Tony didn't continue our banter, I looked his way. He had tightened his lips together and was running his fingers through his cap of dark curls. His expression gave me the first hint the case might not be routine, not even routine for the charge of first degree murder. He confirmed my suspicion.

"Maybe, John. But I'm worried about this one. People care about the victim. We may have to go the distance."

Depressing thought. Death penalty trials were a nightmare for everyone involved.

As we walked, Tony exchanged nods with every cop and clerk who passed by. My roots in this town went three generations deep, but for the present crop of young people working at the courthouse, my twenty-plus years in New Orleans had wiped the slate clean. I had to put in more time to earn Tony's good-old-boy greetings. Even time wouldn't give me the Morgan City High School football headlines he could claim, and I might not live long enough to wipe New Orleans out of my speech.

We mounted the steps two at a time. I stretched my long legs; Tony pumped his shorter ones like pistons. Together, we entered the elevator to ride up to the courtrooms on the sixth floor.

At few minutes before nine o'clock, Tony and I stood respectfully at our counsel tables before the judge's bench in the large courtroom. Beyond the bar that separated the court personnel from the public, a scruffy array of handcuffed men and women in orange jumpsuits—the better to be spotted if they tried to run away—occupied the front two rows of pews. A thin chain tethered each inmate's ankle to its mate. A uniformed deputy sheriff stood at attention at the end of each row. Most everyone else present in the courtroom this morning formed part of the staff. Clerks, deputies, probation officers, and a court reporter busily set up operations for a routine day processing the criminal docket. Very few casual spectators came to watch preliminary proceedings.

Judge Dudley D. Wright entered through a door behind the bench, dipped his leonine head in greeting to the courthouse personnel, and stood erect behind the tall back of his leather chair. The bailiff called the court to order. Judge Wright plopped down in his seat, banged his gavel once, and raised sleepy eyes to address the imposing figure at the end of the first pew.

"Who do you have for us this morning, Warden Dandy?" the judge asked.

"We'd a full house upstairs last night, Judge. I'd appreciate your feelin' real kindly this morning and lettin' a few of 'em go. We need some space."

A bit familiar for an exchange between a deputy and the presiding judge, but most everyone in the courtroom knew that Judge Wright often called Warden Dandy to pick him up after an evening when he'd had one too many to make the drive home.

Warden Dandy had for presentation to the judge the usual assemblage of dopers, fighters, and drinkers produced by a clear autumn weekend, plus a few extra because this was Monday morning after a festival in a neighboring parish. A secretary from the District Attorney's office handed a stack of papers to Tony and walked over to hand another to me. Tony and I only cared about the top sheet—*Affidavit for the Arrest of Daniel Howard, first degree murder, two counts.* When we had dealt with that one, we'd be able to pass off to our assistants the paperwork for the lesser offenders. Second-in-command could handle the run-of-the-mill criminal docket.

Warden Dandy led a slight young man before the judge and announced his name. "Daniel Howard, your honor."

"Are you Daniel Howard?" the judge asked.

The prisoner did not answer or even raise his head.

"Look at me, boy. Is your name Daniel Howard?"

"Uh-huh."

"You are brought before a judge to be told why you are being held in jail. You have been arrested for..." The judge scratched around in his papers to find the one for this defendant and continued his sing-song recitation. "Do you understand you have two charges of—first degree murder?"

"Yes, sir," the prisoner answered, barely above a whisper.

"Your bond has already been set by the judge who signed the warrant for your arrest. Oh, I see that I did that Sunday evening. Your bond is set at... Oh, I see that $500,000 has been deleted and you are being held without bond for these capital charges." The judge raised his head from his papers and looked directly at the prisoner. "Do you understand that?"

Silence.

"Do you understand you are held without bond?" Judge Wright bellowed.

"Yes, sir."

The judge returned to the recitation he'd given a thousand times. "You have the right to a lawyer, and if you cannot afford one, I will refer you to PDO, the office of the public defender. They will provide a lawyer for your defense. Do you wish to have a lawyer appointed for you?"

"I don't have any money."

Not exactly responsive to the question. I took the cue and stood up at my table.

"Fine. I will refer you to Mr. Clark." The judge nodded

to me. "Would you like to speak to Mr. Howard at this time, counselor?"

"Yes. Just for a moment, your honor."

Warden Dandy signaled to another deputy sheriff to take over the presentation of the remaining prisoners and placed a large black hand on the sleeve of the orange jumpsuit worn by his special charge. The warden guided the young man, shoulders slumped, shuffling in white socks and black shower clogs, toward an anteroom behind the counsel table. I joined them.

I greeted my new client. "Good morning, Mr. Howard. My name is John Clark. What do you like to be called? Dan? Daniel?" I asked.

"Danny's fine." Only those in the first few rows could have heard his mumbled response.

"First of all, Danny, don't talk to anyone about what happened unless I am with you. OK?"

"I already told them stuff."

Damn. I waived Warden Dandy out of the anteroom and shoved at the door. I indicated a chair to Danny.

"Just don't say any more unless I'm with you, OK?"

The door popped open. I shoved it again, and the latch caught. I sat opposite Danny and introduced myself a second time. I tried a little small talk as I checked the paper in my hand to find his date of birth. He looked like a boy.

Big dark brown eyes looked up at me. "Can you get me out? I don't like it here."

I didn't answer directly. "I'll be up to see you this afternoon. Then I'm going to talk to the district attorney and look at the reports. Remember what I said. Don't talk to anyone about what happened. OK?"

"I guess so."

I opened the anteroom door and turned Danny over to the warden. His charge on leash, Warden Dandy guided Danny's hobbled steps through the courtroom and into the hall, past a knot of people who had gathered there, and into the elevator that would carry them up one flight to the jail on the seventh floor.

Tony joined me in the hallway. He appeared to be searching the small crowd, but he didn't find the face he was looking for.

I looked again at the paper in my hand and shook my head. "Holy shit, Tony. Did you see the date of birth of that kid? He's just a few days into being eighteen years old."

Tony's eyes didn't meet mine. "Old enough to go to war, as they say. The detectives tell me he admitted he did it."

I felt an onrush of irritation. "Don't flip me off, Tony. We'll see about any incriminating statements he might have made. You know the Supreme Court says you can't take a confession from a kid without his parents present."

"He's of age."

"Barely. Does some miraculous change take place on the very day of an eighteenth birthday? Kids are different, especially boys. Slow to develop that frontal lobe, the part of the brain that controls impulse. The Supreme Court has told us that."

"Easy, John. We've got a long way to go with this one." Tony wore his amiable public face, but his voice had an edge of caution. He ran his hand through his black curls again, and he still avoided my gaze. "For your information, I think the kid's a killer."

Tony turned and disappeared into the stairwell to walk to the offices of the district attorney on the fifth floor, one flight down.

Damn.

* * *

With each step up the narrow stairs that led to the jail on the top floor of the courthouse, the heat and the odor increased. Stale food and sweat. The stench took a bit of getting used to, even when you knew it was coming. My body treated each visit as a fresh assault on the senses. I had left my coat and tie downstairs and carried a bottle of water.

Charlie Dandy, the warden on duty, known around the courthouse as Black Charlie, must have watched my arrival on one of the screens that monitored his domain—the corridor of cells on his side of the heavy metal door that secured the parish jail. At my knock, Warden Dandy turned his chair away from the screens and swiveled toward the door to the landing where I awaited a summons to enter. He buzzed me through.

"Who you wantin' today, Mr. Clark? Your new client?" Charlie asked with good humor.

"Yes." I glanced at the paper in my hand. "Daniel Howard."

"The kid. Sure thing. I've got him back there by himself. I'll put him in the lawyer room for you."

"So what happened to the A/C this time?" I asked. "Broken again?"

"As usual. The motor's running but the breeze ain't what you'd call cool. Thank God we've had our last summer up here. The new jail should be finished by springtime. Hold it a sec, Mr. Clark. I'll go switch on the fan in the lawyer room. That might help a bit."

Charlie bent over as best he could with a gut the size of a watermelon. One fat finger pushed in a button on the ancient device standing on the floor, a rusted cage that covered four wide blades. I couldn't feel any breeze, only heard an aggravating whir.

Charlie disappeared down the hall and returned with his prisoner, prodding him from behind. I stood and greeted my client, but I couldn't shake the manacled hand. He barely grunted a response.

"I don't like it here," he mumbled.

I looked again at the papers in my hand, and then to the smooth young face before me. *Affidavit for the Arrest of Daniel Howard, Black Male, DOB 9/30/1987.* An ink line struck through the word *Black*; a handwritten entry,

White, floated in the space above the line. This morning I had been so fixed on the date of birth that I hadn't noticed the ambiguity about race. An entry at the bottom of the page read *Sworn to by Captain Brett Daigle, Deputy Sheriff, Parish of St. Mary.* A second affidavit, *Sworn to by Sgt. Theresa Wiltz, City of Franklin Police Department,* had an identical correction in the caption. *Black* lined through; *White* written above.

Wait a minute. I reached up to scratch my forehead. White? I looked again at the sepia-toned face before me, the cap of curly hair cropped short, large coal-black eyes, full lips and wide nose. Distinctly African-American features. There had to be a story here.

"For now, I'm your court-appointed lawyer, Danny, but if your family wants to hire someone else, that's cool. I'll just step out of the picture. Do you think they're going to get a lawyer for you?"

"Naw. Can I go home now?"

Oh, boy. A client who doesn't get it.

"Right now you're being held without bond. The usual bond for a capital offense, if we can get one, is a million dollars. I might be able to have that lowered a bit, but unless you have an oil well or a pot of gold, I doubt I could push the number low enough for you to bond out. I think you'll be in here for a while."

"Fuck it!" Danny sank down in his chair. His shoulders sagged; his head fell forward. I sat down across from him.

"Let's talk for a minute. You do know that you have very serious charges? Just about the most serious. First degree murder, two times, it says here. Do you understand that?"

"That's what they tell me."

Danny appeared to be studying his hands. Light brown on top, pink on the underside.

"Tell me a little about yourself. It says here you live in Franklin, at 111 Pecan Street. I think I know where that is."

"South side, off East Main."

"Is that near the McDonald's at the corner of Pecan and Main?"

"Yeah. A couple of houses farther down Pecan."

"That's near the Pecan Street projects. Pecan Gardens Apartments I think they call it."

"Yeah."

"And in front of the cane field where this is supposed to have happened, right?"

"Yeah, man."

Directly across the highway from my house, I wanted to say, but held my tongue. On my usual route home, I would turn left, not right, when I reached Pecan Street, take the shell portion of the road down toward the bayou, and cut into my property from the side. Maybe one day I'd have a front entrance on the highway, but I had twenty-five years of woods to clear out first. The whole place turned wild when we left, and my grandfather became some kind of recluse. Without care, in Louisiana any land that isn't underwater quickly turns into a thicket fit for the Big Bad Wolf or, in Cajun legend, the *Loup Garou*. I'd been doing a lot of work on the place but wanted to clear the backyard slope down to the Bayou Teche before tackling the woods in the front.

Danny sat perfectly still. What gives with this kid? After a night in jail, my first-time clients were usually jumping out of their skins, babbling nonstop about the unfairness of it all. I decided to try to get a few facts.

"This happened Saturday night, I see. Did you go out last Saturday night?"

"Yeah. I went out."

"Where'd you go?"

"A party at the apartments."

"Tell me about that party. Do you know what happened there?"

A slow head bobble, right to left. No. Well, I wasn't

going to give up yet.

"It says here that the two victims were Clyde Carline and a John Doe, a young African-American boy who has not yet been identified. Did you know them?"

"I know the Carline dude."

"How do you know Clyde Carline?"

"I seen him around the apartments sometimes."

"He lived there, I'm told. Right?"

"Yeah."

"Were you and he friends?"

"Shit, no." Aha! A sword thrust of irritation.

"Did you ever talk to him?"

"Not if I could help it."

Hmm. Not good.

"No one seems to know who the boy was. Do you have any idea?"

"No, man. No idea."

I pondered my options. I could question Danny some more, but I didn't usually press my clients for details so early in the game. Squeezed tight at the beginning, they just told me a bunch of lies they had trouble letting go of later. The truth wasn't essential for a defense, but I could do a better job when I had it. If I waited until I earned a little trust, they were more likely to give it to me.

But I didn't wait too long. After a period of feeling sorry for themselves, even the flat guilty had a way of convincing themselves they really didn't do it.

"OK. Tell you what. I bet you haven't had much sleep. This place isn't exactly the Hilton. I'll check on you again tomorrow and we can get better acquainted. For now, is there anyone I can call for you?"

"Naw."

"How about your parents?"

"You could call my mom, but... A very tentative answer.

"What's her number, Danny?"

Danny offered the telephone number and I wrote it down.

"Is there anything that I can get for you? Candy bar? Magazine?"

"Naw."

"OK. I'll see you tomorrow, then—or maybe in a couple of days." I quickly corrected myself so I didn't make a promise I might not keep. "For now, and from now on, Danny, do not talk to anyone about these events without checking with me first. Do you understand that?"

"But I told you I already did. I talked to those two officers at my house."

"Yeah, I know. They tell me you made a statement to Sgt. Wiltz. I'll deal with that later. But nothing from now on. Agreed?" I just wanted to freeze this story until I could get hold of some facts.

"OK," Danny answered.

Danny interrupted me when I stood up and went to the door to knock for the warden to take him back to his cell. He fixed those big eyes on mine. "You know, I don't remember anything that happened that night."

"You don't remember anything?" I turned back to him. Maybe he was going to offer something I could use.

"It's all just a blank," he said.

"A blank? What's the last thing you do remember about Saturday, Danny?"

"I was at a party over there. At the projects. I got really buzzed. After that, nothin'."

Was this the way he was going to handle the situation? Claim memory loss?

"OK, Danny. We'll talk again soon, after I get the initial reports from the investigating officers. Then I'll know more about what we have on our hands."

I looked through the little window to catch the warden's eye. Charlie came and escorted Danny back down the hall to his cell, to one of the singles, not to the bullpen with nine other men. I was glad of that. God only knows what went on in there. There was supposed to be a monitoring system, but the cameras in the ceiling were busted most of the time. The prisoners did that.

I waited for Charlie to return so I could ask a question.

"Charlie, my man, tell me. Is that kid black or white?"

Charlie raised his eyebrows. "The kid says he's white, Mr. Clark, but he sure looks like he got black blood to me. And I guess I should know, bein' they call me Black Charlie!" A big white-toothed smile opened up the dark chocolate face. "Maybe you'd better see what White Charlie has to say about that."

The other Charlie in the sheriff's department ran dispatch. The color monikers, given to the two by their fellow deputies, distinguished one from the other.

"'Till next time, bro!" I said.

I turned to go, but Charlie stopped me with a request.

"Mr. Clark, would you do me a big, big favor? I got a skinny little white girl in here who's bawlin' her head off. They brought her in Saturday night when she got busted in a drug house. She says she had to give her kid to someone she barely knows, and she's freakin' out about it. She wants to telephone her kid every few hours. When she does, she listens to him cry for his momma and afterwards bawls so much she can't eat her next meal. I guess she's never been in an establishment like mine. Man, I don't mind tellin' you, she's gettin' to me!"

"Well, what do you know? Big Charlie's got a bleedin' heart! Sure, Charlie. I'll talk to her."

I took the booking sheet from the warden and read the terse details. *Medley Ann Butterfield, age 26. Possession of Schedule II, cocaine, over twenty-eight but under 100 grams. Bond $500.*

"Wait a minute before you get her, Charlie. This is a mighty low bond for possession of that much coke."

"Right. The arresting officer must have asked the duty

judge to set a low bond. They can't be too serious about pursuing prosecution. Actually I made a few calls, and the narcs told me that's the case."

Charlie had done his homework.

Charlie continued. "The officer who brought her in says she wasn't the target of the raid. They were serving a Mississippi fugitive warrant on her husband. You know how the narcs always tell you so-and-so's 'the biggest drug dealer in the parish?' This time Mississippi sent word that her husband, a guy named Jackson Butterfield, was 'the biggest drug dealer in two states!' When the narcs got to the house for the raid, it was chock full of dope and the tools of the trade. They had to bring her in because she was there with all that stuff."

"And her husband? This Jackson Butterfield? Is he in here, too?"

"No. He was, but he didn't stay long. I didn't have him but a few hours, and he like to tore up the place, but he stayed long enough for me to know he's a mean son-of-a-bitch. Thank God they sent him on back to Mississippi to face charges over there. I would've gladly helped him pack his bags."

"What about her lawyer? Is one of my staff appointed to represent her?" I asked.

"Not yet. Before he left, the husband said he was going to get a lawyer for her, so at call-down she followed his instruction and declined PDO appointment. He probably had in mind one of those Lake Charles or Lafayette hot-shots who are funded by the big boys, but so far no one has shown up to help her. I guess she'll get you guys at arraignment. For now, she just sits here."

"OK. I'll talk to her, Charlie."

A shapeless orange jumpsuit hung loosely on the young woman Charlie brought into the lawyers' consultation room. Curtains of limp brown hair framed a pale, tear-stained face. Blinking, frightened eyes fixed on mine.

"What's all this business about your child, Ms. Butterfield?" I asked.

"Please, sir. Help me get out of here. I've just gotta go get my baby. I'm so scared the State is going to take him away! Please help me. Please."

Now that was normal behavior for someone's first time in the pokey. Confusion, distress.

The woman sputtered out her story. She said she came from Mississippi—pretty obvious from the way she talked—and had no family or friends in Louisiana to put up the little bit of money she needed to buy release. She had a nine-month-old baby boy. The officers who arrested her wanted to call child protection to place the kid in a temporary home, but she begged them to let her find someone herself. She did, passing her child off to an older lady who came out of the house next door to watch the commotion. She barely knew the woman.

The story touched me. I made a few calls to verify Charlie's report that the narcs had no plan to pursue the serious charge against her. I called Judge Wright, explained that narcotics was not opposed to having her released, and arranged for an ROR—release on recognizance. That brought more tears, a torrent of blubbery gratitude, and for me, a moment of satisfaction. Very few of my clients even said thank you.

Walking back down the stairs to the elevator on the public floor, my thoughts turned back to Danny Howard. A killer? Most of my clients were guilty, of something if not the charge brought against them. I knew that. I spent more time with serious felons than with friends or family. But this kid? There had to be a story there. If he had killed, maybe I could figure out why.

GETTING STARTED

After my first visit with Danny in the jail, I headed for the fifth floor office of the District Attorney to find ADA Tony Blendera. The receptionist said he was out for the day. I left word that I needed to see him. By the end of the week, I had become anxious. Tony hadn't returned my repeated calls, and he was never in the office when I stopped by. I also noticed his parking spot frequently empty.

Did he have a personal problem? Did his absence have anything to do with our new case?

I'd always trusted Tony. Perhaps not every defense lawyer felt the same about him, but he'd played straight with me. I didn't play games or plant error, and I always tried to be thorough without being a nitpicker. Maybe I got special treatment because I defended the very serious cases in which he needed vigorous opposition to prevent appeal court reversals for incompetent counsel. But now I had begun to think Tony was dodging me. I finally found him in his office on Friday.

Tony apologized for being out-of-pocket and tossed off an explanation. "A little trouble on the home front, and the big boss had me doing political shit."

I raised my eyebrows in invitation for him to tell me more, but his glance slid off to the side.

I swallowed my pique. "Not urgent. I'm just looking for whatever you've got for me on Danny Howard."

Tony's eyes avoided mine once again. "Nothing new. You have those two affidavits that were attached to the warrant of arrest. That's all I have. Brett and Terry are still working on their full initial reports."

"Do you have the medicals?"

"Not yet. You know we called in Dr. Petain for this one."

Dr. Emile Petain worked all over the area doing forensic autopsies for serious cases. The information that Tony had called him for this one confirmed for me that Tony was putting together a vigorous prosecution.

"You'll get everything as soon as I have it," Tony said. "But Brett did tell me he has physical evidence and an incriminating statement that pretty well nails your client for the deaths of both Clyde Carline and the black boy. Open and shut, he says."

I snickered. "Don't they always say that?"

"Yeah." Tony smiled and his blue eyes sparkled. "Cops never understand why I can't just say good morning to the judge and jury, put the investigative reports in evidence, and get an instant verdict of guilty. Big clout politicians have the same tunnel vision. But I guess no one understands the other fella's job."

'Big clout politicians,' Tony had said. And he started our meeting with a reference to political shit. What did we have going here?

Although I could sense Tony wanted to move me on, I decided to poke around a bit. Maybe the officers hadn't filed official reports, but I knew they loved to talk. They wouldn't be keeping quiet about a double murder, especially one with some political twist. I knew he wouldn't give me a paraphrase of my client's statement—the exact wording would be critical evidence—but maybe there were other questions he might be willing to answer.

"What physical evidence did they get, Tony? I don't think there could have been much left at the scene."

"Hell, no. But they have some. You'll hear about that when you get the initial reports."

Tony just kept trying to close me out. I looked him in the eye and posed the big question. "Tony, are you going to ask for the death penalty in this case?"

He punted. "We have no decision on that question yet, John. It's only been a few days. But looks like it fits."

"For crying out loud. The kid's barely eighteen!"

"That's old enough."

"Technically, yes. But..." OK. So be it. I decided to change gears. "Tell me about Clyde Carline. I don't know the recent history around here, but the word on the street is he came from a family of some importance. But he was living in the projects. He must have been one of the very few white guys in there. What's the story with that?"

"You're going to hear a lot about that story, John. Clyde Carline had a bad accident as a young man—a vehicle hit him head-on and left him with serious head injuries and brain damage. After years of rehab by his family, he finally recovered enough to be able to live on his own. The family picked the Pecan Gardens because they had a connection to the manager and it was close to home. His sister went by every day to give him his meds and to see he had food. Carline could be difficult. He talked with no filter, but he made friends in there. They understood him. He had a community. That's what has the family so upset. And you do know his uncle is the senator. The guy with the big cattle farm in Centerville

"Yes, I know. Senator Robert St. Germain, chairman of Judiciary A, the committee that must bless every proposed piece of criminal law before it goes on to the legislature as a whole. Every DA pays him homage."

"Yes, the one and only."

Had I picked up a hint of disgust in Tony's voice? Was the senator the occasion for the political shit he had to deal with that delayed our meeting?

I thought about one of my grandfather's expressions: "money purifies by volume." Senator St. Germain bred cattle for shipment all over the South and South America, but rumor had it most of his disposable income came from an all-cash business raising much smaller animals— fighting roosters. Bayou Birds, he called that profitable side-line. People who thought about running against him knew they would never match the money he could throw into his political campaigns.

Damn. A victim from an important family would probably drive the capital trial decision once again. When the prosecution considered whether to pursue the death penalty, the character of the perpetrator was of secondary importance to the standing of the victim.

"And what about the black kid?" I asked. "Has anyone figured out who he was?"

"Nope. Still working on that one. Everyone assumed the boy was one of the kids who lived in the projects, but the manager tells us no. And he wasn't one of the neighborhood kids who hung around. No one Brett and Teresa interviewed can make an ID. The boy was probably just somebody's friend who ended up in the wrong place at the wrong time, stumbled on the scene and became collateral damage. I expect we'll get a missing person report pretty soon. In the meanwhile, Brett is full time on this investigation until we get more information."

Tony was trying to get me out the door. Every response had the tone of a closing remark, but I wasn't going to let him off the hook just yet.

"That reminds me of a question, Tony. Why'd the sheriff call in Brett in the first place? I thought he was off that weekend."

"Because Brett's good, that's why. And I suspect the sheriff didn't want to leave the investigation in the hands of Sgt. Wiltz."

That had the ring of truth. Black, a woman, a lowly city cop and not a deputy sheriff, Teresa Wiltz had to contend with a good deal of resistance from the old guard. And

Brett was the deputy the sheriff usually sent out to front for him. Six-two, 210 pounds, a touch of prematurely gray hair added gravitas for his handsome and amiable thirty-five year old face. People gave Brett information without being asked.

A smile opened Tony's face, the first one I'd seen on this visit.

"So what's funny?" I asked.

"Brett was spending the night in Lafayette at his girlfriend's when he got the call from dispatch. Around six o'clock Sunday morning, it was. He well told White Charlie he wasn't on weekend duty and hung up. Three minutes later the sheriff himself was on the line, ordering him to get his skinny ass back over to St. Mary Parish on the double. Brett was pissed. 'Just because the sheriff's ass is the size of a four-wheeler,' was the way he put it. But Brett came back in, of course."

Tony's sober expression returned quickly, as if he'd been instructed to take a certain tone with this case and had been caught in a slip. I was definitely getting the idea that our past camaraderie had been put on hold. Tony continued his story.

"I think everyone in Pecan Gardens got up early that morning. The city police stretched yellow crime-scene tape around a big swath of cane field trying to keep back the half-dressed crowd that had gathered to rubber-neck. Wait a minute. You live pretty close to there, don't you?" Tony asked.

"Across East Main and a little farther out of town. There once was an entrance to my house right across the highway, but I haven't cleaned it out yet. Now I reach my house by way of the shell extension of Pecan that goes left, down to the bayou. I guess you know I'm doing a major restoration of my grandfather's place."

"So I've heard. Everyone is delighted that you're doing so. Beautiful place. I'm told a cypress baron built it during the heyday of logging in the Basin. Big job. You've courage to take on the project."

"I enjoy it. Believe me, work on that relic takes the mind off all this stuff we deal with. You know, I actually heard the sirens early Sunday morning, and it crossed my mind to go over there myself, but I figured that if there'd been some crime committed, I'd learn about it soon enough."

"Yup. And now you have. A major crime."

I persisted in my effort to probe for more info the cops might have turned up.

"The affidavits for arrest say the two victims were both stabbed. Same weapon for both of them?" I asked.

"The coroner isn't certain—stab wounds are difficult to read—but he can't rule that out. Both wounds were probably made by a serrated knife. The size of a kitchen knife, he thinks. Maybe Dr. Petain will find out for sure."

"So Dr. Petain hasn't yet done his autopsy?"

"No. Well, maybe by now he's done it." Tony corrected himself. He added, "but I don't have the report."

Good thing. I was entitled to the report as soon as it came in.

"I'll be wanting to talk to Dr. Petain. Do I need to file a motion or will you give me a general OK?"

"Go ahead." Tony knew Dr. Petain could handle himself with lawyers. He wasn't going to give me any more information than he had in his report.

"Did anybody find the knife?" I asked.

"No. No knife. The city cops had circled the area with a half dozen 4 x 4s with light bars on their roofs, and the EMTs stomped all over the place taking away the bodies. The first responders—the coroner, the EMTs, the cops searching for the knife—did a pretty good job of serious contamination of the scene. Later, the detectives tried a metal detector. Nothing. I don't think there could be any physical evidence left out there that will do either of us any good."

"Par for the course. But they seem to have arrested my client the very next day. That's pretty quick work. How'd that happen?"

Tony paused before answering. "From what they told me, Sgt. Wiltz questioned the onlookers asking if anyone saw or heard anything. Nothing. But later in the morning, when she went back to the apartments, somebody there gave her a tip to go to see your client, Danny Howard. She and Brett went calling. They say they came up with a bloody T-shirt and took down incriminating statements." Tony stood up. "I think this is all I can tell you now. Patience, John. You'll get their reports as soon as I have them. You'd best get your information from the sworn statements. I don't want to pass on what might just be big talk from the cops."

I had learned nothing new here. What he had just told me was in the affidavits attached to the warrants for arrest. Clearly Tony wanted to move me on. OK. I surrendered, but I had to get in one last point.

"I've talked to the boy a couple times now, Tony. You know, he's just a kid."

"The law is clear, John."

I had it figured. Tony had his nose on scent. Nothing was going to change his course. Damn politics. I called it a day.

On my way home, when I got to the golden arches of McDonald's at the Main and Pecan Street corner, I didn't turn left to go down to my house. I turned right, drove the few hundred yards to the entrance of the Pecan Gardens Apartments and pulled up onto the shoulder. The complex stretched back to a sugarcane field in the rear. This cane field was in the third year of rotation, had been recently cut for plant-cane, but would remain untouched for a year. It would be next summer before a big John Deere came again to prepare the rows for the laying of lengths of cane for the next crop.

There were six clusters of structures in the Pecan Gardens apartment complex, three clusters on each side of a wide central drive. Each cluster consisted of four two-story red brick buildings set at right angles to one another. From the air, the layout would look like wooden blocks arranged by a careful child. Symmetrical narrow concrete paths webbed the buildings together. Each building appeared to have eight apartments, two upstairs and two down on the front face, duplicates on the back. Exterior stairs on each structure connected the porches of the apartments below to the balconies of those above.

A few flowerpots graced little patches of dirt on the right side of the central drive. On the left side, some scraggly bushes struggled for life in dry brown beds. A car up on blocks and some metal chairs on each lower porch completed the marks of subsidized housing. But there was no trash around, no broken blinds in the windows. These were the homes of poor people, for sure, but poor with pride. And the management obviously stayed on the job.

I made a mental note. The manager himself would probably be a good source of information about everyone who lived there. I'd ask our investigator to pay him a visit.

I checked out the numbers on the units. Number seventeen, the ground floor apartment on the outside corner of the last building on the left, must have been the home of Clyde Carline. I took a walk down the central drive in that direction. At the rear of the complex, the drive flared out to a large apron the width of the complex and about thirty feet deep. A basketball goal hung over each end of this concrete pad. Beyond the basketball apron on the right side, on an outbuilding constructed of the same red brick as the units, a naked bulb burned futilely in the daylight. I made out two faded signs. One said *Washeteria*; the other read *Telephone*. Telephone? Who had detached public telephones anymore? This must be one of the last ones in existence. Indeed, the apartment manager must have run a pretty good operation if he could keep an external phone from being torn off the wall.

The newspaper report of the double murder said that the Duplantis dog, named Praline, had found the bodies just off the concrete apron at the rear of the complex. I walked to the left and stood on the spot. Looking past the cane field that stretched out toward Main Street, I could see the houses that fronted the highway across from my house. Praline and his master must live in one of those. To my left, I saw the backs of the houses that I had passed as I drove along Pecan Street. One of those must belong to Danny's family. The whole L-shaped area formed a kind of neighborhood. Middle class and mixed race, I supposed. I wondered how friendly they were with each other.

I walked to the right, across the concrete apron to the basketball goal on the far end, in front of the washeteria and telephone. A big barrel held the evidence of a recent gathering. Empty beer bottles, Styrofoam food cartons, plastic go-cups. It was easy to imagine what went on here of a Saturday night. The thump of basketballs, the trash talk of the players, the calls of children on bikes and trikes, the spot must have been a magnet for the young people of the apartments and also for those who lived just a few hundred yards away in the houses across the fields.

While I contemplated the scene, a beat-up car pulled off Pecan Street and drove into the central drive. The car found berth next to an apartment on the right side of the complex. Then, across the central drive, someone came out on a balcony, banged on a portable barbecue pit, and opened up a couple of folding chairs. Perhaps in another hour, when the heat of the early fall had broken, this place would once again come to life. The paved areas would invite a happening for the neighborhood, just as they probably had last Saturday night.

I tried to guess how many people lived there. A few of the forty-eight units could be empty or have been put to another use. But my best guess? Well over a hundred people called the Pecan Gardens home. That was a lot of people who might have some idea about what had happened last Saturday night.

A feeling of urgency washed over me. I had already lost a week of good investigation days waiting to meet with Tony. I shouldn't let any more time slip away. If I was going to get the slow treatment from the district attorney, I needed to meet with our investigator and talk to these people before first-hand information had vanished from everyone's memory.

I returned to my car, turned it around, and started back down Pecan Street to look for No. 211, the home of Danny Howard. I found it. A brick and frame ranch, circa 1960, the middle house of five between the entrance to the apartment complex and McDonald's on the corner. The house was well cared for: grass cut, shrubbery and walks neatly trimmed. A concrete statue of the Virgin Mary perching next to the gas meter in the narrow front yard marked this house as the home of simple country folk who had moved to town.

Danny might never be back home.

Once again I wondered about Danny's parents. Why hadn't they been in touch? Usually the mothers of my felony clients called me right away. When I asked Warden Dandy about what visitors Danny had, I was surprised to learn he was in jail for five days before his mother had come by. His father had not come at all. So far, his most frequent visitor had been a Mrs. Diggers, the mother of a friend.

I would have to make a call on the family, but not until I knew a lot more than I did now. First I needed to confront Danny on the subject of his race. What was the reason for the confusion on the paperwork turned in by the investigating officers? Black lined through; white written above.

I pulled back out into Pecan Street, turned right at

McDonald's on the corner, and drove slowly along the highway. On my left, the tall widow's-walk of my house poked above the overgrown yard. What a jungle! An eyesore, really. I resolved to put 'clean-up of the front yard' higher on my list of restoration chores. Even if I didn't know what to do about the driveway, I could cut the weeds.

Across from my house sat the wood-frame home of Bob and Marie Angelle Duplantis, 1469 Main Highway East. A golden brown lab prowled a dog run in the side yard. Must be that dog Praline. I passed by, made a U-turn at the next corner, and returned home.

I put in a call to our investigator, Mike Donado. We all called him Possum. Five years ago a bullet in his right knee had taken Possum off active duty with the sheriff's office. The sheriff gave him a part time job as a bailiff, but he quickly became bored with managing the courtrooms. We were lucky to get him to come over to the Office of the Public Defender. A stiff leg didn't affect his nose for investigations, and he worked hard to keep himself trim and strong.

"Can we meet in the morning, Poss? I've got a shitload of work to do for the Danny Howard case. I need help."

QUESTIONING DANNY

Danny Howard stared at me across the metal table. "I told you I don't remember anything. I said I was buzzed. I just blacked out. Can't you get me out of here?"

Possum and I sat with my client in the lawyer's consultation room of the jail.

"No, I can't get you out yet, Danny, but I'm trying to put together a defense for you and need some information." I was determined to be patient. "So, you don't remember what happened. But let's go back to the afternoon. I want to know about before you started to drink. Maybe even further back, to when you woke up in the morning. What time did you get up?"

"Must've been around noon."

"OK. Then what did you do?"

"I called the guys."

"Who are the guys?"

"Snap-Dog and Nee-Nee."

I picked up a rustle from Possum who sat at my side.

"What is it Poss? Go ahead."

He addressed Danny. "Snap-Dog? You said Snap-Dog? Is that Mark Diggers?"

"Yeah, man. I know. Snap's had some troubles. But he's straight now. Snap's a good guy."

An exhale of breath told me Possum thought otherwise.

I picked up my questions. "Keep going, Danny. After you called your friends, what did you do next?"

"Nothin'. Just messed around home. Well, I did ask my Dad if I could have the car that night. He said I could if I got it back by eleven."

"Then what?"

"I called the guys and made a deal to pick them up so we could go to the party at the apartments."

"And did you pick them up?"

"Yeah."

"What time was that? What time did you pick them up?"

"Must've been around nine."

"Where'd you pick them up?"

"Snap-Dog up at his house on Willow Street, Nee-Nee at the apartments."

"Does Nee-Nee have another name?"

"Yeah. Neal. Neal Roberts."

Possum wrote that down. So far we had two names for Possum to run down: Mark Diggers, aka Snap-Dog, and Neal Roberts, aka Nee-Nee.

"OK. Where did you go from there?"

"We went get some beer."

"Did you drink a beer then?"

"Yeah."

"How much?"

"Maybe a forty."

My experience with people giving me an amount of beer they drank is that you can triple the number.

"OK. Then what? Back to the apartments?"

"Yeah. To the party."

Possum scribbled on a pad, writing down Danny's answers. Taking notes was an easy job right now. I was dragging the story out of Danny's mouth only a few words at a time.

"So tell me about the party, Danny. Where was it? Whose apartment?"

"Nee-Nee's mostly. But all over the place. You know, the balconies, down in the street. We moved around."

"OK. So tell me everyone who was there."

"Well, lots of us. Ace, Poochie, Snap, Cheese, Nee-Nee, of course."

I nodded to Pos. "Ace, Poochie and Cheese. Danny, what are their real names?"

"Cheese is Traylin Fields. I don't know the others right off."

"Those were all boys, I guess. Were there girls, too?"

"Yeah. Nikki Roberts, Nee-Nee's girlfriend. Maybe LaToya, Lisia. But Christ, a dozen more came and went. I can't tell you everybody."

"Keep going Danny. Everyone you can think of. Boys and girls."

Danny rattled off a half dozen more names. Possum had to scribble fast to get them down. Each person had a special handle. Possum didn't ask me to slow it down; he could go back later and get the real names.

"Everyone seems to have a nick-name, Danny. What do they call you? Do they have a name for you?"

"Yeah, they call me Lazy."

That figures.

"Let me ask you this, Danny. Did anyone have a knife at the party that night?"

Danny sputtered. "Anyone? Shit, yes. I bet everyone did."

"I mean a big knife. A kitchen knife."

Danny hesitated just a moment before answering. Wary. "There was a big knife around."

"Where did you see a big knife? Who had it?"

"It was sittin' on a chair in the apartment."

"Which apartment?"

"Nee-Nee's. Where we started the party."

"Was it Nee-Nee's knife?"

"His mom's, I guess. It came from his kitchen."

"OK. Exactly where is Nee-Nee's apartment? What

number?"

"I don't know the number. Upstairs on the right as you go in from Pecan Street."

"Back to the kitchen knife, Danny. Did anyone pick it up?"

"Yeah. Everybody did. We all picked it up a couple times."

I looked Danny straight in the eye for this question. "Did anyone take the knife outside of Nee-Nee's apartment?"

"Damned if I know," Danny snapped back. Then after a moment he added, "I didn't." He didn't look at me when he said that.

"When and where was the last time you saw that big knife?"

"Last I saw the knife, it was sittin' on the chair at Nee-Nee's."

"OK. Were there any other big kitchen knives around that night?"

"Not that I saw."

So that was going to be his story about the first part of the evening. He saw a knife, handled it, but he didn't take it outside. If someone stabbed Carline with the kitchen knife, it couldn't have been him.

"Did you ever leave the party, Danny?" I asked.

"Well, yeah."

"Where'd you go?"

"Snap and I went out for more beer."

"Did you use your Dad's car for this run also?"

"Yeah."

"And then you came back?"

"Yeah."

"Danny. You said you had to get the car home by eleven. Did you do that?"

Another hesitation. "Yeah. I took the car home and

walked back."

I had my doubts about the accuracy of that answer.

"When was the party over, Danny?"

"I don't know. It's kind of a blur. Maybe one or two."

"And you went home?"

"That's what's a real blur, man. I told you. I just don't know."

"Yeah. You don't remember." I worked on keeping skepticism out of my voice. "So when did you start remembering things again?"

"The next morning.

"And where were you?"

"Home. In my bed. My mom woke me up because the people were there."

"And that would have been Sgt. Wiltz and Capt. Daigle?"

"Yeah. The cops."

An exhale from Possum. Danny had a way not to get his story mixed up; he wouldn't have one. I'd have to find some other way to find out about the later hours of the evening, the time two people got knifed. But there was still the early part of the party to ask him about.

"Back to the party, did you ever see Clyde Carline that night?" I asked.

Danny was quiet for a few moments before answering. "Yeah, I saw him."

"When was that?"

"I don't know what time."

"Before or after you and Snap went out for more beer?"

"After, I think."

"And after you returned the car to your house?"

"Yeah. After that."

"So that means it was after eleven?"

"Shit, man, I can't be sure about times."

OK. I should cut him some slack. Who would know the

exact time something happened at that kind of party.

"Where was he, Danny? Where was Clyde Carline when you saw him?"

"Sittin' outside his place. On the porch."

"He lived in number seventeen, they tell me. That's on the left side of the central drive, farther back. Nee-Nee's is on the right side, to the front. Why did you go over to the left side where Carline lived?"

Danny widened his eyes. Was he trying to recall why he crossed the drive, or was he thinking up a good reason?

"I went after the basketball. Someone tossed it off the court. I ran over to pick it up and saw him there."

"Was Carline alone when you saw him?"

"Maybe there was someone with him. I don't know."

"Maybe?" I tried not to show sarcasm. "Was he maybe a black guy or white guy?"

Danny looked up quickly. "Maybe black guy. I don't notice that stuff. I don't care if somebody's black or white."

Oh, yes. That's his line.

"What were the two of them doing?"

"Just sittin' on chairs on the porch. I think they'd barbecued something."

"OK. Did you speak with Carline?"

"No."

"You two didn't speak?"

"I didn't speak to him, but he spoke to me."

"Oh? What did he say to you?"

"Some shit."

"What shit, Danny?"

Danny didn't answer right away, so I prodded. "The word on the street is that Carline called you a *nigger*, Danny. That true?"

"Yeah. That's true."

"And how did you feel about that?"

"Pissed, man."

I put a toe in the water. "You tell me you don't notice whether someone is black or white, Danny. That color doesn't matter to you. But you were mad about Carline calling you a *nigger*. Why's that?"

"Cause I'm white, man. And anyway, that's not a good thing to say to anybody."

"I get that. So, did you say or do anything to Carline when he called you that name?"

"Naw. I just let it be."

"OK. Did you see Carline again later, maybe when you were going home?"

"Like I told you, man. I just don't remember anything that late."

"So I guess you don't remember how you went home?"

"Well, I walked, I guess."

"Yeah, but what path did you take? Did you go back out to Pecan Street or did you cut through the apartment units, maybe cut in front of Clyde Carline's and across the field to get to your house?"

"Man, I don't know that. I was buzzed."

I sat back in my chair.

"OK, Danny. Possum, here, is going to go over to the apartments to talk to some of your friends. I'll be talking to them too. The cops have already taken their statements, I suppose, but we need to ask them what they remember. We'll be back up here to see you in the next few days. In the meanwhile, try to think more about that night. We need to figure out how everything came down." I stood up. "By the way, you know the cops still haven't yet ID'd the second victim, the young black boy. Do you have any idea who he could be?"

"Not a clue, man."

"He was younger than you, I think. Do you remember anyone around like that? Very dark-skinned. Someone you didn't know but who could have been that boy?"

"I told you, I didn't see nobody like that. I didn't see

nobody I didn't know."

Possum and I were quiet going out past Black Charlie. When we were alone in the elevator going down to the ground floor, Possum spoke first.

"You know that guy they call Snap-Dog, Boss? Mark Diggers? Bad news. I knew Diggers when I worked juvie. We put him on misdemeanor probation a couple times. When he graduated to burglary, he caught a term at the juvenile prison—LTI. The kids from New Orleans have a lot to teach the poor country boys who end up with them in there. For once, Snap found teachers he'd listen to and some lessons he cared to learn. Bad teachers. Bad lessons."

I smiled. "So you think we have *another dude did it* defense and Mark Diggers could be *another dude*?"

"I wish. I'd love to have good reason to see Snap-Dog gone, but Danny is looking pretty guilty to me. It's sad. He's so young. But I wouldn't be surprised to learn that Diggers caused it all to come down."

"Are you saying you think he put Danny up to it?"

"It's a possibility. But, as you know, the talk around coffee and donuts in the cops' break room is that Danny stabbed Carline because Carline called him a *nigger*. They say Carline is simple. He just says stuff. He could have gotten Danny really, really mad. Maybe Brett and Sgt. Wiltz got a confession out of him about that. Think that was it, boss?"

"Right now I think that's the most likely possibility. There was something going on between Carline and Danny, but Theresa was careful not to call what Danny said a *confession. Incriminating statement* was what she called it. Still, I know how juries react. When they hear that a defendant has admitted anything, they find him guilty. I had some serious work to do to either suppress or seriously damage the statement he gave to Brett and Theresa, whatever he said."

We reached our office on the ground floor.

"Pos, on another subject, Black Charlie tells me Mrs. Diggers came to see Danny immediately after he was arrested, and she's been back up to the seventh floor a lot more than his own mother. What's the story there?"

"Beats me. We need to talk to the two of them, Mark and his mother. I know Mrs. Diggers, the mom, pretty well. Sappy woman. When her boy was just a kid getting into little stuff, we tried to work with her, but she was no help. She had no clue about how to get the boy under control. She worked nights and never knew where her son was. She's pleasant enough but kind of simple. Snap thinks circles around her."

"Start with them, Possum. Mark and his mother. See what they know. Then talk to the others who hung around the apartments. We need to know what they're going to say about what went on that night."

"Got it. But what do you think about Danny insisting he's white? What gives with that?"

"I'm not ready to tackle the subject just yet because, quite frankly, I'm not sure how to do it. Let's talk to those kids first. And we've got to figure out about that dead black boy. Was he really just some poor kid who stumbled into trouble? Collateral damage, Tony calls him."

We parted, with plans to meet in a few days.

That night I was too late to do any work on the house and too tired to think about cooking dinner. I stopped in town to find something to eat and didn't get home until around nine. As I mounted the steps from the shell drive, my eyes fell onto a bundle on my front porch. Did someone deliver construction materials at this time of night? Maybe the bundle had been there at noon, and I hadn't noticed. Wait a minute. The bundle moved. I made out the shape of a person propped against the wall.

I stepped warily forward and saw that the bundle was actually alive, a woman who seemed to be asleep. My footsteps startled her awake. She had a child in her arms. I called on the years of practice handling the unexpected and calmly posed my question. "Ma'am, is there some reason why you are here, on my porch?"

The woman stumbled to her feet, clutching the child. She was shivering. From fright, I supposed, because it was far from cold.

"Oh, Mr. Clark. Please. I don't mean to scare you. I just didn't know where else to go. You're the only one who has helped me."

My God! It was that woman I sprang from the jail! I told her to calm herself and sit down on one of the chairs leaning against the side of the house. I stood facing her, confronting her, really.

"Ma'am, just exactly what are you doing here?"

"Mr. Clark, I'm so sorry to be bothering you. I got out of jail OK, thanks to you, and I found the lady who kept my baby. I stayed with her for over a week, but she just couldn't have us stay any longer."

I racked my brain for the name. Melanie? No. The last name Butterfield came to mind. She ran on.

"I'm going back home to Mississippi as soon as I can, Mr. Clark, but there isn't going to be another bus to New Orleans until tomorrow morning. I sold my car for money to live on but now the money's all gone, except what I need for the bus ticket. If I could just stay here on your porch for the night..."

"What? No way, ma'am. Are you crazy? What are you thinking?"

"I'll be gone in the morning, sir. The bus station is just down the road, but I'm scared to stay in there all night."

The woman looked better than she had the day she wore the orange jumpsuit. She wasn't crying out of control now, just soft voiced, pitiful. I wondered if the duffle bag at her side contained all her worldly possessions. No, sleeping in the bus station would not be a safe plan. She'd be a target for every kind of creep, and unless someone her size worked out at the dojo, she wouldn't have the strength to beat off anyone.

The baby in her arms woke and fixed on me wide green eyes and a smile like the map of Ireland.

"Wait right there, ma'am," I said. "I'll go inside and get the number to call the shelter. What did you say your name was again?"

"Medley. Medley Butterfield."

Ah, yes. Medley.

The woman on night duty at the domestic abuse shelter answered my call but said after eight p.m. they could only take in someone brought by the police. Medley overheard the conversation. When I started to punch in the phone number for the city police, she came unglued.

"No, sir. Please don't call the police. They'll take my baby. They told me that if I didn't have a home for him, he'd have to go to foster care. Please, please. Just until tomorrow morning. We'll curl up right here and be gone as soon as the sun's up. I promise."

I took a closer look at the woman. Lovely green eyes just like her baby's. The oversize jump suit she wore in the jail had hidden some very nice curves. And she looked so sweet holding the baby. She'd definitely be a target out on the street or in the bus station. Oh, hell. I couldn't leave her on that open porch. I bowed to the inevitable.

"Ma'am, come through this door. There's a couch inside you can use."

What would one day be my living room held my work bench, all my tools, a couple of light fixtures and boxes of old hardware I'd found on Magazine Street in New Orleans. A stack of cypress driftwood occupied the far corner of the room. I had a good dead-bolt on my new front door and a lock on the one to the finished rooms in the back. She'd be safe from the outside, and I'd be safe from her.

She had other ideas. "That's OK, Mr. Clark. I'm not asking to come inside. I can just stay right out here."

"No, Ma'am. If you found this place, someone else could. I'm insisting."

I showed her to the bathroom, and then I let her sit at the kitchen table to eat a peanut butter sandwich and drink a glass of milk. And I had a banana for the little boy, who kept giving me that smile. Dammit! He was a cute little tyke.

"We'll be gone in the morning, I promise."

But they weren't. When I came into the living room at 7 a.m., they were still curled up on the couch.

"I'm so sorry, Mr. Clark. I know I promised to be gone, but I got to thinking about what they told me when I left the jail. I can't leave the state or they'll call my bond. I just don't know what to do."

Mother and son both gave me those pleading eyes. Damn.

"OK. Tell you what. I'll call the shelter again."

Thank goodness the director answered the phone this time.

"Nanette. I have a situation here."

Nanette laughed. "That's a switch. I'm usually the one with a 'situation.' What's going on?"

"I've a woman and a child who spent the night over here. I'll explain later. Anyway, they're homeless. Her husband went off to prison somewhere so I guess, to be honest, she's not in imminent danger of domestic abuse that would qualify her for your safe house. But..."

"Bring her on over, John. We'll sort it out. This isn't the craziest thing you ever dumped on me and not half as crazy as the situations I've asked you to help with. I'm still way ahead of you in the department of favors. I'll figure out something for your visitors."

After another peanut butter sandwich for breakfast, I put the pair in my car and dropped them off at the shelter.

Then I began wondering how the woman ever found my house. Somehow I had felt invisible behind my overgrown front yard. This woman was probably harmless enough, but I couldn't say the same for many of my clients. Who else might figure out where I lived and come calling?

My grandfather had a collection of guns upstairs, but I hadn't seen the inside of the locked cabinet for twenty years. Maybe I'd be wise to see if he had something in there I could clean up for my own use. The next problem would be getting back the skill to fire a gun. I hadn't had one in my hand since my grandfather took me on a couple of duck hunts when I was fourteen years old.

DR. PETAIN

In search of the morgue, I maneuvered the twisting and gloomy corridors in the basement of the old Our Lady of Lourdes Hospital in Lafayette. Stepping through a pair of swinging doors, my eyelids involuntarily snapped shut and I caught my breath, assaulted by blinding florescent light and a sharp antiseptic smell. In a few seconds my eyes adjusted. Not my nose.

I made out a tall figure standing beside one of the examination tables. Dr. Emile Petain. I needed to see if the forensic pathologist on this case would be able to give me some clue about the identity of the young boy we had come to call the second victim, although we had no way of knowing whether Clyde Carline or the boy had been the first to die. A robed, gloved, and masked man I could be only half sure was Dr. Petain raised his chin and smiled a welcome in my direction.

Dr. Petain did not interrupt his work. His gloved hands continued to caress a slick red object the size of a baseball, turning it this way and that. Smiling with satisfaction at the knowledge he had obtained from his examination, he gently returned the specimen to a large opening in the belly of the cadaver lying on the table before him, all the while giving a running commentary about his work into a microphone suspended from a cable dropped from the ceiling above his head.

"The end, *la fin*," I heard him say.

Dr. Petain beckoned to another robed, masked, and gloved figure standing across the room and pantomimed a sewing motion. He took a few steps away from the mic and spoke to me.

"Come in, counselor. Or perhaps you would rather wait for me right over there?" With a wave of his gloved hand he indicated a small office to the side. "I'll be with you in a minute." He handed a giant needle threaded with twine to his assistant. "Close for me, my good man," he said, a quick smile flashing out from under the clear plastic shield that covered most of his face.

I leapt at the invitation to leave the grisly scene—an array of chalky-pale bodies, their chests decorated with standing levees that evidenced the work of the pathologists. Blood pooled in troughs at both edges of the shiny tables. I didn't need to witness any more of his gory work. And that smell. How could anyone deal with dead bodies all day, every day?

Rumor had it that Dr. Petain had no home but slept on one of the examining tables in the morgue of whatever hospital had provided him with the last task of his day. The rumor was probably false. Maybe someone had once seen him stretch out on a table for a short rest while waiting for the arrival of a body, but every hospital provided a room, or at least a couch in the doctors' lounge, for those caught on duty past bedtime. Indeed, a soft couch stretched across the back wall of the room where Dr. Petain had indicated I could wait for him to join me after he had finished his work.

I welcomed the introduction of Dr. Petain into the case of Danny Howard. Some fortunate and singular set of circumstances brought this brilliant, Belgian-born, Johns Hopkins educated pathologist, to settle in south Louisiana. Perhaps only in this unusual corner of the New World would such an odd bird feel at home. Louisiana loves characters, particularly ones with unflagging good humor and a charming French accent. Odd bird indeed, but I liked the guy. Clearly, he had a first-class brain and an engaging amiability. I spent most of my non-working hours alone.

Looking around for companions who didn't come with romantic expectations—I'd sworn off entanglements—or had wives and children in tow, I often wished I could know Dr. Petain better.

After preliminary courtesies in which we each invited the other to use Christian names, the doctor and I settled down in metal chairs around a plastic table.

"How can I help you, John?" the doctor asked.

"I came to talk to you about the autopsies of Clyde Carline and the young boy found dead in St. Mary Parish two weeks ago. The prosecutor tells me you have performed the forensic examinations."

"No, no, counselor—John. Not yet. And I do not believe that a full forensic autopsy of the body of the older man, Clyde Carline, will be necessary."

"No? Why not?"

"I have seen both bodies and agree with the on-the-scene report of your coroner about the time and cause of the deaths." Dr. Petain rolled back his eyes to tap into his amazing memory. "As I recall, after his examination of the body of the older man, the coroner reported a white male, about 175 centimeters tall, weight 82 kilograms, age between thirty-five and forty-five. A large scar creased his forehead, but that wound had no relation to the mode of his death. The man died in *exsanguination*—a bleed-out, you would say—from a stab wound in the upper stomach."

Someone might describe the grin the doctor flashed as ghoulish.

"From the state of post-mortem lividity—as you no doubt know, that's the gravitational pooling of bodily fluids —and unresolved rigor of the body, your local coroner fixed the time of death sometime between two and five on the morning of the date he performed the field examination. 7:25 a.m. last 3 October, I believe."

The doctor had total recall. As he spoke, he worked his lips as French-speakers do, mouth mechanics that added precision and an imprimatur of veracity to his speech. With his accent, listening took a touch of extra concentration; as a result, his words reached the ear with emphasis.

"The coroner found the time and mechanism of death of the younger victim—African-American, approximately twelve years of age, 150 centimeters tall, weight 35 kilograms—to be the same. However, according to the last information I received from the district attorney, no one has yet made an identification of the boy. Is that still the case?"

"Yes. Still no ID."

"Quite unusual. For that reason alone, a full forensic autopsy might well be warranted for the boy. Our bodies carry a good bit of information about the experiences we have had. But you know, for many people the prospect of an autopsy of their loved one is distasteful. Under circumstances indicating foul play, the permission of survivors is not required for us to proceed, but it is a courtesy to give the family an explanation so they may understand and accept the necessity for the procedure. I would like to allow time for a family to come forward."

"You are kind, Emile. How long can you wait, medically speaking?"

An impish grim widened the doctor's face. "As long as the body rests in one of our facilities, we have time. But maybe another week would be an appropriate deadline."

The doctor knew I was asking how long before a body began to rot.

I sat forward in an invitation to close out our interview. "I'm sorry to have taken you from your work, doctor. I thought you had done the autopsy already. If you need to get on with your day, I'll understand. I could come back."

"No, sir. No hurry. Actually I am through with my work-day."

"In that case, maybe you have a little time to tell me how your forensic autopsy might help us identify the boy.

Perhaps you could run through your procedure."

"Really? You would like to know what I do? Most people would rather not hear about my work."

"Yes, I would. I have heard you testify in several cases, but usually you speed through the details."

"And you want to hear them? The details?" The doctor looked genuinely pleased to be asked to speak about his work. "OK. When I receive a case at one of the facilities where I perform my autopsies, a hospital morgue, I first remove the body from the body bag and place it on a table for an external examination. I take photographs. I note ethnicity, sex, age, hair color and length, eye color, other distinguishing features. I note the clothing in which the body was presented. I look for evidence such as plant material, paint flakes, substances under the fingernails, any foreign objects or substances clinging to the body, especially the eyebrows." That impish grin again. "The eyebrows are one of my favorite sources for information." His francophone lips pulsed in and out.

"The clothed external examination completes step one. Then I undress and weigh the body, which I can do quite easily here on the hospital's beautiful new cadaver dissection tables. Perhaps you saw them on your brief look into this morgue?"

He swept his arm back in the direction of the room where I had found him.

I nodded my head in response. I definitely did not want to go back for another opportunity to be in there. Especially, I didn't want another look at those corpses.

Dr. Petain continued. "When my subject is undressed and exposed, I proceed to an external examination of the naked body, noting birthmarks, old scar tissue, moles, tattoos, possible fractures. I take dental impressions. I clean and examine wounds, if any. Again, I document all findings and lack thereof. That process ends step two. When these external examinations are complete, I proceed to set up to go inside. Do you want me to continue?"

"Yes, I do."

The doctor rubbed his hands together. No wonder people compared him to Boris Karloff.

"I place a body block beneath the upper back, thrusting forward the chest. That position facilitates my next step—a Y-shaped incision, starting at each shoulder, meeting at the sternum, and then a straight cut to the pubic bone. This incision enables me to lay open the chest and belly to expose the essential organs."

The doctor paused. "I will spare you the details of the evisceration, my friend, except to say that I remove each organ and place it in a pan at the side of the table. I weigh and carefully examine the heart, lungs, abdominal organs and their vessels. I usually excise small samples of each for study by others. I examine the stomach and intestinal contents, particularly looking at the state of digestion in order to determine the length of time elapsed since the last meal. You know, counselor, the stomach is often the most helpful organ for confirming time and manner of death and yields a variety of other important information about events prior to demise. We are what we eat, as they say."

The doctor playfully flicked up his eyebrows. "Right now I must be a nonentity. I haven't eaten all day."

What? Was the cafeteria closed? An additional rumor about this guy was that he pursued neither haute nor Cajun cuisine but dined exclusively on complimentary hospital cafeteria fare. He spent next to nothing and sent most of his considerable earnings to his family back across the sea.

I had skipped lunch as well, but at that moment didn't desire to see food any time soon.

"Following the examination of the body, I drill into the head to study the brain. That is the last step in the forensic autopsy. I think I have now told you enough, except to say that my work is often supplemented by toxicological, biochemical, and genetic tests that others perform on the samples that I have taken from the body. In the case of the young boy, if we are still without a positive identification, I will no doubt order these additional studies."

"You do put Humpty Dumpty back together again, right?"

"Oh, yes. Everything back in its place. It is really quite remarkable that after reconstitution of the body, and a little stuffing here and there, the practice of open-coffin-viewing of a deceased, so popular in this part of the country, can proceed with no one aware that I have done my grisly work."

I believed that thereafter when I knelt at the *prie-dieu* to say my prayer for the departed, I would add an apology for whatever post mortem indignity the deceased might have had to endure.

"From that process, from a forensic autopsy of the boy, doctor, what do you think you are likely to learn in his case? Any preliminary thoughts?"

The doctor tilted his dead provocatively. His deep-set eyes twinkled. "Now counselor, how many times have you cross-examined me in court? You dissect my testimony as carefully as I dissect my cadaver. You require that I give you medical findings, no more, no less. You would never allow me one shred of conjecture or supposition."

"Good point, doc! Let me ask you the question in two parts. First, having reviewed the coroner's report, from which you've obtained a few bits of vital information, can you draw any conclusions about the boy's background or lineage?"

Again, Dr. Petain raised his eyes to facilitate the working of his brain. "Slight, small in stature, perhaps under-nourished. No, counselor. You would not let me draw any conclusions from those limited facts."

"You are right. Second question. Perhaps you could tell me some of the findings you might be looking for as you pursue your complete forensic autopsy?"

Dr. Petain now had a chuckle to match his elfin grin. "Yes, indeed. I will look for clues about the boy's physical development, his medical history, his genetic background."

"Don't we already have some? He had very dark skin—blue-black I believe the coroner noted. On the cusp of puberty but small for his age. No one has come forward to say they miss their child, brother, relative, friend. Wouldn't we be able to venture a guess that this boy might be an orphan? Or perhaps a recent immigrant who left all family behind?"

"No, counselor. You lawyers might present a courtroom hypothetical based on such limited information, but you would not let me get away with a medical opinion to that effect. My clinical findings would not rise to the reasonable medical certainty that you, of all the lawyers who question me on the stand, require in testimony from a pathologist. I believe if I tried to spin out possibilities, you would ask me if I had the qualifications of a forensic anthropologist. And I do not."

His eyes twinkled. He also liked the sport we played.

"Good point, doc. When I've had you under cross-examination, I may have succeeded in causing you to emphasize the aspects of your report that favored my client, but I've never uncovered a flaw. Usually I try to get you off the stand just as quickly as I can."

The doctor's precision made me speak precisely as well.

Dr. Petain ran his hand over his shaved head. "One item that will be of interest to me in a forensic examination, counselor, is the wound. Serrated knives shred the sides of entry. We have photographs of the wounds of both bodies, and it appears your coroner believed the mode of death of both victims to be the same. However, the coroner stopped short of saying that the same knife killed them both. I will examine the boy's wounds very carefully. I just might be able to say, more probably than not, the same instrument had been in use.

Not reasonable medical certainty, of course, but enough to support a possible scenario."

And I'd be trying for the flip side. I'd try to get the doctor to say there were some differences in the serrations on the two wounds that made it impossible to be certain the same weapon had been employed in both killings. I'd hypothesize that we had two different perps. *Another dude.*

"OK, doc." I sat back on my chair. "You win. You do your job and I'll try to do mine."

Dr. Petain's passion for his profession engaged me, and I felt emboldened to try to extend our time together.

"Doctor, would you be interested in joining me for a po-boy at Pappy's Oyster Reef around the corner?"

Dr. Petain looked startled, as if to say *doesn't everyone know I don't go anywhere with anyone.* He stammered out a response. "Well, I don't know." He looked down at his scrubs and found his excuse to decline the invitation. "I'm not dressed to go out for dinner."

Another story that circulated about this unusual man was that he had but one set of civilian clothes, the ones he wore to court—a tan corduroy jacket dusted with a patina of age, a blue oxford shirt that showed white threads at the collar points, and slacks that stopped two inches short of fashion. He did not see the need for a more complicated wardrobe; hospital scrubs did just fine for the daytime, thank you. At the end of each workday, he tossed the scrubs into the hospital laundry basket and chose another set to wear as pajamas. Today's costume was baby blue.

"Believe me, doc, you're dressed just fine for Pappy's. Hey, I'm not gay and trying to hit on you or anything!"

The words were no sooner out of my mouth when I bit my tongue. Did my smart-aleck remark offend? No. Dr. Petain tipped his chair back and laughed out loud. But the response he gave me came as a surprise.

"Well, I am. And I promise not to hit on you."

Dr. Petain waited a moment to see that I hadn't reacted

badly to this revelation, then he jumped up from his chair. "Just a few minutes, counselor," he said. "I'll put on a fresh set of scrubs. I don't want you to think about what might have splashed on this suit."

He had a beer with his po-boy, but I didn't. We talked about football and New Orleans jazz. The oysters were great.

* * *

The dinner served to take my mind off Danny Howard. All the way home I thought about my next house project. I had two cypress doors leaning against the wall of what would one day be a dining room. I'd found them in New Orleans at a wrecking company on Magazine Street, stripped off many layers of lacquer, and covered the wood with a light coat of wax. They were beautiful. I had a box of brass hardware I had found at another shop, but I hadn't yet figured out if I had any pieces that would work on my doors. Too late tonight, but tomorrow evening I'd open up the box and see if I had a good marriage. Emile Petain said he'd done some of this kind of work. Maybe he'd give me a hand hanging the doors.

When I stepped into the kitchen, the little red light on my telephone indicated a voice-mail message. I punched the button and heard Tony's voice.

"I'm calling to give you a heads-up, John. When the fall Grand Jury is convened the week of November 15, we're planning to present the case against Danny Howard. I'd like to talk to you about that. Would you meet me in the parking lot tomorrow morning at eight?"

Breath shot out of my mouth. I know I said a few choice words. I had never before heard of taking a case to a grand jury when a victim hadn't yet been identified. What the hell was going on? I called Tony back, but he didn't pick up.

You bet I was in the parking lot at eight in the morning, sitting on a bench waiting for that Camaro to pull in.

"So what is all this *caca*? We don't even know who that

boy was. Since when do you take a case to a grand jury when the victim hasn't been identified? Unprecedented rush."

"I knew you'd steam over this, John. And I think I owe you a little explanation. Not my choice, but the word came from on high."

"What do you mean? From Mr. Strait?"

"Let me just say I have my marching orders."

"Dammit, Tony. Let me guess. Politics. Clyde Carline's uncle is a state senator, and sits on the Judiciary A Committee. The DA needs him now and for the foreseeable future if he wants to get legislation through or to block any bills the DAs don't want. All forty-two district attorneys in the state expect Mr. Strait to keep him happy. Right?"

"You didn't hear that from me. I will say that I've had a few calls demanding I get the case moving. I'm sure he has also."

I was disgusted. "Shit, Tony. That doesn't sound like Mr. Strait. Catering to political pressure like that."

"So go talk to him, John."

I did. Jumped in the car and drove up the road to his office at the courthouse in New Iberia. The receptionist/personal assistant Bonnie, who guarded the door like Cerberus, let me in right away. District Attorney Gerald Strait didn't waste time on small talk.

"Not surprised to hear from you, John. I'm sure you're looking for an explanation for my decision to take the case against Danny Howard to the fall Grand Jury and then set the matter for trial."

"You bet I am, Mr. Strait. I've never heard of trying for an indictment when you haven't identified the victim."

"And you suspect that I've allowed political pressure to influence my decision?"

Mr. Strait had a hand on one of his four telephones and the other held a pen on a stack of papers covered with columns of numbers. He put the pen down on the desk and straightened the papers until he had two neat piles, largest papers on the bottom of each. OCD, I'd say.

"Yes, I do. I've heard Clyde Carline's uncle has been insisting on quick action, and he has been mouthing off about how Danny Howard is going to get the penalty of death. Nothing like the clout of an influential legislator to..." I had the good sense to stop speaking before I said something I'd regret.

Mr. Strait smiled. "There's an upside for you, John. The prosecution is taking a risk the Grand Jury will fail to indict without an ID."

"Give me a break. With no one there to tell them that's exactly what they should do? What's the expression? Any decent DA can get a grand jury to indict a ham sandwich? They only hear one side of the story and the way the prosecution wants it told."

"You're right. But how about this? I say 'yes, sir' to the senator today and tomorrow tell him he already got his favor."

I felt my irritation wane. As was usually the case, Mr. Strait had his reasons. Perhaps the chance a rogue juror would talk the others out of an indictment was a long shot I had no reason to expect, but everyone in the courthouse would see who sat on those hall benches waiting to testify. I might learn the identity of the key witnesses and be able to talk to them myself, which would be a possible advantage for the defense.

In any event, this development required that I put the case against Danny Howard at the top of my list and in fast-fast forward. So much to do: interviewing at the apartments, investigating Danny's background, engaging experts to prepare for the penalty phase. I called Possum, my investigator, to beg him to put aside the hundred other cases he had to cover and get out to the Pecan Gardens Apartments ASAP. I'd take the lead in investigating Danny's background.

I would save the hardest task for myself—breaking down the wall my client had built around his feelings about his race. No memory about what happened at the Pecan Gardens Apartments? Hog wash. Something went down that night and I had to find out what.

PART II—EARLY WINTER

GRAND BOIS

"Danny, the DA is taking your case to the Grand Jury in two weeks."

No response. Those black eyes remained fixed on the scarred surface of the metal table between us. Could he have seen art in the scratches? Or perhaps a message of hope? Hardly. What went on in the circuits of Danny's brain? Maybe nothing. Maybe they weren't even hooked up right.

"The cops still haven't identified the second victim," I continued, "but apparently that's not going to hold the DA back. Double homicide, he says. I guess you know the prosecution has to take murder cases to a grand jury. That's the law, and we don't have any control of the process. We aren't even in the room when the DA puts on his evidence."

It was my duty to explain all this to Danny, but his lack of interest confounded me. Infuriated me, really.

"Usually the DA puts only the investigating officers on the stand before a grand jury, plus maybe a few key lay witnesses he wants to teach some lessons in how to testify. The grand jurors decide if the DA has *p.c.*, that's *probable cause*, to bring the charge, a term of art in the law that means some credible evidence. The grand jury is a slam-dunk for the prosecution, unless the DA has purposely used the process to get cover for a charge he had to bring for political reasons but really doesn't want to pursue. Not the case here. The DA is dead serious about the charges he's bringing against you."

Still Danny didn't speak. OK. I ramped it up a notch.

"The DA tells me he'll be asking the Grand Jury to return two first degree murder indictments against you, Danny. Definition of first degree murder? Homicide when the offender has a specific intent to kill or inflict great bodily harm on more than one person. In your case, that's Clyde Carline and the unidentified boy. A possible penalty for each charge is death."

Still no response, so I gave it some more juice.

"Do you get it, Danny, that the DA will be asking the jury to give you the death penalty—twice?"

At last Danny spoke. "Yeah. I know. So what the fuck can I do about it?"

"Goddammit, Danny. You can give me little help, that's what. I have a job to do here, and I need you to talk to me."

My obvious anger made a hairline crack in his wall. Danny raised his chin and actually looked me in the eye. He spoke with clear diction this time.

"I know nothing about that boy, Mr. Clark. I never seen him."

My God, he might even be telling the truth. But then, it didn't matter if he was lying or not. And it didn't matter if his insisting he didn't know the boy had a flip side—close to an admission that he had something going with Clyde Carline. My job was to mount the best possible defense to both charges. *Ours not to question why, ours just to do or die...*

"I need some facts, Danny. Let's get back to that fateful night. You've told me you don't remember what occurred late in the party, right? That still your story? That the later part of the evening is a blank?"

"I told you, man."

"OK. Then here's what I need. I've got to know everything you *do* remember about that party. Earlier. From the top, up to the time you go blank. Who was there, what they did, when they did it."

"I told you, man. I gave you the names."

"Yeah. And Possum is over at the apartments right now talking to whoever on your list he can find. Do you have any more names to give us? Other than who you told us about already?"

"Naw."

"I guess you know that I have to ask those people what *they* remember. Maybe they saw you do something. Then I come back to see if you have an explanation for what they say you did but now don't remember. OK?"

Danny said nothing.

"It's my job to put on a plausible defense. Maybe I'll be able to figure out if someone else might have done it."

At this Danny looked up and squinted one eye, and gave me just a hint of a canny smile? "Yeah, man. You do that. Find *another dude*."

They all knew that defense. *Another dude did it.*

"What about your buddy, Snap-Dog? Was he out and around Carline's apartment at the same time you were?"

Anger flashed across Danny's face. "Goddammit, no. Not Snap. You just can't do that, man. Don't try to pin this on Snap."

"Why not? Nothing can happen to him if I put him out there as a possibility, to raise reasonable doubt. He's not charged or anything."

Danny put his hands over his face and mumbled through his fingers. "Leave Snap out of this. You want to get me blown?"

Now that was interesting. He was afraid of Snap.

"No, Danny. On the contrary, I want to keep the State from killing you. Are you scared of what Snap might do? What has he to do with all this?"

"I'm not talkin', man. I'm out of here." He stood up.

"Sit down, Danny. I'll drop the subject of Snap."

My thought was to describe this exchange to Possum and see what he could do with it. He'd love a chance to finger Snap. I gave Danny a moment to simmer down before continuing.

"Let's go back to that night, starting with the first statements the detectives took from those they say are the witnesses in this case. Do you know anyone named Marie Champagne?"

Danny looked blank and shook his head slowly.

"A lady that lives in the apartments, in number 15. Across from Clyde Carline and upstairs."

"Don't know the lady."

"The initial report of the officers says that earlier in the night Marie Champagne was inside her apartment watching TV. She heard two men talking—really yelling, she says. She looked out her window and saw Clyde Carline and his friend, a black man named Vic, sitting on Carline's porch. Apparently Vic often came over to barbecue. She heard Carline calling out to some kids who, as she put it, 'sashayed by.' Later, when everything quieted down, Mrs. Champagne closed herself up in her apartment and tried to sleep. About two in the morning she heard commotion again. This time she was pretty sure there was only one voice, and she thinks it was Carline. She looked out again, but she didn't see anything."

"So?" Danny said.

"So, do you know what the first yelling was about? When Vic was there?"

"No, man."

"Was that maybe when you chased the basketball over to the other side and Carline called you a name?"

"No way. There was just Carline when he said that. No other guy."

"Wait a minute. You told me last week there was another guy there when he called you a name."

Danny looked sheepish. "Oh, yeah. Maybe so. Maybe that guy Vic was there."

I took a deep breath. "Danny, you've just got to give me

straight answers. These details are very important. Can you understand that?"

"OK, man."

"So do we have that straight? Earlier in the evening you went by Carline's place and Vic was there with him. Carline called you a *nigger*. I hate to say that, but we're into reality now. OK?"

"OK, man."

"But you tell me that you didn't go by Carline's apartment later on, on the way home? Is that right?"

Danny flared. "I told you, man. I don't know nothin' about later. I was buzzed. I don't remember leavin' the place."

I swallowed hard to keep control. I could look at those big black eyes and ache to help the kid, and then get furious when he pulled that *don't remember* crap. Totally exasperated, I changed the subject.

"Possum and I'll go see who we can talk to over at the apartments. Maybe some of your buddies can fill in the blanks. Then I'll be back. Now, the second big problem I have has to do with your background. I need to get to know your family."

Danny's head twitched, and he drew his lips tight. His full lips. I read anger again, but pure anger, without the fear I saw when I brought up the name of Snap.

"Why you need to know them?"

"A couple of reasons. First, I see in the investigating officers' initial report that they talked to your parents the day the bodies were found, and your mom gave them a T-shirt you had thrown in the laundry. They found a spot of blood on the shirt and had it typed. Same blood type as Clyde Carline. Not yours. Do you know how that spot of blood got on your T-shirt?"

"No clue, man."

"OK. We'll get all that straight in the next few weeks when we get the DNA. The labs are all backed up right now." I got to the real reason I was asking about that meeting between the detectives and Danny's parents. "I kind of wonder about your mom, Danny. She hasn't been to see you but a couple times since you've been in here."

What I really wondered was whether his mom ratted him out.

Danny's mouth tightened. "Just leave my mom out of this, man."

"No, Danny. I can't leave anyone out of this. I need your family to be there for you, for your sake, and also so the jury knows there are people who care about you. And if we have to get to the capital phase of the trial, I have to make a case in mitigation."

"What's that *mitigation*?"

"If the jury should find you guilty, which of course I'll try very hard not to let happen, we have to tell them why they should spare your life. I'll put on experts to say why you might have done what they've just decided you did. That's called *mitigation evidence*. Another term of art. And whether you like it or not, Danny, I'm going to have to discuss your race."

Danny's half-closed eyes shot open."What kind of crap is that, man?"

"Let me ask you this straight out. The story out there is that you stabbed Clyde Carline because he called you a *nigger*. If the jury thinks you had reason to do something crazy like that, it might even be good for you. Understandable anger. They might bring in some lesser verdict that would spare your life. But on the other hand, if you were insulted and then went back to get a knife, that's a problem for us—tends to show intent rather than spur of the moment anger. Danny, these are really important details."

Silence. I bored in deeper. Possum had given me a lesson in investigations. Roots matter. Find out someone's story and you can judge him. He pointed that out when I'd introduce myself to a jury, I'd always begin with "I was born here in Franklin, but I moved to New Orleans when I was seven." Begin at the beginning, Possum said. I had to go to the beginning of Danny's story.

"Apparently the man you live with, your mother's husband, is not your biological father. Is that right?" I asked.

Danny nodded.

"Tell me Danny, do you know who your father was, or is?"

"Who he *was*, yeah. He's dead, but I seen his picture. Mom and my dad at their wedding. It's on the mantle."

"And is he a black man?"

Danny glared at me now, lips drawn tight. "Holy shit, no. He's white like me. How many times I got to tell you I'm white?"

I went at the subject from another direction.

"OK. The house you live in now isn't where you've always lived, right? Where'd you live before?"

"We lived in Grand Bois, out below Charenton, by the Basin. We stayed with my grandmother until she died."

"So your dad and mom lived together out there in Grand Bois?"

"Yeah. Well, no. When they married, they moved away. Houston, I think I heard. My dad died and my mom came back to my grandmother's. I was born after she came back. I never knew my father."

"I'm sorry about that, Danny. Must've been tough for you. Do you remember the address where you lived in Grand Bois?"

"You don't need no address out there. But there's nothin' there now. A ghost town, they tell me."

"Could you give me directions on how to get there?"

"All I know is you go out to Charenton. I can't remember no more."

Less than an hour with Danny and I had a headache

taking up residence between my ears. I was used to difficult clients, and could accept staying emotionally distant, just doing my professional best for most of them. But this kid? He had to be one of the most aggravating I'd ever had. Those eyes kept tripping something in my heart. I thought I had a tough situation when I was a kid, losing my mom, moving to New Orleans under a cloud. Nothing compared to the hand Danny had been dealt.

"I'm going to see if I can find that place called Grand Bois, Danny. Maybe someone out there can give me some help."

Because you sure enough aren't giving me any, I thought but didn't say.

* * *

A few days later I found a clear space of time to take a ride. First I did a bit of research in the office of the Clerk of Court on the second floor of the courthouse. Ten minutes in there and I learned more about Danny's background than I had in three weeks pummeling my client with questions.

On August 7, 1987, Josie Blanchard, age 17, and Willy Howard, age 31, took out a license to marry. She gave her address as Catfish Road, Grand Bois. The license listed Josie's mother as Marie Blanchard; no father's name given. Not much, but Josie had more in her corner than Howard. The box for the groom's address was blank, as was the box for the names of his parents. In the space for race, both parties entered "white." A notation on the license indicated that Father Pierre Blanchard, Church of the Assumption, performed the wedding ceremony three days later in Franklin. Apparently in those days you came to town to tie the knot. I headed out toward Charenton to see if I could find Catfish Road in Grand Bois.

I lowered the car windows, turned off the A/C, and breathed in the cool fall breeze. The fresh, clear October morning displayed south Louisiana at its best, erasing all memory of the white heat of summer that chafed the nerves and turned everyone into creatures of the shade. I turned right on the Irish Bend Road, crossed the Bayou Teche that snakes its way through the parish from north to south, passed through the Indian tribal lands—a much improved area since the advent of casino gambling put money in the pockets of all those who were able to prove their Chitimacha heritage—and came to the Bayou Teche again. The settlement of Charenton. I crossed a rickety bridge and turned south on a narrow strip of blacktop. To the east, the tops of the cypress trees in the Atchafalaya Basin poked up over the levee. Hand-lettered signs that read *Catfish For Sale* decorated several weather-beaten houses. I almost missed Grand Bois. The town existed on my map but on the ground was no more than a wide place in the road. The only life I could find was a couple of scrawny mongrels scratching themselves in the dirt on the side of the road. I had to drive around for few minutes to locate a human being.

"Used to be fifty families livin' 'round here," an old man sitting on his porch on Big Indian Road told me. "We had a store, gas station, syrup mill, and even a one-room schoolhouse. The men mostly did loggin' in the Basin just a ways yonder." He swept his hand toward the east. "You could get in there by pirogue then, down a little canal to the big swamp."

He said his name was Gus. He had only a few teeth in his mouth. His eyes didn't move as a pair.

"The syrup mill was yonder past the grocery; ain't nothin' left of it anymore. Catfish Road goes off that way." Gus waived a thin arm in the general direction of the north.

"What happened to everybody, Gus?" I asked.

"First thing that killed us was the lumber companies loggin' out the Basin. No more giant cypress meant no more work. No point even callin' us the Grand Bois anymore. More like Petit Bois." He scrunched his face in a smile. "After the high water in '29, the Corps built up the levees and everythin' inside went under. Cut us off. We couldn't even get to the crawfish. Our little town done dried up like a ditch in August."

"So, Gus, do you remember a Blanchard family that used to live around here? Maybe on Catfish Road?"

Gus's face cracked open in a smile. "My man, I'm a Blanchard. Over there you got Blanchards. Almost everybody 'round here's a Blanchard!"

"Good point. How about this group? Grandma Marie Blanchard, mom named Josie Blanchard Howard, and a baby boy named Danny? Do those names sound at all familiar to you?"

After scratching the white stubble on his chin, Gus came up with a story. He remembered that Marie Blanchard's daughter Josie got swept off her feet by a traveling Hadacol salesman. She married him, gave him all her mom's savings, and the couple skipped out of town. Within six months Josie came back alone. A few months later she had a baby, and the boy grew up right there. Gus didn't recall anything else about them. They kept to themselves, or 'theyselves' as he said it.

"I'm very glad to have met you, Gus, and I thank you for taking time to think about the old days."

"Lucky, that's what you are. Two weeks and I'll be well gone from here."

I assumed he meant he was dying, so I was quick to say nay.

"Not true, Gus. You look as if you're good for a long time yet."

"Could be, but it won't be here. The State lady says I got to go live in town. It's a sorry situation when you can't stay where you want anymore."

The *State lady* was probably wise. How could an old man manage out here by himself? That rusty truck out back looked about to fall in heap. When I went closer to

Gus for a goodbye handshake, his stale odor wrinkled my nose.

Possum had given me another lesson in investigations. Every kid goes to school, he said. The St. Mary Parish School Board kept records going back at least twenty years. I returned to town to run down that information.

The first record for Danny turned out to be for the second grade at W.P. Foster Elementary in Franklin. Daniel Howard, age eight, transferred in from Grand Bois. Again, the entry for race said *white*. At this point Danny had one parent, Mrs. Josie Howard. That school year, and for several years after, the record showed Danny got all A's on his card. And he had a good many positive comments from his teachers.

The record held up pretty well all through middle school, or junior high as it was then known, but in high school his grades took a dive. He always had an A in PE, however, with the notation *basketball* and *baseball* handwritten on the records. Then his parents were listed as Mr. and Mrs. William Chastant, 211 Pecan Street, Franklin.

I felt I could reasonably conclude that Danny had been born in deep back country, spent the first years of life on the edge of the Basin, and had adequate if not good schooling. His biological father was nowhere in the picture. I could surmise that Danny had been a bright child, with good help at home. A country kid rarely does that well in school without family support. But what might have been the emotional toll of the move to town? Was he, like Gus would soon be, uprooted from Eden, leaving behind a vanished past? Was that what turned Danny into the surly, depressed teenager who aggravated the shit out of me?

Armed with this background information, on my next visit to Danny I felt emboldened to confront him again about his race. After some preliminary conversation about my trip to Grand Bois, his Granny, and his school record, I took a deep breath and plunged in.

"Danny, all the records that I've found list your race as white, and you tell me you are white. How do you know that?"

As before, anger sparked those black eyes at the mention of the subject. His manner of speaking slipped into what we call *gumbo speak*, words tripping over each other on the way out of his mouth. "Because I seen the weddin' picture of my parents, that's how. I seen my birth certificate. Says there I'm white. The school say I'm white. I'm white, man!"

I refrained from pointing out that the school system always listed the race of a child as that of the mother, no matter the color of the child's skin. To compound the absurdity of this practice, if a dark-skinned daughter of a white mother and a black man had a child who married a black man, and they stayed in the same school system, their child would also be registered as white because that was the designation of the mother. Society took an entirely different view of these racial issues. Social custom in these parts embraced the one drop rule. People regarded anyone with a 'touch of the tar brush,' as they called it, to be a person of color.

Wasn't it time to do away with all this? But conflicting considerations played a part. The number of racial minorities an institution could count in their corner often triggered benefits. A conundrum.

I pressed on with my client, more forcefully.

"I look at your face, Danny, and you look in the mirror. You must notice that some of your features resemble those of an African-American. Has your mother given you any explanation for that?"

Danny's face turned darker. He pinched his eyes closed. His left hand balled into a fist, and he slapped the table with his right.

"Look, man. She don't need to. We don't see no color. The way we see it, my mom and me, race don't matter. We all just human beings. All our blood's the same. Equal. That's the way I was raised, and that's the way I be."

"OK. I see you're angry with me. Were you angry with Clyde Carline when he taunted you about your skin color?"

Danny lifted his head and gave me another rare look in the eye. "Yeah."

"Enough to do something about it?"

"I'm not talkin', man."

"Maybe you aren't talking now, but think about this. You're a pretty bright guy. If you were mad, and had reason to be, and you did something in understandable anger, you have a shot at a defense to a capital murder charge. That's my job, you know, to come up with a defense. To save your fuckin' life!"

"I tell you man, I'm not talkin' about this."

I had to get out of there before I totally lost it. My mind swirled with anger all the way down to the ground floor.

A clean-cut young man with no record, Danny would be a good candidate to take the stand to testify in his own case. He might have a story that would touch the jury, but I'd have to know what he'd say before I put him on the stand.

First degree murder of Clyde Carline was only one of the charges against Danny. What about that kid who got it the same night? I had no master plan to defend Danny for the death of the unidentified boy. To tell the truth, I believed Danny when he said he didn't have anything to do with that. If I could figure out who killed the boy, I could keep Danny off death row.

DANNY'S MOM

Unlike the mothers of most of my clients, Danny's mom never called me. When I tried to telephone the number Danny gave me for her, she didn't answer. I called in the morning, at noon, evenings, on weekdays and weekends. I suspected she had caller ID and screened me out. Late one afternoon, taking a slight detour on my way home, I saw a car in the driveway of 211 Pecan Street and risked a cold call.

Parking two houses down so she wouldn't be tipped off, I walked up the front path and rang the doorbell. A solidly built, very local looking woman in loose slacks, bright overblouse, and heavy shoes opened the door. I stepped closer than prescribed by ordinary southern custom. She flinched but didn't step back. Over her shoulder, in the semi-darkness of the living room, I could see a man slumped down in a lazy-boy, beer in hand, eyes fixed on a TV screen where two overweight Asians in g-strings wrestled each other on a bright blue mat.

I spoke first. "Mrs. Chastant, I'm John Clark, your lawyer. May I come in?"

Wary, she cocked her head. Taking a chance on confrontation, I put a toe over the threshold and inched forward. Now she shrank back as I claimed the space.

"I want to talk to you about your son Danny, ma'am. May I come in for a few moments, not long?"

Her eyes cut to a worn flowered sofa that also faced the TV. I took that as an invitation, walked around her, and sat down at the near end. On my way I addressed the occupant of the lazy-boy.

"Sir, I'm John Clark, Danny's lawyer."

"Bill Chastant," he responded. One quick glance was all I got.

Awkwardly, and without speaking, Mrs. Chastant sat down on the other end of the sofa, but she didn't settle into the cushions.

Danny sure didn't live in a chatty household.

I went through the charges against her son and briefly discussed my plan to do the best I could for his defense. Mrs. Chastant offered no reaction, information, appreciation, emotion. Nothing. I cut to the elephant in the room.

"Mrs. Chastant, I want to talk to you about Danny's race."

She sat back, more to steady herself than to welcome me to her company. I fixed my eyes directly on hers.

"What? What are you talking about?" she stammered.

"I'm sorry to be intrusive, ma'am, but I really need some information to be able to be a good lawyer for your son. I have reason to believe that if Danny was involved in these events, his feelings about race had something to do with his actions."

Silence. After a few moments dealing with my intense gaze, she made a response. "What is it you want to know?"

Bill Chastant got up from his chair, turned the TV off at the set, and reoccupied the lazy-boy.

"Of course you're aware that Danny has features that indicate African-American heritage..."

Mrs. Chastant almost hissed her reaction. "Mr. Clark, just stop right there. Danny is white. I'm his mother, and I'm white. His father was white. He's white. It says so on his birth certificate."

"It may say that on the paper, ma'am, but we both know that Danny has the features..."

"Look! That's the picture of his father right there,"

pointing at a dim little snapshot on the mantelpiece, struggling for significance in the swirls of a cheap plastic frame. "Our wedding picture. My first wedding." She cut a glance to her husband.

This woman kept a wedding picture from her former marriage sitting on the mantelpiece? Egads!

I wasn't giving up. "You're not blind, ma'am. You can surely see that your son Danny's face has some African-American features."

"He's dark complected, yes, but so was his father."

"Mrs. Chastant. It's more than his complexion. Surely other people have noticed and talked about this."

Her right hand clutched the arm of the sofa, knuckles white. "Yes. Some people have said that."

Bill Chastant got up from his chair and took a position behind his wife. He put one hand on her shoulder. Reacting to his touch, her face softened just a tad. I tucked away the idea that sometime in the future Bill Chastant might help me, but right now I had Mrs. Chastant in my sights.

"Ma'am, does Danny talk to you about what people say to him? How do you explain those comments to Danny?"

Mrs. Chastant sighed. "I tell Danny what I believe. Race doesn't matter. It's what's inside a person that counts. I told Danny he should just ignore what people say. His father was white. His birth certificate says he's white."

"Come on, ma'am. Was he able to do that? Was he able to ignore race when people made remarks to him?" I pressed.

She said something but I couldn't make it out.

"What did you say, Mrs. Chastant?"

"When he was a little boy, he did that very well. But when he got to high school, he had some problems with people. I'll admit it. He stopped telling me about such things, but I heard about them from other people."

"Thank you, Mrs. Chastant. Thank you for talking to

me about this. I know it's hard, but it's really very important. I want to help your boy. You know that the charges against him carry the ultimate penalty. I want to save his life. Can you understand that?"

"Uh-huh."

That's all she had to say? Uh-huh?

"Mrs. Chastant, let me explain. If Danny had anything do with those deaths, and I'm not saying that he did, there could be reasons why he did what he did. We call that mitigation evidence. It's my job to bring that evidence to the jury. We must make the jury understand what might have prompted him to do something foolish. *If* he did, of course. And I have to talk to the jury about Danny, and I have to find witnesses who will talk to the jury about him. The jury must believe that Danny is a life worth saving. If I don't do that, he'll get the penalty of death. Please, ma'am, understand how very much I need your cooperation."

"Yes, but..."

"No buts about it. I need your help. And Danny needs your help. You need to spend time with him and help him through this. He's facing an ordeal and needs you in his corner."

I had her attention for a moment there but now watched a curtain fall. Her face hardened and she clasped her hands tight to one another.

"I have nothing further to say to you."

"Mrs. Chastant. Tell me, why won't you help me?"

"I just don't want to drag up what can't do any good. Danny's what he is. His father was white. I'm white. And I'm telling you, he's white also. I don't want to talk about this anymore."

She stood up. I stood up also and stepped closer.

"I do not agree with you, ma'am. Dragging this up may do him a lot of good. Please try to understand that. If I don't explain this boy to the jury, he could be put to death."

She was done with me.

"That's all I'm going to say on the subject, Mr. Clark. I have to be getting on to a meeting tonight..."

I stayed in the same position, blocking her path to the front door.

"One more thing, please Mrs. Chastant. On another subject." I offered a smile in hopes of a thaw. "No one seems to know anything about the second victim that night, the young African-American boy. Do you think Danny knew him at all? Was he perhaps a friend, an acquaintance, anything? "

"I have absolutely no idea, Mr. Clark," she said in a dismissive tone. "I don't know him. Bill, have you ever heard of the boy?" Mrs. Chastant asked her so-far-silent husband.

"Nope. Never heard of him."

"Again, Mr. Clark. I'm going to have to ask you to go. I need to be leaving for my meeting."

Now that was a first. Kicked out by my client's mom.

Could it be the kid's own mother didn't want him to beat the charge? I tried to wrap my head around that thought.

* * *

A couple of days later I had a call from Nanette at the shelter.

"John, that was quite an interesting woman you had sleeping with you."

"What? Sleeping with me? What the hell are you talking about?"

"You know. Medley Butterfield."

"Oh, come on. Give me a break, Nanette. It was just one of those impossible situations."

"I shouldn't tease you, especially when I need help. Seriously, we've been working with Medley, and now I need a favor."

I was wary. "I'm hard pressed to turn you down, Nanette, being as you do me favors all the time. But what is it you want?"

"Medley has a line on a job, a good job. She's a nurse; I don't know if you knew that. But there's one little problem. Her boy."

I burst out laughing. "Oh, I know what you want. Now you want her child to come sleep with me. Right?"

"No, no, no. Not that. But didn't you tell me the your secretary's sister has a day care?"

"Yes, so I understand."

"I'd let the boy stay with me here at the shelter, but our board won't allow that. If you could just get her to keep Buddy—that's his name—during the day, without paying, until Medley gets her nursing license transferred from Mississippi and can be on the home health payroll... Not long. Maybe a month, at most. She hasn't a penny to her name right now, you know."

"For you, Nanette, I'll ask. But can't the woman's husband pay support for the kid?"

"From jail?"

"Oh, yeah. I forgot."

"Anyway, Medley is really terrified of him. She says he went to Iraq, saw some pretty bad stuff, and has been messed up ever since. Maybe he was messed up before, but she didn't know it. Medley wants to try to make a go of it here and I want to help her. She's been a godsend around the shelter already. I don't want to see her go."

I made the deal. Once again, I assumed I'd heard the last of Medley Butterfield, at least I hoped so. This woman was becoming a pesky gnat that wouldn't go away.

INTERVIEWING SNAP-DOG

Possum spent several days running down Danny's party pals. They all verified that Danny had a lot to drink—lots of "40s" was the way they put it. They all used the identical word to describe his condition—*buzzed*. But no one would admit to actually witnessing an explosive conversation between Danny and Clyde Carline, and no one had any clue about the identity of the second murder victim. I was now fairly sure that boy never came into the apartment complex. But what was he doing hanging around outside? I couldn't imagine.

Possum did get a better fix on everyone's whereabouts during the course of the evening. He made a list of the partygoers—most with a street name in addition to a real one—and a shorter list of the critical witnesses he thought I should question. Mark Diggers, aka Snap-Dog, headed the list. Poss wasn't rational on the subject of Snap. Out of frustration from past dealings, he had it in for this guy. Poss really hoped I would make a case for Snap being the *other dude who did it*.

We had both read Snap's initial statement to Sgt. Wiltz. Unfortunately for us, Snap said he thought Danny had left the party with a kitchen knife. To do a decent job of defending Danny, I'd have to do something to discredit that testimony. I had doubts I could pin two murders on Snap, but maybe, at the least, I could figure out a way to make the jury disbelieve his story about the knife. That could throw the life preserver beloved by all defense lawyers—reasonable doubt.

We found Snap at his house on Willow Street, a shabby cottage with an unpainted porch along one side. We stepped around a dog turd on the broken concrete front walk. Snap answered our knock and invited us into the living room. He turned off the TV and indicated where we could sit. Snap appeared to be the only one in the house.

Dirty-blond dreadlocks, narrow red scarf, rapper cap, one gold earring, hooded eyes.

Possum raised his chin and sniffed in a couple of puffs. Yeah, I also smelled traces of the noxious weed. There was an idea I might be able to use. Maybe Snap had been too stoned that night to be an accurate reporter.

Possum had warned me Snap would knock himself out to be ingratiating. Clearly he didn't feel he had to look mainstream, but he'd learned from his experience with the juvenile system that he scored points by being extra respectful to the adults who had his fate in their hands.

"Yes, sir. I was at the party. Danny's my bro', you know. No way he offed those two. He's a great kid, Danny is."

Not if he's spending time with you, I thought.

"So start at the beginning, Snap. When did you first see Danny that night?"

"Danny picked me and Nee-Nee up around nine o'clock. We drove around, visited some friends in Lafayette and up the bayou, sir."

"Then you went to the party? About what time would that have been?"

"We got to the apartments around ten thirty, or eleven, I guess."

Next to me, Possum held the back of his hand up to his nose and made a couple more quick sniffs. He did it a third time before I got the prompt.

"What were you guys driving around for? Were you trolling to score something? Weed? Snow? Maybe pills?"

Snap raised his eyebrows and pulled his chin back in horror at the idea. "No way, man. Sir. We're not into that."

"Don't worry about telling us, Snap. We're not narcs. We represent your friend Danny. We're just trying to get the details of the evening straight in our minds."

"I'm not lyin'. I don't use the stuff."

"So, how about beer? Were you two drinking while you were riding around?"

"Not me, sir. I'm on parole."

Aha! Parole. So Snap had an adult conviction on top of his juvenile offenses. I saw Possum making a note. He'd get an update of Snap's jacket.

"How about Danny? Was he drinking?"

"Oh yes, sir." Snap decorated the words with a knowing smile, implying he was an adult on our side of the table, Danny just a kid.

"Did Danny buy the beer?"

"No, sir. I'll admit it. I bought beer for him to take to the party." Snap feigned total openness about his transgression, his wide-eyed expression attempting to convey that he'd just confessed the worst crime he'd ever committed, buying beer for someone underage.

Next to me I could hear Possum exhale. Disgust at Snap's attitude, I supposed.

"How much did Danny drink?"

"On the ride? Best I remember he had a forty—40 oz. beer. Sir."

He had almost forgotten to say 'sir' this time.

"And after that? During the evening?"

"Oh, he had a load on. He was buzzed."

There was that word *buzzed* again.

"OK. So after you rode around for a while, you went to the apartments. What time did you say you got there?"

"Maybe around eleven. Can't be sure about that, sir."

"Where exactly did you go? Was any apartment in particular the location for the party?"

"Yes, sir. Nee-Nee's. We spent some time down in the

street first. Then we went upstairs to Nee-Nee's. His mom works nights."

When the cat's away. I looked at the card I had made to keep track of the street names. Nee-Nee would be Neal Roberts.

"I think Nee-Nee's apartment is in the first building on the right side. Correct?"

"Yes, sir."

"And Nee-Nee's sister Nikki's your girlfriend?"

Snap-Dog gave us a sly smile. "You done your homework, eh? Off and on. That night was mostly on." He rolled his eyes. "Now we're off."

"Could you tell us everybody you remember who was at Nee-Nee's apartment for the party?"

Snap looked to the ceiling as if trying to improve his recall. Like Danny, he described the crowd as changing, people coming in and out, upstairs and down. He gave us names, locations, times, all in a jumble. Possum wrote as fast as he could until, in frustration, he put his pen aside and shook his head. Plan B. I'd try to have Snap freeze-frame the crowd at the time the knife appeared.

"I hear that some time in the evening there was a knife around. Right?"

"Well, yeah. We all carry knives." He patted his pocket.

"I mean a big knife, a kitchen knife, serrated blade."

"Oh yes, sir. I saw a kitchen knife."

"Where did you see it?"

"On a chair. Someone got it out of the kitchen."

"Did you pick up that knife?"

"Probably did. I think everybody did. We were clowning around with it."

"Could you tell me exactly who was there in the apartment when the knife appeared on the chair?"

"Well, I'll try. But you know, as I told you, people came and went. Sir."

For that point in time, his list of the partygoers

matched Danny's pretty closely, except Snap added a couple more girls and a guy they called Cheese. Possum interrupted to have Snap give him Cheese's real name—Traylyn Fields.

Now that I had Snap giving a narration, I closed in.

"Did the knife, the kitchen knife with a serrated edge, ever leave the apartment?" I asked.

"Not that I know of, sir."

"No?" I reached into my pile of papers and pulled out a copy of the statement Snap had given to Capt. Daigle. I handed it to him. "Isn't that your signature there at the bottom of the page?"

"Yeah. That's my signature, but..."

I read from the statement. "'I saw Danny leave with a big knife.' That's what it seems to say here."

"Man, I didn't ever tell them that. You know how they take a so-called statement? They talk to you for a while, go away, type something up, come back later and ask you to sign. I signed, all right, but I didn't read the whole thing. No, sir. I didn't read that."

Actually, I knew the practice. For good reason, the cops didn't count on their witnesses to be able to compose a decent account all by themselves. And in many cases they wanted to launder the language and get the story down in the way they wanted the witness to testify down the road at trial. I might have to throw a little mud on law enforcement to get the jury to consider that explanation for a discrepancy, but it wouldn't be the first time I'd done so. Part of my job.

Anticipating my need to cross examine Snap at trial, I thought I'd better dig a bit more.

"You say you never told the cops that you saw Danny leave with the knife. But *did* you ever actually see him leave with it?"

"No, sir."

I glanced at Poss and made sure he wrote down those

exact words.

"But you weren't with him all the time, were you?"

"Well, no sir. Nikki and I went next door to Toya's, Danny went out to the telephone, or at least that's where he said he was going. Look, everyone moved around a lot."

"Do you know what happened to that knife?"

"I don't know, sir. Maybe Danny had it." Snap thought better of how that statement sounded, blinked, and made a quick revision. "I think it was on the chair when I left."

"You think?"

"Yeah. I think."

Snap was a mess to deal with, but he could be good for us if he stuck to what he just told me—that he didn't see Danny leave with a knife. Of course I would have to make the jury skeptical about police practice because the statement to Lt. Daigle was clearly different. Part of a defense lawyer's job, but not behavior that endeared us to the cops.

"Let me go back to when you all were at Nee-Nee's apartment, Snap. Did there come a time when Danny told you about someone calling him a bad name?"

"I don't remember anything like that. Not then, anyway." Snap looked me right in the eye. Now he wasn't remembering to call me 'sir.'

Did that mean Snap was being truthful? Actually I didn't think Snap had any conception of the truth.

"But that happened sometimes, didn't it? People calling him *nigger*? The Carline guy, for instance. I'm told he just said stuff to people."

"Yes, sir. I heard about that, but not that night. I don't know nothin' about Danny and Carline having any conversation that night."

I moved on to the last line of questions I wanted to bring up with Snap—the route he took when he left the apartments at the end of the night. Possum was waiting for me to get to this. Maybe on the way home Snap became the *other dude.*

"OK. When did you leave the party for good?"

Actually I was ready to leave that damn party myself.

"I guess it was about one, one-thirty. Sir."

"Did you leave alone?"

"Yes, sir."

"Where did you go? Home?"

"No, sir. To Billy Bulliard's. I spent the night at his house, a couple of doors down from my house on Willow Street. I slept on the porch."

"Just you two, you and Billy?"

"No. There were a couple more guys there too."

"When you left the party to go to Billy's, was Danny still at the party?"

"We went downstairs together, sir."

"Could you describe Danny's condition at that point?"

"Yes, sir. Buzzed."

"In what way did that show? Could he walk OK? Did he tell you good night?"

Snap gave us a broad smile, and that con expression. "Oh, he was smashed, all right. He didn't say anything, really."

Now I tried to use exactly the same tone I had for the last few questions. I didn't want to tip him off to my trap.

"Which way did you go to Billy's?"

"What do you mean, which way? Down Main, then up Willow."

"Which way out of the apartments? Did you cross the field behind the houses and go that way?"

He tilted his head. Wary. He hadn't figured out why I was asking about this.

"Cross the field, sir?

"Yeah."

"No. I went out to Pecan Street, down to Main."

Next to me, Possum sighed. Sorry Poss. I tried.

"How about Danny. Which way did he go?"

I wondered if he was going to finger Danny right here.

"I don't know. I must have left a minute or two before him. I didn't see him actually leave."

On to the next chapter. "This Billy Bulliard, can he verify that you were at his house after one-thirty that morning?"

"About then. Took me a while to get to his house, sir."

"OK. After two?"

"Yeah. Two."

"And he could verify when you arrived?

"Yeah. All the guys could. Sir."

And I knew they had done so in their statements to the police.

"Tell me, Snap. Any drugs on Billy Bulliard's porch that night?"

"Well..."

"OK. We don't need to go into that. What if I told you that Billy says somebody in the crowd on the porch said there'd been a stabbing at the apartments, and he thinks maybe that somebody was you. Can you explain that?"

"Wasn't me, sir."

"How did Billy know about the trouble at the apartments if you didn't tell him?"

Snap gave us that open, innocent look again. "Must've been someone else, someone who came later. I told you. I left Nee-Nee's party before there was any trouble, walked to Billy's, and went to sleep. There was a bunch of us sleeping on Billy's porch. If he heard me say something, maybe I just repeated what somebody else told me later on."

I had read the detectives' interviews with Billy Bulliard and his buddies. They didn't know who said what and couldn't give exact times about anything. Clearly there were too many mind-altering substances on the porch that night. If the DA used Bulliard's statement against Danny, I was pretty sure I could get the jury to see the picture.

I changed the subject. I had to get Snap's take on the racial issues.

"Danny seems to insist to us, to everybody, that he's not black. He says he's white. What about that, Snap? Do you agree?"

Snap gave me the open, straight-in-the-eye look he had learned so well. "Mr. Clark, I say Danny is what he says he is. And anyway, color makes me no difference and makes no difference to him. No difference to any of us. We're brothers."

"But color does matter to some people. Like Clyde Carline, for instance. Right?"

"Yeah, so I've heard. But I don't know nothin' about that, sir."

Next to me, I could hear Possum fidgeting. I knew he wanted to get into all kinds of irrelevant subjects, to dig around about past grievances he had with Snap. I glared a warning.

I couldn't let him do that. We had what we wanted. Snap had recanted his statement to the cops that Danny left with the knife. We needed that and sure didn't need to tick him off.

"My last question, Snap. Do you have any idea who the one we call the second victim could be? The black boy who also got stabbed to death that night?"

"I have no idea, sir. I never saw him before."

"There were no strangers around at your party, downstairs, anywhere on the center drive? No one you hadn't seen before?"

"No, sir. We knew everybody around."

Possum couldn't sit still any longer. "Snap, I hear nothin' happens at the Pecan Gardens Apartments that you don't know about. My guys all tell me you're the man around there. My guess is that you know everyone who comes and goes, and if you don't, you find out pretty damn quick. Surely you've been digging into who that boy might be. Who do people say he was?"

Snap kept his cool better than Poss. "No, sir. No one has any idea."

That was it. We shut it down.

When Possum and I left Willow Street and drove the few blocks to the apartments, Possum didn't speak, but he shook his head the whole trip.

"Sorry we didn't get what you wanted, Poss. But we got good stuff. The DA is counting on Snap to finger Danny. If Snap sticks to what he just told us, Tony is going to get a nasty surprise."

"Yeah, I know. But you just can't trust that one. Come trial, he could flip again."

"But in the meanwhile, unless we can uncover someone who fingers your old friend Snap, I'd say you will have to give up on him as our *other dude*. Billy Bulliard and his pals may have been impaired, but they place Snap with them from around one a.m. on. And I can't figure a motive for Snap to have stabbed Carline. As for a motive concerning the boy, we don't even know who the kid was, let alone what he was doing there."

"The narcs tell me Snap's the go-to man in the apartments, boss. Nothing happens in there he doesn't know about. He's a con, a petty hood. Unfortunately for mankind, he's also smarter than the crowd he runs with. And now it looks like Danny is afraid of him. I'm going to do some work on finding out just what goes on with our boy Snap."

We pulled up in front of the apartments and parked the unit. "Whose next on your short list, Poss?"

"Let's try for some of the girls."

Poss wouldn't let go of his pique. "Snap-dog makes me sick."

I laughed. "Not enough, Poss."

MORE PARTYGOERS

We found Toya Vallot perched on a lawn chair on the balcony of the apartment next door to Nee-Nee's. Her right foot stretched out to rock a car seat cradling a baby only a few months old. Toya carried a several extra pounds around the middle, but wasn't fat. She returned a broad smile when we introduced ourselves. Deep dimples.

"Is that little one your sister, Toya?" I asked her.

"No, no."

"No?"

"I'm just babysittin'."

Whew! For a moment I thought I'd stepped in it, that the baby was hers. Teen moms were common here.

"We came to ask you a few questions about the party last October, the night when two people got killed at these apartments. You were at the party that night, right?"

"For a while."

"How old are you, Toya?"

"Almost fourteen."

That explained our welcome. Just into her teens, and not yet old enough to be wary of two white guys coming up to her apartment.

"That's kind of young to be at a party like that, isn't it? Did your mom know you were over there?"

Toya tucked her chin. "Mom was at work. My grandmother was home, in the back."

If I'd had Toya on the witness stand instead of her own porch I would have asked a follow-up. *So the answer to my question is "no?"*

"Danny Howard is your boyfriend, right?"

Toya tilted her head. "Kind of. But we had a disagreement. I got pretty mad at him that night."

"Why was that?"

"He was drinkin' too much. I don't like that."

"So what happened?"

"He got mad about me bein' mad and said he was gonna' call another girl. So I left out of there."

"Out of where? Where did you two have this disagreement?"

"Next door. On Nee-Nee's balcony." She swept her hand in that direction.

"Did Danny call another girl?"

"I guess he did. I don't know. He went downstairs and out toward the back to where the telephone is. I went on home."

"Do you know what time you two had the disagreement?"

"No."

"Can you guess? Was it early in the party? Or late?"

"Oh, early. I left and went home early."

"Did you see Danny again that night?"

"No."

"And have you seen him since? Maybe been to the jail to visit him?"

Her eyes dropped, then lifted up to meet mine.

"Mom says I can't go there."

Danny was mighty short of friends. Sad. But if I were Toya's parent, I'd probably say the same.

"I guess you've heard that we're all looking for information about a knife that was around at Nee-Nee's apartment. Did you see a big knife over there? A kitchen knife?"

"No, I never saw a knife, but then I didn't go inside Nee-Nee's" She paused. "That's one thing Danny was mad at me about. I wouldn't go in there."

Toya lowered her eyes, which told me she'd refused Danny more than simply his request for her to cross the threshold.

"How about the young boy who also got stabbed that night, Toya? Do you have any idea who he could be? Could have been?"

"Naw. No idea."

"Did you ever see anyone around that you didn't know?"

"No."

Toya had been no help, but I liked her. I tucked away an idea. With careful work, Toya could be a witness for Danny. She cared for him, and she had jury appeal. Her grandmother wasn't much of a chaperone. I wished her mom could stay home and keep better track of the friends her daughter chose. It wasn't easy for a young girl to stay safe in the apartments.

Our next stop was the apartment next door, the scene of the party. No answer there either, but as we turned to go back down, Nikki Roberts appeared, picking her way up the stairs on sparkling, Wizard-of-Oz-red four-inch heels. Upthrust breasts challenged the strength of her low-cut, sequined T-shirt; a black leather miniskirt cupped her rear end. Her hair had been marcelled into careful furrows across her forehead, a flapper hairdo that must have set her back sixty bucks. Nikki couldn't afford the clothes or the style on her part-time minimum wage job at McDonald's.

When I introduced myself, Nikki shrugged and looked skyward. *Oh, what a bore it is to have to deal with you!*

"Nikki," I began, "We'd like to talk to you about the night of the party where the two people were stabbed to death."

"So?"

"You were there?"

"No."

"No? You were not at the party?"

"No one got stabbed at a party I was at."

Oh, boy. One of those.

"OK. I'll ask my question more precisely. Were you here at a party at your apartment on the night of October 2 to 3, the night two people were stabbed to death in a cane field off to the side?"

"That's what they tell me, about the stabbin'. I didn't see no stabbin'." She pronounced the word *stobbin'*.

"Right. You didn't see it. But you heard it happened, right?"

"Yeah. Hear tell." She rolled the words, and her tongue pushed out a bulge at the corner of her mouth.

"OK. When you were at the party, at your apartment, was Danny Howard there also?"

"He there."

"OK. Did you see a knife, a kitchen knife in the apartment that night?"

"Yeah, I seen a knife."

"Did there come a time when Danny picked up the knife?" I'd learned my lesson. No imprecise questions.

"Yeah, one time he had it. Everybody did. Everybody took a turn with that knife."

"Did you see Danny leave the apartment with the knife?"

Nikki took a breath and stood straighter.

"I seen him with the knife. I seen him leave. The knife wasn't on the chair no more. One, two, three. That's it."

"So you didn't see him leave with it."

"I don't know if he left with it or not. You figure it out, man." She sighed and tossed her head up at an angle. "Hey. I'm sittin' down."

She did, on a metal folding chair. She swung one leg provocatively over the other, letting her sparkling shoe dangle from her toes.

"OK. Before that, before you saw Danny leave, did you hear anything about anyone talking ugly to him?"

"You mean that dick Carline callin' him a *nigger*?"

Next to me, Possum smothered a laugh. I took a couple of deep breaths to keep from doing the same.

"Yes, that's what I mean."

"Hear tell."

"Where was Danny when you heard that?"

"What you mean 'where was Danny?' He came in and said it himself. 'That shit-faced Carline bastard called me a *nigger*.'"

"Danny's words?"

"Yeah. His words."

Nikki drew a circle in the air with her pointer finger, which meant nothing to me. I glanced at Possum, but he also appeared to draw a blank. I could sense Nikki's heightened impatience, so perhaps that's all she was expressing. The next few answers came to us through tightened lips.

"Then what happened, Nikki?"

"Nothin'."

"The party went on?"

"Right."

"Did Danny say anything else? Like he was going to do anything about that statement by Clyde Carline?"

"Not so's I know."

"And Danny. Did he leave after that?"

"He left."

"Where'd he go?"

"Damned if I know. Look, I've had about enough of this."

"Just a few more questions, Nikki. What did you do then?"

Nikki's eyes flashed with anger.

"Got in a fuckin' fight with Snap, that's what."

"What about?"

"Some crazy shit. I'm through with that jerk." She tossed her head back and rolled her eyes. Big, brown eyes, well defined by heavy liner and glittering purple shadow on the lids.

"Did the fight have anything to do with what went on at the party?"

"Who the hell knows? I don't. Snap's just pissed at me and I've had enough of his crap. Snap and I weren't just conversatin', you know. We got into it. Physical, like. I hauled ass outa' there. I got me a new boyfriend now."

A sassy move rippled her torso from her shoulders down to her waist. She patted the side of her head with long plastic fingernails painted to match those ruby slippers. The new boyfriend probably paid for the hairdo *and* the manicure. Maybe he bought the shoes.

"Back to the party a minute, Nikki. After Danny said Carline called him that name, did you ever see the knife again?"

Nikki actually spit out the answer to this question. "It-wasn't-on-the-chair, man. You retarded like shit-face Carline? Danny? I seen him with the knife. I seen him leave. The knife wasn't on the chair no more. One, two, three. That's it."

The exact words she'd used before. That was going to be her story. Her testimony would be a problem.

I thanked Nikki and steered Possum down the stairs. We walked to the basketball court at the rear of the complex so I could cool off. I took a few more deep breaths and watched the afternoon sun cut across the cane field and light up the backs of the houses on Main.

"I've talked to a dozen of those kids, boss, and haven't put together any plausible alternative. I thought maybe Nee-Nee would have a contribution, but I came to the realization that dude doesn't even know where he was.

Stoned or drunk, I guess. Got to admit it, boss. Looks bad for Danny."

"Possum, have you talked to Carline's friend, Vic Diamond? As I remember his statement, he said Carline called out to 'boys passing by,' but said he knew nothing about what might have happened later in the evening."

"I talked to him, all right. That guy has a serious credibility problem, boss. He says he never, ever heard Carline say the word *nigger*. Flat denial. I guess the DA will put him on the witness stand, at least if he keeps the deal he made with the jury that he'd bring them everyone who was in the picture. If Tony doesn't put Diamond on, I know you'll tell the jury Tony failed to give them the one person who might have heard the remark. But I don't think Diamond will matter. Like Carline, he's got mental limitations, and the jury will see that right away."

If Snap-Dog let Tony down—always a good possibility—Nikki would be the key witness for Tony's theory of the case. With careful and brief questions, he would get her to say she saw Danny come in mad about Carline's remark. The knife and Danny disappeared at the same time. Not great evidence, but maybe good enough.

"Here's my plan of attack, Poss. I'll put Nikki through the wringer under cross. If I can make her mad, she'll disintegrate into her vocabulary of choice. The jury will hate her guts. Maybe, just maybe, they'll see *reasonable doubt*."

Possum laughed. "I like your chances, boss."

The fallow field of cane stubble stretched before us. I pictured the scene last October: a boy, stabbed, left to bleed to death, and no one even missed him.

"And still no one knows the other victim." I mumbled the statement. Not a question.

"In Nikki's vocabulary, boss, "'it's a real fucker.'"

I had an idea.

"Poss, the guy who found the bodies, Duplantis is his

name, has an eighteen year old son. I wonder if that boy ever came over this way. Maybe."

"Still lookin' for your *other dude*? I'll give it a shot."

"Let's get out of here. I've about had enough of this bunch for one day." We turned to go back through the complex.

"One more stop, boss. If you can stand it. We'll pass right by apartment number 40, the home of the one they call Cheese. Traylyn Fields. He's a friend of Danny's from school, and he's probably the one who introduced Danny to the Pecan Gardens Apartments in the first place. His statement says he didn't see anything, but it might be a good idea to talk with him. Let's give him a try."

"OK. If your leg can handle mounting one more flight of stairs."

We knocked on the dirty door of number 40, in the building next to Nee-Nee's, also upstairs. A slip of a boy, no more than eight, appeared. He looked at me with an open, steady gaze.

"Oh, I thought you was the nurse. My mom's gone to the sto'," the little fellow said.

"And your brother? They call him Cheese, I believe. Is he home?"

"Not here either."

In response to Possum's query about Saturday night, the boy answered, "No, I'm not out at night. I always stay in with Gramps when my mom goes to work." A TV set flickered in a dark corner of the room. Down a narrow hallway, farther into the gloom, I could make out a covered figure on a mattress. I smelled the need for long overdue personal care.

The boy knew nothing about the party and was no help on the subject of the identity of the second victim. We thanked him and left the apartment.

When we stepped to the metal stairway, we almost collided with two women coming up. The older woman in front wore pink scrubs. Possum gave her a quick hug and introduced her to me.

"My sister, Lizzie, boss. Liz, this is my boss, Mr. Clark."

Behind her... My God, it was that woman again! Last time I saw her was the morning I delivered her to Nanette at the shelter. Medley Butterfield.

I was just absorbing the fact of Medley's presence, and wondering if I should introduce her to Possum, when Lizzie exploded. She chopped the air with her left hand and launched into a rant at her brother.

"Brer Possum, Christmas dinner is only a week away, and I may kill our brother before it gets here! Every damn night I get a call. First he says he can't come to dinner. Fine. Who needs all his *traca*?. Then it's yes, he'll come, but he can't bring any food. OK, that's fine. Who needs a pie from the grocery store? Now he says he'll be there with his two girls. Look, Poss, I'm happy to have the dinner at my house, and the girls are sure welcome, but I need two things. I gotta have my peace at night to recover from the day, and I gotta know how many will be at the table for dinner. Do something about him, Possum."

"Easy does it, Liz. What do you expect me to do?"

"Call him up. Get the straight skinny. Tell him to make up his mind once and for all and that's it."

"Maybe he can't know. You know how teenagers are. They have no idea what it takes to put on a holiday dinner. They want to keep their options open to see if they get a better deal. Let's talk. We're done here and on our way to McDonald's for a cup of coffee and to write up our notes. If you won't be too long, you could join us when you're finished. We can talk there."

"Fifteen minutes, Poss. We'll join you."

I guessed that "we" included Medley.

* * *

Lizzie resumed her rant to her brother when she and Medley were still four feet away from the little orange table where Possum and I were seated reviewing our notes from the interviews at the apartments. She slammed down her coffee cup, spilling a few drops on Possum's notebook. He threw up his arms in frustration.

"Does all of McDonald's need to hear our family shit, Liz? So we have a difficult relative. We're Italians, already! We're just going to have the classic Donado holiday dinner. Remember Thanksgiving? Aunt Carmela ended up hurling a gob of cranberry sauce at our dear brother."

I tuned out Possum, Lizzie, and their family drama. My eyes were on Medley. We had a reverse Dorian Gray going on here. Every time I saw this woman she looked better. Color rose in her cheeks, and I realized I had been staring.

"Mr. Clark, what brings you over to the Pecan Gardens?" she asked.

"I think that's a question for you, Ms. Butterfield."

"I'm finishing my first day of a new job, thanks to you, your secretary's sister, and your friend Nanette at the shelter. Not really my first day on the job. I'm only in training. I'm a home health nurse."

"Possum and I have a case that took place at the apartments," I explained. But that isn't what I had let into my consciousness. I was intensely aware of a lovely face, a warm smile, a soft voice. And an unwelcome stirring.

Luminous green eyes looked directly at me. "I really appreciate all your help, Mr. Clark. Now Nanette is arranging for Buddy and me to move into the building next door to the shelter—in return for some work fixing the place up."

What could it hurt to have a little conversation? Just one little bite of the apple?

"Sounds as if you're not planning to go back to Mississippi."

"No. I'm staying here, at least for now. I'm very glad I didn't get on that bus back to Magnolia. I miss my grandmother, and she chokes up when I put Buddy on the phone, but I'm hoping I can figure out a way to get her over here."

Oblivious of the Donado family drama going on around us, Medley and I had a casual conversation, slipping into calling each other by our first names. The shelter had received a gift of the house next door, made a connecting breezeway, and planned to create a playroom for the children and an area for classes. Medley and Maria Rodriguez, another resident, would be on the payroll to do some painting. I found myself telling Medley about the restoration of my grandfather's house, my pride in the woodworking, and my anxiety about tackling the plumbing and electrical work that lay ahead. Until I heard Medley say, "You must really enjoy getting back to your childhood home. Why did you leave and go to New Orleans? Maybe after the holidays we could..."

She had torn the scab off a wound. I stood up abruptly. No! I did not, not, not want to get involved again. And I certainly didn't want to start telling her about the reason we left.

"I'm going to get another cup of coffee." I turned to the other two at the table, "Anyone want a refill? I need one."

I really didn't. What I needed was to prevent opening myself to the possibility of a reprise of pain I had left behind.

When I returned to the table, Medley had her eyes fixed on her coffee cup. Obviously my abrupt departure had cut.

Lizzie's diatribe seemed to be winding down. With a deliberately casual tone, I directed a question to her. "Did you and Possum figure out how to restore family harmony in time for your Christmas Dinner?"

Possum answered. "Impossible! So what are your holiday plans, John?"

"I'm going to attack the kitchen or a bathroom. Enough of the meticulous process of refinishing old cypress boards! I feel the need to get a crowbar and do some major destruction. Plumbing will be a new trade for me to learn. My only question is which room I should tackle first."

Possum asked Medley about her holiday. Her answer was subdued.

"I'm going to visit my Gram in Mississippi. It'll be a long drive, but my friend at the shelter—Maria Rodriguez— has offered to come with me." Medley smiled bravely, but the sparkle had left her eyes. "I don't know what kind of holiday dinner we'll have. Maybe Maria will be fixing turkey enchiladas."

Bless her. She was making this easy on me.

I decided to use the crowbar on the old kitchen.

A BREAK

On Monday morning after the holiday, in the middle of monitoring a new PDO staff attorney who was getting her feet wet representing felony defendants charged with violating their probation, the courthouse switchboard receptionist delivered a message that I should drop everything and come directly up to the DA's office on the fourth floor. Not an invitation but a command. Damn. Why was I always the one who had to jump? Defense lawyers get no respect, especially ones who work on the state tab.

"You're doing great, Maggie," I told the new hire. "You can handle this on your own. Give me a call when you're through, and tell me if you had any problems."

I didn't like to leave her like that because I was determined to give young staff more support than I had when I started in the Public Defender's Office in New Orleans. They just handed me a file and sent me through those swinging doors to defend an armed robber. Traumatic, but I needed to get out of my father-in-law's firm no matter what the circumstances. Six months later I had learned to love my PDO job. I'd have been there still, but Orleans Criminal Court just wasn't far enough removed from a marriage gone sour. Katrina evacuation provided me the opportunity to relocate—and reclaim my grandfather's old house.

Tony stood up to greet me.

"We have a break in the Danny Howard case, John. Come with me next door to the sheriff's office. They've got a lady from Houston in there, and she says our unknown boy is her sister's adopted kid."

"Positive ID? She's seen the boy's body?" I asked, my heart racing at the news, even though the information had a downside. My argument against going for a grand jury indictment before identification of the second victim had just been shot to hell.

"Yup. The sheriff took her to Lafayette to the hospital morgue. She came apart at the sight of the body, wailing her head off, but her ID is good enough for me. She's shown up just in the nick of time, I'd say. A few more days and that little fella' would have been in the ground."

For two months, hundreds of inquiries had come in from all over the southern half of the United States. A dozen frightened parents had made the trip to St. Mary Parish, hoping—but really not hoping—that the body kept chilled in a drawer in the basement of Our Lady of Lourdes Hospital in Lafayette, covered with only a three foot square of cotton on the privates, would be their missing child. A deputy sheriff accompanied each parent to the morgue. Each one left drained and disappointed, but relieved as well. Hope remained.

The odds of ever knowing the identity of the boy had grown slim. Inexplicably slim. An adult John or Jane Doe was not unusual, but a kid? Children usually, really almost always, had someone to care for them. Caretakers shift into overdrive when their charges go missing.

Apparently no one missed this boy. In a few more days, St. Mary Parish would fund a pauper's burial, leaving no trace of him on this earth save for police reports in the sheriff's murder pack, the readout of his DNA, and a couple of photographs of his dead eyes staring into the night. His name wouldn't even show up in any law enforcement database of unsolved crimes. This John Doe file would become a cold case tucked away inside a closed investigation—the second victim of the crimes attributed to Danny Howard.

"Has Dr. Petain already done his autopsy?" I asked Tony as we walked out of the DA's office to go next door.

"Right. I have the report for you right here." Tony pointed to the red file his secretary carried. She pulled out a thin manila folder and handed it to me. "There are a couple of interesting findings in there, but we won't really need them now that we have someone who can make a positive."

Tony may not have needed the findings, but I did. I was still scrambling to develop a plausible defense for my client, and maybe there'd be something in there I could use. Unfortunately, a positive ID of the victim strengthened Tony's case.

"So this lady from Houston says the boy is her sister's adopted kid?"

"Yes. Named Jerome Davis, known to her as Ti-Boy."

"But she's from Houston? What was her nephew doing around here?"

"It's complicated. The Sheriff called in Brett to take the lady's statement, and that's no easy job, she's so distraught. We may need to give her time to bury the boy before we can get it all straight. The sheriff and I left the interrogation room in the hope she'd feel more comfortable."

I could hear the woman wailing when we went through front door of the sheriff's office. Capt. Daigle waited for us. He threw a polite glance in my direction to acknowledge my presence, but he spoke directly to Tony.

"I sent Theresa in there so the woman would have a shoulder to cry on. Here's what I have so far. Name: Jerome Davis, known as Ti-Boy. Mrs. Duncan, the lady we have here, is his aunt. Not blood. Mrs. Duncan's sister was caring for the boy, maybe had actually adopted him. *Auntee's* not sure. Anyway, the sister floated away in the floods of Katrina. Mrs. Duncan and this boy were picked up by a passing boat and ended up in the Superdome. She's spent a good bit of time telling me horror stories about that experience. After six days in that dome, they got loaded onto a bus and were driven to the Cajundome in Lafayette. That's when she lost the boy."

"Lost him?" I asked. "How do you lose someone in there?"

"He just disappeared. One night Ti-Boy lay on a cot next to her when she went to sleep. The next morning he wasn't there. She says she about went crazy. Finally, someone told her the boy had gone off with some man they'd noticed hanging around him. The only name she could get for that man was something that sounded like Ma-Loo."

"Ma-Loo? I've never heard that handle, Ma-Loo,"

"Neither me. I guess if I was trying to run him down I start with Louviere, but who knows."

"The Cajundome in Lafayette must have a record of the guy. I know for a fact they ran a really tight ship in that shelter."

"No luck. The Cajundome has no record of Jerome Davis checking out, or of anyone checking out who could be the man Mrs. Duncan was told he left with. Actually, they say they never had anyone come in they can't account for, and they never heard of the name Ma-Loo. The Red Cross tried to help, but they had no success, at least until last week. The Red Cross lady is upstairs with Mrs. Duncan right now."

I had a bunch of questions, but I didn't want to interrupt. I let him go on.

"After a couple weeks in the Cajundome, Mrs. Duncan says they herded a bunch of them into another school bus and shipped them off to Houston—to the Astrodome. Her third 'dome.' She didn't want to leave without the boy, but they made her. Ultimately she got a job cleaning motel rooms over there in Houston and moved to an apartment. For the past year she's used every spare penny trying to find the boy."

"Brett," I couldn't hold back any longer. "You say Ti-Boy may have been adopted by this lady's sister? I assume the adoption took place in New Orleans."

"That's where Mrs. Duncan gets kind of fuzzy. She says her sister brought the boy home from church about six months before Katrina. She's never seen any paperwork for an adoption and isn't sure there is any. Mrs. D. only saw the kid a couple times when her sister would bring him to family gatherings, and she never learned anything about where he came from. The boy 'talked funny,' as she says, which makes me think he might be some kind of a foreigner."

"How old was he, did she say?"

"She says the boy claimed to be fourteen, but he didn't have any kind of ID. She thought he looked a couple years younger than that."

Emile Petain had hit the age on the nose. He was good.

"So I don't suppose she has any idea how the boy came to be here at the Pecan Gardens on the night of October 2nd, early morning the 3rd?" I asked.

"None whatsoever. She's totally mystified. The Red Cross is going to help her stay around a few days—to bury the boy, I guess. We'll get a chance to talk to her some more. She may remember more when she gets over the shock of it all."

"I'd like to talk to her, Brett."

"That's not the best idea right now, Mr. Clark. She's pretty distraught. Is there something in particular you'd like to know? I'd be happy to try to ask her. I think she's built up a little trust in Theresa and me."

"I guess the only question I have right now is about where the boy came from. The church might know. Could you ask her the name of her sister's church?"

"Yes. I'll do that tomorrow. The Red Cross lady is going to bring her back in the morning."

Capt. Daigle assured me they would do their best to locate the man called Ma-Loo. I wasn't convinced. The assignment was destined to slip far down his priority list. With Mrs. Duncan back in Houston, there'd be no local victim to put pressure on the sheriff or the DA to find the man, and both the sheriff and Tony believed they had closed the case with the arrest of Danny Howard. They had ID'd the second victim, and that would be enough to go forward with the prosecution. What good would it do them to find a man named Ma-Loo? Just a side complication that might delay things. He didn't fit anywhere into their theory of the case.

My conclusion? If I wanted Ma-Loo, Possum and I were going to have to find him ourselves.

I went down to our office on the first floor and put in a call to Possum. Then I opened the folder I got from Tony. The autopsy report was there, yes, but something else as well. A DNA read-out of the bloodspot found on Danny's T-shirt. Comparing the T-shirt bloodspot evidence with the DNA report on Clyde Carline, if I read the probabilities correctly, there appeared to be less than one chance in a million the two samples came from the same person. *The only shared loci are ones highly frequent in the population.* I'd have to check with Emile to be sure I understood what that all meant, but one in a million had a good ring to it.

So much for the only piece of physical evidence on which Brett and Theresa had based the arrest warrant that sent Danny to jail in the first place. Reading further in the report, I saw that the DNA of the blood spot evidence had even less correlation to the DNA of Jerome Davis or Danny Howard.

Thank God for modern forensic science. In days gone by, before DNA, finding the same blood type on Danny's T-shirt as that of one of two victims killed at the same time, apparently by the same instrument, might have been enough to convince a jury of Danny's guilt. He might have taken a fast trip to death row. End of story.

Which made me ponder the possibility that sometime in the future another blockbuster scientific achievement would revolutionize forensic certainty. That bit of progress wouldn't do any good for the people we'd already put to death.

But back to the case against my client. It took me a few minutes to bend my mind around the implications of Dr. Petain's autopsy report, and as the information sank in, I felt the heat of anger take up room in my chest. Face it, the cops had no fucking idea whose blood was on Danny's T-shirt, and Tony hadn't pointed out that fact when he handed me the file.

OK, I was pissed at Tony. But I was also pissed at my client. Wouldn't it be grand if Danny could give me a lead on where that blood came from? Then I might be able to get a line on *another dude.*

I settled in for a close read of the pathologist's report. On the first two pages, Emile Petain detailed his meticulous external examination of the body. Nothing extraordinary. But page three, his internal examination, told a story. *Examination of the bony structure reveals eight remodeled ante-mortem injuries to the tibia, clavicle and mandible... and bony deformation of the vertebrae and feet, probably resulting from bearing heavy loads.* Wow! This boy's little body had suffered some serious mistreatment early in his short life. Perhaps child labor?

The ringing of the telephone interrupted my thoughts. "It's Nanette, John."

"What's on your mind, girl? Somebody over there at the shelter in trouble with the city's finest?"

"Not this time. I'm calling about Medley Butterfield." Oh my God.

"Nanette. Not again." I couldn't hide my irritation. What was it with this woman that she didn't move on?

Actually, Medley had been creeping into my head ever since our cup of coffee at McDonald's. Her face had a way of appearing to me in the middle of the night. Each time that happened, I woke up with stirring down south. Then I recalled the hurt on her face when I had frozen her out.

"Yes, Medley again. I know you've already helped with the day-care problem, and I really appreciate that, but now she has another issue. By the way, she has begged me not to ask you for help. I insisted."

My guess was that the state of Mississippi hadn't sent on Medley's nursing license. I was going to be asked to run the traps of two state bureaucracies to get her out of an interstate paperwork snafu. I could do that without entanglement, right?

"A problem with her license?" I asked.

"No. Not that. The license came, and she has a job at ABC Home Health. Good job. In just a few weeks she'll be able to pay back your secretary's sister for daycare for her little boy. You know, I guess, that the district attorney dropped all charges against her."

"Good." I wasn't going to be asked to cause that to occur.

"She handled her charges herself, and a lot of other things. She's more than just any old nurse, that one. She's invaluable to me. She's moved to the shelter annex next door but still comes back here to volunteer when I'm in a bind. Right now she's in the back playing a quiet game with seven ordinarily hellacious kids whose mothers had to appear in court this morning, and she's been doing night shifts for me since I lost the intern I had on that duty. I don't usually get residents who are this put-together. I can't imagine how she ever ended up in her predicament."

"So, what's the problem?" Get to the point, Nanette. What is it you want me to do?

"Medley thinks someone is following her, someone she recognizes from the night when she and her husband were arrested in that drug bust. She doesn't recognize the man's face, but she does remember a tattoo on his lower arm. A nest of snakes."

"Really? Following her?"

I didn't say what I was thinking—that I had the idea the woman was following *me*. Or maybe haunting me would be a better description. But I trusted Nanette's antenna for trouble. If she was concerned, I needed to hear her out.

"Yes. I don't think she has enough to call the cops about, but maybe you could come over here and talk to her. You could give her some guidance about what to do. I'm used to angry husbands following my clients, but that could not be what's going on here. Her ex is in prison in Mississippi."

What the hell could I do? It appeared the fates, God, whatever, kept putting this woman in my path.

The shelter was just three blocks from the courthouse. I told Nanette I'd drop in during lunch. First I wanted to finish reading Emile's report on his forensic autopsy of the body we now knew was Jerome Davis. Maybe with a bit of time to let Nanette's request sink in, I'd think of some way I could get out of this unwelcome assignment to make another contact with Medley Butterfield.

I noticed that now I had no trouble remembering her name.

"Thanks, John. I owe you another favor. When you get here I may be gone to pick up the women who had to appear in court today, but that will only be a few minutes. Just come on over. The entry code is 462121, the citation to the domestic abuse statute. Medley will be with the children in the back. I'll tell her you're coming."

Medley had apparently garnered Nanette's complete trust.

I turned my attention back to the autopsy report and read a few more interesting findings: serious liver damage and tooth decay. What had our little T-Boy endured in his short life? Maybe Emile wouldn't want to speculate about the cause of these problems, but I figured I'd need to inquire.

And I had an idea. I called Brett Daigle and asked him to handle another question when he spoke with Mrs. Duncan about her sister's church. Did the sister ever mention any health problems that Ti-Boy may have had? Malaria, maybe? When I had the name of the church, I planned to send Possum to New Orleans and to add health issues to the list of questions he had for the people down there.

Thoughts of Medley kept wiggling their way into my mind. I gave in to them, put aside my papers, and walked over to the shelter.

I found Medley just where Nanette said she'd be, sitting on the floor with a half circle of children, all ages, around her, every eye fixed on her face.

"And then Lisette the Lizard tip, tip, tiptoed her four little feet over to the grass and disappeared." Medley made her hands tiptoe over the carpet. "No, Lisette the Lizard didn't really disappear, did she? What happened to Lisette, do you suppose? Why couldn't the children see her?"

"Because she turned GREEN!" the children called out in chorus.

"Right. And now Thomas the Tuxedo Cat couldn't see her any longer either. She was safe. Lisette hid there, green in the green grass, until Thomas got tired of waiting. He stretched his back, shook his head, stuck his little nose in the air, and wandered off to look for some other wiggly creature to capture."

Medley noticed me and stood up. She moved away from her charges and spoke just to me. "Dogs can't see color, and I'm not sure cats can either, but the story of Lisette the Lizard works for me every time."

Medley tried to tell me about her problem, but as soon as the children lost her total attention, they began to act up. All I could get out of Medley was that she had seen a tattooed man in the grocery store and again at the park where she took the shelter children. And now she'd seen him a third time. The day before, when Nanette was out, she'd spotted a tall blond in a truck parked across the street from the shelter. She couldn't see the tattoos this time, but the man looked like the one she'd seen before. And the one she had caught sight of the night of her arrest.

"I don't suppose you got a license number?" I asked.

"The plate was covered with dirt, even though the truck was shiny clean."

Not good.

"And you say he's someone you saw the night you were arrested?"

Medley looked up to me and shivered. "I'll never forget those tattoos. That night he and another person, a boy, ran out the back of the house."

OK Nanette. This one's for you. I extended an invitation to Medley.

"Tomorrow's Saturday. Are you free for lunch?"

"I can be."

"I'll come by around noon. You can tell me about him without distractions."

LUNCH WITH MEDLEY

I arrived at the shelter shortly before noon. I found Medley in the yard. Her little boy was tumbling around in a mix of children on the swings and monkey bars. She turned to a pretty Latina girl there with her.

"They're all yours, Maria. An hour or so, OK?"

"Take your time."

"We could walk the two blocks to the sandwich shop on Main Street," I offered. "Or, if you have any interest in oysters, we could drive down the road a bit to the Yellow Bowl. Your choice."

"I have a pretty tight budget..."

I laughed. "My treat. Or I may put the bill on Nanette's IOU."

The idea of a date made me nervous, but I was just returning a favor to Nanette, right? She had begged me to evaluate whether the man following Medley posed a threat. I still felt a little guilty about hurting the woman's feelings the other day, but I'd keep the conversation strictly professional.

Medley wrinkled her nose. "I have never eaten an oyster, but I do like the thought of getting out of town." She changed the subject, looking solemn. "You know, I begged Nanette not to bother you, but she insisted."

"That's OK. Yellow Bowl it is."

I must have anticipated that a ride in my car might be on the program. Last night I'd spent some time cleaning out Blue Betsy. It had been a long time since I cared what anyone thought about my old Toyota, but apparently I didn't want Medley to see what a slob I was.

"How about an appetizer of a few fried oysters?" I asked Mary, the waitress who was always on hand for the lunch crowd. "I have a newby here. Even though I've given her my enthusiastic recommendation, she isn't sure. We'll decide on what to order after that."

Medley laughed. A lovely rippling sound. Today, up to this point, she had barely smiled.

"I'm relieved, Mr. Clark. I thought I was going to have to be a good sport and face a plateful of those critters."

"John. Call me John."

"OK." And another smile.

Medley tried an oyster, and looked up at me with those wide green eyes. "An acquired taste. I think I'd rather have a shrimp sandwich. Po-boy, I guess you call it."

We ordered, and I got to the reason for our meeting.

"Nanette tells me you're concerned that someone's following you, someone you think you saw the night you were arrested."

"Yes. Maybe I'm being paranoid, but . . ."

"Go ahead. Tell me about it."

"Three weeks ago I was at the grocery store doing the shopping for the shelter. I saw this tall man who looked vaguely familiar, but I didn't know why. Instinctively, cheery little Mississippi girl that I am, I smiled and said, 'Hi, there!' The guy acted as if I'd hit him with a stick. He literally turned tail and ran out of the store, leaving his half-full basket of groceries sitting smack in the middle of the aisle. Then bammo." Medley hit her forehead with her fist. "I remembered when I had seen him before—the night of my arrest. I didn't actually recognize the face, but I couldn't forget the tattoo—a nest of snakes poking out from the turned up cuff of his shirt sleeve."

Medley drew in breath and straightened her back, seeming to need strength to continue her story. I prodded.

"You say you saw the same tattoo on a man who was at

the house the night of the bust? Was he arrested also?"

"No, he didn't get arrested, but he was there. He was in a back room and ran out."

"Maybe you'd better tell me all about that night. Let's finish our po-boys first. Time is not kind to fried food."

We wrestled the hard crusted bread into our mouths, liberally squirting globs of spicy mayonnaise onto our plates. Medley laughed at the mess.

"'Face over your plate, Medley,' my Gram used to preach at me! Good advice when you're tackling a po-boy."

How had this gentle young woman ended up in the company of a known drug dealer, in a house chock-a-block full of the tools of the drug trade? It didn't make sense.

We polished off our po-boys and sat back. "OK. Start at the beginning."

She looked puzzled. I guess she was trying to figure out just how far back to go. "Starting when?"

"Starting with what brought you to Louisiana."

"OK." She put one hand on the table and I could see she had made a fist. "Jack, that's my husband, Jackson Butterfield, had come to Louisiana to join his old seismic crew. They'd gotten a contract for work in the Basin. He'd worked with that crew about five years ago, in Mississippi, before his National Guard unit got called up and deployed to Iraq. I was all for the move. We'd been having some personal problems, and I thought a change of location would be a good thing. New start and all that."

Medley stopped and took a sip from her water glass. Her soft brown hair, that had been pulled tight in a rubber band the first time I saw her, now swung loosely around her face.

"And?"

"Jack really hadn't been the same since Iraq. Now I know I should've realized what was going on. He went out at night, slept until mid-morning, and talked on the telephone with people I didn't know. But nurse's hours aren't nine to five either. I believed him when he said he was doing hotshot deliveries for an oil service company." She paused. "That isn't really what you asked me about, is it? Girl talk. You asked about the man with the tattoos, and I'm dumping my whole life story on you."

I was curious to hear her whole life story, but wary. When I didn't rush to give her encouragement, she sensed my diffidence and got to more recent events.

"After Jack had been over here about a month, he called and told me the job was going well. He'd rented a house and wanted us to come meet him. I hated to leave my Gram—my grandmother who raised me, and who babysat Buddy while I worked—but I came.

"Three days, two nights. That's how long I'd been here when all this happened. Yes, Jack had rented a house, all right. That was the truth, but he didn't tell me everything. Two other guys from the seismic crew were living in the house with us. A pretty big bit of information to leave out, wouldn't you say?"

Medley took another sip from her water glass and ran her tongue over her teeth.

"The first day after I arrived, I mostly slept. It had been a long, hard bus trip with the baby. The next two days passed uneventfully. I went to the store to buy groceries, cooked some, and took Buddy to the park to play. When I think back on it now, I realize that I barely saw Jack those few days. That night, the night when it all happened, he told me to stay in the back 'cause he had some people coming over. I did that."

Medley's voice quavered. She bit the corner of her bottom lip.

"Around eight o'clock, there was all sorts of commotion. Shouting, and voices ordering everyone in the house to come up front. I was terrified. I picked up Buddy, opened our bedroom door, and did just that, went up to the living room. But two people I'd never seen before came out of the other bedroom and rushed right past us. Not the two guys that were staying there; two others. They fled out the back door. It was just bedlam in the living room. Cops in combat gear, guns drawn."

Her voice broke completely. She couldn't speak.

I gave her a few moments, and then brought her back to the subject of the two that fled. She seemed to have less trouble talking about them, and they were really what I needed to hear about.

"Two people went out the back? Can you describe them?"

"A man. Tall, blond. And a boy. A black boy."

"The man is the one you think you've seen again. Right?"

"Yes. As he ran by me, he caught his sleeve on the doorknob of the bedroom and tore his shirt. I saw a crazy-looking tattoo. A nest of snakes. That's the same tattoo I'm pretty sure I saw on the man in the grocery store."

"Nanette tells me you think you've seen him again, recently. Right?"

"Well, I can't be positive of that. These last times I didn't see the tattoo."

"Tell me about them."

"First, about two weeks ago, coming out of a house on Willow Street where Lizzie and I were seeing a patient, there was this man who looked the same—blond, tall, thin face—sitting in a green truck parked across the street. I felt he was watching me. Then last week, when I took the shelter-kids to the park..." Medley paused and swallowed hard. "I'm probably just over-reacting. I don't know how I've gotten myself into this situation. I once had such hope that Jack and I could get back to how things used to be, especially for Buddy's sake. That's totally gone now, of course. Now this business about being watched. I'll admit, I'm kind of scared."

I had questions on the tip of my tongue. Did she have

any reason to believe the man who ran out of the house thought she knew something that might be a problem for him? Was he intimidating her to keep her quiet? I decided on just one question.

"Have the police talked to you at all since that night?"

"No. They haven't."

That was a good sign. Sending Jackson Butterfield back to Mississippi had apparently closed their file. If the police had no interest in Medley, maybe Jack's Louisiana connections had no reason to be interested in her either.

"Then I'm not too concerned, Medley. I'm going to see if I can find out anything about this man with the tattoo, but it really doesn't sound as if he has any harmful intent. Keep your eyes open, of course, and let me know if you think you see him again."

I had my plan. I'd dig out the arrest reports connected to the drug bust. They might contain use useful information. And I'd talk to the narcs. I wasn't only interested in the white man. What about the other person who came out of the room that night? An unknown, black boy. Could it be coincidence that on the very same night a black boy, name also unknown, was stabbed to death about a half mile away behind the Pecan Gardens Apartments? I carefully went back to her for a little more information.

"Tell me about the black boy who ran out of the back of the house. Can you describe him for me?"

"Not really. He was small, thin, very dark skin."

"Could you guess his age?"

"No. I couldn't. But not a big teenager or anything."

"Did you hear him speak?" I have learned that how someone sounds can be very helpful in identification.

"No. He just scooted by behind the white man."

Dead end. I had no idea where I could go to find out more about the boy. If these two escaped, they wouldn't be in the arrest report. But perhaps if the narcs had been watching the house, one of them might have some ideas.

Something else snuck its way into my mind. How did Medley stand with that no-good husband of hers? Was there any way he could be behind the activities of the person following her?

"Where is your husband now? Do you know?"

"Parchman, I guess. Gram told me when he left Mississippi he was on parole from a long-ago charge that neither of us knew anything about. When he got sent back over there, he went straight to prison to serve the twenty years of the sentence he had hanging over his head. Gram says there might be a trial for some of the recent stuff, but no one is in a hurry. They know they have him off the street." Medley's voice cracked. "I've been very stupid. Very, very stupid."

Her face twisted in an effort to keep back tears. Without realizing I was doing so, I reached across the table and covered her hand. Was she regretting the loss of her husband, or was she just ashamed of what she'd been involved in?

And just exactly why did I need to know that? Watch out, you idiot.

Some bread pudding might make her feel better. With two fingers, I signaled Mary to bring two instead of just one of my usual dessert. And I cast about for a lighter topic of conversation.

"Tell me, how's the job going?"

Her face relaxed. "Really great. I guess some people would say making house calls on the poor and dying is a demotion—back home I managed a home health service in two counties—but I like it. The pay is actually better here and I have some flexibility arranging the hours. That's a good thing since I have to arrange daycare for Buddy. The patients take my mind straight off my problems. I'm sorry I had to sell my car because now I need one, but in a few months I'll have saved enough for a down payment. I'll find something."

"What about your Gram?"

Now, why the hell was I asking these questions?

"Yes, Gram. I've got to work out something for her. She's relying on her younger sister to help her out right now, but I don't think that'll last. Aunt Dell may go live with her daughter in Meridian. I dream about getting Gram to come here, and she just might do that. I've talked with Nanette and she has a few ideas."

Medley changed the subject. "I guess you know you have quite a blessing in Nanette. Her job title may be administrator of the shelter, but she is so much more. Social service advisor, employment agency, confidant, counselor. Nanette can get you to think about yourself in a whole new way. She's really helped me."

"She says the same about you, you know." My next question just slipped out. "How has she helped you, Medley?"

"I was beating myself up pretty bad about getting into this predicament. But you don't want to hear all that past history. And anyway," Medley looked at her watch, "I need to get back. I don't think I can impose on Maria to watch the kids any longer."

I confronted the realization that I wanted to spend more time with this lovely young woman. Just company. I'd be very careful, of course. No complications.

"So can the story be continued?" I asked. "Maybe we could have lunch another day?"

She lifted those luminous green eyes, and I didn't take a breath until she answered.

"That would be very nice, provided we leave time for your past history as well."

"Well..." I'd have to think about committing to disclose any of that. There was absolutely no need.

She said she'd give me a call after moving day. I dropped her back at the shelter, and I caught myself humming all the drive home.

The rest of Saturday I fooled around with the hardware I'd found in New Orleans. It fit the cypress doors quite well. I called Emile Petain. He was in New Orleans for the weekend but said he'd come back early Sunday afternoon to help me with the project.

Each time I passed by the mirror I'd hung in the hallway, I could see a smile on my face.

* * *

"Blind hog found an acorn," was the way Lt. Marcus Magrette, Chief of Narcotics, put it to me when I questioned him about the cocaine bust he had led last October. Almost six feet tall, shaved head, biceps bulging in a tight black T-shirt, handcuffs hanging from a loop on his jeans.

"Mississippi was burning up the wire for us to go out and find this dude called Jackson Butterfield, wanted for flight from state and federal charges of trafficking crack. They had information saying he'd come with a work party to an address in our parish. Jude, my partner, and I went to the house. We knocked. The door opened, and we just kind of slipped our feet over the threshold nice and easy. A couple of guys were crouched over a table on one side of the room. One of them had on green rubber gloves and held a metal ruler. Tools of the trade. Right away we recognized Butterfield from his picture. Big dude. You could put a gray uniform on him and he'd pass for Robert E. Lee."

Lt. Magrette laughed at his own joke.

"There was a bunch of other people in the room, and every pair of eyes shot up to look at us, like a conductor had waved his baton, or something. Bags, rocks, scales, you know, all the usual paraphernalia of the retail dealer decorated the table." He smiled. "All in plain view, right?"

Sure, Marcus. Plain view.

"Then, everyone in the room began scurrying around like we'd stepped in a pile of red ants. I think we got ten people all together."

"You got them all? Are you sure? Do you think it possible that some people got away from you, maybe out the back?" I asked.

"What? Out the back? No way."

I asked the killer question. "Had you secured the back door to the house before you went in?"

Marcus had been open, comfortable, downright boastful up to this point. Now his eyebrows pinched. The policeman's distrust of the defense lawyer showed all over his face. He thought I was trying to make him look bad.

"Well, no. But..." He recovered his bravado. "No fucking way, man. This bust came down real fast. No time for anyone to escape. We had the place shut down stat."

"Good. Had you narcs been watching this house? Did you know any of these people beforehand?" I asked.

"No, we weren't watching the house. Turns out we knew some of the people in there and some we didn't. But they were small potatoes. Just a few customers and retail dealers. Nobody really high up the ladder except Butterfield, and we sent him right back to Mississippi. If Mississippi hadn't been so antsy to get him, we wouldn't have busted the place. We'd have worked to turn some of them to get information on the suppliers."

That's the way the game was played. Law enforcement tried to make deals with the lower level dealers to get at ones higher up the food chain.

"What happened to the charges against the people you arrested?" I asked.

Magrette snickered. "Whatcha think? The usual crap. Some charges got dropped; some guys pled out to lesser offenses and went on probation. They're probably all back out on the street doing it again. One crack house closes down, another takes its place. We've got job security, you know."

"And Butterfield's wife?"

"Charges dropped." He smiled. "But I think you know that."

Word spreads quickly through the courthouse. I was an idiot to ask the question.

Lt. Magrette got me the offense report for the bust. I found the names of those who were arrested and passed them by a couple more narcotics officers. They had the same opinion; the operation involved merely low-level salesmen. No one knew anything about two people who might have slipped away in the night.

Law enforcement had no professional interest in Jackson Butterfield's wife. I felt relief, and then a jerk of annoyance with myself. Why did I care? No involvement, remember?

I didn't heed my own caution. We had another lunch together and then I asked her to go to dinner.

PART III — LATE WINTER

REQUESTS FOR THE JUDGE

As I predicted, the Grand Jury returned two true bills against Danny Howard. Two indictments for first degree murder. Tony filed notice he would try the cases together and seek the death penalty in each one. Damn overkill.

The Ping-Pong device in the office of the St. Mary Parish Clerk of Court shot out a green ball assigning the trial to Judge Mari Johnson. A former assistant district attorney, yes, but we could have done a lot worse. Young, African-American, energetic and known to spend time reading the law. Thank God we didn't pull Judge Wright. He was the best argument around for mandatory judicial retirement. As far as the courthouse crowd was concerned, the day he would reach seventy years of age couldn't come soon enough.

I camped out on the worn pew outside the door to the judge's office and settled in to wait for Judge Johnson to finish her day in court.

My mind kept slipping sideways to Medley Butterfield, and to a review of all the reasons I didn't need personal complications right now. I had enough on my plate with my regular work duties and the case of State v. Daniel Howard. Yes, I had lonely evenings, and my methods for sexual release left me depressed, but a quick rerun of the hell of the last few years set me straight. I didn't need that again.

But I wouldn't necessarily have to get involved. Maybe just a date now and then. I could be very careful and take care not to deceive.

No. Forget about it, dummy.

I lengthened my breaths, stretched out my legs, and tipped my head back to pass the time with progressive muscle relaxation. I didn't get above my ankles. Water stains on the ceiling tiles morphed into the shapes I had imagined as a boy lying flat on my back watching cloud patterns in the summer sky. Was that the head of a lion rising from the African bush? The Bounty on the Main? Or maybe the head of Black Charlie?

No muse created this art. No. The prisoners upstairs in the jail relieved their boredom by stuffing the toilets with whatever they could lay their hands on, causing a disgusting overflow to seep slowly downward, stain the tiles, and in a good hard rain seep through the walls. Then came the redolence of mold.

A few years back, when a federal order required the parishes to supply local inmates with law books, Black Charlie did as ordered. Soon the prisoners had a generous supply of material for their pastime. Page after page of the criminal codes met the water. Charlie gathered up the remains of the books, tossed them in the trash, and defied the feds to come 'do him somethin'.

No matter the grunge in this building, I'd grown fond of the place. Courtroom law practice requires a lot of waiting around. I much preferred killing time with these easy-going country people than in the pretentious and tense atmosphere of the federal court in New Orleans. I'd spent four years in those cold marble halls, doing the bidding of my father-in-law, taking a client out to a stuffy lunch, and then trying to rack up billable hours until late at night while my wife waited at home alone—alone until she found someone who was available. If I had spent the first few years of my law practice in the country, I might still be married.

At least, the years in New Orleans allowed me to get past the circumstances under which my father and I left

Franklin, to live through and beyond the nightmare of the accident in which my mother lost her life. Now I look at the corner of Pecan and Main, where that huge truck barreled down Pecan Street and crashed into our car, as a memorial to my mom. My dad couldn't get through his grief, and in his grief I read his accusation. *If you hadn't cried out to tell her to stop, she would have sailed through the intersection before the truck reached Main.* Years had to pass before I could bury the guilt.

Maybe. So what was keeping me from clearing the front yard and rebuilding the driveway opening onto Main?

I ran my hand through my thinning hair. For sure, if I'd started practice in the country, I'd have a few more strands on my head. I sat back, closed my eyes, and let time slip by.

I had told Tony that I'd like to meet with the judge on the Danny Howard case. Given the nature of what I would be asking, Tony had no problem agreeing to let me talk to her alone. I needed the meeting face-to-face because my requests were all tricky. That was what judges were elected to do, right? To make decisions that have no easy solutions? Right now Judge Johnson was in court doing exactly that.

In spite of the lateness of the hour, I was pretty sure she'd hear me out. She took time with the lawyers. Although she used to be a prosecutor, or perhaps because of that fact, she respected the job the defense had to do. But I knew not to waste her time. Which of my requests should come first? Sitting out here waiting provided an opportunity for me to ponder and to make a plan.

Judge Johnson returned from court shortly after six o'clock. She must have been tired, but she didn't let it show. She actually seemed pleased to see me.

"What can I do for you, Mr. Clark?"

"Just a couple of things on my mind, Judge. If you have anything left after what I can see was a long day."

"They're all long. I'm not complaining. I actually

campaigned for this job, you know. Have a seat."

She sat down behind her eight-foot desk. Her secretary and her law clerk had gone home over an hour before, leaving behind a stack of pink telephone messages by her phone. On the other side of the desk, a foot-high pile of routine civil orders and a few dozen warrants waited for her signature. Focus on one issue at a time was the judge's motto. That's how she got through the workload.

"I want to run a couple of things by you on the Danny Howard case, Judge Johnson. You got the lucky ball on that one, I guess you know."

"Yes, I saw my docket. He is so young." Her eyebrows pinched together. "Tony is proposing I set this case for trial next month. What's the big rush here?"

I had started to sit down, but with this information I actually fell into the leather chair across from her desk.

"What? Next month? No way."

"Right. No way. Tony knows better than that. The earliest I can find time in my court calendar is May. Clyde Carline's uncle has the heat on, I hear, but Tony can just tell Senator St. Germain it's the judge's fault that we can't go to trial. The political big shot will be mad at me instead of District Attorney Strait." She rolled her eyes. "But I guess that's why we wear the black robe."

So Mr. Strait called it when he went for the quick grand jury. The senator got his one favor. One and done.

"So what's on your mind, Mr. Clark?" the judge continued.

"I know we can't have a substantive *ex parte* conversation about the case, Judge. The DA has to be present for that. So if I step over the line, please stop me. But since we've been notified that this will be a capital case, I know you've a high duty to safeguard the process itself, to assure the defendant gets a competent defense. What I have to talk to you about falls into that category. Competent defense."

"Duly noted. I'll be on guard." She pulled a yellow legal pad off the back table. She would make careful notes of the discussion and put them into her file. The clerk of court kept the official records, but Judge Johnson had plenty of her own.

"I have a situation here. May I give you a peak into how we underfunded defense lawyers manage with what little we have?"

"Sure. Shoot."

"Usually the defense doesn't need to worry about a thorough investigation of a double murder. The prosecution digs deep and uses all the resources of law enforcement: the sheriff's office, city police, State Police, Crime Lab, experts, whatever. Sometimes they call in the FBI. Then the district attorney turns over the entire work-product to me, to the defense. We benefit from the investigation without spending the money or doing the work. We have a pretty good deal, I'd say."

Her face opened in a knowing smile. "I agree. Very good deal for the defense. I used to be on the other side, you know."

"I do know. But in this case? Not such a good deal, Judge."

"No? And why not?" She tipped her head to the right.

"Because law enforcement thinks they finished their work when they ended their investigation into the death of Clyde Carline. I will admit to you the DA has a triable case against my client for an offense against Carline—alone. But there is no capital crime without intent to harm the second victim. And the DA is ready to go forward with a capital prosecution of my client for the death of the boy. All he has is weak circumstantial evidence where the boy is concerned. I object."

Her eyebrows shot up. "Really? You object? Is his decision to bring either case to trial any of your business?"

"No, but..."

Judge Johnson sat forward in her armchair, her full frame filling the seat from one armrest to the other. She ran her long fingers over her head, a close crop she had worn since her days on the basketball court at ULL. "If the DA feels ready to go to trial, that is his prerogative. *Entire charge and control of every criminal prosecution instituted or pending in his district.* Isn't that the way the statute defines his authority?"

"Yes. The DA calls the shots. I understand that."

"And isn't it in your interest to be able to point out in the trial that the investigation is incomplete? That proceeding to trial at this point is premature? A rush to judgment? The jury might go for that argument."

"Yes. But what about the flip side? Clyde Carline could have been collateral damage during the murder of the boy, for which my client has no known motive. You know I will make those arguments. But..." I took a deep breath to prepare my request. "Law enforcement has stopped looking for an explanation of the second murder."

"So?"

"Please understand that I don't accuse the prosecution, or law enforcement, of not being on the up-and-up, but how can I prepare a defense if I don't know of any connection between my client and the second victim? The only strategy left to me in the guilt phase of this trial is denial. And my only strategy in the penalty phase is to argue there is no reason my client would do this. Not much of a defense. And even for that defense I'll need to research his background."

Judge Johnson's dusky skin grew darker, camouflaging the freckles that covered her cheeks and nose. She narrowed her eyes. "Mr. Clark, I smell something. You are about to ask for more time than the four months we have between now and when I have the next possible trial date."

When judges have found three weeks for a capital trial, they hate to upset their calendars. "No, ma'am. I can make a trial date four months from now if..."

"If what, counselor?" She narrowed her eyes.

"If the public defender's office gets some funding to do our own investigation into the death of Jerome Davis."

Her reddish eyebrows shot upward again.

"I should have anticipated you would want money, Mr. Clark. Time and money are really all I have to offer, and you just told me you don't need time. Do you have any specific line of investigation that you want the court to fund?"

"Not at the moment, but..."

The judge settled back in her chair, the way she did when her pondering had finished and she had made up her mind. I'd seen it a dozen times. She tented her fingers and smiled like Queen Latifah.

"File your motion, Mr. Clark. We'll have a closed hearing on the issue of funding your investigation. When it's over, here's what I'll probably say. If there's some specific line of inquiry that should be done by the investigating authorities, and you can show me that they're not doing it, I will order them to do so. But making the parish government give you funds to run your office? No way."

Her long fingers swept outward, ridding the air of my distasteful request.

I thought better of pursuing the issue any further. "Thank you, Judge." I said. But I kept my seat.

"Something else on your mind?" Judge Johnson asked. Those rusty eyebrows rose again. Somewhere back there one of her ancestors must have been a redhead.

"I do have in mind some additional investigation that we can do on our own, on the cheap, but I need some help for that as well. Not money, not time, but your signature on a piece of paper. I need you to bless my access to some records."

"Oh, yes. I guess my John Hancock is one of my

powers." Her cheeks swelled in a smile. "What records?"

"There must be some reason why Jerome Davis visited the apartments that fateful night, some connection to someone who lives there. There must be some reason he had no ID and not a cent in his pockets. To answer those questions, I'd like to study every single person who lived in, or regularly visited, Pecan Gardens."

"Sounds like good thinking to me. Something or someone brought him there. And for that you will need... "

"Judge, I would like permission to look at the juvenile records of everyone who was around that night, both those who are juveniles now and those who've aged out. If I study the incident reports of all the offenses of all of the residents, I just might run across some connection to our second victim."

Again Judge Johnson ran her fingers over her head. "Now you have cut yourself in for a shitload of work, if you'll pardon the expression."

Judge Johnson's language slipped when she was tired, which I'm sure she was by now. She continued. "That's a pretty big apartment complex, Mr. Clark. Probably a third of those residents are underage now or lived there when they were kids. And the list of residents isn't going to look like the social register. I've only been doing the juvenile docket for a couple of years now, but I bet I would recognize half of those kids if they walked in my courtroom."

"I know. But I have a law student intern who can help with some of the tedious work. You may know Kaniesha Morris."

The judge clouded. "No, I don't know her."

"Her mother is Sheila Morris in the clerk's office."

"Oh, yes. I apologize. I thought you were giving me the 'you're from New York so you must know my friend.' You're black so you must know..."

"Kaniesha has already done an amazing project for us.

She took every statement the DA got from the apartment dwellers—you know Tony gave us the entire investigative file—and made a chart. The x-axis is the hours of the evening; the y-axis is the names of the witnesses; the intersecting boxes have the statements by each one of them about what happened at that time. Then she did the same with the information from the interviews Possum and I did over at the apartments. Revealing."

I didn't know if I would be trying to introduce Kaniesha's chart as demonstrative evidence—pointing out a raft of inconsistencies in the witness statements—but I thought I'd put my toe in the water. Before I could bring up the topic Judge Johnson smiled, anticipating my thoughts. She liked to spar with the lawyers.

"The admissibility of that chart will be an interesting pre-trial motion, counselor. But here we're touching on a conversation that should include the district attorney."

"I agree. Sorry. Another day."

"File your motion for the juvenile records. I'll need a complete list of those you want. If I grant your motion, my order of disclosure will include a condition that you assure protection of the confidentiality of the records, and I'll need to have a good long talk with your intern to be certain she understands what that means. As for that chart? Not today's problem."

"Right, judge."

I was reasonably certain I would win the motion for disclosure of the juvenile records. I was even more optimistic when Judge Johnson told me a story from her juvenile court experience, and when, for a little while, she didn't address me as Mr. Clark.

"John, I had one of the girls whose name is on the preliminary witness list—I won't tell you which one—on probation to me for being ungovernable. That's a fancy term for running away from home, if you can call what she ran away from a real home. The elderly grandmother who raised her had no clue how to control a teenage hellion with raging hormones. She could do little more than wring her hands. The frustrated probation officer kept bringing the girl back for me to give her a talking to.

"One time, after the officer picked her up during school hours at the apartment of some forty-year-old creep, he brought her to court for revocation of her probation." Judge Johnson smiled at the memory. "The girl sashayed into court in an itty-bitty, skin-tight denim mini-skirt. She flopped herself down in front of the bench. Expensive hairdo, no doubt funded by the guy. Surly expression. Then her knees gaped apart. A dark bush. I had an unobstructed view of the wares she was peddling in the 'hood.'"

A rosy blush colored the judge's cheeks, and she continued.

"When I recovered my composure, I gave the girl a blistering earful and sent her to detention. But I had to hand it to this one. She had found a brand new way to say f--- you to the whole judicial system!"

I laughed out loud. "Her poor lawyer. Some other judge might have held *him* in contempt for the girl's behavior!"

"You're used to dealing with garden variety crime by grownups, John. Let me tell you, these kids today can drive you to the brink." The judge tipped back her chair and raised her eyes to the ceiling. "I wonder what happened to that girl."

In spite of her exasperation, Judge Johnson still cared about every kid who crossed her path.

I wouldn't have been a bit surprised to have her tell me the girl was Nikki Roberts, Snap-Dog's girl friend. Ha! I looked forward to having the judge see Nikki as the chief witness for the prosecution.

"I have no experience with juvenile offenders, judge, here or in my brief time in the New Orleans PDO, but I have found adult crime here to be quite different. All the murder cases I handled down there were pretty much the same. 'Stick 'em up! Give me your money. Bang, bang. You're dead.' Here every case I get has some weird twist. I just finished defending a guy who loved his wife so much he put rat poison in her chili supper to deliver her—immediately—to her savior in heaven. The jury didn't reward his religious mission. And now we have a child victim who seems to have sprung full blown from the head of Jupiter."

Judge Johnson looked puzzled at my reference. Education in her background did not include Roman mythology.

"Came from nowhere, I mean, Judge."

"Is that it, Mr. Clark? Is that all you need today?"

"Judge, one thing more. I need some guidance." I saved my most interesting request for last because I believed she'd hang in there to hear this one to the end. "I need a certain kind of expert for this case, and I don't know where to find him."

Judge Johnson turned her chair and brushed her hand toward a stack of pamphlets, paperback books, and a few hard covers on the table behind her desk. "That pile is filled with ads for expert witnesses, Mr. Clark. You're welcome to take them *all* off my hands."

"Let me explain. Clearly, the issue of race is at play in this case. You know that Danny says that he's white, but he has distinctly African-American features. Danny's mother swears up and down that her boy is white and that his father was white. Our first victim, we call him that although we actually have no idea which one died first, was known to taunt with racial slurs. The prosecution theory is that Clyde Carline used the 'n' word and Danny flew into a rage, went back to the party to get a weapon, and then returned to stab Carline five times. I'm not sure about that going-back-for-the-knife testimony, but in any case there are several issues I need to explore in order to give Danny a good defense to that scenario. How did Danny handle his racial ambiguity? Did his understanding of his parentage have an effect on his behavior?"

Judge Johnson shook her head slowly. "Apparently his Mom thinks being African- American is nothing to be proud of."

"She's quite a puzzle to me, Judge. She keeps the wedding picture from her first marriage, to a white man, on the mantel piece, right in front of where she and her second husband sit to watch TV."

Judge Johnson chuckled. "That's a good way put the gris-gris on a second marriage! I don't think Oprah would approve."

"Danny won't talk to me about any of this. It is all well and good to teach your child that race doesn't matter, that we're all created equal, but what does it do to a kid to be told to deny his heritage?"

Judge Johnson's eyes narrowed. I couldn't see any of the specks of green I had noticed on other occasions.

"You're not going to argue to me, or to the jury, that something like this should justify murder?"

"No, Judge. But I need a psychologist or psychiatrist who can do a couple of things. First, to probe Danny's mind to learn how these ambiguities might have directed him. Then, if we get to the penalty phase, I need this person, or some other expert, to explain the issue to the jury. And lagniappe, really before any of that, I'd like the guy to get my client to talk to his lawyer. You know, he just sits there and tells me he's a white boy who has no memory of the evening. A bit hard to believe."

Now I saw the green specks sparkle.

"Are you thinking that because I'm African-American I might know such an expert?" she asked.

I swallowed hard. Had I again stumbled into offense? Everyone is more prickly when tired.

"No, but perhaps you may know where I could begin to look for one."

Her brows tucked together, and she thought for what seemed like a full minute before she answered.

"I do have an idea where you might start to look, John. The whole business of capital defense is ass-backward, you know. The Capital Post Conviction Project out of New Orleans is a very effective organization, but they don't step in to help with prosecutions at the trial level or even on state appeal. You defense lawyers struggle along on your own, with limited public resources. Come the federal post-conviction phase, *after* a sentence of death has been upheld by the state Supreme Court, CPCP pulls out all the stops. Wouldn't it be dandy if we could get them on board before the horse left the barn? You're a persuasive kind of guy. Maybe you could convince them to help you now."

"I doubt it, but you have a good thought. Maybe they know of an expert who could help me. I know they're deep into study of whether sentences of death are unconstitutionally affected by the race of a defendant. They also study whether the decision of the DA to seek the death penalty is affected by the race of the victim. CPCP must know of a psychologist who studies these issues, one who might be able to transfer some of that expertise to this case. Good suggestion. I'll give them a call."

"Another thought, John. I can give you the names of some organizations of black lawyers. They might also have ideas."

The judge showed obvious interest in my situation. I wondered where she stood on the death penalty. My best guess? Personally opposed, but sworn to do her duty, to uphold the law of the state. I knew better than to put her on the spot by asking.

"If they do know of someone, Judge Johnson, it may become necessary for me to seek funding..."

She sat forward in her chair. "Ah, yes. Back to the bucks. We'll take that up when you have a plan. First, see who you can find. I can tell you right now I'm going to require you to exhaust the PDO funds before I go to the parish government to order them to pay for your expert. A capital murder trial is a budget breaker as it is."

"Agreed."

"And a tip. There are advantages for you if you fund your own inquiry and keep your effort in-house. If you find your own money, you may not have to reveal the details of your strategy to me or to anyone involved in the so-called closed hearing. As you know, the walls of this old building leak more than rainwater and overflow from the toilets upstairs."

I left the judge's office with renewed hope—not necessarily for getting my client off, but for giving him a decent defense and a fair trial.

THE SHRINK

The St. Mary Parish jail is as unpleasant in winter weather as in the heat of summer. Hot air blasts from two high vents—one at the front of the central corridor and one at the rear. The heat rises to the ceiling between the two and stays trapped there, impotent against the cold below. In the side cells, dampness leaks through barred windows and settles on the bare concrete floor. Baggy cotton jump suits provide poor protection for the prisoners shivering on their cots.

I only visited Danny every few weeks now, usually as a sideline to consultations with my other clients. The visits didn't go well. I had nothing to report and Danny had nothing to say. He continued to claim no memory of what happened after he left that fateful party, a claim I thought unbelievable, pigheaded, and downright stupid.

He refused to talk about race. As far as I could tell, Danny had lived a completely unexamined life. He could not be persuaded to start taking a look inside himself now.

At first, I had feigned credibility when in my client's presence. But now, with crunch time around the corner, I felt I had to crack Danny's shell. I tried every trick in my book, including the old 'good-cop/bad cop' method of interrogation.

On one visit I sympathetically prodded Danny to talk about himself.

"You liked sports, Danny, right? Baseball, I think, was your favorite, at least according to what I see in your school records. What position did you play?"

"Wherever they put me," came the flat answer.

"Did your team win a lot?"

"Sometimes." Danny shrugged one shoulder. He couldn't even be bothered to lift them both at the same time.

"Spring training has begun. Do you watch the majors on TV?"

"Not much."

"Are you a Red Sox fan? They may finally do it this year."

Silence. I got back that same empty stare, with shadows deep behind his eyes. I shuddered, remembering my father's eyes during the last weeks of his life.

On other days, out came the bad cop—a mean one.

"I see by the sign-in sheet that your Mother hasn't been to see you in a month, Danny."

"Yeah."

"So tell me, how does *that* make you feel?"

Danny sputtered air through his teeth. "Like shit, man. Why you bring that up?"

"Looks like Mrs. Gibbers has quit coming too."

"So what?"

"So you think they've all forgotten that you're in here maybe?"

"Fuck off, man."

One day I pulled out all the stops.

"Look here, Danny boy. You better remember something about leaving the Apartments that night or I won't be able to do a thing to help you. One fine day, not too long from now, those big fat black-and-red-uniform dudes at Angola are gonna strap your ass onto a gurney. They're gonna stick a needle in your arm, hook up a couple of rubber tubes, and shoot your veins full of three kinds of poison. You'll twitch and twitch and twitch." I jerked my head from one side to the other, miming the scene. "And you're gonna die, Danny. Not too quick either. Yup! Might take a bit of time, but pretty soon you'll be dead, dead, dead."

Danny dropped his chin. "So? I'm fucked, man."

No doubt about it, this boy needed professional help. And I needed help also. If Danny wouldn't talk to me, how could I ever put together a viable theory of defense? How could I persuade a jury Danny's was a life worth sparing?

"Danny, I'm going to make an appointment for a doctor to come here to see you." Danny scowled. "Yeah, I know you don't like that, but it's the law." Not so, but I was reduced to many lies dealing with this client. "Someone of the shrink profession has to see everyone charged with a capital offense. Yeah, I know. That's a bummer."

"Shit, man."

"The good news is that the defense gets to pick the expert, Danny, and I'm going to find someone I have a lot of confidence in. He may give you a written test or two, but mainly he'll just come visit you and ask a few questions."

"Which I don't have to answer."

I tucked away that reaction. Was Danny admitting that his failure to answer questions was a choice? No amnesia here.

"Whatever, Danny. I don't care if you answer the questions or not. But the law says the doctor has got to come."

* * *

Judge Johnson helped me get the Parish Government to pay for a psychiatric evaluation of Danny Howard and to foot the bill for the expert to return to testify at trial, should that become necessary. Most likely would be; the defense had the burden of proving any mental impairment affecting criminal responsibility and, should the trial move to the penalty phase, the defense was required to present evidence mitigating against the imposition of death.

With the help of material sent to me from the Louisiana Public Defender office, I scoured the medical literature for biological and genetic causes of criminal behavior, behavior that prosecutors prefer to paint for juries as just plain wicked. I found the name of a renowned New York forensic psychiatrist, Dr. Nicholas Hibou, who was making a reputation for himself with his studies of the etiology of violence in young men. Dr. Hibou currently examined a possible genetic predisposition that turned some individuals to violence when they were exposed to an inciting event. I sent off a package of Danny's records and put in a call. Bingo! Dr. Hibou responded.

Dr. Hibou expressed interest in studying Danny Howard as pilot data for his next research grant. Unlike most of the subjects available to the doctor—inner city youth from the ghettos of New York and Los Angeles where social restraints had completely dissolved—Danny did not possess what Dr. Hibou called "the usual complicating confounds." He was of average intelligence, had neither big-time substance abuse nor prior history of violent behavior, had not suffered a head injury. He appeared to have had only one trigger inciting him to violence—racial taunts. In a most fortunate circumstance, Dr. Hibou was scheduled to deliver a paper at an upcoming medical conference in New Orleans. He said he could cut out some time to slip away to visit my client in the St. Mary Parish jail.

Dr. Hibou had his goals in mind, but I had my own agenda. First and foremost, I wanted my client to talk to me. Second, I cared about my clients. If Danny needed treatment for what appeared to be depression, perhaps Dr. Hibou could cause that to occur.

I sent out an SOS to Reginald Denny, the contract counsel the State Public Defender Board frequently sent to assist in capital defense. In preparation for meeting with the psychiatrist, I needed a crash course in the current scholarship on the etiology of violence. Could Reg put together some pertinent reading material and get it to me?

Reg Denny spent a couple days in the library at the

State Office and collected medical textbooks, a dozen pamphlets, a score of scholarly journals, and copies of everything Dr. Hibou had written on the subject of violence. He drove to Franklin with two laundry baskets of material in the trunk of his car. From the right hand side of each publication, a clothesline of sticky notes marked material Reg thought might be helpful. So much for spending the weekend on my renovation projects. I started with a pamphlet that dealt with self-esteem. "A child internalizes negative messages from being ridiculed and teased." That could be Danny, all right.

He didn't talk to many people, except Mrs. Gibbers, and Possum told me she's bananas. He said a conversation with Snap-Dog's mother flowed in only one direction—out of her mouth.

"With low self esteem," the pamphlet explained, "a child suffers consequences. He may rebel, blame others, break rules, fight authority, suffer from depression."

Aha! When I asked Danny how he felt about being taunted, he said "depressed."

But could depression make someone stab two people to death? Make someone blank out for hours? I tackled a scholarly journal for a deeper explanation.

Under Louisiana law, the presence of a mental disease or defect is one of the two prerequisites for a defendant to escape criminal responsibility, the other being a finding that the defendant did not know the difference between right and wrong. Good old McNaughton Rule. Low self-esteem wouldn't give Danny a pass to being found innocent. An article in *The Psychology Journal* made it clear to me that low self-esteem fell far short of any of the conditions listed in the compendium of psychological diagnoses, the current edition of the *Diagnostic and Statistic Manual* known as *DSM-IV*. I wouldn't rule out presenting evidence on the subject, however. If I could raise a dose of sympathy for a kid who was taunted and dissed, some jurors might start looking around for another reason to cut the boy some slack. And, I reminded myself, I only needed one juror with me to save his life.

Should the jury find Danny guilty of the crime of first degree murder, heaven help us, low self-esteem would be relevant in the penalty phase as a factor in mitigation. Surely the jurors would empathize with a kid who didn't ever get positive reinforcement.

Next I tackled a marked article in another issue of *The Psychology Journal*, "Internalized Oppression." Tough sledding. After consulting a dictionary five times while trying to read the first two paragraphs, I took refuge in the executive summary on the front flyleaf. There I found a layperson's short explanation of the thesis.

> In sociology and psychology, internalized oppression is the manner in which an oppressed group comes to use the methods of the oppressor against itself. Sometimes members of a marginalized group hold an oppressive view toward their own group, or start to believe in negative stereotypes of themselves.

I got that. Danny seemed to have a very dim view of himself. I skipped down until my eye caught sight of the word race.

> Internalized racism occurs when a person begins to believe that racial stereotypes are true, like that he is less intelligent or academically inferior to those of another race.

I got that, too. No one ever told Danny to be proud of what he was. At some point in his childhood, he must have realized that some people thought his race shameful. Some people indeed—his own mother! For a reason of her own, Josie Chastant continued to deny to him the obvious facts. Danny never heard the message of 'black is beautiful.'

What was left for him? Depression, for sure.

But would these feelings cause Danny to be violent? Dr. Hibou might shed some light on that subject. Would depression give him amnesia? I had a bunch of questions for the psychiatrist.

I picked up another journal, this time one step deeper into the business of understanding the mind, *The American Journal of Psychiatry*. The title of one tagged article made no sense and the subheading only a bit: 'A study of genetic predictors of impulsive violence.' Two more cups of coffee failed to dim my throbbing headache. The rest of the morning slipped away. Still I wasn't getting it.

After a break for lunch, I tackled one of Dr. Hibou's supposedly less scientific articles. My eyes fell on a few paragraphs in an article entitled "Violence" in *The Psychiatric Review*.

> Although murder rates vary from place to place, the pattern of violence does not. Most violence occurs between unemployed, unmarried young men; 80% of both perpetrators and victims are between the ages of 15 and 19. Success in work and marriage, coupled with the passage of time, appear to dampen a criminal career.

> An evolutionary biologist would explain this pattern by positing that violence is an understandable response to competition for sex and status. For a nonevolutionary biologist, an area appropriate for scientific inquiry would seek to study a correlation and possible causative relationship between abnormal serotonin receptor genes and impulsive behavior.

Danny fit right into the pattern of violence the author described. But how on earth did one study the genes of violence? A few paragraphs further on in the article and my mind spun in complete confusion.

These two formulae are mathematically identical. The first: a genetic predisposition plus an inciting event leads to violence. The second: an inciting event coupled with a genetic disposition leads to violence as well. In both cases, if neither the cause nor the modifier is present, the resulting violence does not occur. Nor does the result occur if only one is present. However, the proportion in which violence is 'caused' by one or the other, the initial cause or the modifier, is not an empirical question. Taking an example from another field of the law, the extent to which debilitating injuries sustained by the so-called eggshell plaintiff are attributable to a preexisting condition or to the inciting event of an accident also defies scientific determination.

He had lost me. I'd tackle this stuff again the next day, after a good night's sleep. But even if I couldn't understand my expert's scientific work, surely he'd be able to help me frame questions to pose to the experts on the other side.

* * *

Dr. Nicholas Hibou was late. He and an assistant planned to slip away from the annual meeting of the American Psychiatric Society. They would rent a car and drive to my office on Wednesday, arriving well before noon. They planned to spend that day and the next in the St. Mary Parish jail conducting an evaluation of Daniel Howard, then return to New Orleans in the evening, in time to deliver his scholarly paper at the conference the following day.

I waited. Noon passed, then one o'clock. Close to two o'clock, I looked out of my office window and saw an odd bird standing in the parking lot, chin upturned, pivoting his head from side to side, surveying the scene. My psychiatrist. Only a New York shrink would wear a hat and overcoat to Louisiana.

A taller man, carrying a briefcase, unfolded from the driver's side of the car. The pants of his dingy black suit stopped a good four inches off the ground. He took a position at the left side of the man in the hat. Heel, good dog. A big dog at that.

The doctor responded to my greeting. "I beg your forgiveness for the delay, Mr. Clark. As advised, I left New Orleans on Highway 90, but when I saw the road sign for a *Scenic Bayou Ramble*, I could not resist. I was not disappointed. Lovely country. My apologies to you."

The bridge of the doctor's nose rose to a crest between two round black eyes, and then hooked down to a tight mouth. My God! I thought. He's looks like a barred owl! Danny is going to totally freak out at the sight of him.

The doctor accepted my offer of a chair and a cup of coffee. When he lost the coat and hat, revealing a narrow double-breasted jacket and a halo of wild curls on his head, he didn't look quite so peculiar. He was perhaps forty years old, a good twenty years younger than I had thought at first glance. No discernible accent. I began to warm to his soothing voice. That he could be a therapist became somewhat credible.

The assistant didn't speak at all, mutely nodding when addressed.

I reminded himself of the doctor's superb credentials: an Associate Professor of Psychiatry at the Medical Center of the University of New York; a practicing clinical psychiatrist working with teams of professionals in the treatment of violent young men; holder of many international appointments; author of scores of scholarly works. My initial reaction, however, was that I'd never put Dr. Hibou up on the witness stand before a local jury. Too weird.

While I sized him up, the doctor initiated discussion of the business at hand. "I have read the documents that you have sent to me, Mr. Clark. The arrest reports, witness statements, school records, medical history, your summary of your client's social history, et cetera. I would like to meet him this afternoon, if that is possible, for an unstructured interview, just to establish rapport. Then tomorrow, if all goes well, my assistant and I will do the full clinical interview. We will assess for the presence of mental disorders with a variety of oral and written tests. Then we will conduct additional assessments: memory; malingering; physical impairments; substance abuse history—whatever is prompted by our prior observations and results. Over the next few weeks we will compile our findings and submit a report to you of our conclusions. Will that be satisfactory for your purposes?"

"Absolutely, Dr. Hibou."

"Then, without further ado." The doctor stood up.

"Dr. Hibou, a moment please. Let me apologize to you for the accommodations upstairs. The Warden has tried his best to spruce up the consultation room for a distinguished visitor, but it's impossible."

"I am quite used to that, Mr. Clark. When I chose to study violent young men, I accepted the conditions where I would find them. Incarcerated."

"And you do understand, Doctor, that Danny has absolutely refused to open up to me about the crime. He talks about what he did in the early part of the evening, but then says he 'blanked out.' I'm certainly hoping that you can get him to talk—to you and then to me—because it's very difficult for me to devise an effective theory of defense without his cooperation. However, if he gives you the kind of cooperation he's given me, you may be in a lot less time than you expect."

"Oh, I am used to that behavior, and I have my procedures. I do not start with what the patient did or did not do; I start with the patient himself. Very few people can resist talking about themselves. If they do resist, I use tests. Anyone who ever went to school is conditioned to take the piece of paper from the teacher and set about to answer the questions."

Hmmm. This guy might know what he was doing. "OK, Dr. Hibou. Let's go upstairs."

I led the pair to the narrow stairs leading up to the jail. The doctor surprised me again. He took the steps two at a time.

* * *

The doctor and his assistant emerged from the consultation room three hours later, close to five o'clock. I had waited at Black Charlie's desk the entire time, certain that any minute Danny would terminate the interview and bounce Dr. Hibou and his assistant straight out of the room. I sent Charlie in twice during the course of the afternoon to ask if anyone wanted water, coffee, a break. Charlie reported back that they all seemed to be getting along just fine.

I offered dinner and an evening's company but the doctor declined. He and his assistant had work to do. The doctor donned his coat and hat, and in doing so gained back that twenty years of age he had hung up on the coat rack three hours before.

The next morning played out in the same manner. Shortly after noon, the doctor pronounced himself satisfied with his assessments and ready to leave. He proposed to analyze the results and submit a report in due course. He reached for his coat.

"Please wait, Doctor," I pressed. "Can you talk to me about Danny for a few minutes, give me some preliminary findings? I'd very much appreciate an idea of what you've found, particularly with respect to that convenient amnesia."

"I could do that. But please wait for my full report before taking any action on what I may say."

The pair sat down before my desk.

"At the outset, let me say that my testing indicates the intelligence of your client is in the normal range. That is consistent with his school record; he passed his grades without difficulty. He has no noted physical or motor impairments. Also, with the one exception of my attempts to discuss the period when he says he 'blanked out,' he was responsive and truthful throughout the tests. Oh, you look surprised."

"Yes, I am surprised. Responsive and truthful you say? He tells me nothing."

"We are asking different questions. To continue, I believe that you have correctly diagnosed depression. Rather mild, I would say. I am going to recommend that you have your client treated by a clinical psychologist."

"I may not be able to get him treatment, doctor. Medical care for prisoners is pretty gross—broken bones, raging fever, major mental illness. Minor problems are ignored. But I will try."

The doctor again attempted to leave.

I pressed again, "Can you tell me, Dr. Hibou, if you believe that Danny's racial issues have a connection to his behavior, his violence?"

"Ah, yes. Indeed, I do, to some extent. I have done fairly sophisticated testing on your client, based upon my studies in this area. I have developed questions that probe reactions to stressors, including racial insults. My prior studies indicate that some of us are predisposed to hair trigger response. Danny has told you that his reaction to insults is to be depressed. He has accurately described himself."

"So depression caused his violence?"

"No, no, no. We cannot say that. You and I do not use cause in the same way. I dare say, if you tested a sample of violent offenders, there would be a higher incidence of depression than in the regular population. But one cannot say depression triggered his violence." The doctor smiled, "If he *did it*, that is. I believe you lawyers might say alleged violence. The violence that he *allegedly committed*."

The doctor was proud of his attempt at legal

sophistication.

"As you are aware, depression is not a mental illness that ordinarily results in diminished responsibility for criminal acts. It is a common symptom found throughout the *DSM-IV* but not, in itself, a major mental illness. Perhaps in bipolar disorder, or another extreme manifestation, but not the mild depression we see in someone like your client."

I now knew I'd have limited use for this information during the guilt phase of my client's trial, but if we should get to the penalty phase, another story. An explanation of Danny's depression could be powerful mitigation.

"I will explain all this at length in my report, Mr. Clark. As you know from your preparatory reading, my current area of interest is genetic predisposition to violence. Unless and until we can measure abnormal serotonin receptor genes, for example, we can only hypothesize the presence of a genetic predictor of violence. We do not know for certain exactly what kind of incident would set someone off. Daniel Howard, however, is proving to be a good subject for me since it appears we have only one inciting incident. I will be able to explain all this to a jury. They will have to make the decision whether these issues should mitigate the penalty for Danny's conduct. That is not a question about genetics. It is deeply personal. I explain; I do not judge."

"Nor do I, sir. And the amnesia? Can you figure that out?"

"Ah, yes. Your client persists in his declaration that he has no memory of the events. Amnesia, however, is not a characteristic of depression or of any psychological condition that he manifests. Preliminarily, and please remember my caveat about taking no action on these findings until you have seen my final report, I believe that my tests will show that Danny is not being truthful in that regard."

"Doctor, I'm not surprised. I have to agree with you."

"What is the true story? I am not here to say. The determination of guilt or innocence is not for me; it is for the jury."

"Another question, sir, if you would." I found myself slipping into the stilted language of my expert. "As you know, sir, there were two persons stabbed to death that night—Clyde Carline and a young black boy. Were you able to learn, or even surmise, anything at all about what we are calling the second crime—the stabbing of the boy?"

"No, I was not. And that is a finding in itself, preliminarily of course. If Danny were involved in that poor boy's death, I would have expected something about the event to have come to the surface in all these assessments. It did not. I submit to you that you may need to rethink the generally held assumption that Daniel Howard had anything to do with the stabbing of the young boy."

"Sir, I have questioned that assumption for some time."

I thanked Dr. Hibou, again offering the hospitality of the area. The doctor and his silent assistant insisted on returning to New Orleans. On went the coat. The hat returned to cover the halo of prematurely graying ringlets. The doctor reacquired the twenty years of age.

After fifteen minutes, I stopped talking like a New York psychiatrist.

DINNER WITH MEDLEY

Medley chose a restaurant from the list of my suggestions. Pat's, up the levee in St. Martin Parish, a ramshackle collection of unpainted sheds perched on the west guide levee of the Atchafalaya Basin. Her selection pleased me. We were too early in the season for the best Basin crawfish, but I'd hoped she'd be enticed by my description of the sunset show. And she was.

The first part of the drive out to the Basin took us by rice fields, sugarcane fields, modest homes and camps. We passed through the settlement of Catahoula.

"What are all those little tents in people's yards?" Medley asked. "Are those chickens I see chained underneath?"

"Ah, ha! I guess that looks mighty odd to you. Fighting roosters, they are. Really splendid animals when you see them up close, strutting their sleek copper bodies, glowing blue-black tail feathers splayed out in a sassy fan."

"Fighting roosters, you say?" Her nose crinkled.

"Yup. Louisiana is the last state in the union where cockfighting is still legal—for now, that is. The humane society people and half the legislature think there's too much bad stuff connected to what people in this part of the state call a 'sport.' Animal cruelty, of course, but also gambling, drug use, smuggling, you name it. But the locals are fighting tooth and nail to keep the games legal. They think cockfighting is part of their culture. Our state senator is front and center leading the cause for preservation."

"Roosters fight? You call that a sport?" Medley was

incredulous.

"Not me. Remember, I was transplanted to 'New Awlins.'" I pulled out the word even longer than usual, and she reacted with her rippling laugh.

"Where do they have the rooster fights?" she asked.

I pointed out a wooden structure in a side yard, next to a cluster of trailers. "See that shed over there? That's a rooster pit. Dirt floor, bleachers all around. The handlers attach razor-sharp gaffs to the roosters' legs and let the birds loose in the middle. The roosters go after each other until one of them is dead, or he gets his eyes pecked out and can't see to fight any more." Medley shuddered. "The crowd sits up there to watch the battle, drink beer, cheer, and place bets. High stakes ride on which cock will survive the fray. Lots of money changes hands, and of course Uncle Sam never sees a bit of it."

"That's horrible! Surely that's animal cruelty."

"A lot of people agree. I hear lately several of the handlers have been hassled, so they've taken to hiding their pits—and the blood—in the middle of some cane field. The tide is turning against them."

"Good."

"Have you ever been to a farm where they raise the chickens you and I eat? Compared to those birds, fighting roosters live like kings. And they live longer. Anyway, the legislature solved the problem of people claiming the fights were cruelty to animals by passing a law that says a rooster is not an animal. Our senator masterminded that bit of sophistry."

Medley shook her head. "A rooster is not an animal? Sure isn't vegetable or mineral. Gimme a break!"

"Crazy, I agree. The locals put tremendous political pressure on the legislators and they came on board. They just redefined the word. But perhaps more important to the economy than supplying the roosters for the fighting pits, folks around here raise chickens for export. They ship birds to Mexico, Central and South America to stock the *palenques*, the cock fighting ring each little village has in the center of town. They all think gringo cocks are the very best fighters. Good nutrition, good veterinary medicine, vitamins, and steroids. I'm told our local birds can fetch up to $10,000 apiece."

Medley shook her head. "Promise me a rooster fight isn't what you have in mind for an after-dinner event."

"That's a promise. I went to one only once, out of curiosity, and got out of there very, very fast. Blood and deafening noise are not my idea of fun."

Past Catahoula, we mounted the levee and took the shell road along the top.

"This is a beautiful drive, John." We were John and Medley now.

"But stay in the car! Around here it's always the season to hunt something. It can be dangerous to roam around in the woods if you aren't wearing hunter's orange."

I looked over to check out Medley's outfit—black pants and a soft pink shirt. Nice.

We arrived at Pat's early for supper. The sun had just begun its descent. Just as we sat down on the screened porch, a storm rolled in. Medley sat transfixed by the curtain of crystal created by the sun shining through huge raindrops. She shivered in the fresh chill, and must have felt the splatters through the screen, but she declined an invitation from the waitress to retreat inside. She tipped up her chin and breathed in the fresh smell. Driving rain soon billowed folds of white gauze before our eyes, turning the sunlight to dusk, obscuring the trees that a few minutes before had been a verdant backdrop to the scene across the water.

"Daytime darkness is spooky," Medley whispered, in awe of the wild exuberance of Mother Nature. We sat in silence.

A short twenty minutes later the misty curtain rose,

and returning sunlight sparkled through the last of the raindrops. White specks dotted the sky as flocks of egrets and ibis came in to roost. Hundreds of birds. They landed in the trees, pulled in their necks, tucked their beaks under their chest feathers, and settled down for the night. Then came the roseate spoonbills, an armada of pink sails heading for port. Medley's face glowed with wide-eyed delight at the spectacle. I silently thanked the birds for their performance.

The harsh voice of our waitress broke the spell.

"OK, *mes chers*. Dinner's ready inside."

The crawfish were especially small at the beginning of the season. It took a good hour for us to empty our three-pound tin trays—the energy derived from eating one crawfish being exactly equal to the energy expended to peel the critter. We washed our hands at the basin on the back wall of the dining room, returned to our table and ordered coffee.

"Are you ready to continue your story, Medley?" I asked.

"You really want to hear my past history? I'm just an ordinary girl from a small town in Mississippi."

"Maybe, but you've got to admit it's pretty unusual for a classy girl like you to end up in the St. Mary Parish jail. There must be an interesting explanation"

Medley laughed. "Classy? I am not, John. Country, country. OK. I'll share. But only if your story comes next."

I didn't say that it would.

"My mother was a beauty queen," Medley began.

"I can believe that."

I was looking at a lovely young woman. Gone was the pinched expression she had when I first saw her, and she had lost most of the nervousness she had shown at our lunch. She had seemed scrawny in the jail jumpsuit, but now I could discern very nice curves.

She continued. "Seriously, a queen with a crown and

all. Mom took the stage for her first pageant when she was two years old and had won a dozen trophies and ribbons before she went to the first grade—I don't believe they had kindergarten in Magnolia in those days. They curled her blond hair, put on globs of make-up, taught her how to swing her sassy hips and flash a smile. I've seen the pictures. She was adorable, if you aren't bothered by selling sex with a baby." Medley raised her eyebrows into a lovely arch to emphasize that she was bothered. I was rewarded with a better view of her luminous green eyes.

"She dropped out of competitions for the few awkward pre-teen years, but by the time she was fifteen she was back up on the boards. She pushed out the boobs, fluttered the eyelids, and brought home the hardware. Gram and Pops built a special shelf for the trophies and displayed them proudly."

I heard a tinge of bitterness, but not much, considering what came next.

"By the time my mother became the youngest Miss Magnolia in the State of Mississippi, she was dating one unsuitable guy after another. Gram and Pops said they tried to warn her about falling for what they called 'the wrong sort,' but Mom was the queen. She didn't listen. Queens think they don't have to take orders from anyone.

"Mom became pregnant—with me—in the middle of her junior year of high school. She fled out of town straight from the hospital, with some slick-haired roustabout, not my father. Gram and Pops took me home. That's where I grew up, with my grandparents."

"Are you in touch with your Mom? Do you ever see her?"

"She visited three times that I remember. She sent me cards at Christmas and my birthday, but she never came home to stay. Gram and Pops, God bless them, were all I had, and vice versa. Today I have no idea where my mother is."

"Tough. And your father?"

"Who is he? No one claiming to be my father has ever surfaced. I have to think he doesn't know I exist."

"You don't have any idea who he is?"

"No."

I wanted to take Medley's hand, but her fingers were busy picking at a paper napkin on her lap.

"With their second shot at child-raising, Gram and Pops did an about-face. They regretted what they had done the first time and vowed not to let me turn out the same way. The pendulum swung way, way to the other side. They put me in granny dresses and shoes that looked like a missionary had issued them. Straight to school, straight home, few friends, no boys permitted anywhere around."

I must have looked pained because Medley hastened to add, "Don't give me that expression, John. I really didn't mind. I was a shy thing. Sticking close to home was fine with me. I admit sometimes I fantasized about my father appearing in Magnolia and sweeping me away to live in one of the big houses I saw on television, but those thoughts passed quickly. I much accepted the situation. And Gram and Pops were wonderful, really. Unconditional love, I think you'd call it. I had that."

"You only talk of Gram now. Is your Pops gone?"

"Yes. He died when I was fifteen. He had run the local Western Auto Store, so after he died Gram took over. She did a good job keeping it going—until Walmart came to town, that is. We couldn't compete with one-stop shopping."

"The fate of small town America, I'm afraid."

"Right. After graduation from high school, I was lost. College was never on the table. No money. Our store could barely support Gram, let alone pay tuition. My high school counselor suggested I go to the local community college to become a nurse, and she found a scholarship to help me with the cost. Gram approved. I worked part time at

Walmart—in the hardware department, of course—and continued to live at home with Gram. I found out I liked nursing. Do you really want to hear all this?"

"Yes, I do."

"OK. After a while I had a boyfriend. It's hard to believe now, considering how he turned out, but Jackson looked like the answer to a girl's dreams. Handsome, hard working, money in his pocket. He worked seven and seven for a seismic crew. He didn't smoke or drink, was polite and respectful to Gram. Mr. Right, we both thought. Jackson used to take me to the clubs, which opened up an exciting new world, but he always got me home on time. He was a great dancer."

Medley paused for a sip of water. Her hand went back to twisting the napkin. I didn't speak for fear she wouldn't continue.

"Once, when he came home from a hitch with the crew, I thought I smelled marijuana. But I figured I must've been mistaken. After six months of dating, we married. Everything was still fine.

"We'd been married about a year when Jack joined the National Guard, for the best reason: so he could be home more. His boss had to give him time off for the monthly training. We were happy, didn't fight, or even have any serious arguments. We were even happier when I became pregnant.

"Then came 9/11 and Operation Iraqi Freedom. Jack's unit got notice they were to be called for active duty. They were shipped to some place in Texas for two months training, then came home to wait for deployment."

Medley paused. Her napkin now in tatters, she placed it on the table. I kept still, afraid she'd stop talking if I moved a muscle.

"Jack had been acting different for a while. He stayed out late and then moped around the house the next day. I thought maybe he had anxiety about becoming a father, or perhaps fear of going off to Iraq. At times I even looked forward to his deployment. I thought going overseas might be a good thing for both of us. I thought the service discipline would straighten him out. But when I heard about casualties over there, I felt really guilty. I was scared, I guess.

"Life wasn't turning out quite like I thought. Then his unit shipped out.

"After only three months overseas, Jack returned, just before Buddy was born. I was glad to have him home for the birth, of course, but the circumstances of his coming home are still a puzzle. His unit stayed over there. I say Jack came home, but he wasn't the Jack I knew."

She paused and took a sip of water.

"Before Iraq he never touched me except in love. Now, he was cross, he slapped my arm, or my backside, and so rough..." Her voice cracked, and she didn't finish the sentence. "One night he hit me in the face and gave me a black eye just because I asked him where he'd been. I got so I was scared to leave him home with the baby. Come to find out, it was drugs. Jack had been dealing cocaine to the guys in the unit—and sampling the wares. Later, much later, I found out he had drug charges from the past, long before I knew him. Back then he was put into some kind of diversion program that left his record clean—provided he didn't get into trouble again. But he did."

"If only you girls would check a guy's rap sheet before going out on a date."

"You can do that?" Medley asked. "Oh, you're kidding."

"Yes. Sorry. Not a laughing matter, I know."

I had wanted to break the tension, and I had. Medley drew a deep breath and gave me a weak smile.

"Anyway," she continued, "the Army sent him to counselors, and I had to go too, which I really didn't like. I went, anything to help, but the shrinks were worthless. Someday I'll tell you what I think of the medical care we're giving our returning troops.

"When Jack told me his old seismic crew wanted him back, and they had a job waiting for them in Louisiana, I was happy. A change of location seemed like a great idea. In twenty-four hours he packed the car and drove over here. I quit my job and followed a week later. I've already told you what happened when I got here."

The waitress returned to the table with the check and an expression that clearly said she was ready to close down the place for the night. I gave her my credit card, and we got ready to leave.

"You owe me, John. We didn't get to your story."

"Saved by the closing! I guess that means you'll need to come out to dinner with me again. Right?"

"Yes."

Wait, I told myself. No entanglements. If some disclosure became necessary, I could give her an edited version.

Pitch black now, we didn't get back up on the levee but took the paved road below. Medley remained quiet, but I couldn't resist giving her more background. I found myself wanting her to connect with the area.

"Just a bit farther north from here is the place where the Bayou Teche begins, first a trickle in a dense copse, then gaining water from coulees carrying rain runoff and from a few underground streams. After about twenty-five miles the bayou becomes a waterway wide and deep enough to carry gunboats in the War Between the States and now barges of bagasse from the sugar mills. Long, long before that, my friends who know about such things tell me the Red River rolling down from north Louisiana took a turn through here on its way to the Mississippi—thus the terrain of deep gullies just north of Lafayette. Now we can find patches of both red and black dirt in spittin' distance of one another."

"I'd like to see all that, John. When it's daylight and I

have on my hunter's orange!" she teased.

"In my own back yard I have both kinds of dirt, which makes me think of our racial history—native tribes, white settlers, and the Africans they brought as slaves—living close but not mixing all that much."

I changed the subject. "Would you like to stop off and have another beer?" I asked when we were almost to Franklin.

"I'd better not. Buddy seemed very comfortable with Maria, my new housemate, but this is the first time I've ever left him with someone other than Gram."

I stopped the car in front of the shelter annex. Without speaking, we turned our heads to face each other. I reached over and gently put my hand behind her neck, drawing her to me. I kissed her lips, soft, warm. They responded with an invitation for a deeper connection. My hand moved lower, controlled by a mind of its own, seeking territory to claim. Thirty seconds or three minutes passed; I couldn't tell you which.

"John, we shouldn't... "

"Medley, we shouldn't..."

We spoke the words in perfect unison. Medley reached for the handle and opened the car door, stepping out before I could think about going around to do so myself. Her shoes tapped up the sidewalk as she walked quickly, head down, to the front door.

For the next few weeks we were very cautious. We had lunch—at the Yellow Bowl, the Forest Restaurant on East Main Street, and sometimes farther afield. I attended Buddy's birthday party at the shelter. Only once did I ask her to an evening event—a Bar Association reception for the retirement of Judge Wright. Truly a celebration. We thoroughly enjoyed each other's company. Several times our conversation tiptoed close to an emotional precipice— but we stepped back. Without discussing why we did so, it appeared we were of one mind. Too soon. Too risky. Too something we couldn't define.

As for me, I wanted a clear head. I had to focus on the upcoming trial, without distraction. I knew from experience that working through any strong emotion could be like driving to New Orleans in a heavy fog, straining to find the lines on the surface of the road so you wouldn't be hit head-on by a eighteen wheeler. I needed to get this trial behind me.

I had the feeling Medley understood.

* * *

Three weeks later, on a Sunday morning, when I took my coffee cup out on the porch to savor the beginning of the day, my eye fell on the spot where six months before I had first seen Medley huddled with her little boy. I turned a page. Why not take a chance? These days intimacy didn't require commitment. What did my old DKE brothers call it? Pulling down a little low hanging fruit.

I got in the car and drove to the shelter. The annex door stood ajar. I pushed inside. Medley stood two rungs up on a ladder, a paint roller in hand. One wall gleamed newly yellow, three others were still dingy green. Yellow paint splattered the front of her oversized shirt and on the kerchief that held back her hair. Maria lay on her belly on the floor, taping the baseboard. I watched them for a moment before they realized I was there.

"John! You startled me!" Medley exclaimed.

"Keep going. I don't want to interrupt, but could I come pick you up for a miracle-in-the-microwave supper tonight? I still have no kitchen, you know. About five? Buddy, too."

Medley brushed back a strand of hair escaped from her kerchief, and in the process placed a yellow stripe across her cheek. A wide smile crinkled her face up to the outside edges of her eyes. Clearly, she welcomed my invitation.

"I'll be ready."

She was ready, but didn't have Buddy. Maria had

insisted this be her night with the boy, or so Medley told me.

I don't remember much about the first part of the evening. I know I showed her the work I had already done in the kitchen, and we talked about what remained. I grilled some fish on the outdoor grill. Medley made a salad and fixed a couple of baked potatoes in the micro. I guess we cleaned up.

I do remember the second part of the evening, every magnificent moment.

"Medley, would you like to stay?" I asked.

"Yes." That's all she said.

We locked up the house and went back to the bedroom. Slowly, tantalizingly slowly, we took off each other's clothes. My loins caught fire with the warmth of her body against my chest. The passion that followed was so natural, without doubt or nervousness, without thought at all. I sank into the rhythm of the act. Inside her, I felt totally and completely at home. After we both came, I kissed tears from her eyes.

"John, I won't have to go home early tomorrow."

I awoke to the comforting sounds of Medley in the kitchen preparing a microwave miracle breakfast.

GUNS

"Good God, Mr. Clark. This baby's older than I am. It's an antique!"

Theresa lifted my grandfather's handgun out of the dusty box with one hand and shook a fur coat of dust off the faded red velvet liner with the other. Standing barely three inches over five feet tall, she tipped her head back to look at my eyes.

At nine o'clock Saturday morning, Sgt. Theresa Wiltz had opened up the gun range—an array of weather-beaten wooden stalls set out in a remote woods two miles from Vermilion Bay on the road to Burns Point. Each stall held a stand for a 3-by-5 foot cardboard poster on which the outline of a man had been drawn with a thick black line. I once heard about a state-of-the-art FBI facility that provided firearms training to federal officers on interactive, shoot/don't shoot scenario devices located in a National Guard armory occupying an entire city block in Washington, DC. The parish of St. Mary offered the simplest possible alternative. But the St. Mary Parish range was fine for my purposes. I just needed to know if my grandfather's pistol would shoot straight. And if I could.

The Colt .45 I had found in the gun cabinet upstairs looked to be clean, still had traces of oil, and felt good in my hand. Granddad was a hunter. He had three other guns in there: a deer rifle and two shotguns. I might want to take them out in the fall for squirrels, deer and ducks, but they weren't appropriate for what I needed now—a weapon to have handy in my nightstand in case of emergency. If

Medley had no trouble finding my house, there were other people who might make their way behind the overgrown semi-tropical jungle that was once my grandfather's front lawn. I met too many house creeps in my line of work, and I generated a long list of the disgruntled who would have more in mind than lifting something to pawn for drugs or caging a place to sleep.

That's what had pricked my worry center when I had awakened at 2 a.m. a week ago. That night, not wanting to disturb Medley, whose long breaths whispered softly beside me, I slid to the floor and walked barefoot to the kitchen, passing by Buddy's crib. I stood still and listened. A rustle, a knock. Probably an animal, but I should check it out. With one hand on the door to the front porch, I stopped dead. What was I doing? If there was something out there, I had no way to protect Medley and her little boy.

I turned at Medley's voice.

"Trouble sleeping?"

Medley stood silhouetted in the doorway, my robe folded double around her and trailing on the floor.

"I thought I heard something," I answered.

"Of course you did. This place is alive with animals of the night." Medley took my hand, opened the front door, and led me out onto the porch. We could barely see the stars through the thicket.

"Listen," Medley whispered.

Hoo-hoo-oo, a great horned owl called from the top of a large live oak and received an answer from a companion on the far side of the yard. At the base of the porch, the night breeze in the banana bushes shuffled the leaves like a deck of cards. When I had become accustomed to the darkness, I made out a pair of shiny eyes below us. A possum rooted for grubs. I could swear the critter dismissed our disturbance with a disdainful toss of his long snout before continuing to dig in the dirt for his supper.

Medley squeezed my arm. "I must have awakened a

half dozen times the first few nights I spent here, and you never even turned over. Once I came out on the porch and watched a raccoon using those amazing fingers to harvest satsumas, feast on the fruit, and scatter the peels like crumbs for Hansel and Gretel. Now I'm accustomed to all the nocturnal activity and sleep like a baby."

Medley and Buddy were giving me more reasons to love my house.

"John, Nanette told me about the accident out front there, the one where your mother was killed."

I was startled, but in a moment was relieved we would put this topic out on the table. "I'm glad she did. I needed to tell you but just didn't want to."

"I know something about losing your mother, but under those circumstances? That must have been hard on you."

"Worse for my dad. He just couldn't live here without my mother—not that he did much better after we moved to New Orleans. He died ten years later and I don't think he laughed in all those years. But I was only seven, you know, and kids get over stuff. Even get over the guilt of thinking I was the cause. You know, I guess, that she hit the brake when I called out to her about the truck coming. If she hadn't, the truck would have tucked right in behind us."

"Maybe. That's the story, but how can you be sure of all that?"

"Right. I can't be sure. I think I first got that dumped on me by my father when he was out of control with grief— and now I know it isn't fair to judge someone on what they do or say at such a time."

Medley squeezed my arm.

"I realize now that the accident is what has been keeping me from cleaning up the front of this house, and from restoring the driveway."

"Is there some way to redesign the driveway so that the intersection is less of a danger? Maybe you could bring it out to Main Street farther from the corner."

"You know, Emile and I were talking about that last Sunday. He had some ideas. I think when I get the front fixed up I'll really wipe out the last of what haunts me about the past." I put my arm around Medley's shoulders and kissed a delicious soft spot at the back of her neck. "I think we fell asleep too quickly tonight. Perhaps we need a little more of our own nocturnal activity."

In the morning, one thought chased around in my mind. What if someone dangerous had actually been out there in that thicket? Having people to care for changed my perspective. We were defenseless. Right then, I had made up my mind to check out my grandfather's collection of weapons and called Theresa for a session at the range.

Theresa balanced the gun in her right hand and then raised it, steadying with her left, and squinted her right eye to sight down the barrel. Theresa wore fatigues and combat boots when she was out on patrol, but even dressed for power she had to straighten her back and widen her stance to develop what might pass for menace. She didn't have to put on a show for me. I knew her abilities. She was a dead shot and had the combat skills to take down a man twice her weight. Today she had on blue jeans and pulled her ponytail through the hole in the back of her ball cap. Cute.

"The piece looks to be in great shape, Mr. Clark. Soldiers in World War II used them, you know. You can get some serious bucks for this baby at any gun show that handles old weapons."

"But then I wouldn't have anything for protection, which I told you is the whole idea."

Why was she smiling at me?

"Have you fired it?" she asked, twinkling her eyes.

"No. That's what I came here for."

"OK. Let me try first. Ammo?"

"I hoped you'd have some."

"I suspected you wouldn't bring any. Brett gave me a

box of rounds that should work. He's a bit of a collector, you know."

Theresa opened her canvas gun bag and pulled out two sets of ear protectors and a box of shells. She put on the ear protectors, loaded my grandfather's pistol, raised it and fired, both eyes open this time. She shook her head.

"I'll be honest with you, Mr. Clark. You need more than this. Sell it, take the money and get yourself a new Glock."

"Really? This one isn't any good?" I asked.

"Sure it's good, in fact it's great. For anyone who loves old guns. But for what you need? No. You can do much better. For one thing, when you use up Brett's stash, you're going to have a little trouble finding ammo. And you can't lock the Colt. You don't want to have a gun hanging around that someone can just grab and fire. This one handles well, but not as good as the Glock. Go ahead and fire. You'll see what I mean."

"No, I won't. I haven't had a gun in my hand for fifteen years."

Sgt. Wiltz passed me the other set of ear protectors, unholstered her sidearm, and handed it to me. "Go ahead. Shoot each of them and compare the two."

I quickly saw the difference. I couldn't get inside the target outline with the Colt. After six tries with the Glock, I actually got one shot centered on the chest. A kill.

"Wait until you've had some practice, you'll see even more. My Glock is a .45. The Glock .40 and the Glock .45 are both good. Every shot you take feels the same. The .40 has greater felt recoil, so the sheriff requires that we carry a .45. There's also a Baby Glock if you want to have a smaller gun to strap with Velcro onto your lower leg."

She was serious. No. I hoped I wouldn't be creeping around with a concealed weapon.

"I don't think I'll need that," I said.

We took turns firing, and the morning slipped away. You could tell Theresa had affection for her weapon, loved to shoot, and wanted to make a believer of me. The only part of the morning I didn't like was the mosquitoes.

"I'm persuaded. Where do I go buy one of these?" I asked.

"Any gun shop in Lafayette. But promise me that you'll come out here at least once a month and practice. No one who doesn't keep up training should have a gun hanging around."

"That's a promise, if you can arrange permission for me to use the firing range."

"You bet. You can come with me. I want the company. I like to shoot, but somebody to shoot with motivates me to get here. I try to come the last Saturday of every month."

"Thanks, Theresa. You know, my clients never understand something like this, that you'd work this out for me, and that Tony and I fish together in the Gulf every fall."

"Well, they'll get the opportunity to see us spar. I expect your talons will be plenty sharp when you have me on the stand in the Danny Howard case."

"You can count on that," I said with a smile. "I think Tony has brought a serious overcharge."

An understatement. I didn't know which of the investigating officers would be testifying for the prosecution of Danny—probably Brett who was the senior of the pair and a parish deputy not just a city cop—but I anticipated my cross examination of the testimony of one or both of the investigating officers would put a chill on pleasant times at the firing range, for a little while at least.

I planned to spend that very afternoon taking a good hard look at their initial reports. Theresa and Brett had told the same story. When confronted by Theresa on the morning of his arrest, Danny made an incriminating statement. As Theresa wrote in her report: "I asked Danny if he became angry when Clyde Carline called him a *nigger* and went back to the party to get a knife. In response to that question, Danny mumbled 'yeah' and shook his head in the affirmative."

Theresa and Brett were both careful to characterize Danny's "yeah" as an incriminating statement and not a confession, but juries do not draw such a fine differentiation. I knew from experience that jurors are quick to convict any defendant who says anything close to an admission of guilt. And in spite of an instruction from the judge that everyone has the right to remain silent, I was quite sure the officers would make certain the jury learned Danny stonewalled after his arrest. Yes, Theresa and Brett were not going to be good for our team.

Well, that just meant I had a job to do.

First line of attack: convince Judge Johnson, on a Motion to Suppress, to exclude every reference to what Danny said as a violation of *Miranda v. Arizona.* When the officers talked to Danny, they didn't first inform him he had the right to a lawyer, the right to remain silent, or tell him that anything he said could be used against him. I'd make a strong argument for the exclusion, of course, but my chances of success were slim to none. Danny hadn't been in custody, the prerequisite to the need for that legal protection. He was sitting in his own living room, with his parents present. If anyone kept him on that sofa, it was his own mom.

A more promising strategy would be to learn everything I could about the circumstances in the living room that morning and paint a picture of subtle coercion. I would question to learn the exact time Theresa and Brett arrived at the Chastant house. What did the officers say to Danny's parents before his mom woke him up? Exactly what did they say when Danny came into the living room? How long did the questioning take?

This line of inquiry sent me to find my material on the sophisticated methods of interrogation that have now replaced old time brutality by the fist and the billy club.

Almost all civilian police forces, as well as the military and government agencies such as the FBI and the CIA, are now trained to use psychological methods to extract admissions. In fact, the more widely known training company, Reid & Associates, boasts 80 percent success in getting what they call "the truth" from those initially unwilling to provide it. Have the psychological techniques of interrogation honed over the past fifty years cured the problem of false confessions? Hardly. More than a quarter of defendants exonerated through post-conviction DNA testing had previously "confessed" to the crimes.

In the absence of a videotape of the entire morning the officers spent in Danny's living room, I'd have to get them to recreate their interrogation. I'd ask for details, but I knew from experience I'd get the short version. Did the officers prey upon Danny's depression and feelings of hopelessness to the point where he acquiesced in a suggested response?

If I lost the Motion to Suppress, and Judge Johnson allowed their testimony to go into evidence as I expected, I'd go to work on the officers when they testified at the trial.

Jury selection would afford me another opportunity to lessen the impact of Danny's words. I'd explain to everyone called for service the difference between a confession and an incriminating statement. That's an explanation of law, a permitted topic during jury questioning. And I'd ask potential jurors whether trying to answer a two-part question had ever fooled them. My point? Did Danny's answer "yeah" apply to both parts of the question or only one? Perhaps he was answering in the affirmative to the query about whether Carline had called him a *nigger* and not that he went back for the knife.

For sure, I'd work hard to eliminate jurors who indulged in simplistic labels. I needed people who could appreciate the complexities of communication.

Here was a humbling thought. For six months I had been totally unsuccessful in getting Danny to tell me anything. These officers brought him to heel in a matter of hours.

But only for one crime. Theresa and Brett didn't claim to have any statement about the death of T-Boy Davis. From the first moment I would speak to the jury, distinguishing the investigation into the death of Clyde Carline from that of the death of the boy would be critically important.

PART IV — EARLY SPRING

JURY SELECTION

We were on the cusp of spring. The daylong dreary skies of mid-winter had brightened. Almost daily, brief afternoon showers vanished in sunset glory. Soon we would awake to the surprise of swollen azalea buds transformed into crimson blooms.

The season of new birth raised the spirits of those of us who enjoyed the open air, but that category did not include the residents of the courthouse jail. The inmates were largely oblivious to the season's change. Danny must have felt spring warmth on the rooftop where he went for his hour of exercise, but his disposition didn't improve. My client remained glum, detached, reticent, downright surly.

Through scores of meetings with me, with Possum, and with Dr. Hibou, Danny failed to impart any further information about his conduct on the night his freedom came to an end. He repeated his mantras: *I have no memory of the last part of the night of October 2 to 3. I know nothing about the boy you say was Jerome Ti-Boy Davis.* Danny had no reaction to Possum's report that Snap-Dog had been caught dealing drugs in Lafayette Parish, faced conviction as a second felony offender, and might be gone for a while. To every probing question about his feelings, Danny returned indifference or a hostile glare. And of course he denied he ever thought about race. *I'm white, and I don't care what race anyone is.* I had long since ceased to be frustrated by this incredible statement. Just resigned.

Medley and I had settled into a pattern of spending the

weekends together at my house. Buddy even had a bedroom he could call his own. I felt no pressure for commitment and gave none. A very comfortable arrangement, for me, at least.

Judge Mari Johnson set capital jury selection for the last week of March. Not yet daylight savings time, the eastern sky had just begun to lighten when I left my house for the five-block walk to the courthouse. As my front door closed behind me, the firm thud infused me with pride. Emile Petain and I had spent a few Sunday afternoons refinishing and hanging a half dozen of those doors I had found in the wrecking company on Magazine Street in New Orleans. The doors were worthy companions to the giant cypress beams my grandfather had used in the initial construction of the house. My renovated kitchen now had a black marble tile floor and granite counters where, after our labors, Emile enjoyed teaching Medley to cook like a Cajun while Buddy amused himself on the Fisher-Price jungle gym I had built in the corner of the room.

Emile enjoyed a couple of glasses of cabernet; Medley took a glass sometimes, but not me. Sometimes, when Emile was pouring and I shook my head in the negative, I thought she had a question in her eyes, but she didn't press. Which made me realize I owed her an explanation of our family problem, at least if we kept being together. My father found solace in alcohol, which shortened his life, and I had a fear that the weakness might be heritable.

I took five steps down to a pebble path that led to the Pecan Street extension, walked up to Main, and turned toward town. Too early for traffic, the morning dog walkers and runners had the street to themselves. I opted for the sidewalk and followed the five quiet, tree-lined blocks to the square. Almost there, the ugly, mold-streaked, seven-story box we all called the *new* courthouse loomed into view.

One of my earliest memories is the day the wrecking ball came to town to demolish the turn-of-the-century courthouse that once proudly owned that square. My grandfather, the first John Clark, duly elected District Judge of the Parish of St. Mary, had spearheaded a campaign to replace the totally inadequate building with a modern facility capable of serving the growing population of the parish. The day the old courthouse met its demise he adjourned all proceedings in the temporary courtroom he had set up in the parish hall of the Church of the Assumption across Main Street. He topped his mane of snow white hair with a straw boater, retrieved his brass-headed ebony cane from the coat rack in the vestibule of the church hall, and strode the few blocks to his home to fetch me from playtime in the back yard. On the return trip to the courthouse square, he shortened his steps to match mine, and I bounced along beside him to join the celebrating crowd.

That day, all work downtown had come to a halt. Police officers blocked off the streets on three sides of the courthouse square; the Bayou served as a barrier on the fourth flank. The bell of the Church of the Assumption tolled eleven times, marking the beginning of the last hour of the morning.

As the final note of the church bell faded, the brick street beneath our feet began to tremble. An ominous thunder rumbled in from the north, and the head of every spectator turned toward the sound. An earthquake? Frightened, I clung to my grandfather's leg. Within a few minutes, a parade of heavy equipment appeared, advancing slowly but resolutely toward the crowd. Immune from the restrictions confining ordinary folk, one truck after another commandeered the street, then rolled across the banquette and onto the courthouse lawn. Men, women, and children scattered like chickens in the barnyard as the vehicles brazenly claimed their space.

A flatbed truck brought up the rear of the procession and came to rest directly in front of the old courthouse building. Two-dozen strapping men in black and white

striped jumpsuits monogrammed LSP—the initials of the
Louisiana State Prison at Angola—spilled out. Directed by
a uniformed guard with a rifle spanned across his
shoulders, the crew offloaded three truckloads of hollow
iron pipe and laid them in a neat stack on the lawn. Last, a
heavy black orb the size of a cannonball rolled off the back
of the truck and landed with a thud, flattening the grass
and molding out a shallow impression in the soft lawn.

Each man picked up a pole and lashed it to another. My
fear faded, and I watched in fascination as a metal scaffold
towering fifty feet into the sky miraculously took form. A
heavy chain hung from the apex. To the end of this chain,
close to the ground, the men affixed the black ball in a
center point within the structure.

For the next stage of the operation, the guardian of the
LSP prisoners called forward the five strongest men he had
in his charge. An unintelligible call from the mouth of the
head deputy pierced the air. Ten sinewy black arms
reached up inside the scaffold and grasped a lead rope
attached to the base of the ball. Grunting with exertion, the
men drew the lead backwards towards Main Street, away
from the building. On the count of three, the men threw
their hands off the rope and let the ball swing free.
Shoowsh! Gathering speed along the arc of the pendulum,
the iron ball swept through the center of the scaffold and
out the other side, spot-on for the front wall of the gentle
old building helplessly awaiting its fate.

The orb struck with a horrendous thud, and my little
body shuddered as if I had been the target. My grandfather
encircled my shoulders with his arm, conveying comfort. A
cheer erupted from the crowd but abruptly hushed as the
wall prevailed. The impotent ball quivered in diminishing
shivers until it resettled, ominously still, in the center of
the structure.

The deputy again issued a call to arms. The men
reentered the enclosure, drew back the rope, let it go, and
the crowd cheered on a second tremendous crash. The

target shuddered this time, but again prevailed.

On the third assault, the wall of brick trembled, buckled, and fell. A billowing cloud of choking dust drove us backward, and the entire scene disappeared from view. We heard but could not see the onslaught continue. In less than one hour, when the miasma lifted, a lovely, turn-of-the-century architectural treasure had been reduced to little more than a pile of pink rubble.

The church bell tolled again—twelve times now, the sound mysteriously transformed from the mark of a neutral timepiece to a lugubrious lament. The crowd stared, pulled in by the sick fascination that draws people to rubberneck at the scene of a highway crash. Beside me, my grandfather stood in stunned silence, regret creeping in. But the ramifications of what I had witnessed didn't occur to me. For months after that morning, oblivious to the loss of an irreplaceable landmark, I spent hours with my erector set trying to duplicate the magnificent destruction.

From the day the new courthouse took shape on the same location, the structure offended the eye. Miami and New York may have fine examples of the architectural style of the nineteen sixties, but there are few out in the country. In an ugly manifestation of mid-century modernity, every contract let to a favored political friend or to the lowest local bidder, sharp angles took the place of pleasing curves. Blinding white stucco and marble of questionable provenance replaced soft brick tones of pink and gray. The flat roof of the new building soon sprouted radio antennae like weeds in a fallow field. Pigeons came to roost on the ledges of the small high windows, their excrement bleeding unsightly black streaks down the facades.

One could see the eyesore above the treetops from any vantage point within ten miles of the courthouse square—a lighthouse warning of the downside of progress. My grandfather realized too late that tearing down the courthouse had been a grave mistake. If they needed a new facility for a new age, he soon admitted, they should have built one at another location and saved the treasure.

But the old man always had the vision to find a silver lining in a cloud. There's a bit o' good in everything, he would say, twinkling the blue-green eyes of our ancestors—the wagonloads of the descendants of hardy Celts who, after the Louisiana Purchase, came from the Carolinas to settle among the Acadians. More ambitious and better financed than the carefree Cajuns who preceded them, the easterners established large plantations along the Bayou Teche. They grew sugar cane, cotton, and indigo and, thanks to the importation of slaves from the Caribbean islands, they prospered. Their children became the bankers and businessmen, and the judges, who over the years called the shots in the northern half of St. Mary Parish.

Indeed, when the citizenry realized what they had lost, 'Remember the Courthouse!' became the battle cry for historic preservation. Throughout Acadiana, dozens of citizen committees sprang to life. Local legislation sped through the usually slow process of passage and implementation as saving other historic public buildings, grand old mansions, plantation homes, genteel neighborhoods, and carefully tended green spaces, became a passionate cause. Now, almost thirty years later, the little boy who had witnessed the destruction of the old courthouse and watched the building of the ugly replacement benefited from this love of the past. My passionate restoration of my grandfather's house gained me appreciation and notoriety in the area, along with a good dose of wonder at my willingness to undertake such a task.

Unfortunately, I had to go to work each day in the seven-story graceless box that had inspired the change of heart.

* * *

A crowd packed the courtroom, but they had not come

by choice. Judge Johnson ordered three hundred and fifty ordinary citizens to appear for jury selection. On prior calls for jurors for a capital case we had exhausted that number and had to call even more. That's what it takes to find twelve people, plus a couple alternates, who are willing and able to be part of a jury that must decide if someone is to live or die.

"Ladies and gentlemen," Judge Johnson began, sending out over the crowd her most engaging smile. "Louisiana law provides that a jury may impose the capital penalty for the crime of first degree murder—*if* every juror thinks death is appropriate for the facts of a particular case. This jury term we will have for trial a defendant who is charged with first degree murder, and the prosecution has given notice that they will seek the penalty of death. Twice. It is the law of the United States, given to us by the Supreme Court in the case of *State v. Witherspoon*, that a person is only qualified to serve on such a jury if, and only if, he or she is willing to *consider* the capital penalty. It is also the law, from the same case, that a person may not serve if he or she is committed to impose the penalty for *every* conviction that qualifies. For the next few days the lawyers and I will be talking to you, individually, in order to find people who qualify for this service. We call the process Witherspooning a jury pool." Judge Johnson paused and allowed a sardonic smile to pass her lips. "I daresay, before we are through, you will have thought of a few more words to describe the ordeal."

Judge Johnson could muster up a lot of charm, put spin on the process, but her humor was lost on the jurors. The sober faces in the room revealed they were quite aware of the stakes, and their emotions ranged from aggravation to outright hostility. Those of us who worked in the system understood the necessity for the Witherspoon questions, but John Q. Public resents being required to endure the intrusion into their time and their private thoughts.

You have to feel sorry for ordinary people who have

never before given serious consideration to the death penalty and now must interrupt their lives to do hard thinking on the subject before God and everyone. They had to reveal their innermost thoughts to strangers. Even when we choose the President of the United States we can keep our counsel, go into the voting booth, and cast our vote in private.

Jury selection is the most critical part of a criminal trial. Legal experts who study the process tell us that not the evidence, not the argument of the attorneys, not even the actual guilt or innocence of the defendant, has as much effect on the ultimate outcome of a trial as the selection of jurors. Funny that TV cop, court and crime shows never depict jury selection. Probably because the process is as deliberate and painstaking as microsurgery on the eye. Is there any alternative to this tedium? Could we just pick fourteen people by random and give them a capital case to decide? Not if we expected the decision to be made by persons who respect the statutes passed by the legislatures rather than their own idea of what the law should be. We call our system the rule of law for a very good reason.

Both Tony and I had put days into researching the backgrounds of the people subpoenaed to appear for jury service. His investigator and Possum had each studied the questionnaires the jurors had returned—home address, age, occupation, marital status, prior jury experience, and other personal information. They had also scoured every pertinent public record they could uncover—criminal records, property assessments rolls, credit reports. They consulted old timers and notorious courthouse gossips. And in this digital age, they hit Google and the blossoming social media. Both sides were ready.

The judge excused one after another of the prospective jurors for admitting they would be unwilling, even in the face of horrendous circumstances, to impose the penalty of death. The reasons varied: religion, morality, too nervous. A few, a very few, had the polar-opposite view. They stated they would automatically vote death for anyone who murdered. They were excused as well. People demand that their public officials be tough on crime, and are quick to blame the police officers and the prosecutors for criminals on the street. But just try to get those same people to man up to make the hard decisions necessary to take someone out of the picture. When summoned for jury service, a raft of excuses come out to play.

I think the response that most raised my ire was when I heard this answer: "Yes, I believe in the death penalty, but I couldn't actually vote for death myself." It was all I could do to keep from giving the juror the same lecture on personal responsibility I might have heard from my father or my grandfather.

Doesn't the fact that it takes hundreds of candidates to find twelve jurors willing and able to serve on a capital jury tell us volumes about the appropriateness of the penalty?

Two days later, at the end of the Witherspoon process in State v. Danny Howard, we had seventy jurors still in the room. Only those unfamiliar with the process of jury selection would be certain that number would be sufficient to get a jury. We still had all the questions necessary to ferret out other biases and predilections that might be obvious enough to prompt the judge to excuse a prospective juror for *cause*, the term of art we use to describe unwillingness or inability to apply the law we're sworn to uphold. And then each attorney had twelve peremptory challenges he could use for no reason except that he didn't detect empathy for his particular side.

At the end of the fifth day, one little scene injected a tense moment in the selection process.

"Ladies and gentlemen." Tony addressed one of the last pared-down panels. "I apologize for the language you are going to be hearing in this case." He stood at the podium, facing the box. Respectful, earnest, downright charming. "Much as I hate even to use these words, I am going to ask how you feel when you hear bad language, even racial slurs."

He came around the podium and stood facing the box. He directed his question to a middle-aged black woman in the back row. "Ms. Picard, please tell me, has anyone ever called you a *nigger*?"

Half the air in the room sucked into the throats of the startled crowd. Judge Johnson could usually sit still for anything, but this question put her to the test. She scowled and her complexion darkened

Ms. Picard responded, "Yes."

"Tell me, please. When that happened, how did it make you feel?"

Five seconds of silence seemed like an eternity.

She spoke softly. "I sure didn't like it."

Tony took a step closer to the jury box. His voice was gentle, but he spoke with enough precision for his words to be picked up by the microphone and broadcast throughout the room. "I can certainly understand, Ms. Picard. I apologize for asking these questions. Unfortunately, for this case, how people feel about that word is very important."

Another step forward.

"When something like that happens, when someone uses that word to you, Ms. Picard, what do you do?"

The juror thought for a moment before she responded, but now her voice sounded clear and strong. "Well, it depends. Time was, I used to not do anything. But now?" She paused. "Now I say something." Another pause, then she threw off a dismissive answer. "'Really, I just consider that attitude's their problem."

Tony turned and returned to his position behind the podium. Whew, that's over, I thought.

But no. It wasn't.

"Now, please tell me, Ms. Picard. Do you think it's OK, when someone says something like that, when someone uses that word, to physically attack them?" Tony spoke even louder now, enunciating his words. "Like do you think it is OK to stab someone five times for using the word *nigger*?"

I exploded from my chair. "Objection, your honor."

Tony's response was immediate. "I withdraw the question, your honor."

"We will be in recess for fifteen minutes," Judge Johnson boomed. She rose, spun around, and exited through the door behind the bench, letting the door slam behind her.

I was furious, but I also had to admire Tony's guts. How could he have predicted Ms. Picard's response? And he'd hit a bulls-eye. Every juror, black or white, had heard a black woman say that the appropriate response to a racial slur should be temperate. Damn good at his job, Tony was. I walked to his table and told him so.

"Tony, I have to hand it to you. The question was brilliant."

"You think so? A bit of luck, there," he responded. "What the hell would I have done if she'd been a Black Panther?"

There was a lot of luck in this business. Whether or not Danny Howard succeeded in having on his jury the one person who, come deliberation time, choked at imposing a sentence of death, might depend on the skill, lack of it, or damn blind luck, of the lawyer who tried his case. Me.

At the end of the seventh day we had our jury. When they were being sworn, I put my arm around my client's shoulders, letting the jury see a paternal attitude I hoped they'd adopt toward the boy as well.

"I'm pretty happy with the jury, Danny. Almost every one selected has kids, and we have four black jurors." Danny raised his head and looked at me, a rare occurrence.

I continued. "Yeah, I know. You say color doesn't matter to you. But let me tell you this from my experience, it does to a lot of people. And African-American jurors, men and women, are the most reluctant to bring down the hammer on anyone, black or white."

Danny looked drained, younger, even lower than when we started jury selection the week before.

"And Danny, I think every one will take great care to try to figure out exactly what you might have told the officers in that so-called incriminating statement."

Silence.

"How do you feel?"

"Where's my mom?"

I looked to the pews. "I saw her earlier, but I think she had to go."

I was lying. I hadn't seen her since the very first day.

OPENING STATEMENTS

A low hum wafted through the air over the crowd in the large courtroom of the St. Mary Parish courthouse. Spectators had filled the pews to hear the opening statement of the prosecutor, Tony Blendera. A capital trial draws an audience, and even impresses thirty-year veterans of the process. Yes, I would be making an opening statement as well, but a defense lawyer doesn't have a following unless, of course, a defendant has snagged Johnny Cochran or some other celebrity counsel. Not the case for Danny Howard. He had to make do with what the state provided: me and Reginald Denny, the regular co-counsel sent by the State Public Defender Board to be my second chair.

This morning Reg had surpassed even his customary sartorial splendor. He sported a gray, European-cut sharkskin suit, yellow bow tie, matching yellow handkerchief, and alligator boots that added just a tad to his five-foot five-inch height. His neat Afro seemed an inch longer today, another attempt to increase his stature. To me, sparkling eyes, a quick smile, and even quicker mind, made him ten feet tall.

I had the help of Kaniesha Morris as well, newly barred, with a computer on her lap and five boxes of research and evidence at her feet. I was willing to bet Kaniesha's mother, who cleaned houses and offices downtown, dipped into her savings to buy Kaniesha's black pantsuit.

The surfaces of both counsel tables were clear. No

messy papers. Trial lawyers are supposed to look as if they have everything under complete control.

The prosecution table was, of course, located on the same side as the jury box, the better for the ADAs to maintain eye contact with the jurors. A tradition, and another example of the prosecutorial edge. Just to be certain no defense counsel became presumptuous, one of the bailiffs always arrived early to unlock the courtroom and guard the left-side counsel table until the district attorney's staff moved in. Today, Tony had two additional assistant district attorneys at his side.

About five dozen, solid-looking country people, dressed as for Saturday afternoon Mass, occupied the first ten rows on the left side of the courtroom. The bailiff had also saved these rows this morning, an accommodation for Clyde Carline's family. They mattered.

At the head of the Carline crowd, next to the center aisle, in the most prominent seat in the room other than the judge's bench, sat Senator Robert St. Germain. Senator Robert *McAdam* St. Germain, the political moniker he used to tap into his connection to another prominent family in St. Mary Parish. A large man. Shiny silk suit, golf course tanned ruddy complexion, full head of silver hair, everything about him said *look at me*. The senator hadn't diluted the impact of his presence by sitting through the five days of jury selection. He knew how to make an entrance by arriving for opening statements. *The whole state will be watching what you do here, his presence warned the jurors.* The various uniformed personnel who would serve the proceedings—the deputy sheriffs, city policemen recruited for extra security, deputy clerks of court—cast smiles and nods in the direction of the Carlines. The family was well known to all the men and women who wore the white hats.

Paranoia bubbled up into my consciousness, and I shot an accusing glance over to Tony. Had he orchestrated the presence and location of the senator in order to intimidate the jury? Tony's eyes were fixed upon his notes. Lose the road rage, John, I told myself. You'll say something stupid. Just do your job.

Behind, and slightly apart from the Carline crowd, one middle-aged black woman sat alone. Jerome Davis' aunt from Houston.

On the defense side, behind my counsel table, a couple hunched low in the first pew. Danny's mother Josie Chastant and her husband Bill. Chins tucked, eyes on the floor, they didn't search the crowd for friends or family; there would be none.

The three main doors to the courtroom opened along the side wall of the room, directly at our left. In addition to being given a less favorable position in the room, we had to contend with the distraction of the clanging doors. I looked up each time they opened and swung shut.

A few minutes after nine, Medley slipped through in her pink home health scrubs. Up on the balls of her feet so as not to squeak her rubber soled shoes on the tile floor, she scurried along the wall up to the first pew, just behind the bar. Agitation flushed her cheeks; I could hear her rapid breaths. She sank down, leaving a little space between herself and Danny's Dad. I started to go to her, but Kaniesha shook her head. She went back to join Medley, sitting close.

"Where've you been, girl? I was afraid you weren't going to make it."

"Whew! Lemme tell you. I nearly didn't. I got caught in a restroom stall!"

"What? The lock didn't work or something? You're skinny enough to slither underneath."

"I'm not kidding. Two of the Carlines were at the washbasins, Clyde Carline's mother and his Aunt Aimee. The aunt kept running water on paper towels and daubing them on the mom's forehead. I knew they'd seen me with John during jury selection; I thought if I came out they'd totally freak out!"

"I can picture it! You pinned down in the stall! But what were they so upset about? This is the day they've been waiting for."

"The mom said through her blubbering that she knew Clyde would want her to be brave, but she just didn't know if she could do it."

"Do what? All she has to do is sit here. I don't see her name on the witness list."

"She kept saying she didn't know if she could go into the courtroom and look into the face of the monster who cut up her boy. Then she'd collapse in another torrent of tears. Aunt Aimee was doing her best to calm her down. 'Clyde would want you to be brave,' she said. 'If you don't go through with the trial, that boy will go back to his family just as if he never did what he did. He'll see each and every sunshiny day. He'll enjoy all the good things he took away from Clyde.' To tell you the truth, Kaniesha, I felt for them."

Kaniesha touched Medley's arm. "I understand. Kind of makes you wonder how you'd feel about the death penalty if someone took away the most precious person in your life."

"I hope I know how I'd feel, but..." She didn't finish her sentence. Losing Buddy must have crossed her mind.

"All rise!" The booming voice of the bailiff stopped every conversation mid-sentence. My body temperature obeyed the bailiff's command. I lengthened my breaths—the well-tested technique I used to settle my nerves.

Judge Johnson entered from the door behind the bench. She remained standing, her expression amiable but showing deference to the solemnity of the occasion. The twelve jurors and two alternates filed in from the jury room, entered the box, but didn't sit.

"Take your seats, ladies and gentlemen," the judge instructed. When they had done so, she continued. "You will probably notice that when you come into and when you leave the courtroom, we all stand. We do that out of respect for you; you are now the judges of this case."

Nice touch. She was good at making jurors feel proud about their participation in what is really an ordeal.

Seven men and seven women, only one below the age of thirty. There were only four African-Americans, all middle class: an accountant and three schoolteachers. A jury of Danny's peers? Hardly. I'd done my best, but would it be good enough? Was there a single person there who would care about a mixed-up kid? Was there anyone who could relate to life in the projects?

I stood erect and, with a head nod, bid each juror a good morning. I knew a good bit about these men and women, both from research and from jury selection questioning the week before. I believed I had made a connection to each one. If I hadn't felt that way, I wouldn't have let them on the jury.

Danny hadn't budged. He didn't even acknowledge the presence of the fourteen people who'd decide if he lived or died. Without taking my eyes from the jurors, I pinched his shoulder, pulled him to his feet, poked him in his side, and hissed out of the side of my mouth. "For God's sake, Danny, look 'em in the eye! And it wouldn't hurt a bit if you could manage a smile!"

Tony walked to the podium, still set directly before the jury box. He had polished himself to a bright shine for the occasion, and a whiff of Brut followed in his trail. The overhead lights gleamed off silver streaks in his black curls, adding to his gravitas. Damn, he looked good.

Even before Tony had finished reintroducing himself to the jury, he broke free of the podium, leaving behind any notes he may have placed there. He strode up and down before the rail, appearing totally at ease. He wasn't, of course. I detected the quiver of his trousers and the stiffened fingers of his left hand.

"During the next few days, ladies and gentlemen, you are going to hear a very sad story. On a warm, October night, six months ago, two people were stabbed to death behind the Pecan Gardens Apartments. You probably know where that is, off Main Street, on the north edge of town. Clyde Carline was stabbed five times with a large serrated instrument, probably a kitchen knife. Jerome Davis, a fourteen-year-old boy, was stabbed three times, with a large knife as well. Both Clyde Carline and Jerome Davis bled out, dying right there off the concrete pad behind the apartments, their blood pooling together in a furrow between two rows of stubble cane. The State is bringing into this courtroom the young man whom the grand jury accuses of committing these two murders."

Following standard prosecutorial practice, Tony didn't give the defendant a name. Personalize the victims; treat the defendant like a nameless fiend.

"You are going to hear from the group of young people who were partying on the night of October 2 to 3, at and around the apartment of Nee-Nee and Nikki Roberts, the defendant's friends. You will hear from them and from many other friends as well. They will tell you, under oath, what they know about everything that happened that night. They would rather not come to this courtroom, but as the prosecutor for the State, I subpoenaed—ordered—them to come. I am determined to give you every bit of information we have about what happened that night."

The prosecutor always tells the jury how noble he is!

"The testimony of the defendant's friends will tell you the story. The defendant was partying, and you will decide for yourself what that means. He left the group to use the telephone at the rear of the apartment complex. He encountered Clyde Carline. Clyde called him a name and he got mad about it. He went back to his friends, asked for a knife, then left again. No doubt about any of that."

Well, maybe some doubt. I hoped I could raise

reasonable doubt about how those events tied together.

"Clyde Carline, who had some very well known mental limitations, lived in the rear area of the apartments, on the other side of the complex from where the kids had the party. You will hear from someone who lived near Clyde, Marie Champagne. Earlier in the evening she saw someone, probably the defendant, in the very same place where the stabbing occurred. She heard an argument. Later on that evening there was another exchange. In the morning, Clyde Carline lay dead. Next to him, a fourteen year old boy lay dead as well."

I studied the jury. Every eye watched Tony as he spoke.

"I will be completely honest with you, ladies and gentlemen. This witness, Marie Champagne, is not absolutely certain that the person speaking to Clyde Carline that night was the defendant. But you will hear her testimony and judge for yourselves. She is pretty darn sure. And we have important corroboration. An incriminating statement by the defendant himself.

"Turning now to the other person who was killed *at almost the exact same time as Clyde Carline, in exactly the same manner,* I will admit to you, ladies and gentlemen, that no witnesses tells us they saw him anywhere around the apartments. No one knows what he was doing there. I submit to you that the poor unfortunate boy, Jerome Davis, known to his family as Ti-Boy, must have come upon the scene, saw what he should not have seen, and suffered the same fate as Clyde Carline. That is the only reasonable explanation for his death.

"For proof of the stabbing of Ti-Boy Davis, the State will present to you circumstantial evidence—which term was explained to you in jury selection and which the judge will instruct you about at the end of the trial. As you know, you can only convict on circumstantial evidence if there is no other reasonable explanation for what occurred. I submit to you that there is no reasonable explanation for the death of Jerome Davis other than that he was stabbed by the defendant. Same time. Same weapon. No one else around."

Got to admit I had no other reasonable explanation.

"Ladies and gentlemen, you will also hear from the person who found the bodies of these two persons. You will hear from the police officers who investigated their deaths. You will hear from the doctor, a renowned pathologist, who performed the autopsies. You will learn how the victims died, how many wounds they had, how they must have suffered as they bled to death. And lastly, you will hear what the defendant did and said at the time of his arrest.

"As your prosecutor, my job is to bring to you all the people who know anything about what happened on that night six months ago. You will hear them, and from what you hear, you will decide what should be done. From this evidence, I know you will agree that the State has proved, beyond a reasonable doubt, that the defendant stabbed Clyde Carline. And I know that you will agree that the State has proven to you, beyond a reasonable doubt, that when he did so, the defendant had the specific intent to kill or inflict great bodily harm. From the circumstantial evidence you will also agree that the State has proved, beyond a reasonable doubt, that when the defendant stabbed the other victim, Jerome Davis, who so unfortunately happened upon the scene, he had the specific intent to kill or inflict great bodily harm on him as well. Ladies and gentlemen, that is first degree murder, two counts."

Tony returned to the podium. "At this time, ladies and gentlemen of the jury, you will not consider the penalty for these crimes—just guilt or innocence. Penalty is for another proceeding, after the determination of guilt is over."

Tony stood motionless, looking each juror in the eye. After fourteen seconds, one second for each of the twelve jurors and two alternates, he picked up his papers.

"Thank you," he said, and returned to his table. The

eyes of every juror followed his steps. He had them.

Behind me, I heard Kaniesha whisper to Medley. "Yeah, I know. Tony's smooth. And he's good. But so is John. Just wait."

I wasn't so confident. As late as last night I had worked on Danny to try to get him to let me admit he stabbed Clyde Carline in anger so that I could work on the DA to accept a plea to manslaughter, death penalty off the table. Danny refused. He held firm to his position that he had blacked out and knew nothing.

"Keep it simple," Reg had told me. "Closing argument is time enough to give them the intricacies of the intent required for first degree on two counts. Now, just drive home that not one of the State's witnesses, all in impaired condition, saw Danny do anything."

Kaniesha had agreed. "For whatever may be the value of the opinion of someone licensed to practice law for all of four weeks, I believe the safest course at this point is to deny everything and hold the district attorney to strict proof of all that the law says he has to prove. There'll be plenty of time for admissions later on."

Showtime. I gave a reassuring smile to my motionless client, more for the benefit of the jury than for him—today he was into studying those hands again—and rose to make the opening statement for the defense. I clutched the sides of the podium.

"Ladies and gentlemen."

I looked from one juror's face to another, willing my energy to flow to each one of them.

"I agree with my worthy opponent that you are going to hear a very sad story. But it is not quite the story the State has just said you will hear. Yes, you will hear from witnesses who were in the Pecan Gardens Apartments that night. Yes, you will hear that Danny Howard was there with them some of the time. But listen to these witnesses very carefully. When you listen carefully, ladies and gentlemen, you will hear not one story but many different stories. Not one story matches another. No one was with Danny Howard all of the time. No one saw either victim receive the fatal wounds."

Was I getting through? Maybe. I saw two women on the front row lean forward.

"Remember in jury selection we talked a lot about burden of proof? Remember that the State has the burden of proving to you, beyond a reasonable doubt, every element of the two crimes? Remember that you assured me you would hold the State to that burden? I submit to you that the State will not bring to you any witness who can prove that my client, Danny Howard, stabbed anyone."

I came around in front of the podium. Like Tony, I wanted to pretend we were just having a casual conversation.

"Danny and his friends were drinking. They were probably pretty obnoxious folks to have around. Picture it. Late on a warm night at the beginning of October. Kids playing loud rap music, yakking and yelling back and forth to each other, from balcony to balcony and beyond. I believe one witness will tell you that someone tossed a six-pack of beer from the balcony of the party apartment to waiting hands below—but missed his target. The bottles smashed in an earsplitting crash. I daresay not one of us would want to have been there that night, let alone try to sleep through the racket."

I gave them a brief smile, then returned to my sober description of the scene.

"Danny had been drinking more than most. You will hear plenty of testimony about that. The last thing he remembers is that he and Clyde Carline got into an argument when Clyde provoked him with an insult. Clyde called Danny the worst racial slur, the 'N' word. After that," and here I spoke very slowly, "Danny remembers *nothing*. He blanked out. And no one knows what happened. Not one witness for the State can tell you that he or she saw Danny do *anything to Clyde Carline or to Ti-Boy Davis.* Burden of proof. I submit to you there is no proof beyond a reasonable doubt that Danny did *anything.* And, for sure, there is absolutely no proof at all that Danny Howard had *anything* to do with the death of Jerome Davis."

I took a step to the right, just to make a juror in the back row, clearly not on my side, look up to see if I was done. No, sir. Just trying to get your mind back to the business at hand.

"Over the next few days you will be learning a lot more about Danny Howard." I stopped and looked back at Reg. He was shaking his head. Don't go there, he signaled. Don't talk any more about the provocation. Wait until you see how the prosecution witnesses hold up before you argue what may not be necessary. Wait until closing argument for legal stuff.

OK, Reg. I took his advice. I returned to my position behind the podium.

"Next thing we know for sure, some time later that night—morning by now—Danny is walking across the field toward his house in the neighboring subdivision. Ladies and gentlemen of the jury, listen carefully to what Danny did and said from the time he left the Pecan Gardens Apartments. I think you will agree that his actions are not those of someone who, moments before, had murderous rage. He bought a hamburger at McDonald's on the corner and made his way home to bed."

I paused and took a sip of water. Enough? Literally, only heaven knew.

"Remember, ladies and gentlemen. Do not make up your minds until you have heard all the evidence. And remember the burden of the state, *proof beyond a reasonable doubt.* Thank you."

I returned to my seat behind the counsel table. The judge dismissed the jury for lunch and, after an update on the schedule, left the courtroom. Danny had turned around to look for his mother. Gone. Medley and Kaniesha sat alone in the pew behind me.

"Sorry, Danny. Your mother seems to have left." I tried to sound matter-of-fact. "But you saw her, right? She was here."

"Yeah, man. *Was* here."

I could have strangled the woman.

When I started to go back to join Medley, she was standing up, distress drawing her brows tight together.

"Was I that bad, Medley? Don't tell me you think Tony made a better case?" I teased, charged up with relief that my opening was over.

"No, no, John. Not that. The guy is there, in the back of the courtroom!"

"What guy?" I asked. I had been totally into the trial and hadn't a clue what she was talking about.

"The guy with the snake tattoos. You know, the one who was following me before."

"What?" I almost shouted when I realized what Medley was saying. "Where? Where is he?"

"About five rows from the back, on the other side. See him? Tall, blond. Whoops, there he goes!" The big blond scurried around the back of the courtroom and slipped out the last of the three side doors.

I darted through the front one and grabbed the arm of the uniformed deputy standing duty at the security station. "Benny, I need a favor right quick. See that fellow on the way to the stairs?" Benny followed my pointing finger. "Tall blond man with the stringy hair? We've gotta stop him. You take the jail elevator back there; I'll take the front one. Use some pretense or other. Say we need to make a security check. Anything. Stop him. And radio narcotics to get here p.d.q. We've got to find out who he is."

The deputy signaled his partner that he was leaving the security station and ran to the service elevator at the end of the hall. I punched the button for the regular one, but waited an eternity for it to appear. When I got to the ground floor the deputy was waiting for me.

"I don't see anyone, Mr. Clark."

We dashed out the front doors of the building, down the steps, checked the front lawn, and around the corners. Not there either. He had vanished.

My heart was banging in my chest. What the hell was this all about?

When I returned to the courtroom, I spoke sharply to Medley, more sharply than I would have if I hadn't been in major alarm. "Whenever, if ever, you see that man again, don't wait a second. Call me. Call Possum. Call Kaniesha. Make a beeline to a deputy sheriff or a policeman."

Medley's eyes watered, the way they had in the jail the day I first saw her. "That's just what I did."

"I'm sorry, Medley. I've got a few hundred things on my mind." I put my arm around her shoulder. "This guy's been around for six months now, and all he does is show up once in a while. If you were in any danger, we would know by now. But if we can find him, we'll put an end to this business. OK?"

Medley set her jaw. "I won't be hanging around the courtroom, John. I'm just a distraction. I'm going back to work. Kaniesha, give me a call now and then to tell me how everything is going."

Medley touched my arm and added, "Whenever you want to call..."

I had to agree. She was a distraction. But what the hell was going on? She hadn't seen the guy for months. What rattled his cage? Was he interested in the trial or just in Medley?

Kaniesha and I walked back up to the front of the courtroom. "Kaniesha, one more task for your list. Keep an eye out for that fellow." Then, in imitation of myself a few minutes ago, I gave her the same harsh command. "Call me; go to the deputy sheriff or to a policeman. Tell them to contact me immediately. Promise!"

"Yes, sir!" Kaniesha saluted, and drew my attention back to the task at hand. "Tony may get to the kids at the apartments this afternoon, right?"

"Yes, that's what he says."

"Well, I have their statements for you in a folder on the counsel table."

"Thanks. I was planning to organize that material over lunch."

"I have something else for you—almost finished. I made a chart, kind of like the Synoptic Gospels we used to study in Sunday school. Instead of three columns showing what Jesus said according to Mathew, Mark, and Luke, I have set up four columns comparing what the partygoers said happened at the apartments that night. The first column contains the statements by the girls: Toya, Nikki and Alicia. Second column, the facts according to the boys: Ace, Poochie, Cheese, and Nee-Nee. Then I have a special column for Snap-Dog—I set him out separately from the others because Possum is still trying to make him our *other dude*. The fourth column is the evening according to Danny."

"Girl, you continue to amaze me. Come with me to the sheriff's office for lunch. The inmates are cooking jambalaya."

I went to the sheriff's office, but I totally forgot about jambalaya. I searched out Lt. Marcus Magrette, Chief of Narcotics. I found him and laid out the situation with Medley's shadower.

Marcus showed no trace of the defensiveness he had shown when I'd questioned him about the possibility of someone escaping out the back of the house on the night of the Butterfield arrests. He said little, but I could tell from the intensity of his gaze that his mind was at work.

"I'll be in touch," he said. "And of course, let me know if

Medley spots the guy again."

They say sharing doubles joy and cuts worry in half. Arithmetic didn't work on this problem. My anxiety hadn't diminished.

THE PROSECUTION CASE

When I came back to the courtroom, Reg had already settled at our table. He rolled his eyes across the aisle to direct my attention to that prominent location at the head of the Carline clan.

"I see Senator St. Germain is still favoring us with his presence," he said.

"Who cares? I have no time for celebrity watch."

"It's curious, John. The senator is one nervous cat. All morning he's squirmed in his chair like a teenager at the family dinner. I thought he'd jump out of his skin when he turned at the same time Medley spotted the blond dude in the back of the courtroom."

"Really? I hadn't seen that."

Other than being the uncle of the victim, did the senator have another connection to all this business? I didn't care if the courtroom gave him the fidgits, but his interest in Medley's shadower got my attention. Maybe I should tell Lt. Magrette.

Tony led off the prosecution case with Bob Duplantis, the offshore oil worker who had discovered the bodies of Clyde Carline and Ti-Boy Davis. Straightforward, matter-of-fact testimony delivered in a monotone. Early on the morning of October 3, following his disobedient dog into the cane rows past his back yard, he stumbled first on the body of a young black boy and then on the body of a white man. He didn't know either one. They lay just off the concrete behind the Pecan Gardens Apartments and looked quite dead.

Duplantis had trouble when Praline wouldn't leave the bodies alone, but he finally got his dog on leash, pulled her back to his house, and called 911. Praline had put her teeth into the back of his hand so he missed most of the subsequent commotion. He had to go to the hospital to get his hand stitched.

As Tony turned his witness over to me for cross-examination, and I was sharpening my talons to go to work, Reg tipped back in his chair and muttered. "Dull, dull, dull. Duplantis couldn't sell crawfish to a Cajun. His testimony might have had impact on the jury if he could've brought Praline to show and tell."

The opening-gun tension in my shoulders eased. Reg was going to do an important job—keep perspective. I should pass up nit-picking the witness. But in my quest for reasonable doubt—all I had going for me at the moment—I could probe for a red herring.

"Mr. Duplantis," I asked, my face a guileless facade. "I believe you have a son about the same age as Danny."

"Yes, sir."

"Do you know if he ever spent time with Danny or with his friends in the apartments?"

Tony shot to his feet. "Objection! That topic was not covered in direct examination and has no impeachment value."

"Sustained." Judge Johnson used her gavel for this ruling, leaving the jury to speculate about what they weren't permitted to hear. I had planted a seed, really a smoke screen. I had no idea if his son knew the players.

Tony glared in my direction. I deserved his censure. I wouldn't stoop to such tactics in my routine criminal trials, but as U.S. Supreme Court Justice Blackman had written, 'death is different.' With the life of my client on the line, I pushed the envelope.

"I have no more questions, your honor."

Tony called Sgt. Theresa Wiltz as his second witness.

An investigating officer usually sets out the roadmap for the prosecution case, letting the jury see how law enforcement puts together the evidence. But Tony's choice of Theresa surprised me. Why didn't he go with Lt. Daigle, the senior member of the pair? Tall, handsome, Brett had presence in the witness box. Then I got it. Tony wanted to make an immediate connection to the four black jurors to blunt their possible empathy for a black defendant.

Some people say we're are at the point in this country where race no longer matters. Maybe one day that'll be true, but we aren't there yet. In our line of work, you'd better consider the relevance of race at every turn. At least if you want to win. Clearly Tony had that lesson down pat.

When Theresa described the first person who implicated Danny Howard for the two found dead behind the apartments, I knew she had encountered Nikki Roberts. Theresa cut her description of the girl short with a sibilant s-s-s; she had come close to labeling the girl a smart-ass.

"No, I won't give you my name, fuzz," Theresa quoted the girl's response to her first interview question. "All I say is, Danny was mighty interested in a big-ass knife hangin' around at the party. Where was it after Danny left out o' there?" Theresa said Nikki threw her hands in the air. "No mo' knife on the chair."

Theresa testified that two other kids told her Danny was steaming mad about something that had happened outside that night.

Those two tips, Danny's rage and Nikki's statement that the knife had disappeared after Danny left the party, sent the investigating officers to find Danny Howard. Everybody seemed to know where he lived. Late in the morning, Theresa and Brett paid a call at the home of Josie and Bill Chastant, 211 Pecan Street.

"Danny's mother woke him up, escorted him into the living room, and began to bombard him with questions about his activities the night before," Theresa testified. "He wouldn't respond. I took over the questioning. Eventually, Danny gave a very brief account of his evening. He had taken his friend Snap-Dog, real name Mark Diggers, for a ride and then to a party at the apartment of Nee-Nee Roberts. Danny said he remembered a knife around, but he didn't know what happened to it."

I had tried to persuade Judge Johnson to exclude Danny's statements on the grounds that Theresa and Brett had not first given him his Miranda warnings—the right to remain silent, have a lawyer, that what he said could be used against him. I lost the motion. Judge Johnson ruled that Danny had not been in custody at the time. Probably correct. Any compulsion the boy might have felt came more from his mother than from Sgt. Wiltz.

"Did you ask the defendant if he encountered Clyde Carline in the course of the evening?" Tony asked Sgt. Wiltz.

"Yes, sir. He said he heard Clyde Carline yelling some stuff when he went to the back of the complex to make a phone call. He said he didn't 'pay it no mind.' Then I asked Danny if he became angry when Clyde Carline called him a *nigger* and went back to the party to get a knife. In response to that question, Danny mumbled 'yeah' and nodded his head in the affirmative."

I'd have to go after that two-part question in cross. Damaging, and confusing. Did 'yeah' apply to both the anger and going back for the knife?

"Did you obtain any physical evidence when you were at the home of the Chastants?" Tony asked Theresa.

"Yes. I asked Danny for the clothing he had worn the night before. He said he didn't know where it was. Mrs. Chastant stood up, went to the laundry room, and came back with a stained T-shirt. She willingly handed it to us. I suspected that the spot on the t-shirt was dried blood. I asked Danny if he knew his blood type. He said O-positive."

Theresa said they delivered the shirt to the Acadiana Crime Lab. Within two hours a call informed them the stain was indeed human blood, A-positive, like Clyde Carline's.

"And were those the facts that you wrote into your affidavit for the arrest of the defendant?" Tony asked.

"Yes, sir. The fingering by his friends, his admission that he went back to get a knife and stabbed Carline because of his use of the word *nigger*, and the blood on his T-shirt matching the blood type of Clyde Carline."

"And did you arrest the defendant?"

"Yes, sir. We returned to the Chastant's house around two that afternoon, gave him the Miranda warning, and we executed the warrant of arrest."

"Did you see the defendant again that day?"

"Yes, sir. Around 7 p.m. We went to the jail to take a written statement. No luck. The defendant had lawyered-up."

I went to work on cross.

"Let me ask you first about your last statement, Sgt. Wiltz. About Danny lawyering up. Are you telling me that Danny spoke to a lawyer sometime during that day?"

"No, sir." Theresa answered. "He just told me he wanted a lawyer, so of course we didn't try to talk with him at all after that. I understand he used his one phone call to speak with Mrs. Diggers, his friend Snap-Dog's mother."

Hm-m. I hadn't known that.

I grilled Theresa about her characterization of Danny's response as *an admission*. She agreed with me that Danny had never spoken an identifiable word in response to her killer two-part question. He had only mumbled incoherently and wagged his head. Wagged, I asked? Up and down in the affirmative or side-to-side in the negative? She had to admit she wasn't certain. At least she didn't claim Danny had confessed; the newspapers did that. Yes,

Theresa said, she had learned later the DNA tests excluded both Clyde Carline and the boy as the source of the blood on Danny's T-shirt.

"Do you know how Mrs. Chastant knew she'd find Danny's T-shirt in the laundry room when he had come in late, had gone straight to bed, and was just then getting up?"

"No, sir. I have no idea. But she found the shirt quickly, and Danny didn't deny that he had worn it the night before."

Theresa freely admitted that the investigating officers had absolutely nothing tying Danny to the other victim that night, the then-unknown African-American boy.

"And yet you swore out a warrant for Danny's arrest on that crime as well?" I asked. I hoped I hadn't overdone my feigned incredulity. Jurors don't like inadequate evidence pointed out to them with sarcasm. They like to discover it for themselves.

"Yes."

"And what was your justification for that warrant? What was your probable cause?"

"The coroner had informed us that his examination indicated the two stabbings occurred at the same time and at the same place. The wounds were sufficiently similar for him to conclude they were most likely administered by the same weapon. We had no information that anyone else had access to the scene before the bodies were discovered."

Good answer. During the remainder of the cross-examination I hammered Teresa Wiltz on what she did not know.

Things might be a little chilly the next time Theresa and I got back to the shooting range, but we'd get through it. Both of us had loyalty to the system. We each knew we had to do our jobs. I had to ask hard questions; her investigations had to stand up to heat.

An older white lady in a flowered housedress and

bedroom slippers came as the third witness for the prosecution. Marie Champagne. In response to Tony's questions, she told her story about hearing Clyde call out, pulling aside her curtain, and seeing some black boys walk by. Later in the night, really early the next morning, she didn't know exactly when, she heard commotion again. This time she peeked through her window and saw nothing. Maybe because the stabbings took place just off the concrete pad and not in the path between the two buildings, she suggested.

I could see from their smiles that the jury liked the lady. They wouldn't appreciate me giving her a hard time.

I caused Mrs. Champagne to repeat her statement that she could not identify Danny, either by the voice she heard or by her observation, as the person who was near Carline's apartment. And I made sure that she clearly stated she couldn't make out the actual words that Clyde Carline yelled out to the passers-by.

"But *you* know what Clyde was like," she added to her answer.

I glanced at Reg, and he nodded his head in the affirmative. Best to get information about Clyde Carline's limitations out in the open with Mrs. Champagne, a neutral person.

"No, I don't know. Tell me, ma'am. What was Clyde Carline like?"

"Well..." Mrs. Champagne sighed. "Clyde comes from a very nice family, but he's not quite right. When he was a young man—the best of life ahead of him—he had that bad accident. One morning when he was driving to work a drunk came out of nowhere and smacked him head on. The family nursed Clyde to an incredible recovery. He finally got so he could take care of himself and came to live on his own in the apartments, but he was damaged in the brain. I used to fuss at him all the time about his bad language. I told him he could get in trouble saying those things. He'd just laugh it off. I have to say, though, no one seemed to mind. His friend Vic Dominique, he's black, heard that kind of talk and didn't care. But I worried."

"And why did you worry, ma'am."

"Well, the kids. With them, that kind of business can get you hurt."

"Racial slurs? Did Clyde use racial slurs?"

"Yes, he did." She quickly added, "but I didn't hear anything specific that night."

"Did you ever hear Clyde Carline use the word *nigger*?"

"Yes, Mr. Clark. I did."

"You say you saw some kids walking by, sashaying by, that night. Were they black kids or white kids?"

"I couldn't tell for sure." A twitch of a smile played on her thin lips and disapproval edged her voice. "No doubt both. They're together around here, you know." She cut a glance to the jury box and rushed to cover her tracks. "Really, we're all friends in the apartments. Clyde said things but everyone seemed to know that was just the way he was."

"And you're sure you didn't see anyone later that night, early morning really, when you heard the commotion?"

"Not at the time of the commotion."

"Any time?"

Mrs. Champagne squeezed her eyes shut. "I saw the bodies in the morning. Poor Clyde. He was kind of a mess but he didn't deserve anything like that. Big gashes in his stomach, five of them. And that boy! When they turned him over and I saw those big eyes looking at nothing, I... Holy Mary, Mother of God!"

I wish I hadn't given her the opportunity to say all that.

I had planned to ask Mrs. Champagne if she could identify the boy from some post-mortem pictures, but when I looked at her tight upper lip and her chicken-beak fingers picking at her skirt, I realized I would tick off the jury if I made her cry. I opted for a simple question.

"Did have any idea who the boy was, ma'am?"

"I just assumed he was one of the kids who hung around there."

And then came Danny's erstwhile girlfriend, Toya Vallot. She told the same brief story she had agreed to when she signed her initial statement—not written in her own hand, as I was to learn later—and the same story she gave to Possum and me when we visited her in the apartments. She really had no information that bolstered or hurt the prosecution case. So why did Tony put her on? She was Danny's girlfriend, lived next door to the party, and Tony had told the jury in opening that he would let them hear from everyone who was significant to the story. He guessed correctly that the jury would like her.

Nee-Nee Roberts testified next. He and his sister gave a party and everybody came. The knife was there, Danny was there, Danny left and came back mad. But Nee-Nee didn't make a connection between those events. He didn't know if the knife was on the chair when Danny left or when he came back. They all handled the knife and he didn't know who had. By this time, he said, he had left the party.

Nee-Nee had a little gold nugget for me; he thought the last time he saw the knife Snap-Dog had it. I could use Nee-Nee's testimony in my closing to raise some reasonable doubt. I looked forward to getting Snap-Dog in my sights to raise even unreasonable ones. Possum would be delighted.

The big difference between the way Nee-Nee told his story now and how he told it to me when Possum and I came calling was the absence of profanity. His testimony now resembled the initial written statement taken by the investigators. I'd seen this practice before. The investigators talk to a witness. They write out a version scrubbed of profanity and phrased the way they want a witness to testify. That version is what the witness signs and reviews again before the trial. The scrubbed version is what the jury hears.

I also knew Tony did a lot of work teaching his witnesses to speak in language a juror could swallow. But then, I did the same with mine. All that is just part of the trade we practice.

Tony panned his own nugget from Nee-Nee's testimony.

"Did you ever hear Clyde Carline use bad language, bad racial language to African- Americans?" Tony asked Nee-Nee.

"Sure, man."

'Did he ever direct racial slurs to you?"

"Sure."

"Neal, tell me. Did he ever call you *nigger*?"

No hesitation. "Yeah. He did that."

"And what did you do when he talked like that?"

"I gave him some of his own medicine. Called him a few names back."

"Neal, tell me this. Did you ever physically attack Clyde Carline about that, about anything he might have said to you?"

"Naw."

"Think back now to the night of October 2nd. Did you hear Clyde Carline use any racial slurs that night?"

"Yeah. He always did."

"Were you with Danny when that happened?" Tony asked.

"Might have been. The white guy talked like that to everybody around there. That's how he got his kicks."

"Did you see Danny or anyone else do anything to Clyde Carline after being called bad names?"

"Do anything? What you mean?"

"Confront him about what he said."

"Yeah, we called him a few names back."

"That's all you did, talk back?" Tony asked.

"Yeah. That's all we ever do."

Tony was following up on the questions he had asked prospective juror Ms. Picard almost two weeks ago. He scored again. 'Saying something' is how decent, reasonable people react to unacceptable racial slurs.

I did my usual work on cross-examination—trying to persuade the jury that the details of the evening would forever remain in a fog.

We heard from a couple more girls, and the boy they call Poochie. Other than supporting Tony's case about Danny losing his temper and handling the knife, and supporting my case that sorting out details of this evening would be impossible, they added nothing remarkable. Inconclusive. No silver bullets for either the prosecution or the defense. End of the day.

Kaniesha had taken detailed notes on the testimony and handed them to me. I knew I should spend some time that night looking for inconsistencies that might be useful when we heard from the remainder of Tony's witnesses, but I had a splitting headache. I weighed whether or not I should impose my sour mood on Medley.

Kaniesha interrupted my considerations. "Mr. Clark, I have something I would like to talk to you about."

"Shoot, girl," I said, and then kicked myself for using that word girl. She didn't seem to notice, thank God.

"I get *African Americans in Acadiana*. That's a weekly newspaper you've probably never heard of. Published in Lafayette."

"No. Never heard of it." I was just making conversation, my mind thick with funk.

She smiled. "It's kind of like *The Times of Acadiana*, but for us black folks. My boyfriend writes for them. We call it *3As*."

"And?"

I kept packing my briefcase.

"I'm not sure, of course, but *3As* has been following a

story that might be important for us. Over the past two years, in towns around here, the bodies of two kids—one twelve, one fourteen—have been found. John Does.

"And?"

"The first was a Hispanic kid found two years ago in an apartment complex in Lake Charles. Bad death. The cops have his name, but no one ever figured out where he had been or what he had been doing for a whole year before his body was found. About six months ago, an African American kid was found dead in Alexandria. He has never been identified. Both of these kids had empty pockets."

I woke up and tuned her in. "Two deaths of unknown kids? Are you thinking there could be a link between those deaths and the death of Ti-Boy Davis?"

"Yes, sir. That's exactly what I'm thinking. But wait. There's more. Last week there was a third boy found with no ID, fourth boy if we count Ti-Boy in this company. African-American, stabbed repeatedly, behind an apartment complex in Lafayette."

My pulse quickened. "Good grief. Why haven't we heard about this stuff? I haven't read about these crimes or heard about them on TV."

Kaniesha smiled. "So, what's new, Mr. Clark? The regular media doesn't knock itself out trying to connect the dots where we're concerned. But this time we may have caught a break. The last boy isn't dead. He is in Little Charity—University Medical Center in Lafayette, that is—in critical condition."

My brain now revved up a mile a minute. A serial killer of unknown kids? Wow!

"This could be really important. Let me get Possum on it right away."

"Do that, Mr. Clark. But if you don't mind, I'd like to give it a shot myself. According to the article, no one can talk to the boy right now, but I know the reporter; he might talk to me. I'd like to go up there and see what I can find out."

"Go for it, Kaniesha. Do you have the names and places of death of those other boys? I'd like to give that info to Possum?"

"Here, take these copies of 3As. You might actually find them interesting."

Suddenly my headache had gone. Were we finally going to get a break in the mystery of the dead boy? I called Medley and asked if I could pick up something to eat and come over.

That was what was happening to me these days; whether I was high or low, bored or busy, I wanted to be with her. I did have enough of my brain still functioning in the normal, non-trial-of-Danny-Howard world to ask whether she'd seen her tattooed follower since Monday. Negative. Then she sat quietly while I bounced off my theory about Kaniesha's revelations. A serial killer?

"You know, out here in the country we don't have international arms dealers, conspiracies to bring down the United States government, or any of those other exotic crimes you read about in crime thrillers. But we do have serial killers. Just down I-10, in Jennings they've found the bodies of a dozen women, sketchy backgrounds all. They can't find the perp."

"I've heard about that."

"Serial killers usually pick victims who have characteristics in common. And the killers mark their victims. We've seen initials left in blood, a note, sometimes the manner of death itself is a signature. Maybe our killer picks young, minority-race boys and leaves them with no money, no ID."

As we were finishing our Chinese food, my cell phone buzzed. Kaniesha.

"I want to spend the night here at UMC, Mr. Clark. With Lee Drayton, the 3As reporter. I should be back by noon tomorrow. We haven't talked to the boy yet, and may not be able to tonight. But I don't want to miss an opportunity if it comes."

"Stay with it, Kaniesha. Call me if you learn anything. Anytime. In the night, if you get in to see the boy."

Medley picked up Buddy to take him to bed. When I took the boy from her and carried him to his room, his blond head settled into my shoulder. He was as comfortable with me as with his mother. I tucked him in.

Medley and I slowly kissed goodnight.

It wasn't until I was home in my own bed, trying to go to sleep, that I asked myself another question. How did the killer find boys no one would look for? Was there something connecting these kids to one another? Had to be? What could be the connection?

* * *

"The State calls Nikki Roberts, your honor."

The following morning, Nikki entered the forward side door of the courtroom, but instead of walking directly across to the witness box like every other person called to the stand, she headed to the back of the room—and stopped dead. One minute, two minutes, three minutes, until every eye in the room had been drawn in her direction. Then, and only then, she began her runway walk, modeling a thigh-high, shimmering slip of a dress, favoring her audience with nods to the right and to the left. Smart-ass Nikki. I sat back in my chair to enjoy the show. This was going to be good.

Standing at the podium awaiting his witness, Tony's trousers had the same quiver I saw during his opening statement. He must have come to know Nikki as well if not better than I did.

"Please stand to be sworn, Miss Roberts," he instructed.

Nikki thrust out her hip; she bent up her right wrist until her pink palm flanked her high-pointed breast. Reciting the oath, Minute Clerk Eloise, usually the beauty in the room, seemed as plain as a nun.

Nikki smirked and wiggled her finger as her assent. Judge Johnson scowled.

"You will answer the clerk out loud, Miss Roberts."

I held my breath. I saw Tony bite his lower lip.

"Ye-ah," the girl snarled.

"What did you say, Miss Roberts?" the judge demanded.

"Yeah-es, ma'aaam."

Judge Johnson gave the girl an extra measure of patience, but wariness had narrowed her eyelids. Any challenge to authority in the courtroom would be hers to handle. Nikki took her seat in the witness box, crossing her legs to display an expanse of thigh.

"Please state your name for the record, Miss Roberts," Tony began.

Slack-jawed silence.

The judge leaned forward. She couldn't sit still for another challenge to authority. She boomed out her terse demand.

"Your name, Miss Roberts?"

"Nikki Roberts." Hooded eyes, a defiant tip-up of the chin.

"May I call you Nikki?" Tony asked.

"That's my name, dude."

"And where do you live, Nikki?"

"The Gardens. Pecan Gardens Apartments."

With great care, Tony asked a minimum of questions. He clearly wanted the girl to deliver the bare bones of her version of events and get the hell off the stand.

Nikki told her story without incident. She and her then boyfriend, Snap-Dog Diggers, along with a number of their friends, were together at a party at her apartment. Her mother was at work, her grandmother asleep in a back bedroom. Someone got a large, serrated knife out of the kitchen. A couple of the guys played around with the knife, swinging it through the air in imitation of a swashbuckling pirate, then left the knife on a chair. In the course of the evening, Danny Howard, she called him Sleepy, came in and out. At one point he got mad about something someone had said to him outside and asked about the knife. He left again.

I heard the practiced words. *I seen him with the knife. I seen him leave. The knife wasn't on the chair no more. One, two, three. That's it.*

"Thank you, Nikki. Please answer the questions put to you by the defense."

I made my way slowly to the podium, gathering my thoughts about how to disparage this key testimony against my client. Step one: I would ask Nikki to supply details for every observation she had made. *Tell me exactly what happened, Miss Roberts? And you heard those words? And you saw that clearly?* Then I moved on to stage two. For each observation she made, I asked her to pinpoint an exact time. *I can't be quite sure about that*, she answered time after time. Finally, stage three: location. *Where exactly were you located when that happened? When you heard that? Where was Danny when this occurred? Where was your brother Nee-Nee? Where was Snap?* Nikki again repeated the phrase, *I can't be quite sure about that*. Through all this she held her cool.

Then I administered the *coup de grace*. I returned to the beginning of her story and began to ask the questions all over again—but in a different order. She stumbled on her words.

Tony sprang to his feet. "Your honor, I object. Counsel is asking the witness to repeat her testimony for a third— no, really a fourth time."

When we approached the bench to argue about his objection, I convinced the judge that my request was only for a second telling of exactly what happened. I had valid impeachment if the witness told the story differently on a second try. I won the argument. Objection overruled.

I dug in, and Nikki got even more confused. Recounting the events, she listed different people in the apartment from those she had previously given. Instead of being inside when Danny came back mad, this time she said she was on the balcony. She said she and Snap hadn't noticed the knife missing. When Danny left again, Snap had already gone next door to Danny's girlfriend Toya's apartment. I reviewed each of Nikki's answers and reminded her of her previous testimony, suggesting a version more favorable to my client. I watched the mercury rise in her thermometer—until she lost it. She sprang to her feet and her vocabulary turned blue.

"Listen here, you dick-shit. Quit your mother fuckin' questions. It was a party, man. It was a fuckin' party. Who knows what anybody did? We was drinkin', rappin', who knows what the fuck else. I'm out of here."

She sprang up and swung her rear end to the jury.

"Miss Roberts," Judge Johnson boomed from the bench. "Stop right there. You will remain in the witness box until you are released. And while you are on the witness stand, young lady, you will use language appropriate for a court of law. You are just one inch short of open contempt that will land you in jail!"

Nikki slumped back down and scowled even more deeply than the judge. His witness dead meat, Tony had his head in his hands. I had done enough damage to be able to argue that neither Nikki nor anyone else could be sure what happened that night.

The first rule of cross-examination is this: do not ask a question unless you already know the answer. I decided to break the rule. But first, I took a page from Nikki's book and used silence to capture the full attention of the jury. I waited until Nikki had settled down, the judge knew she had the witness under control, and the jurors were beginning to squirm in their seats. They were uncomfortable thinking about more embarrassing fireworks they might be required to endure.

"I have a few questions on another subject, Nikki. Tell me, were there any drugs around the apartment that night?"

She twitched. "No way, man. Not that I know of." Her startled eyes told me, the judge, and the entire jury that she was lying.

My co-counsel tapped his pencil on the counsel table in warning. I heard it. I was skating close to the edge. The rules said that save for legitimate impeachment, I couldn't cover in cross-examination any topic that hadn't been raised on direct unless, if challenged, I could honestly tell the judge I would have testimony in support later on in the trial. The truth of the matter was I had no idea whether anyone would testify to the presence of drugs. I let the subject drop.

But I couldn't forget the second victim. That poor boy had a way of slipping from everyone's mind.

"Nikki, let me ask you one more question. Do you have any knowledge of a young African-American boy, maybe fourteen years old or younger, one you hadn't seen before, hanging around that night."

"Negative."

Tony brought Nikki back on re-direct to try to get her story out again, in the sanitized version he had schooled her to give. That was a mistake. She went over the edge. "Look, man. I have no fuckin' idea what happened that night. And nobody does."

Bingo! Tony's witness made the point I would repeat in closing argument. Tony was going to have a hard time hanging his case on the testimony of Nikki Roberts.

Then Tony called a witness I didn't expect. Traylyn Fields, aka Cheese. I cut a glance to Reg.

"Cheese? Possum and I didn't talk with that guy. What the dickens does he have to allow?"

"We have his initial statement, John," Reg whispered. He dug a paper out of a carton under the table and handed it to me. "Cheese told the officers he thought there was a knife at the party, but he was out on the balcony when Danny came back. He said he never saw Danny with the knife. That's on Kaniesha's chart of the testimony of the kids."

Cheese had experienced a miraculous restoration of memory. He now testified that he remembered Danny being steaming mad, fed up with "that dick Carline and his shitty mouth." "I saw Danny leave with something in this hand, and it could have been the knife." Cheese spoke clearly, with an open expression. He looked at the jury as he answered the questions, and they smiled back. They liked him. Ouch.

I could make no legal objection to Cheese's testimony; Tony had the name on his witness list and I had a copy of his initial statement. Problem was, that statement was quite different from what he told us now. The day I had gone to Cheese's apartment came back to me. Cheese hadn't been home; Poss and I had talked to his younger brother, and then Medley and Possum's sister Liz came up the balcony stairs. Why hadn't I made a point to return and speak to Cheese another day? Because he'd said nothing damaging in his initial statement, that's why.

Or did I get distracted by the reappearance of Medley and forget all about Cheese? Guilt. I took long, deep breaths to gather myself for my cross-examination.

"Cheese. Do you mind if I call you that?"

"No, sir."

Oh, boy. He called me sir. Had he been schooled in ingratiation by Snap-Dog Diggers?

"Did you give a statement to the officers who investigated this case?"

"Yes, sir."

I handed him a copy of his initial statement.

"Would you read the second paragraph of the statement you made the day after the crime?"

He did so, silently.

"That is not the testimony that you are giving today, Cheese. Right?"

"That's right, sir."

"Tell me. How do you explain changing your story like that?"

Cheese had an explanation. A big white officer had barged into his apartment early one morning when he was busy taking care of his invalid grandfather. Cheese didn't want to tell the cop anything. To get rid of the officer, Cheese signed an initial statement right there and showed the officer the door.

Dammit, Cheese sold the story. I did what I could with the old bit about *are you lying now or were you lying then*, but I had to hand it to Tony. Nikki may have been discredited, but Tony could hang his case on the testimony of Traylyn Fields, aka Cheese. I had to know what part Tony played in this fortuitous turn of events.

"When exactly did this change of heart occur, Cheese?"

"What you mean?"

"When exactly did you tell this version of events to the district attorney?"

"That would be yesterday when we all came to his office to prepare for court."

OK. Tony just had a great stroke of luck. He didn't know he had a back-up to Nikki until the eleventh hour.

Tony called Billy Bulliard as his last witness before lunch. When the bailiff announced the name, Danny sat up in his chair and snarled to me under his breath. "That guy is a shit." From my point of view, he turned out to be.

"Snap showed up at my house sometime way late, maybe two or three o'clock in the morning," Billy testified. "We were all sleeping on the porch. He crashed there with us."

"Did Mark Diggers, the one you call Snap-Dog, have anything to say about what had gone down at the apartments that night?"

I jumped to my feet. "Objection! Mr. Blendera is eliciting hearsay testimony from the witness, your honor."

After a fifteen-minute argument out of the presence of the jury, Judge Johnson made the close call. She let Billy do the damage. Had she ruled against me because I got the last ruling? Billy's repetition of Snap's statement came into evidence. *Snap told us there was big commotion at the apartment, and Danny stabbed a guy.*

My co-counsel was livid—no, irate. I couldn't use the word livid to describe his dark skin going darker. I calmed him down. I thought we could repair the damage when we had Snap in the witness box. Snap hadn't fingered his friend Danny in either his initial statement or in our interview.

In any event, should we lose the guilt phase verdict, we had a ruling from the judge that would be useful for seeking reversal on appeal.

Tony closed out the morning. "Your honor, I have finished with my fact witnesses. My experts will be ready after lunch."

"What?" I was stunned. I swallowed my objection until the jury had left the courtroom, then made a beeline for the district attorney's table. "What the hell's going on, Tony? What about Snap-Dog?"

"I'm not putting him on, John. Frankly, I don't trust the guy. You never know what will come out of his mouth."

"Dammit, Tony. You said you'd bring the whole crowd. He's the only one you're skipping, and he was in the thick of it. Snap was probably the last one who had hold of that knife. Where is he? I'll call him myself."

I didn't let Tony know I had in mind trying to set Snap up as the *other dude*. How would I do that? *Tell me Snap, what route did you take when you left the apartment complex to walk to your friend Billy's house to sleep—or do drugs.* I would imply to the jury that Snap could have gone right by the scene of the crime. Snap was my best bet for reasonable doubt on the Carline case and for *reasonable explanation* that I needed to counter the circumstantial evidence linking Danny to the stabbing of the boy.

"Calm down, John. I just changed my mind. He's here. I had them bring him from Angola."

"Angola? He's been at Angola? I heard he picked up another drug charge in Lafayette, but I didn't know he'd been convicted."

"He took a deal for parole revocation. Three years, and Lafayette would drop their new charge."

It would be impossible for the district attorney to try every case, but this plea deal had an odor. So did everything about Snap.

"Shit, Tony. I counted on you calling him. If you release him, I have no way to call him unless I get the judge to order him held, and I don't know if she will. You've sand-bagged me old buddy."

"Calm down, John. I'll tell them to keep him here for another couple days. You can have that S.O.B."

"And his mom. I need to put both of them on. Hell, I think the judge will enjoy a little juvenile court reunion with her old friends Snap-Dog, Snap's Mom, and Nikki Roberts as well. Possum may sell tickets."

* * *

Over the noon break, Possum and Kaniesha checked in from their vigil at the ICU in Lafayette. The unknown African-American boy had gone into surgery again that morning. He survived—five hours, five doctors, all working on his gut. Lafayette Sheriff's Office now had a deputy posted at the door of the ICU. His orders, and the doctor's orders, were that no one was to get through to the patient.

Possum had spent the morning gathering background

at the Lafayette apartment complex where the boy had been found. He had calls in to his contacts in Alexandria and Lake Charles; he planned to hit those sites in the afternoon.

I pondered the implications of our investigations into the attack on the young boy in the Lafayette apartments. So far, we had nothing warranting notice to Tony that we had information about crimes that could be linked to the case in trial. So far, that is. But I had hope.

I returned to the courtroom for the continuation of the prosecution case. Tony put on a hematologist as his first expert. I had the reports so knew what the doctor would say. Unfortunately, it took him two hours to say it. No surprises. I gave my co-counsel, Reginald Denny, the nod to do the cross-examination. I really hadn't wanted him dealing with the kids. Not having worked on the case for the past six months, he would've been hard-pressed to keep in his head the many versions of their stories. Even I got confused sometimes. But Reg always did well with experts. He'd been at my side before, so I knew he understood DNA better than most. Piece of cake for him, really. Several jurors nodded their heads as Reg made those DNA probabilities comprehensible.

Next came the psychiatrist who examined Danny for the State. No, Danny had no conditions that affected his understanding of what he was doing. Again my co-counsel did a good job on cross. He led the expert to talk about a few of the many other personality disorders that did not excuse, but could explain, what might have been Danny's motivation.

By mid-afternoon I could feel my impatience about to overflow. I was ready to bolt. Good thing. It was probably best I wouldn't be in the courtroom when my friend, the coroner Dr. Emile Petain, took the stand. Our friendship would just add the possibility of a confusing side issue. I gave Reg a handshake, wished him luck, and left.

UNIVERSITY MEDICAL CENTER

The dirty yellow brick buildings of University Medical Center in Lafayette sprawl three blocks long on the north side of Cajun Drive, as long and as deep—and almost as important—as the university sports complex on the opposite side of the road. At UMC, designed and built fifty years ago by the political friends of one of the governors who earned our state a reputation for favoritism and corruption, the signs of old age now showed all over. State appropriations for upkeep are always hard to come by; repair money doesn't provide nearly as many opportunities for skim. In the last mini-make-over of the facility several years previously, pressure washing, a honeycomb of new concrete sidewalks, and fifty crepe myrtle trees, did little to mask the decrepitude at the core.

I parked Blue Betsy near the emergency entrance. Winding through the maze of corridors created by dozens of renovations, I came to the green double door marked ICU Family Room. Inside I found Kaniesha slumped in an orange plastic waiting room chair, eyes closed, head tilted back against the dirty wall behind her. In a chair that matched Kaniesha's before someone used shiny grey duct tape in a vain attempt to contain the foam stuffing, a young black man with a camera around his neck had also slipped into slumber. At his side, a plastic lined trashcan overflowed with the detritus of the fast food nation.

"Kaniesha," I called softly, wakening her.

"Oh, man." She shook herself awake. "Mr. Clark! What on earth are you doing here? What about the trial? Who's minding the store?"

"Reginald Denny. I left him to handle the testimony of Emile Petain, the coroner."

"That should be OK."

The young man with the camera shook himself awake also. He stood up and put out his hand. "Hello, sir. I'm Lee Dayton, reporter with the *3As*."

I picked another split chair and dragged it to the pair, and sat down. Kaniesha asked me for an update on the trial.

"For us, one good witness and one bad one. As I had hoped, under pressure of cross Nikki Roberts totally lost it. I doubt the jury will take any stock of her testimony. But Traylin Field, the one they call Cheese, changed what he said in his initial statement. He nailed Danny. A very bad witness for us."

"Oh my God! I feel bad about letting him fall through our pretrial prep."

"As much my oversight as yours. I impeached him with the 'are you lying now or were you lying then' routine, but I have to tell you, things look bleak for Danny for the death of Clyde Carline. To save the boy's life—to knock out the capital penalty—we've just got to do better with the second charge. Buck still has only circumstantial evidence against Danny for that one. I have to come up with another reasonable explanation of how Jerome Davis ended up stabbed to death at the same time, in the same location."

"Well, we sure as hell are working on that!" Kaniesha stretched out her back and rolled her coal-black eyes around the grim surroundings. "This vigil takes patience."

"And in the other significant trial development, Buck tells me he isn't going to call Snap-Dog."

"He's not? Why on earth not? The guy's initial statement is good for the prosecution."

"I don't understand either, except that you never know how that snake will slither. I'm caught. I'll have to call Snap to put in the jury's mind that he could be the *other dude*, or at least the cause of some reasonable doubt."

"I agree. How's the schedule?"

"We start our case tomorrow. Dr. Hibou is here and he'll be good, I know. I haven't quite decided whether to put on Mrs. Diggers, or Danny, for that matter. But catch me up on the story here, guys."

Lee Dayton gave me the rundown. "No story so far. We're just waiting, hoping to be on hand when the boy can talk. I did question the EMTs who picked him up. He was going in and out, but kept rounding his lips and trying to say something like 'oo-oo, oo-oo.'"

Kaniesha looked at her watch. "Possum and the investigator with the Lafayette Sheriff's Office should be back over here pretty soon. All day they've been taking statements at the apartment complex where the kid was found."

"Here's something interesting," the reporter said. "We've been here since last night and nobody, not one body, has come by to see about the boy. Earlier today we had to fight a couple of families for chairs, but nobody's here for this kid. Very unusual. Ordinarily, whenever you have a stabbing victim, especially a kid, you get people in droves—family, friends, rubber-neckers of all sorts. For our boy, nobody here but us chickens."

I swallowed a smile. I bet Lee didn't realize that was an old Amos and Andy line, now politically incorrect.

"Maybe nobody knows about the attack on this boy yet. There's been nothing in the papers," I suggested.

Kaniesha was amused. "Sir, the friends of stabbing victims don't read the newspaper. Radio and TV, maybe. But in our community, news mostly spreads by the Rumor Review—word of mouth or the cell phone. I'm surprised Lee can keep a job."

"Can I spell either or both of you so you can take a break, get something to eat?" I offered.

Kaniesha declined. "Maybe after the Lafayette detective comes back with a report from the projects I could go to the corner store for some yogurt and a granola bar. I can't swallow one more bite out of the vending machine."

We three settled in to wait.

Around six p.m. our patience was rewarded. The door to the hallway opened and the doctor on duty strode into the family room. Detective Antonia Gray of the Lafayette Sheriff's Office trailed behind him, took a skip step to keep up with the doctor's long stride, and gave us a nod as she passed by.

The doctor wore a long white coat—a good sign. The longer the coat, the farther along in the medical training. Run, run, run from the students or brand new interns whose coats barely cover their belts. Blood had spattered the doctor's Hush Puppy shoes. Maybe he was the surgeon who'd been working on putting the poor kid together.

The doctor swiped his ID card through the keypad at the door to the ICU, and he and the detective disappeared inside. Ten minutes later the doctor poked out his head.

"Miss Morris, I think that's what you said your name was, and Lee, come on through. If the boy had family, at this point I would let them in for a few minutes to hold his hand. You two seem to be all this patient's got. But no questions—just be there for him. The nurses tell me he hasn't spoken."

Kaniesha intervened for me. "Mr. Clark is my boss, doctor. Can he come too?"

The doctor looked me over, smiled, and flicked up his head in the affirmative. "Come on, boss of Miss Morris."

We followed him into a curtained station just inside the door. We kept a distance from the bed, not sure about the extent of our invitation.

A small body lay flat out, naked, spotlit by the blinding bright bulbs of a five-foot diameter light fixture overhead. Grey pallor lurked under the boy's almost translucent black skin. His eyes were closed; the body perfectly still save for the slight rise and fall of his chest. A few layers of gauze covered his privates.

Machines on each side of the bed ticked and blinked. A clear tube snaking from a tall stand pumped fluids into his thin left arm; other tubes exited every natural orifice and a few unnatural ones that had been cut into his body during the surgeries. A uniformed nurse sat motionless on a high chair, her eyes moving between the screens of the machines and the boy's face. She had a mumbled exchange with the doctor but never looked in our direction.

The doctor stepped forward and placed long, gentle fingers on the boy's wrist.

"He's breathing evenly, now. Nurse Boudreaux says he opened his eyes a while ago, and we are encouraged," the doctor said to us. "He looks pretty good."

"Good to you, maybe." I whispered. "Scenes like this are why I didn't follow my father into medicine. "

The doctor motioned to Kaniesha to come forward and take the boy's other hand.

"May I talk to him, doctor?" Detective Gray asked.

"Softly. Give it a try."

Detective Gray stepped to the bedside. "Son, can you hear me?" No reaction from the boy. "Can you tell me your name?"

His closed eyelids fluttered and then fell still.

The doctor nodded permission for the detective to try again. She leaned in close.

"Son, if you can hear me, tell me your name."

A little rumble in his throat.

Detective Gray whispered a suggested interpretation of the gurgle. "Maybe he said 'Bob', or 'Rob?'" Turning back to the boy, she said softly, "Son, you're going to be all right. We want you to know that."

"He's squeezing my hand," Kaniesha whispered.

"Rob, if that is your name, can you tell me where you

live?" Detective Gray asked.

A groan. I guess this exchange was what you'd call "being responsive." Not much, I'd say.

"Give him a minute," the doctor instructed.

Detective Gray tried again. "Son, is there someone we can call for you? Your mother, perhaps?"

Only another groan.

"That's enough," the doctor announced, and directed us all out of the ICU.

Back in the waiting room, the doctor stood with his legs apart, in a top sergeant's command position.

"All of you, no more questions tonight. Perhaps in the morning. I'll make a decision about that when I'm on rounds later tonight."

The doctor addressed Detective Gray directly. "Your deputy must not try to talk to the boy at all. Understood? If he appears to be responsive, the nurses will ask him his name again. And for the name of anyone to call. They will tell you if he communicates, but they have my order not to go any further until I arrive."

I interjected myself into his instructions. "Doctor, the reason I'm here is that I'm defending someone..."

"Yes, yes. I know. This young lady has told me the story. The patient may be just the latest young black boy who has suffered this fate."

"I'm not only thinking of my client, doctor. Because of what we've learned, we have a genuine concern that what's left of *this* boy's life may be in danger."

"I understand that. For that reason I am going to have him moved into the inner isolation area. The rest of the ICU can function without anyone being near him. The deputy will be stationed there. Detective Gray, you may post a guard out here in the family room as well. In fact, I insist that you do. I will instruct the staff to keep me informed. Right now the boy needs to rest. His body needs to accommodate to what has been done to him."

"Doctor, I..."

He cut me off. "Bear with me, boss of Miss Morris. My orders are that no one may see the patient other than the nursing staff. You may as well all go home."

I offered my hand. "I'm forgetting my manners. Thank you."

"And thank you, sir." He looked over at Kaniesha and Lee. "I am glad he has someone here for him."

Detective Gray spoke to the reporter, their acquaintance apparent from her easy manner. "Lee, no story yet. OK? Our sheriff's office press release tonight is going to be very short. Boy found stabbed. In critical condition. Investigation underway."

"Fine for now, but in the morning..."

"We'll see."

The detective turned to leave; Kaniesha stopped her.

"Wait a minute, detective. What about your investigation at the housing units? What did you and Possum learn over there?"

"Zilch. Zero. Nothing. Absolutely nothing. And we must have talked one-on-one with fifty people. No one owns up to knowing who the boy is."

"Shit."

Actually that fact told me something. Here was another unknown boy no one seemed to have seen anywhere around the area where he had ultimately been found severely wounded.

After the detective left, Lee gave Kaniesha a wink and patted his camera. He must have taken a shot when we were in the ICU. Bad boy.

Kaniesha had a question for me. "Mr. Clark, have you told Tony—Mr. Blendera—about any of this?"

"Good thinking, girl." I appreciated her sensitivity to the professionalism that keeps the judicial system from becoming armed conflict. "Not yet. And if I tell him now, he'll just think I'm trying to stall the trial. But if we can make *any* connection between this situation and Ti-Boy, or any connection between either of them and the other killings, of course I'll inform him right away. And I'll tell Judge Johnson."

On the trip home from UMC, my mind went into overdrive, spinning possibilities a mile a minute. Who could these kids be? How did they get where they were found without anyone knowing? It made no sense. My questions vanished as anger took up space in my chest. We were out here knocking ourselves out trying to solve a mystery while Danny and his parents didn't do squat to help us.

I drove though town on Main Street, passed the courthouse square, and as if compelled by some external force, turned right instead of left at Pecan Street. I pulled up in front of number 211, the home of Danny's parents, Josie and Bill Chastant.

I strode up the walk and knocked, banged really, on the door. One eye peeped at me through the blinds of the living room window. I heard the deadbolt turn. Josie Chastant let me into the semi darkness.

I walked straight to the TV and pushed the *off* button, nodding to the mound of flesh sunk deep into the lazy-boy. Josie's husband Bill. I turned and took a position of command, much like the doctor had a few minutes ago. I leveled my eyes at Mrs. Chastant. She stood stunned before me as I spit out my words.

"Mrs. Chastant, I'm trying as hard as I can to save your boy's life. Do you want the baby you bore, who was the apple of your mother's eye, the toddler you read stories to, the little boy you took to T-ball and Little League, to be strapped to that table at Angola. Do you want them to pump three kinds of poison into his veins, for him to twitch and die before your eyes?"

Silence.

"What is wrong with you, woman? Tell me the truth.

You loved a black man and we both know it!"

Mrs. Chastant squeezed her eyelids shut. The curls on the sides of her face began to quiver. I stood before her, my lips tight, allowing my fury to waft in her direction. Standoff. She blinked first. She turned to the flowered sofa and sank down.

"Sit down, Mr. Clark," she whispered.

I did. Bill Chastant got up from his lazy-boy and stood behind his wife, his hands on her shoulders, his face contorted in concern. Was he trying to conduct his strength into her backbone? Maybe I had misjudged the guy.

Slowly, softly, Mrs. Chastant told her story. At one point, a particularly difficult part, she reached across her chest and covered her husband's left hand with hers. When she had finished, we three sat in silence.

I spoke first. "Thank you, Mrs. Chastant. Thank you very much. I know how hard it is for you to talk about these things. You understand you'll have to tell your story to the jury."

"If you think it's necessary to save Danny's life, I'll do it," she whispered.

"But first you need to tell Danny. I'll arrange for that tomorrow morning."

The tears came back, and also a hard set to her mouth.

"No. No. I'll tell the jury, Mr. Clark, but I won't tell Danny. I just can't do that. Just put me up on the stand and I'll do the best I can. Then he'll know."

"But..."

"That's it, Mr. Clark."

I couldn't persuade her otherwise, no matter how hard I tried. She just didn't have the guts to tell her boy she had lied to him for all his life. She had one last thing to say to me.

"Mr. Clark, you say that I loved a black man? Now you see that I didn't even know his name."

THE DEFENSE

"The defense calls Mark Diggers, your honor."

Snap did not enter the courtroom like the other witnesses, through one of the side doors from the room where the witnesses were kept sequestered so they couldn't hear the other testimony. Snap came through a door behind the bench, from the holding cell for prisoners.

Flanked by two puffed up chests in the black and red uniforms of the Department of Corrections, Snap wore the washed-out light blue denim of an inmate. His escorts stationed themselves directly behind the witness box, eyes fixed on their charge.

I was looking at a Snap transformed. The dreadlocks and earring were gone. He was fit and tanned. He smiled to the jurors as he took the oath. Ah, ha! Still the same Snap. He hadn't lost his ingratiating manner.

Before walking to the witness box, Snap's eyes scanned the Carline family, stopping for at least five seconds on the face of Senator St. Germain. Did I imagine that? I'd check with Reg, but I suspected something passed between them. Under Snap's gaze, the senator's eyes dropped to the ground. Could these two have a connection? Not likely.

I began my questions. "Tell us your full name, please. Mr. Diggers."

"Mark Diggers, sir."

"Are you also known as Snap-Dog?"

"I was. Not so much anymore."

"And your address?"

"Angola."

"Louisiana State Penitentiary at Angola?"

"Yes, sir."

"And where did you live before that?"

"Here in Franklin. On Willow Street."

"How old are you Mark?"

"I'm 22."

"I understand that you have met with your attorney here today and discussed whether or not you would testify, correct?"

"Yes, sir. He told me I did not have to testify, but I want to. I have absolutely nothing to hide."

Snap may have looked different, but he hadn't lost that ingenuous look he used on older people. The con.

"Fine. But just to be sure we understand each other, if you choose to testify, you understand that you will be cross-examined. You have sworn to tell the truth, and you will be legally responsible for what you say."

"Yes, sir. We understand each other. I will tell the truth."

Snap sat up straight and smiled engagingly at the jury. He could just as well have been the president of his college class. I wasn't fooled by him, but the jury might be. I'd be anxious to hear how Reg thought they took him.

I began by asking Snap for his account of the evening. He went through the same party scene the others had described. Nee-Nee brought a knife from the kitchen; they all played with it; when they were done, the knife was laid on a chair. Tony had characterized this part of Snap's story correctly. Repetitious.

"Did there come a time when Danny left the group?" I asked.

"Yes, sir. Danny went out to smoke a joint. He said it was good."

That was an addition. A little reality here. Dope on the scene.

"Where did Danny get the joint, Snap?"

"I don't know. Not from me, for sure."

I hope the jury saw me raise my eyebrows and smile at that answer. The official transcript that goes to an appeal court never shows unspoken comments.

"Now, about this knife that you saw laid on a chair. Could you describe the knife?"

"An ordinary kitchen knife. Big, serrated blade."

"You say Danny left. When he did so, did he take the knife with him?"

"No, the knife was still there after he left."

Ah, ha! So that's why Tony didn't call him. He must have known that Snap was going to change his story.

"Was Danny mad about anything when he left?"

"Not that I could see."

"OK. So he left to smoke a joint and came back. Did he leave again?"

"Yes, when he left for good. He said he was going to get a coke and go home."

"Snap, would it be possible that he left some other time and you didn't see him leave?"

"Well, sure. Nikki—she was my girl friend—and I went next door to Toya's early in the evening. He could have left then. I don't know."

"But are you telling me that when Danny left to get a coke and go home, the knife was still on the chair?"

"Yes, that's what I'm telling you."

Good old Snap. Count on him for total confusion, but clearly he wasn't going to help the prosecution case on the most critical issues. I could have asked if there had been more than one knife around, but I'd let Tony try that line.

I was feeling good about having called Snap, but I looked over at Tony and he was smiling. In his hand he had that initial statement Snap had given to the police; he probably thought he could score with it. Maybe. I decided to leave party-time alone and see if I could get Snap into a corner about his route home.

"So, you're saying Danny left to go home before you did?"

"Yes, sir."

"Did you see what route he took when he left?"

"What do you mean, route? He walked across the field to his house."

"Did he go out the back towards the coke machine and the telephones or did he go between the buildings? What was his path?"

"I don't know. I just saw him as far as the courtyard?"

"So you really *don't* know that he walked across the field?"

"I guess not. I just assumed so because that's what he always did."

OK, there goes Tony's argument that a witness saw Danny leave by way of the crime scene.

"And what route did you take home, Snap?"

"I went out to Pecan Street and walked toward the McDonald's."

I decided to anticipate Tony's cross and let the jury get the story with my spin. I whipped out Snap-Dog's initial statement. "I want to show you the sworn statement you gave to the officers the morning after these events. Didn't you say in your initial statement that you and Danny went downstairs and left together? If he crossed the field, and you were together, wouldn't you have had to cross the field also? You would have had to pass by Clyde's apartment on the way. Right?"

"Wrong, man. I didn't go that way."

"No? This is your signature on the statement, right?"

"If I said it, I must not have been thinking. I know I went out to Pecan St. I don't know which way he went."

Reginald Denny was smiling. He must be thinking the jury looked skeptical about everything this guy had to say. That was fine by me.

No, best nail it home. "And you are quite sure the knife

was on the chair when Danny left?"

"Yes, sir."

"Thank you."

That was as good as I was going to do. Snap wouldn't support the prosecution on the key element of their case—that Danny went outside with the knife. But he wasn't going to let me tag him as the *other dude* either. I took a few steps to the right, changing position and changing the topic of my questions.

"One more question, Snap. You and Danny are good friends, aren't you?"

"Yeah."

"How long had you been friends when these events occurred?"

"Maybe a year."

"But you are a good bit older than Danny, right?"

"Five years, about."

"And you are of the Caucasian, white race, aren't you?"

"Yes, sir."

"And Danny? What race is he?"

"He's African-American."

"Really? What race does he consider himself?"

"Danny doesn't talk about race."

"Does he ever talk about whether other people are white or black?"

"No." Snap stated firmly.

"Surely the topic comes up now and then. What does he say?"

"He never says anything. He says race doesn't matter, and he acts that way."

I could hear shuffling at my counsel table and whispers between my co-counsel and Danny. I ignored it.

"Do other people ever talk to you about your race? Like say that you are white and he is black and you are good friends?"

The DA stood with an objection? "Invitation for hearsay, your honor."

"The witness may answer. Allowed as a topic of peoples' conversation." Judge Johnson ruled.

"Go ahead and answer the question, Snap. Do other people talk about your race?"

"Yeah, people say that I'm trying to be black and he's trying to be white. And they give us flack, just because the two of us get along."

I returned to my seat, terminating the direct examination abruptly. "I tender, your honor."

I had left unexplored the topic of what Snap may have said to Billy Bulliard on the porch in the early hours of October 3. I knew Tony wouldn't be able to resist getting in that point of evidence against Danny. I wasn't going to object to him cross examining on a topic I hadn't covered in direct; I wanted to come back on redirect to impeach Snap with what he had said about Billy in his initial statement. The testimony heard last is considered to have the greatest impact on a jury, and the last word would be favorable to the defense. Tony fell into my trap.

"Good, morning Mr. Diggers," Tony began.

"Good morning, sir."

"What are you in prison for, Mr. Diggers?"

"Parole violation."

"And how did you violate your parole?"

"Well, I think it was distribution."

"That would be distribution of marijuana and distribution of cocaine at the housing project here in Franklin, right?

"Yes."

"And you made a deal with the State to have those charges dismissed in return for revocation of your first conviction, distribution of marijuana in the Pecan Gardens Apartments. Isn't that correct?"

"Yes, sir."

"Isn't Billy Bulliard your neighbor and your friend?" Tony asked, oh so innocently.

"He's my neighbor, but he's not my friend. When I went down, I left behind all that dope crowd."

"Wouldn't it be more accurate to say that when you went down you turned Billy in as a another purveyor of drugs in the projects, and that's why he's not friendly anymore?"

"Fuck, no."

Judge Johnson reacted. "Watch your language, Mr. Diggers."

"Yes, Ma'am. Sorry Ma'am."

"Snap, you are aware, of course, that Billy Billiard has stated you came to his porch and told him that Danny stabbed Clyde Carline?"

"Lies, man. Lies."

"Did you write out a statement for the police where you said that Danny went away mad, came back, and then left with the knife?"

"That's not the way it works. I didn't write anything."

"No? How does that work, Snap?"

"First the cops talk to you. They write up something and come back, and you sign it. I signed something but I didn't read it."

"So it is your testimony now that Danny did *not* leave with the knife?"

"Right."

"And it is your testimony that you *never* told Billy that Danny stabbed someone?"

"Right."

"That's all I have for this witness," said Tony.

Tony wasn't even going to bring up Snap's initial statement fingering Danny. He wanted to get rid of Snap ASAP.

I had gotten Tony to sum up Snap's testimony in which

he blasted the prosecution case about the knife. For icing on my cake, he gave the jury a good reason why Billy Bulliard might have fingered him, that Snap had turned Billy in. Good day's work. I couldn't see any need to keep Snap on the stand any longer.

I checked in with my co-counsel. Did he think the jury believed anything Snap said? Their smiles told Reg they didn't. I'd made my point on reasonable doubt. Even if I couldn't find *another dude*, I had demonstrated again that you couldn't ever know what went on that night. "That is all I have as well, your honor. I will not be needing anything more from Mr. Diggers."

"Nor I, your honor," Tony chimed in.

The judge dismissed the witness. "You are free to go, Mr. Diggers."

Snap's eyes popped wide open. Judge Johnson smiled and corrected herself. "I misspoke, Mr. Diggers. You are free to go *with the officers*."

Only a couple jurors smiled. Indeed, they had had enough of all of us.

Even if jurors are told they can't hold it against a defendant if he doesn't testify, human nature cannot be denied. Everyone wants to hear both sides of a story. There's really no choice if a defendant has prior offenses that can be brought out in cross-examination; they poison the jurors' minds. And if you have a hothead, a skilled questioner can cause him to lose his cool. But Danny was a good candidate for the witness box. Young, so young, really. No prior record. And he was proving trainable. We'd been working on getting him to sit up straight, look at the jury, and not mumble. I thought the jurors would soften when they heard him speak.

I didn't make the decision for Danny; he made it himself. I took one precaution. I asked Dr. Hibou, my expert on violence who was scheduled to testify in the afternoon, to be present in the courtroom when Danny took the stand.

"The defense calls Danny Howard."

Slight movement and a low rustle passed through the jury box. The jurors sat taller, chins raised, eyes opened a bit wider.

We went through a brief rundown of Danny's history, where he lived, schooling. He spoke fairly well, loud enough but not too loud. He told his story with a minimum of the slurred speech of the 'hood. I had drilled him well. Then we got to the party.

Danny admitted that Clyde Carline made him mad with the racial epithet but denied he went back for the knife. And of course, in spite of my effort to persuade him to admit to stabbing Carline and throw himself on the mercy of the jury, he refused.

As for the unknown boy who met death that night, Danny said he knew absolutely nothing about him. He never saw any unknown boy around the party. And he insisted that he had absolutely no memory of what happened between the time he left the party and woke up the next morning in his own bed—except that he thinks he got a coke at McDonald's.

On cross-examination, Tony couldn't shake Danny—not with questions, disbelief, or with sarcasm.

Was testifying a good idea? Yes, agreed Reg. The jury seemed to like him and he made no mistakes.

I asked the judge for a brief recess so I could prepare Danny for what would come next—the testimony of his mother.

"Danny, your mother will be my next witness. Sit tight here at the table. I'm going to go back to talk to her for a moment."

If only Kaniesha were here! I needed some kind of therapeutic person at the kid's side during the time ahead. Law school does nothing to prepare you to handle stuff like this. Mothers, wives, and girlfriends know how to buffer the hard knocks of life. Maybe psychiatrists? Dr. Hibou was in the courtroom but not at the table with us. Reginald Denny would have to do.

I walked back to the second pew to speak with Mrs. Chastant.

"Ma'am, I will be calling you to the stand as my next witness. Are you sure you wouldn't like to spend a moment with your son beforehand? I can arrange a recess to have you talk with him in the anteroom."

Josie Chastant sat low in the pew, her head down, closed off from everyone. Her husband held her hand. "No sir. I just want to tell the jury that Danny's father was a black man. Nothing else. That's all they need to know."

Oh, boy. It's not over yet.

"No, ma'am. That's isn't all they need to know. Of course, we need that information to make sense of the expert testimony from our psychiatrist, but we have much more at stake here. The jury needs to feel for Danny, needs to think he's a life worth saving. I'm afraid you must go through the whole story for us, just like you told me last night."

"No, sir. I will not do it." She pressed her lips together and dropped her chin even lower.

I had a hostile witness on my hands. I took a deep breath and went for broke.

"Yes, ma'am you will. When you are called to the stand, you will be under oath to answer all the questions, and to answer them truthfully, under penalty of perjury. You will have to answer all of my questions and all of those asked by the district attorney. If you don't tell the story, the whole story, in your own words, we two lawyers will go to work on you. We *will* get it out of you one way or another. You *will* be very uncomfortable. You need to tell it straight, your way. If you do, I won't badger you. And the district attorney won't either."

I felt sure of that. If he drew blood on her after her

story, the jury would hate his guts.

Mrs. Chastant hissed her response. "I'm sorry I ever spoke to you, Mr. Clark. I thought the district attorney's job was to convict Danny and yours was to save him. You two are together on this."

"No. We are both pledged to bring out the truth and let the justice system deal with the results. And the system works, ma'am, I assure you. Mr. Blendera wants the truth and so do I. In this case, only the truth will save your boy."

Mr. Chastant put his hand on his wife's. "Josie. You can do it. You have to do it."

I returned to my table.

"Danny, your mother is going to testify now. She's going to tell you some things that she doesn't want to tell. I am making her testify to the truth. If she hurts you, please forgive her. If you get mad, get mad at me, not at her."

Did I say that right? Please God, help me through this one.

"The defense calls Mrs. Josie Chastant, your honor."

Danny twisted in the direction of his mother, open-faced and expectant—more emotion than I'd seen on his face in two weeks of trial, perhaps ever. In response to his gaze, Mrs. Chastant's grim mask briefly softened, but hardened again. The momentary distraction of that exchange was all it took to tip her off balance, literally. She caught her foot and stumbled into the aisle. Only her husband's strong arm saved her from a fall. Deep breaths propelled her slow steps to the witness box.

I'd thought a lot about how I could get Mrs. Chastant to testify with the emotional impact the story had when she told it to me. Actually, half the impact would be enough. Now I was afraid she wouldn't be able to speak at all. I prayed the judge would sense her terror and let me use leading questions on my own witness.

I started by asking for her name and address and a few other routine questions I knew she could answer. She sat back in her chair and did well.

"Mrs. Chastant, what I want you to do today is tell the ladies and gentlemen of the jury about your son, Danny. Will you do your best to do that?"

"I'll try." A dry whisper.

The judge leaned forward and signaled to the bailiff to bring her a cup of water. "Ma'am, you will need to speak up so that the court reporter will be able to hear your testimony. She needs to record every word that is spoken in the courtroom."

A soothing tone. I nodded my thanks to Judge Johnson.

"Tell me, before you were married for the first time, you lived with your mother in Grand Bois, out by Charenton, right?"

"Yes."

"And you met your first husband, I believe his name was Johnny Howard, when you lived out there?"

"Yes. My first and only husband, according to the church." Bitterness edged her voice.

"Tell the jury how you met your first husband."

I had instructed Mrs. Chastant to speak to the jurors, not to me, but she couldn't. Her eyes remained firmly fixed on my face. She had taken one glance at the jury box and recoiled as if she were watching starving lions waiting for prey. I moved to the far side of the podium, closer to the jury box. When she looked at me, the jurors might see her expression. That was the best I could do.

"I met Johnny one night when I went with some friends to a club in Franklin. He had a regular job at a radio station in Lafayette, but he traveled around being a DJ on the side. No doubt used his boss' equipment." That bitter edge again.

"Did he have a third occupation as well, in addition to the radio station and the DJ business?"

"Oh yes. He sold Hadacol from the grandstand. You

remember the tonic that was supposed to cure everything? He was a pitchman, really."

"Was Johnny Howard older than you?"

"Oh, yes. He was thirty-one. I was eighteen and just starting my senior year in high school."

"So what happened? Did you buy a lot of Hadacol?" I tried a light touch in the hope I could loosen her up, maybe take the deer-in-the-headlights look out of her eyes.

"No. He just paid attention to me, and I fell for him. Hard. Soon I was sneaking out at night to follow him around to the clubs where I knew he'd be working."

"Tell us how your mother felt about that. Did she approve of Johnny?"

"Not at first, but when she met him, she fell as hard as I did."

"And then what happened?"

"Johnny said he and a friend had an opportunity to buy a club in Houston. Chance of a lifetime, he said. We could get married and go there, *if* he just had his share of the down payment. In no time he sweet-talked my mom into giving him all her savings."

"So your mom gave him money?"

"Yes."

"And you got married and went to Houston?"

"Yes. You've seen our wedding picture on the mantelpiece."

I rejected the idea of having her show the photograph to the jury. I was afraid she'd tell us where she kept the picture and the jury would write her off as a weirdo.

"Yes, I've seen it. You found a place to live in Houston?"

"We lived over the garage of his friend."

"Tell the jury, Mrs. Chastant, what happened in your new life in Houston?"

She swallowed hard. "Johnny turned out to be a rat."

"And how was that?"

Silence. The little ease she had developed during the first part of her story vanished. She stared down at her lap. Judge Johnson looked over her glasses and said softly, "You have taken an oath to answer the questions, Mrs. Chastant. You must do so."

"Let me help," I suggested. "Did Johnny and his friend buy a club like he said they would?"

"No. He worked at a club, as a DJ, and I went to work at the Seven-Eleven. It was OK for a while, about three months, I believe. Then..." She froze.

"Then it wasn't OK?"

"No." Her lips tightened.

"What went wrong, Mrs. Chastant?"

Her voice cracked. "He stopped coming home every night."

"And then what?"

She took a deep breath. The dam broke, and the story came pouring out. "One night I was at the club where he was playing. The singer—she was probably no more than seventeen—was pawing all over him. Dumb me; at last I realized what was going on. I got mad, drank a whole lot, and I screamed at Johnny about being unfaithful to me. His response? 'So what are you going to do about it?' I screamed back, 'I'll show you what I'm going to do about it.' I stood up and took the arm of a black man at the next table who'd been watching me all night, and I stormed out of there with him. With the black man."

"Did he take you home? Did that black man take you to your apartment?"

Mrs. Chastant reached for the glass of water the bailiff had placed on the ledge at the front of the witness box, but her hand shook so much she thought better of trying to pick it up. Her hand returned to her lap and that tattered Kleenex.

"Yeah. He took me home, all right." She paused. "He seemed nice enough, but I was too drunk to know what I was doing anyway."

"And?"

"When we got to the apartment—the garage apartment where we lived—he came around the car and pulled me out the door. He was on me in a flash, threw me up against the hood of his truck and..."

Mrs. Chastant stopped talking. She dropped her chin onto her chest.

"And then what happened?"

"He raped me."

I knew to stay silent. She'd gotten this far; I didn't think she'd stop. I kept my eyes fixed on hers, trying to send her the courage to keep going. It worked.

"With every thrust of him, some kind of ornament on the hood of his truck dug into my arm. I still have a scar." Mrs. Chastant reached across her breast with her left arm and clutched her right forearm, rubbing up and down. "I remember staggering into the apartment, blood all over me, carrying what was left of my clothes." She swallowed hard. "Johnny didn't come home that night either."

I let a bit of time go by for the jurors to absorb what she had said.

"Did you leave Houston after that?"

Tony didn't object to my leading questions. I think he wanted to get this over with as soon as possible.

"Yeah. The next day I called home. I had just enough money for a bus ticket, nothing more. It took me two days to get back to Grand Bois. That's about all there was to it."

"That was all?"

"Yes. I never saw Johnny again."

I'd have to try another leading question.

"Not quite all, Mrs. Chastant. Did you find out you were pregnant?"

"Oh, yes." A weak smile. "I guess that wasn't all there was to it. Yes, I was pregnant."

"How did you feel about that?"

"I was pretty much of a wreck, humiliated."

"Did you know who the father of your baby was, Mrs. Chastant?"

"I honestly thought Johnny was the father. I thought that even after Danny was born. Johnny was real dark complected, and we'd been having sex for ages."

"How was your mom about your coming home? About the baby?"

Mrs. Chastant smiled. "Mom was wonderful."

"Did you go to work out there in Grand Bois?"

"Yes. I got a job at the syrup mill, and Mom took care of Danny during the day. She adored him."

"Did you eventually come to the realization that Johnny was not Danny's father?"

The fingers of one hand twisted those of the other. "Yes, eventually I did, but by that time there didn't seem to be anything I could do but keep on saying he was, being as I had no one to replace him with."

"Let me ask you this. Did you ever tell Danny that Johnny Howard was not his father?"

"No."

"Never? Not to this very day? You've never told him?"

"No."

"Why not? Why didn't you ever tell him the truth?"

Mrs. Chastant looked down at the twisted Kleenex in her hands and gave her pitiable explanation. "I thought that was the best thing I could do for Danny, the way things were back then. I thought he'd be better off as a white boy." She looked up at me. "You know, he isn't very dark."

She had gotten through the critical part of her story. I was dying to know how the jury reacted, but I couldn't risk taking my eyes away from hers. I felt my gaze was her anchor. Reg would have to tell me later if the jury felt her pain.

"So, you raised Danny in Grand Bois and later you

moved to Franklin, is that right?"

"Yes. My mom died when Danny was eight. He took the loss of his grandmother real hard. About the same time the syrup mill closed, so I had no job out there anymore. A friend with a car worked at a grocery store in Franklin and she got me a part-time job there. Then Bill came along." She looked over to where her husband sat. "We married and we moved to town."

"How did Danny get along after you moved to town?"

"Fine at first."

"Then?"

"When he got to high school, not so good. But, you know, teenagers often have problems. I didn't think there was anything serious." She paused. "You asked me the other day if I'd noticed Danny being down, drinking too much, maybe drugs, that kind of thing. Well, looking back, I should have noticed some of that, but he was seventeen years old and just about on his own. I just wanted people to leave us alone. Mostly they did, and that was fine by me."

"How did you feel when the officers, Sgt. Wiltz and Capt. Daigle, came to your house that morning, Mrs. Chastant? That morning when they came to ask you about the two people who had been killed at the Pecan Gardens Apartments the night before?"

"When the officers walked in that morning, I just felt powerless all over again. And really scared." She looked down at her hands in her lap and then back to me. "You know, Mr. Clark, when you first came to my house to talk to me, you wanted me to tell the jury that I'd loved a black man."

"And what was your response to that?"

"I said, 'Love a black man? I didn't even know his name!'"

I was done. I let myself look at the jury. I thought I had them.

"Thank you. Mrs. Chastant. As I explained to you, you

must answer any questions the district attorney may have." I returned to my table.

Tony stood in place. "I have no questions, your honor."

Mrs. Chastant stepped down from the witness box, wobbled a bit, and walked back across to her seat. She sank down next to her husband. His arm went around her shaking shoulder.

Judge Johnson bolted to a standing position, knocking over her cup of water.

"We will take a fifteen minute recess."

"I couldn't watch the jury, Reg," I said to my co-counsel. "How'd they take it?"

"You rocked! When Mrs. Chastant got to the part about being thrown against the hood of the truck, the nurse sitting in the middle row began rhythmically rubbing her forearm with exactly the same motion. And the judge was leaning so far forward I thought she'd jump into the box and give the woman a comforting hug."

"Danny, Do you want to talk with your mother for a few minutes? I can arrange that."

He stood up. "No way. I want outta here."

"OK. It is up to you.

"I told you man. I'm outta here."

The deputies took him away.

I found Dr. Hibou and sent him to see if he could help the boy. Reg and I headed for the anteroom to put our heads together about the next move. Big decision coming up. Do I put Dr. Hibou on the stand?

Reg listened to me argue with myself.

"What I do next depends on my best guess about the verdicts the jury will return. On the first charge, first degree murder of Clyde Carline, I'm fairly sure I destroyed the testimony of Nikki Roberts. But Traylin Roberts hurt us bad. Maybe I need the testimony of the psychiatrist to have any chance at anything less than the max. The shrink has some really good stuff about how growing up without pride could trigger violence."

"So now you're liking your little owl?" Reg teased.

"I am. He looks kind of weird at first, but after a while those twinkly elfin eyes get to you. Now that I've worked with him some, I find he's a charmer. You know, people around here like characters. My plan would be to keep him on the stand long enough for him to grow on the jury the way he grew on me. But..." I closed my eyes to take away any distraction. "Maybe the cause is lost. For good reason, I fear."

"Don't go there, John. Keep the faith."

"Right. But if I put Dr. Hibou on now, the impact of what Mrs. Chastant has just told them will be dissipated in the wrangle most certain to follow as Tony cross-examines, and I'm forced to counter and rehabilitate the doctor's testimony. Big brouhaha. After all that, if the jury comes back with guilty of first degree, the doctor's testimony will be stale when he takes the stand with mitigation evidence in the penalty phase. And, by God, I know we need him there."

"We're in a lot better position on the second charge, first degree murder of the boy, than we are on the first."

"Right, Reg. I think my closing argument will persuade at least one person that Tony has not proved Danny had anything to do with the second killing. If there is no second crime, no death penalty. But what if I'm wrong?" I paused. "What if they find him guilty of both? What's your opinion, Reg?"

"You're lead counsel, John. Your call."

With a prayer to the heavens, I made my decision. If the jury should find Danny guilty of killing Clyde Carline, which was likely, I'd need Dr. Hibou in the penalty phase to make my pitch for mercy. Fresh testimony would have the most impact, and I'd need it.

"Reg, go tell the judge we have concluded our evidence for the guilt/innocence phase."

* * *

The following morning we made our closing arguments. The judge delivered her charge. Before noon, the jury went out to deliberate. At four o'clock that afternoon the bailiff heard a knock on the door of the deliberation room. The jury had reached their decision.

When we had reassembled in the courtroom, Judge Johnson took the verdict sheet from the bailiff. Brows knit together, she studied the paper in silence for a good two minutes before she read it aloud.

"On the first charge, the charge of First-Degree Murder of Clyde Carline, the verdict is Guilty as Charged. On the second, the charge of First Degree Murder of Jerome Davis, the verdict is Guilty of Manslaughter."

I was stunned. I've lost cases before, in fact often, but this one stung more than most. The death penalty was still on the table. I barely heard Judge Johnson shutting court down for the night.

"Ladies and gentlemen of the jury. In due course I will sentence the defendant in keeping with your second verdict —manslaughter of Jerome Davis. However, your first verdict requires us to proceed to the second stage of the trial—the penalty phase. The law says that we must wait twelve hours between the verdict and the beginning of the penalty phase. You will now go with the bailiffs and remain sequestered until we reconvene tomorrow morning at 10 a.m. to consider the penalty for the first conviction. Thank you, and good evening."

I put my arm around Danny's shoulders and spoke words of sympathy and hope. He seemed totally oblivious to what had just occurred and to what we would be doing the following day. Where the hell was Danny's Mom? Gone.

Danny mumbled something.

"What did you say, Danny?"

"So, he was right."

"Who was right, Danny?"

"That dick-shit Clyde Carline."

"Right about what?"

"I *am* a *nigger*."

Breath left my chest. I exploded.

"Dammit, Danny, that word is just a nasty way for very small minded people to feel important. It has nothing to do with who you are. The blood in your veins is doing exactly the same job as the blood in mine, taking oxygen to all parts of your body. Just like me, you have genetic material from your father and your mother. Maybe mine is from a horse thief or a philosopher, who knows. It doesn't matter. I am who I am and you are who you are, and..."

I was screaming, but stopped. Danny wasn't listening, and even if he were, a lawyer's reasoned argument would never penetrate the carapace he had grown to protect him through eighteen years of messages of denigration. He needed way more help than I was capable of providing.

"Danny, Dr. Hibou is going to be up to see you tomorrow."

I called Medley. "We closed down early. I'm picking up at the Viet Kitchen. I'll be at your house in twenty minutes."

BACK TO UNIVERSITY MEDICAL CENTER

I pulled up in front of the shelter annex. As I opened the door of Blue Betsy, I heard the squeak of a swing in the back yard and caught sight of Maria Rodriguez digging in a flowerbed on the side of the house. I stepped over a tricycle on the porch and walked in the open front door. The smell of new wood and fresh paint told me how Medley had spent her time while I had been totally consumed with the trial of Danny Howard. A bookcase created from cinder blocks and eight-foot boards now decorated the far wall of the bright yellow living room.

"Sorry about the smell, John. I guess you can tell I've been painting again. The kitchen this time. I'm trying to air out the place."

God, I was glad to see her.

Our arms around each other's waists, we walked back to review her handiwork.

"I love the color."

Something else we had in common; we both found renovations regenerating.

"I've missed you, John. And I'm so sorry about the verdict," she said through a hug that sent a thrill down my back. I picked up her chin for a deep kiss.

"I never get used to losing a case, although unfortunately my job gives me plenty of practice. But, as Scarlet said..."

I didn't tell her how hard a time I was having trying to make sense of the jury's decisions. What were they thinking? That Danny intended to kill Clyde, but only lost his cool over the boy? Or that he accidentally killed the boy in the course of the other murder? I tried to think back to the judge's jury instructions, but I couldn't remember the details. Reg had handled that part of the trial. I was quite certain we had a raft of issues for appeal. Right now I should probably be at my computer writing motions to present tomorrow morning, but I just couldn't think any more tonight. The hell with the whole business.

"So what's next?" Medley asked.

"The penalty phase."

"I meant when. When do you go back into court?"

"Tomorrow morning, but my part won't be up for a couple days. The ADA, Tony, will be putting on Clyde's family first. I'm sure we'll see Aunt Aimee and the other one who had you cornered in the bathroom." That made Medley laugh, the sound I loved to hear. "Tony has to be very careful about pulling the jury's heart strings because the Supreme Court says the prosecutor can't induce them to make an *emotional* decision. Gimme a break. As if there is any other kind! I have some good stuff on tap. I think my psychiatrist will be effective."

"You like him now? The little owl?"

"I do. But you and I both know what I need is help from my client. His testimony on the guilt phase was OK, but I really need him to make a connection with the jury. He is so damned detached."

"The doctor went home to New York and has to come back, right? That must cost a bundle."

"Sure does, but I quit feeling bad about the money spent on this business a long time ago. If the public wants to have a death penalty, they're going to have to pay for it. The trial is just the tip of the iceberg. If Danny should be convicted, we'll be spending a fortune in public money."

I was trying to be upbeat, but my basic concern surfaced. Dr. Hibou was going to have to explain my client to me as well as to the jury.

"I've had enough of Danny Howard for today, my dear. I need a break from even thinking about the case. Where's Buddy?"

Medley opened the back door and called, "Buddy! Mr. Johnny's here."

Buddy jumped off the swing and came running. The front-end scoop into my arms brought a warm smile to Medley's face. Buddy reached little fingers into my shirt pocket and pulled out scraps of paper.

"Hey, little fella. How will I know what I'm doing in court if I don't have my crib notes?" I buried my nose in his neck.

"Maria made a salad. She'll join us for supper, if you don't mind. Look what I found at Goodwill!" Medley said, indicating a high chair and a gate-leg table set with knives and forks for three.

Medley set the food on the table and placed Buddy in the high chair. She called out to the back. "*Hola*, Maria!"

"How's it going with you two—three, I guess? You and Maria getting along OK?" I asked.

"Great. Buddy loves her, and I'm doing better with her accent. I sure wish I could speak some Spanish. Maybe Buddy will pick up a little."

"Not too much, I hope. I have enough trouble understanding his English words right now. Maybe it's the Mississippi accent."

"Speaking of Mississippi, I still hope to get Gram to come to Louisiana, although I don't know where I'd put her in this house."

"And the job?" I was determined to drive Danny out of my mind by directing full attention to Medley's life. She regaled me with stories about her patients, some funny, some poignant. I could tell she cared for them. Eating with more relish than I had all week, we polished off the contents of all the cartons of food and Maria's salad. Buddy tried a few of Medley's noodles. Just as we kicked back to pass the time in small talk, my cell phone jangled a marimba.

"Mr. Clark," a breathless Kaniesha shouted over background din. "Can you get up here right away? Something crazy's going down. Sorry for the noise. Can you hear me?"

"Yes, I hear you. Slow down a bit. Where are you?"

"I'm still at UMC. Two men tried to force their way into the ICU, where the boy is. Now the place is swarming with cops. I'm in over my head here, Mr. Clark. Please come."

Kaniesha was not one to panic easily, and she was definitely at the edge.

"I'll come right away. Who are the men who tried to get in, Kaniesha? Do you know?" Although Medley's living room was dead quiet, I found myself shouting into the phone.

"I can't hear you, John. No, the boy hasn't spoken yet, if that's what you asked. Just get here. We may be having the breakthrough we've been looking for."

"A breakthrough? What do you mean?"

"I can't hear a word. Please just come."

I gave up trying to understand her. "I'm on my way."

Medley came out of the back carrying her purse.

"Medley, you should just stay..."

"I'm coming with you, John. Maria says she'll put Buddy to bed." She didn't have her hands on her hips, but her tone was just that certain.

"Me come too. Me come too," squealed Buddy, raising his arms." I could understand those words.

Medley turned him down. "No, sweetheart. You stay with Maria. Mr. Johnny and I'll be right back."

Maria lifted the boy from the high chair, took his hand, and led him to the kitchen for the traditional bribe—a dessert of ice cream and an Oreo cookie.

Whatever could be happening up there in the hospital?

Possibilities danced around in my brain all the way to Lafayette. Not one made any sense. Kaniesha was shaken. She did say the boy hadn't talked, so that meant he was still alive. Some good news.

Medley put her hand on my arm. "You're driving kind of fast, John."

"I'm sorry." I lifted my foot from the accelerator. "My mind is swirling. I'm trying to think, and I don't know what to think about. I'm glad you came to keep me straight." Understatement. I was very glad to have her at my side.

We found no empty parking spots near the emergency room. I slipped my car into the lot at the restaurant next door, and we walked—double-time—a long block to the hospital.

Flashing lights and a swarm of uniforms swirled in confusion at the emergency room entrance. Medley and I skirted the commotion and pushed our way through the door. I sought out Kaniesha in the waiting room of the ICU. She was on her feet, pacing, showing the effects of her long vigil—eyes bloodshot, her shirt wrinkled, strands of hair springing from the opening at the back of the baseball cap on her head.

"Oh, thank God you're here! I'm in way over my head. I called for Possum but can't find him. But..." Kaniesha started at the sight of Medley. Wide-eyed, she grabbed Medley's arm and pushed her out of the waiting room and into the hall, away from the crowd.

Medley protested. "What are you doing?"

"It's the guy, Medley! The tattoo guy!" Kaniesha explained in a stage whisper.

"What?" Medley and I asked in chorus.

"Sh-sh." Kaniesha's words tumbled on one another. "Mr. Clark, we gotta get Medley out of here."

When we were away from any listeners, she explained. "OK. Here's what happened. Lee and I are sitting there in the waiting room where we've been for most of the last two days. Two guys come in—a young man, black, maybe about twenty, and an older white man. Know what? It was the guy you chased out of court, boss, not that I realized who it was right away."

"What?" Again, Medley and I spoke the same word.

"Yeah. The pair goes to the ICU window and the white guy speaks through the little hole in the glass. He indicates his sidekick and tells the nurse they came to see his buddy's little brother who's the one inside. The nurse was very cool, very good. She told them to take a seat while she made arrangements with the duty staff. The white guy protested, arguing hard, but she stuck to her guns. 'No sir. I can't let you in until I notify the nurses in ICU. You just take a seat a moment, sir. I'll be right back to let you in,' she said.

"So the two of them come and sit, right here with Lee and me. By this time I'm getting the feeling that he's that guy, Medley, so I call Lee outside and tell him. I'm struck dumb, actually terrified, to tell the truth, but Lee is super cool. He casually tells me that he'll be right back, goes around the corner into the hall, actually right to this spot, and puts in a call to Detective Gray.

"God! Then we have a long few minutes! Maybe twenty minutes, I don't know. Seemed like an hour. After a bit, and the nurse doesn't call the two guys to come in, they get wise that something's not right. They mumble to each other, stand up, and go to the ICU door. They put their hands on the door and try to push their way in. The door doesn't budge, of course, without a security card.

"The nurse orders them to get away from the door. She says she's calling security. That's when things start to get real hairy." Kaniesha finally takes a good deep breath. "The white guy grabs the black guy's arm and pulls him toward the exit. The black guy kind of stumbles, looking as if he doesn't really know what's going on. As soon as the pair gets through the door to the outside, they run smack into the cavalry. The cops are all over 'em. That's when I called you."

"You're telling me that the white guy is the man we saw in court? Are you sure?" I asked. I put an arm around Medley, who was shivering.

"I'm pretty sure, yes. Long sleeves so I couldn't check him for the tattoos, but he looked the same—the same as the man you chased down the courthouse stairs. Tall, stringy blond hair, thin face."

"Where is he now?"

"The cops have both of them out there, next to the patrol cars. Detective Gray read 'em their rights and has begun questioning."

I physically handed Medley off to Kaniesha. "Honey, stay right here until I get back." This time I was careful not to be too stern with my order. Kaniesha didn't protest her assignment to stay inside while I went out to see the detectives with the pair. Actually she looked relieved.

Outside, Detective Gray stood with the two men. Not as drop-dead gorgeous as a detective on a TV cop show, but close. Young, fit, very professional manner. I'd heard Amanda Gray came from a family of law enforcement officers.

"Tell me your name again?" Detective Gray asked the black man.

"Cliff Chenier."

What? Named after the zydeco musician? Not likely. I guessed he had said the first name he could think of.

"So tell me what you're doing here?" Detective Gray asked as she frisked the pair for weapons. They were both clean.

The black guy mumbled out his story. "Dude, here, give me twenty bucks to go with him to the hospital. I got no idea who dat sick boy be." The black man's clothes hung on his spare, unhealthy frame. He had the slack jaw and faraway look of a junkie.

The white guy was another story. Really, had another story, told with a wide-eyed expression of innocence. He gave his name as Manny Landry. He claimed he heard that the son of his good friend was real sick in ICU. No visitors. He thought of getting in by having someone pose as a relative. "I know about that ICU; it's only for the family. That's all there is to it," he said. "I just wanted to see about him for my friend. I'll just come back another time when the boy's feeling better and can have company." He turned to leave.

"Not so quick there, man. What's your friend's son's name?" Detective Gray asked.

Just a moment's hesitation, a skipped beat, before Landry answered. "Davy Dobbs."

Detective Gray reached into the breast pocket of her jacket and pulled out a photo of the boy, covering up all but the face. Where did that picture come from? I wondered. Then I remembered; Detective Gray and Lee Dayton the reporter acted like old friends. Maybe, on one of those visits into ICU to see the boy, Lee just slipped his hand down to the camera on his chest, pushed the button, and then passed a photograph on to the detective.

"Is that him?" Detective Gray asked. "Is that Davy Dobbs?"

"Naw. That's not him. That's not Davy. I must've heard it wrong. I'm sorry for the trouble." Manny Landry made another effort to leave.

"Just a minute, man. A few more questions."

I pushed into the scene and stepped up close. Detective Gray stiffened, visibly objecting to the intrusion on her investigation. Kind of "accidentally on purpose," I brushed up against the white man's sleeve. He yanked his arm away, but not before we both caught sight of the edge of a blue tattoo under the cuff. The nest of snakes.

Detective Gray asked for the white man's driver's license to verify his ID. Surprise, surprise. The license carried another name. Maurice Louis.

"I'd planned to charge you with criminal trespass, but now let's add another charge to that one—misrepresentation," she informed Mr. Louis.

I exploded. "What did you say, Detective? Criminal trespass? Is that what you're going to charge him with?"

"Yes. Hold your horses, Mr. Clark. Mr. Louis, it says here that your address is 5055 St. Leo Street. Do you still live there?"

"Yes, Sure."

Detective Gray finished writing on her pad and tore off the top sheet. The charges were both misdemeanors; she gave Louis a summons, released him, and told him to be present in court on October 21, bringing enough cash to pay a big fine.

I was steaming. "Detective. You can't just let him go!"

"Easy man, I've got it covered." She signaled for a deputy to put on a tail, her wink telling me she wanted to know a lot more about Maurice Louis. When Louis disappeared into the crowd, she assured me she'd banded the bird before he flew away. Cops. They always want to set a trap for the perp next up the chain. I just wanted Medley's stalker on ice.

Kaniesha and Medley were pacing the ICU waiting room where I rejoined them.

"You are right, Kaniesha. Something's up. We're having some odd coincidences here, not that I understand a single thing. Hold tight for a while. I'm going back outside to give Tony a call. Cell phone coverage is bad in here, but it's time for me to tell him what's going on.

My call reached Tony at home, finishing dinner. I took him through the history of the man with the snake tattoos: in a drug house on the same night that Clyde and Ti-Boy were stabbed, sighted tailing Medley at work, in the courtroom at opening statements, and now showing up at the hospital where another unknown black boy lay seriously wounded.

"Tony, according to the investigative reporter for *3As*, this one is the fourth young unknown kid who's met tragedy. I don't know what the hell is going on, but I strongly suspect it's all relevant to your prosecution of Danny Howard."

The phone was silent for a few minutes as Tony processed what I had told him.

"What do we need to do to find out what's going on?" Tony asked.

"I have one investigator. You and I both know he's limited in time and resources. I think I need five detectives! Five good ones, right now."

I had Tony's full attention. "John, I don't have five men —or women—to put on this, but I can scare up at least two. Brett Daigle, of course, and I think the city will lend us Theresa again. She's good and she's already been on this case."

The natural competition of the courtroom had vanished. Tony and I were back to being professionals doing our jobs. I gave Tony a report on what I'd done so far.

"My investigator has run down the investigative reports on the two prior victims we think are tied together —the kid stabbed two years ago behind an apartment complex in Alexandria and the Latino kid killed six months ago in Lake Charles. Somebody really good needs to go to each of those places and dig, find out what the people over there suspect but cannot yet prove valid enough to put in a report. Then we need two people to work with Detective Gray in Lafayette. Who is Maurice Louis? Who is that poor kid in ICU? And last of all—at least last for right now—we need someone to do a real good job finding out about drug activity in the Pecan Gardens."

"Drugs?" Tony asked.

"When you have a mystery, it's usually sex or drugs.

And this one sure looks like drugs. Who sells? Who supplies? Tony, there's a hell of a lot more going on here than a stabbing by a confused young man who got called a *nigger*!"

"Hold on, man. I'll call you right back."

He did.

"I found Brett at the girlfriend's apartment in Lafayette. He's on his way."

"Tony, about the trial." I eased into this topic.

"Not now, John. No continuance, no mistrial, no nothing until we can actually eliminate Danny as the stabber. We just keep on keepin' on, as usual. Penalty phase begins tomorrow morning."

I didn't argue.

I re-entered the building. Kaniesha ran smack into me.

"John, she's gone!"

"What?"

"I looked everywhere, the bathroom, down the hall, everywhere. She's gone."

"What? Who's gone?"

"Medley's gone. I can't find her!"

Fear stabbed my chest and curled like smoke down into my belly. Searing hot smoke. "What are you saying?"

"We were right there in the hall, and all of a sudden she wasn't there anymore. I was looking for you, but I didn't go but a few steps away. I didn't hear anything. She just disappeared!"

PART V — EASTER

THE NARCS AT WORK

I couldn't say how much time I spent running all over the hospital like a madman. I remember tearing down the hallways, crashing into an old lady in a wheelchair. I remember wide eyes staring at me when I burst into an x-ray waiting room. I remember circling the outside of the building to scour the parking lots for a truck the description of which I had forgotten. And I remember getting into it big-time with two white-haired pink-ladies manning the telephones when they refused to broadcast all over the hospital that my Medley was missing. How could everyone just go about their business as if nothing had happened? Didn't they realize that a crazy guy with a nest of snakes tattoo had taken Medley who knew where, to do who knew what?

I remember Kaniesha with her cell phone to her ear but being unable to hear what she was saying. Actually, I couldn't hear anything, not even my own rants, over the wind that seemed to be rushing through my head. And then I remember when security had me flat against a brick wall with both my arms pinned behind my back.

Sgt. Theresa Wiltz appeared from nowhere. She flashed her creds to the elderly hospital guard. "I've got him, officer."

Teresa's voice came to me echoing in the hollow of my panic. "Mr. Clark, we're going on over to the Lafayette Sheriff's Office. Brett is already there setting up the search operation with their Criminal Investigation Division. They're going to need your help. They've sent a missing persons report on Medley and a BOLO—*be on the lookout for Maurice Louis, aka Ma-Loo.*"

They had made the same link I had. I leaned against the wall to steady myself and looked Theresa in the eye, my thoughts beginning to line up straight. "What happened to that tail Detective Grey was supposed to have put on him?"

Theresa just shrugged.

"Damn."

We stepped outside into darkness. I shook myself to get control. "How long has Medley been gone?" I asked.

"A couple of hours, now." Theresa had my arm, pulling me along to her unit.

"My car..."

"Forget it. You're in no shape to drive."

"We need to get word to Medley's roommate Maria. She's got Buddy."

"Done, Mr. Clark. Maria's on the job for the night, but she has to go to work in the morning. Nanette will take over."

"The trial..."

"I'll leave that one to you. Here, I've got Tony on the line."

She handed me the phone. I told Tony I didn't give a flying fuck about the trial of Danny Howard. He and Reg could do whatever they wanted about the penalty phase coming up in the morning. I would be off the grid until further notice.

The mental discipline required to make that simple pronouncement brought order to my thoughts. "Theresa, you went to Lake Charles today to check into the murder of the kid over there, right? What did you learn?"

"Lots. I found a Lt. Chretien, the case agent for the murder of one Claudio Garcia, age fourteen, who was discovered dead in the Liberty Apartments in downtown Lake Charles six months ago. Chretien hadn't closed his file, but he had buried it beneath four more recent murders of important victims, as he was honest enough to admit. No one was pushing him for action on this one. The name of the vic came from another Latino kid who had seen Claudio a few times walking through the complex late at night. They'd exchanged greetings in Spanish, but that's about all. The kid probably wouldn't talk because he didn't want what happened to Claudio to happen to him."

"So exactly what did happen to Claudio?" I asked.

"You don't know? Shit, it was crazy. For a couple days this old junker car sat on blocks at the rear of the complex. One day a lady notices oil leaking out from under the front. Second time she passes she looks harder. It wasn't oil—it was blood. She freaks out. When the cops come and open the hood, they find a boy's body jammed, shoved, twisted into the space, crushed by the hood, with a rag stuffed in his mouth. There were some pictures in the file. I thought I'd seen enough dead kids to be immune, but... " Theresa shuddered.

"I asked Lt. Chretien about drug activity in the projects. Just retail trade, he said. Guys went to Lafayette to get the product—mostly marijuana and crack. Some pills in the past three months, but that was kind of new. Nothing big-time went on in there—no kitchen, no farm, no repackaging stations."

"Did he check out the name Claudio Garcia?"

Theresa tossed back her head. "He laughed in my face when I asked him the same question. 'Do you have any idea how many people in the United States are named Claudio Garcia?' he asked. 'Add another one-third of that number for those with that hyphenated mother's last name our computer always picks up for the Latinos.'"

"Did he know anyone named Ma-Loo?"

"Negative."

We walked into the squad room of the Lafayette Sheriff's Office and confronted what looked like the set for a war room of a World War II movie—except for the incongruity of a half dozen computer screens. The doors to the side offices were opened to create one large area for the operation. Tables, radio equipment, charts on the wall, plus maybe three dozen men and women in uniform, no one smiling. Capt. Brett Daigle anchored one end of the squad room with a phone in one ear and a radio in the other. He stood tall, his handsome face alive with the thrill of command. General Patton. Why were all these World War II images coming to me? I wasn't even born then.

"Detective Gray got our boss's permission for St. Mary Parish S.O. to bring us in as partners on this operation, Mr. Clark. A few of the guys came up to lend a hand."

We may have had years of being on opposite sides of the aisle, but we were comrades nevertheless. And now I was one of the victims they were sworn to serve. Amazing how quickly they could put all this together.

Brett briefed me on his plan. "We're setting up the standard protocol for a missing person with priority one. APB to all law enforcement within a hundred mile radius. Detectives are scouring this parish for our number one suspect, Maurice Louis and variations on the name, and our computer geeks are mining the databases for his trail. Unlike those four unknown kids, this guy has lived and worked in the parish. He left footprints."

Did I feel any better? No, but I said thank you.

Lt. Marcus Magrette, St. Mary chief of narcotics, had joined his Lafayette counterpart. Tonight Marcus wore a black ball cap on his shaved head, but beneath the bill I could still see his lumpy features and found them comforting. A half dozen other deputies in tight black T-shirts, the uniform of the narcs, manned computer terminals for him also. Another score stood around. Deputies, yes, but you wouldn't know from looking at them. Two-day beards, unkempt hair, pants hanging six inches below the crotch, they were ready for a night in the field. The men smelled like yesterday's gym clothes, the better to fit into the great unwashed they would have in their cross-hairs. Marcus was delivering a briefing. He knew how to lead; before speaking he made sure he had the eye of every one of his crew, especially the Lafayette deputies who didn't know him well.

"Our best intel says everything here is tied together: the murders in the Pecan Gardens in St. Mary Parish six months ago; the deadly assaults on the young boys in Lake Charles, Alexandria, and here in Lafayette; the mysterious stalker of Medley Butterfield. What ties these events together? The one common activity in every area of low income and dense population. A more accurate answer: the one common activity in every housing project in our part of the country—maybe anywhere. Drugs. And you guys are the experts."

Yes, he had their attention. He had honored their work.

"Here is what we need to know. Suppose someone in the Lafayette projects wants a joint to smoke, wants a fix, wants some pills. How does he go about getting the product? Suppose he wants to make some money from sales of marijuana, crack, pills, or—heaven help us—H. Who does he contact for supply? Who brings him the stuff? Who collects the money? What is the business plan? Guys, I need an education in the whole show." He nodded in my direction. "John Clark, here, is going to tell you about how we need to find a tall, blond guy with a tattoo of intertwining snakes on his right forearm who's been shadowing this case from the beginning."

A sputter of disparaging snorts broke out in the group. Somebody mumbled, "How about going all the way, man. Tell us to find a bushy-haired stranger."

Marcus continued. "Listen up, guys. I've verified this information and am even willing to own up to a major fuck-up to get it all out on the table. Six months ago we busted a drug operation in Franklin on the same night that Clyde Carline and Ti-Boy Davis were stabbed to death. You

St. Mary guys may remember that raid. Doc and I were serving a fugitive warrant on Jackson Butterfield, Medley's ex, and ran across a repackaging operation. John called me about that raid some time ago. He wanted to know if I had any idea about some people who had given us the slip that night. I told him that was impossible. I'm not proud to admit it, but I was wrong. Medley Butterfield is quite certain that two people got out the back door, and now I believe her. Take over, John."

I addressed his crew. "Medley tells me a tall blond guy with tattoos and a black boy maybe twelve to fourteen years old slipped out the back of the house when the St. Mary narcotics officers came in the front. Of course, since those two both got away, they weren't anywhere in the incident report. My investigator, Possum, has been digging, but he's had no luck. No informant talks." I paused. "Now for the rest of the story. Since then, Medley has sighted that tattoo guy on three more occasions. Tall, blond, thin face. Then last week he appeared again, in the courtroom, on the day of opening statements of the trial of Danny Howard."

One of the guys mumbled, "Probably quite a few guys would want to follow Medley around. She's a looker."

I ignored the comment. I felt more in control of myself now that I had a part to play in this operation.

"Yesterday, a tall, thin, blond guy with snake tattoos, we think the very same guy, showed up at the intensive care unit at UMC here in Lafayette. He tried to force his way in to see the fourth of our victims—that poor kid now fighting for what is left of his life. The Lafayette P.D. responded to the 911 call at the hospital—and totally screwed up. They collared the guy, asked a few questions, charged him with a couple misdemeanors, gave him a summons, and let him go, supposedly with a tail. According to our latest bulletin, the guy has shaken his tail and disappeared. Probably with Medley. She vanished from the hallway of the hospital—without a trace."

Marcus exhaled a slow hiss. "So, guys, in addition to looking at the drug trade in the projects to see if phantom kids could have been playing a role, I'm asking you to beat the bushes for a tall blond with snakes tattooed on his lower arms. Maurice Louis, aka Ma-Loo. I know our usual procedure is to watch and wait while we try to nail someone higher up the drug distribution chain, but not this time. We've got a missing girl. We go in for the kill— figuratively speaking, of course." His conspiratorial smile belied the correction, which was OK by me.

"While you're getting chapter and verse on the Lafayette drug operations," he continued, "I'll have my guys in Franklin do the same. Then we move on to connect the dots with what we learn in Lake Charles and Alexandria. When we know how these four kids fit into the game, I bet we'll know how and why they met tragic ends." He turned to me. "And we'll find Medley Butterfield."

That was a statement I wanted to hear.

Marcus' eyes fell on Sgt. Samantha LeBlanc, a black jacket covering her hooker outfit of a thigh-high skinny-skirt and shiny red boots. Dollar Store perfume.

"I know you guys trade undercover personnel all the time." Marcus flashed a facetious smile, which didn't stay but a few seconds on his face. "Sam, you seem to be ready to go teasing in one of our neighboring parishes. While you're wherever you're going tonight, call in the chips for all the help you can get. We need it."

At a desk on the other side of the squad room, the Lafayette deputy who handled their amphibious fleet thundered into a walkie-talkie to his crew set up in the parking lot behind the courthouse. "Make sure the units are fully equipped and gassed up and ready to go." The "units" he had at his disposal were an airboat for the swamp, a speedboat for the Bayou, and a Search and Rescue unit for deep water. "And check with St. Martin Parish to put their divers on call."

There's a lot of water to cover in a search of this area of the world, but that these units could be needed scared me to death. What might Medley be enduring? I held my breath for the wave of dread to pass.

A K-9 officer came strolling through the squad room with a big German shepherd on leash. Three dogs were ready, he reported to Brett—this one, another shepherd, and a bloodhound. The last two were outside in the dog wagon, rested and hungry.

"Do you happen to have anything of Miss Butterfield's you could give to us? A coat maybe?" the officer asked me.

"Her sweater's in my car, but that's parked at the restaurant near the hospital."

"Give me a description and your keys, which I'll bring back pronto. You'll be here for a while, right?"

"I'm not going anywhere until we find Medley."

Another contingent of officers gathered around folding tables in the center of the room—Lafayette deputies being briefed as they came on duty. Only half of them would go out on regular patrol; the rest would stay here, close at hand, waiting for orders. For this night, response to domestic disturbances in the parish would be a bit slower than usual. None of the deputies wore the dark blue dress uniforms of the department; tonight everyone dressed in camo, their pants tucked into heavy boots. And no one had the usual bored and distracted look of the night shift. This kind of operation raced their motors.

Many times I'd given patrol cops a rough time on the witness stand, but right now I thanked God for every macho gene in their bodies.

And then we had a guest. Col. Terrence Lancon, Commander of the Louisiana State Police, loped his tall, rangy self into the room. This Friday, like many others, he had come from headquarters in Baton Rouge to spend the weekend with his mother. He'd picked up the report of the abduction on the radio as he drove in.

A commanding presence, you'd have to say—very handsome, especially when decked out in the royal blue and gold LSP uniform, complete with Smokey the Bear wide-brimmed hat set at just a few degrees off regulation square. That hat askew signaled the touch of rascality for which he was well known. His mom, and most girls, loved to see him dressed like that.

"Remember this, Brett," Col. Terry said, "I can put a unit at any spot on any state highway in no more than fifteen minutes. You need help? You just get on the horn. Louisiana State Police at your service." The colonel knew his staff would jump at the opportunity to do real law enforcement. Roaming the highways, going from one accident investigation to another, or dishing out speeding tickets to earn the money to run law enforcement in every parish, got to be a bore.

Face it. Everyone but me was having fun with this operation.

Into this bullring came the rodeo clowns. Two older men pushed a squeaky cleaning cart into the center of the room. Oblivious to the significance of the activity afoot, they proceeded to unload mops, pails, disinfectant, and a large floor polisher, and they threw a thick extension cord across the floor to a plug on the far wall. I may have been a madman in the hospital looking for Medley, but at this sight, Brett met my measure. He screamed at the cleaners to get the hell out until the poor old guys were shaking as if they faced a firing squad. A bottle of pungent Pine Sol smashed on the floor as they packed up their equipment and rattled out of the room.

All the activity encouraged me. Brett was in charge of a well-practiced search for a missing person. And Marcus had joined Lafayette narcotics to figure out why four boys met tragedy. Solve these puzzles and we'd find Medley. I was sure of it.

Around ten o'clock, I had two visitors. ADA Tony

Blendera and the District Attorney himself, Gerald Strait. An Assistant District Attorney often paid a call on a victim's family vigil—a courtesy call, really, lasting no longer than the socially acceptable twenty minutes—but the appearance of the DA himself was unusual. Tonight they both stayed over an hour.

Tony walked in with a bucket of Popeye's fried chicken, a stack of paper plates, and a package of napkins. I realized that I hadn't eaten anything for many hours. They ate with me, without a lot of conversation. Apparently they were working all this night as well.

"It's a beautiful night out there and this place is beginning to smell like a bus station." Tony said when we had finished. "Grab your phone and let's take a walk around the building. We won't go far."

I breathed in the cool, fresh night air. We walked across the street to the church lawn where floodlights on the fairy tale castle of St. John's Cathedral transformed the area into a huge outdoor room. The darkness of the side streets formed the walls, a sliver of new moon peaked through the ceiling of branches canopied overhead. Shadows of the trees and shrubs grew and diminished as the occasional car cast beams of light as they passed.

Tony had something on his mind.

"John, we probably need to bring Judge Johnson up to date on the developments. No doubt she's going to bed thinking she'll have a routine penalty phase starting tomorrow morning."

"I agree. Judges, like wives, are always the last to know. What's the prosecution plan?"

"I'd like to present a joint motion to continue the penalty phase until this all shakes out?"

"Speak to Reg. I'm out of it."

Tony smiled. "I believe you described your position about the trial with more colorful words! But I'm sure you've a few thoughts you'd like to convey to Reg."

"I mean it, Tony. I'm out. I'm a walking case of incompetent counsel because I have only one thing on my mind. But while you're thinking about motions, how about a joint motion for mistrial of the whole shootin' match? The boy's death is coming from an entirely different set of facts. No second murder, no capital case."

"John, I haven't lost the motive I had; I've just added another. I had thought that Danny did in Ti-Boy in order to wipe out a witness. Now, for all we know, Danny saw an opportunity to pick up a wad of drug dough. I've still got a good case for first degree murder: when the offender has specific intent to kill or inflict great bodily harm on more than one person. Manslaughter is a responsive verdict to the original charge. But I do think we should delay until we can get the full story. What about sending word to bring the jury in the afternoon when we've had a chance to meet with Judge Johnson?"

My professional faculties never went far below the surface, no matter my personal concerns. I didn't like his plan.

"Tony, we're in the process of uncovering major exculpatory evidence, evidence that the jury did not have an opportunity to see before they came in with their guilty verdicts. The whole trial is crap. But, as I say, not my call. Talk to Reg." I changed the subject. "This is hell, you know, and I do thank you for coming by. "

I meant that.

Mr. Strait had stayed out of this exchange, but now he spoke up.

"John, right now I'm not at liberty to tell you another reason we need to keep the trial simmering on the stove. I'll just say that people farther up the line are interested in what is going on around here. They're baiting the hook for a very big fish."

He wouldn't say any more, but I really didn't have much interest in the big picture. I had only Medley on my mind.

An hour later Marcus called me over to sit down with the narcs.

"Interesting stuff from the guys, John. Some we had already, some of this is new."

"Shoot."

"They're still at work on the cases, but we've picked up a pattern in both Lafayette and St. Mary. Someone owns the territory in each of the projects. He's known to be the 'go-to' guy. You want some stuff? You let him know. He may go get it himself, or he may receive a delivery, but he's 'the man.' You deal with him and only him; you deal with anyone else at your peril.

"Sometime in the course of a night, a good party night, 'the man' might need some more product. He calls the supplier on a pay phone; the supplier sends some in. And who delivers? Who might pick up the money? For the past year or so, in both of the projects it's been a kid, and not necessarily the same one each time. The buyer never knows the kid's name. The buyer just appears at a designated spot, silently turns over the money, and collects the product in return."

I felt a shot of excitement. "Marcus, this sounds like our scenario! The deliveries are made by a clean kid, no identification, nothing to connect him to the supplier. Then if something goes wrong..."

"Yup. And in our cases, something went wrong. A white man and a black boy ended up stabbed to death in the cane field behind the apartments, their blood pooling together in a furrow between two rows of stubble. All evidence points to those deaths being connected to drugs."

And probably my silent client Danny could shed some light on how that all came down, but he won't talk. Damn that kid.

Marcus continued. "Here's the kicker. The 'man' for Pecan Gardens Apartments used to be your friend and mine, Mark Diggers, aka Snap-Dog. Around about the time of the events in question, Snap knew we were on to him. As a precaution, he was in the process of training an assistant to cover when things got hot. And guess who that assistant was going to be? Danny Howard!"

"No, shit!"

"Yes, shit."

"I'm getting a picture here, Marcus. Danny went to the telephone at the rear of the Apartments and made a call. Do you suppose he was putting in a request for some more product?"

"Very probable."

"And what about that riding around he and Snap did earlier in the evening? Do you suppose they were getting the first load then?"

"Could be."

"Does anybody have information about the identity of the delivery boy for Pecan Gardens Apartments? Can you say it was Ti-Boy?" I asked.

"Not yet. We're still digging. And we don't know who might have killed him, if indeed Ti-Boy was the delivery boy that night. The killer could have been Danny, Snap, or even the person who dropped him off for his evening's work. Could have been a stranger who just stumbled onto a way to pick up some easy dough. But the more we know about how the system works, the better chance we have of getting an answer."

"Thanks, Marcus. But who killed Ti-Boy Davis is down on my list of concerns. I haven't heard you tell me anything about Ma-Loo. Or about Medley."

"It's all tied together. We solve one riddle we'll have the other. Stay with me. Now for your part. We need you to get your client Danny Howard to talk."

My face scrunched up and my hand covered my eyes. "You think I haven't tried to get him to come clean with me? Not even the prospect of the death penalty has opened him up."

"Not necessarily about the murders. He knows more than he's told you about the drug trade in the projects and that information could help us run down whoever took Medley. John, it's important."

"OK, Marcus. First thing tomorrow, I'll hit on him again. This time, without mercy."

Kaniesha called in from the hospital. The doctor said that tomorrow, at the six a.m. visiting time, the boy could answer a few questions. Just a few. Theresa said she'd be there.

Sometime around midnight Marcus rolled a cot into an office off the squad room and asked me to follow. "Get some rest, John. Unlike you, we'll get relief in the morning."

"I'm having a thought, Marcus. How long would it take to get someone to Angola?"

"Four hours, maybe. Why?"

"As you suggested, I'm going to take another shot at getting my client to tell me what he knows of the drug trade in the projects, but if your intel is right, there's somebody who knows a hell of a lot more. Mark Diggers. We need to get Snap to talk."

Marcus pondered my suggestion and raised me. "Perps don't cooperate unless they get something in return. When Snap got revoked, they hit him with twenty years. He'll want a deal. I'll call Tony and ask whether the DA would make an offer that might loosen his tongue." Marcus gave me an atta' boy punch on the arm. "You've got a good idea, there, Mr. Clark. When you get tired of helping these guys avoid paying for their crimes, think about coming over to our side of the street. We can use you. Now get some sleep."

I tried, cranking up my usual stress-reducing routine. *Imagine you are lying on a warm sandy beach. Relax the toes of your right foot, relax the toes of your left foot.*

Relax the ankles... I got no higher than my knees when yet another terrifying vision of Medley and Ma-Loo together threw the exercise into the trashcan.

I needed help. What's the expression? There are no atheists in foxholes? I droned through the liturgy of the Book of Common Prayer. I pleaded for intercession by my favorite saints, by my mother, by the nuns of my New Orleans Catholic school childhood, and by all the departed I believed had made it to the right hand of God. I tried personal prayers, but drew a blank. Oh those lucky Baptists. They're trained to deal direct. I begged God to spare Medley from a list of perils—terror, pain, rape, death, until visions of what torment she might be enduring rendered me mute. A long night.

REVELATIONS

At first light, a deputy took me to pick up Blue Betsy at the hospital, and I drove down to the St. Mary Parish jail to confront Danny.

I started slowly. Danny had no reaction to hearing that a black kid lay in ICU with half his stomach sliced away. He didn't look up from his hands when I recounted the stabbing of the others now also believed to have been on the very lowest rung of the drug trade in the projects. He stayed motionless when I told him we had reliable information that he and Snap had been part of the business. I kept my cool. But when he continued to sit there as I told him of Medley's abduction, I lost it. I stood up, leaned over the table, my face close to his, and shrieked until spittle dropped.

"What are you anyway, boy? Some lousy little piece of shit? I'm bustin' my ass trying to save your neck and you don't care. When I tell you about kids getting stabbed and crushed, kids peddling death just like I suspect you did, you still don't care. When I tell you a woman who has nothing to do with all this, totally innocent, has been abducted by some creep, you don't care. What do you care about? Nothing? Nothing but your sorry little self. Goddamn you!"

I barely paused to take a breath.

"But, you little fucker, now you've gone too far. When what I love most in this world is in the hands of some sadistic monster, all because of you, I have a mind to walk out of here right now and let the jury go ahead and give you the needle. They'll strap your sorry ass onto a table and pump poison in your veins. And if they can't find the right drugs, you *will* suffer agonies. You know what? I won't give a shit."

Danny raised his eyes "I just can't, man. Snap said he'd..."

"There's nothing Snap could do to you that I couldn't do in spades. If I do my job only *half* well, you'll spend the rest of your life in the pen as some big dude's toy boy. And that would be just fine by me too."

Danny cupped his ears with his hands, and blubbered. "OK, OK, man."

I kept going. "OK what, man? You want to talk to me now? Let's hear it. Get going. Come clean with me right now, or I swear to you, I'll see to it that if you live, you'll get put into the worst possible hell-hole in the entire prison system. There are some guys in there who'd do anything for me, and I'll tell them exactly what I have in mind for them to do. You'll wish you *had* gotten the needle."

Danny broke. He put his hands down on the table, picked up his chin, and looked me straight in the eye.

"So, man. What is it you want to know?" he whispered.

"Start at the beginning, Danny. With the drug trade. I know you and Snap were into it, and you were on the job that night. I want to know all about everything you two did, starting with that ride you and Snap took up the line. Where did you go and why did you go there?"

"OK, man. Could you get me some water?"

"Hell, no. Just talk, you little piece of shit." I wasn't going to let up on the pressure.

"OK. I picked Snap up—must have been some time after nine. We went by this place in Lafayette. That's where we was supposed to get the stuff."

"Details, Danny. I need details. Where exactly was the place?"

"Man, I don't know. Snap said drive here, drive there."

Looking at my fury, Danny sped up his answers. "Look, I'd tell you where we went if I knew, honest. I just don't."

"Describe the area for me, Danny. What part of Lafayette? Did you drive to the north, south, east, west?"

"North Lafayette. I drove the four-lane through the city, and then went a way past where you turn off to go downtown. We ended up in a not-so-great part of town and turned left on a little street."

"OK. North Lafayette." I had my pad out now, taking notes. I'd stopped screaming. I questioned him just like any witness I might interrogate. "Did you go to a store, house, apartment, what?"

"We went to a house, not an apartment."

"A frame house? Brick?"

"Frame."

"OK. Then what?" For maybe the first time ever, he began to speak to me in sentences longer than three or four words.

"When Snap spotted the house, he had me drop him off and take the car around the corner and park. I waited. He came back holdin' a paper sack, a small one, and he handed me a joint. We drove on back to the apartments."

"So did you two do this often, Danny? Were you and Snap working together regular? Like were you working for him?"

"Yeah, in a way. Or maybe I hoped I'd be regular. I'd been buggin' him for months to get me a piece of the play. I was pretty fed up with what I was doing then—slinging burgers, always the last shift, always broke, my Mom on my case to go look for a better job. Tell me, man, where do I get a better job? There's nothin' here to find. Snap had money, and I knew where it came from."

"Keep going, Danny."

"A couple of weeks before all this came down, Snap came through with an offer. He agreed to put me on as his assistant. I could get a hold of a car now and then, you know, and Snap needed wheels. He could have bought a car, I suppose, but his license was suspended. I did a few things for him—took a package here or there, called up somebody—but mainly I just hung around waiting for my chance. The trip that night was about the most I'd handled with him so far."

"Good, Danny. Now let's get back to that night. You and Snap took a ride to Lafayette and back. And then?"

"We just partied. I had a few beers. After a while Snap asked me to make a phone call for him. He gave me the number on a piece of paper."

"You got that number now?"

"Naw. I gave him back the paper. I don't remember it."

"OK, so that business about calling a girl, that was crock?"

"Yeah."

The DA got him good on that one.

"OK. Go on. You made the phone call. Who'd you talk to?"

"Shit, I don't know. All I heard was 'hello.' Snap told me to say 'Snap needs 120.' I have no idea what that meant. Honest, man. That's all I know."

"And then? Did someone come and make a delivery to you there at the apartments?"

"Not so's I know."

"OK, then what happened?"

"The next is like I said in court. Carline got after me again."

"What did you do about Clyde Carline going after you? Did you go get that knife?"

He hesitated. "Yeah."

"Danny, did you stab Clyde Carline?"

Danny didn't look at me when he answered this question.

"Yeah, man. I dropped him."

"Dropped him? You stabbed him? You killed him?"

"I stabbed him. I guess I killed him."

"What did you do with the knife?"

"I think I just left it there. Don't remember. Really."

OK. Got that one. Now for the other victim.

"And what about that black boy, Ti-Boy Davis?" I asked Danny.

"Honest to God, man. I swear I never saw him. When I left outta there, the white guy was on the ground. There wasn't nobody else. That's all I know."

Danny sat back in his chair. I think I saw relief on his face. Bottled up the way he had been for the past six months must have been tough to pull off. I'd pass his revelation on to Reg, and he'd have to deal with whether Danny came clean when he testified during the penalty phase. Right then, I thought for him to come clean with the jury was the best strategy, but I wasn't in charge any more. My mind focused on how the drug operation might lead me to find Medley.

"Back to the 'package' Snap picked up in Lafayette, Danny. Are you telling me you don't know what was in it?"

"Right, man. I didn't see inside."

"What did Snap do with it?"

"I don't know. When we got back, he disappeared for a while."

"OK. Back to the person who gave the package to Snap. Do you know anything about him?"

"No, man. I never saw him."

"Now think real hard, Danny. Have you ever heard of someone named Mario Louis or Maurice Louviere, anything that might get shortened to Ma-Loo? Anything close to that?"

"No." Danny gave a firm negative, but then raised his head with a quizzical expression. "Well, when I think about it, way back when, in the beginning, when I asked Snap to give me a place in the operation, I think he said he'd have to talk to Lou. That's the only time I heard the name Lou. Never heard the rest of them names."

I'd been standing over Danny for all this entire exchange. Now I sat down on the other side of the metal table. "Danny, for the first time I think I'm believing you. Think some more. Please. Can you remember anything, anything at all that Snap ever said about where he got the drugs."

"That's all there was, man. Honest."

"OK. Now think hard about that trip to Lafayette, or any trip you made there. Any thought about who might have been in that house where Snap got drugs? Maybe some other name or description? Anything?"

"Nothin', man. I never knew a thing about the guy or the place."

"How about when you made the phone call? Do you remember anything about the voice of the person you talked to?"

"Voice? A white man, I think. Kind of a hoarse voice. Maybe an accent. I don't know. All I heard him say was 'hello' and 'OK'. Can't tell much from that."

Danny knew very little. Snap was probably the only one who might have the players farther up the chain. If the District Attorney wanted that information, he'd have to arrange a deal for Snap. I stood up.

"Thank you, Danny." I meant it. "Dr. Hibou is coming back to town today and he'll be up to see you. It sure would be helpful if you could give him some cooperation. He can help you deal with all this shit. Really."

It was all I could do to keep an appreciative attitude in my voice. I really thought I could have done a much better job of his defense if he'd been straight with me from the beginning. Let go, I told myself. Don't say or do anything unless it helps find Medley. Except for one thing. The mother.

"Danny, I hear you've been refusing to let your Mom

visit."

"Yeah. That story she told in court pissed me off."

"Story? You don't believe she told you the truth about your real father?"

"I guess she did. Yeah, I guess my Daddy was some *nigger*."

"Danny, don't start that again. "

I'd done what I could on this subject, but I planned to tip off Dr. Hibou that he needed to do a lot more work on self-worth.

"I'm going to call your Mom and ask her to try again. We've turned a corner here, and you two have a bit of catching up to do. Like about ten years of conversations you two should have been having all along."

When I got back to the Lafayette S.O., Brett and Marcus were both still on hand, waiting until Theresa got off duty and called in from the UMC. I told them my conversation with Danny had been helpful for his trial defense but really contributed nothing to our knowledge about the drug operation. The only bit of information I picked up was that maybe Ma-Loo had an accent. Snap was the one who might know more.

When the call came in from Theresa, they put her on speaker.

"Guys, the boy will pull through," she reported. "That's the good news. And we found out why no one could get much out of his mumblings for the past two days. He speaks English well enough when he's rational, but English isn't his first language, and definitely not the language of his delirium. Name: HaNome Dinga. An African immigrant. And he has a story. When he was about eight years old he walked for five days from his burned-out home in Ethiopia, across the border, to a refugee camp in Kenya. The only identification he ever had was a scrap of paper from the Red Cross that gave the date of his appearance at the camp. HaNome was none too clear on how he first got into the United States except that he and another kid came in on an airplane. That's right, a lost boy. Not a *lost boy of the Sudan*, but a lost boy from Ethiopia.

"A year ago, a man he calls Ma-Loo found him and the other kid and offered them a home, food, and a job—an attractive offer for undocumented aliens living with fifteen other illegals in a walk-up tenement on the North side of Houston. Ma-Loo brought this kid to Lafayette; the other boy went away with some church people and HaNome has no idea where he is now. For the past eight months, HaNome did whatever Ma-Loo wanted him to do. He followed his boss' orders to tell no one where he lived, what he did, or for whom he did it. Off the grid."

We were standing around a metal table, eyes fixed on the instrument that carried Theresa's voice.

"HaNome didn't want to talk about what happened to him on that dark night less than a week ago. To persuade him, we made a promise we're not at all sure we can keep. We told him we would see to it he wouldn't be deported."

I saw Marcus raise his eyebrows to Brett, and Brett roll his eyes in response. To pull off that kind of help, they'd need the feds.

"HaNome opened up. Here's his story. Ma-Loo dropped him off at the projects, telling him to wait right on that spot for a man on a bicycle. He was to give the man a package and get a fat envelope in return. The task was a routine assignment for HaNome; he'd followed the same instructions a dozen times before. This night he stood in the dark for over an hour, and no one came. Then someone came up behind him, put a knife in his gut and vanished.

"Who stabbed him? HaNome had no idea. Of one thing HaNome was absolutely certain— Ma-Loo would never do such a thing. Ma-Loo had saved him, been the father HaNome never had."

Cynicism twisted Marcus' face at that last statement.

Theresa said she cranked up her motherly routine and

HaNome 'remembered' a little more. The person who came up behind him smelled like cigarettes and had a heavy wheeze. She asked the boy if Ma-Loo smoked. He said yes, but lots of people do. HaNome repeated his opinion that Ma-Loo wouldn't harm him, not for anything. Poor shmuck.

When Teresa finished her report, Marcus took my arm and led me out of earshot of his crew.

"John, I've talked to Tony about a deal for Snap. He's positive about it, but he has to talk to the big DA. Right now they're in deep discussions about what to do with the trial. It may be this afternoon before we get an answer."

"We need it bad, Marcus."

"Yeah, I know. I'm hard on it."

Late in the morning, I had a welcome visitor. Emile Petain.

"What can I do for you, my buddy?" he asked. The word *buddy* jogged my brain. Buddy. And Gram. I couldn't put off telling her about Medley's disappearance any longer.

I made the call I dreaded—to Gram to tell her that Medley was missing. Gram insisted she was going to come on over to Louisiana to take care of Buddy. Dr. Petain grabbed the phone from my hand and introduced himself to Gram. He put his hand on the instrument and told me now he knew how he could help. Speaking to her, he said, "Ma'am, I'm going to come to Magnolia and pick you up."

Gram agreed. I almost cried. Three hours there and three hours back was more than I wanted to be away from ground zero, but I couldn't make that old lady take a two-day bus ride by herself. Now she could have Buddy in her arms before dark.

The day was endless. The shifts changed but the pattern remained the same. Calls came in, but no one had any good news. A grim calm settled over the squad room. What had been a bustling beehive went into slow motion. The officers kept at their tasks more quietly now. Outside, deputies drank coffee and tended the boats on trailers. A couple of officers clustered around the High Sheriff's Humvee, speaking softly. Periodically, the dogs in the K-9 unit patrolled the lot, and relieved themselves in the grass. The movement of the deputies just served to remind me they were poised and prepared for a dire assignment— which scared me shitless. Medley had been missing now for twenty-four hours.

From what I knew of the search for a missing person, if you don't catch a break in the first twelve hours of a disappearance, the chances of a quick resolution nosedive. After twenty-four hours, settle in for a long haul. After thirty-six hours, brace yourself for bad news.

Early afternoon Marcus had two visitors—agents from the FBI and the DEA. I wasn't included in their conversation, but when they left two hours later, Marcus was smiling. He handed me a newspaper.

"They brought me *The Baton Rouge Advocate*, Acadiana edition. There's a short article about all this on the front page of the second section. You can see we've gotten the word out."

The missing person report about Medley, and an APB for a tall white male, twenty to thirty years old, fell well below the fold. Much more prominent, the half above the fold featured a large color picture of cattle being loaded onto an AeroMexico airplane at the old Navy base in New Iberia. 'Local Cattle Mexico Bound,' read the caption.

"The FBI is onto something, John. I sent them to see Mr. Strait. They're with us on making an offer of a deal to Snap Diggers. There's a chance we'll be able to get higher up the distribution network after all."

And I had another visit from Tony. Of course, I wanted to know what he had done about the trial.

"Penalty phase continued. Jury dismissed," Tony reported. "We'll convene another jury for the penalty at another time."

"You think you can do that? Break it in two?"

"Happens every time an appeal court reverses the sentence. Makes for a long penalty phase since these jurors haven't heard the story, it but can be done."

"Hell, I don't know. Let's go outside and take another walk around the church." We did, and found a bench.

Tony was pensive. "John, I've been talking to Mr. Strait about getting out of capital prosecution."

"Really?"

"I've come to the conclusion that asking for the death penalty is just not worth the cost in time, money, and the wear and tear on our guts it takes to get a conviction. And we can hardly say the process is even. The outcome is ultimately determined by an incredible collision of circumstances. If we prosecutors do succeed, there's a ten to twenty year post-conviction process before anyone ever gets close to the actual penalty. We keep two recent hires on our staff doing nothing but preparing and arguing responses to federal *habeas* motions. Defense talent comes from all over the world to the remaining death penalty states to think up arguments to spring these guys."

"You're just tired coming off this last trial, Tony. You'll recover your steam. And anyway, do you think your boss is going to be persuaded by your attitude? He wants to keep the prospect of a capital prosecution on the table to get defendants to plead guilty to a lesser charge."

"They're getting wise, man. Something that never happens isn't much of a threat."

"And politics keeps him in office. You think he's going to agree to give up the big show? In this state, the public still polls in favor of the penalty—not that they're willing to be part of the jury when we call them to serve on one. Actually, my thoughts are going in the other direction. Your attitude changes when it's your person who is the victim. We've got some really bad dudes out there, and they don't belong on this earth with decent people. If that guy does anything to Medley, I'd be more than happy to see him strapped on the table."

Tony picked up on my fear. He looked me in the eye. "That guy followed Medley for six months and did nothing. I don't know what kind of weirdo he is, but I don't see violence in the picture. I think he's got her stashed somewhere. John, I'm confident Medley's going to be fine."

"Thanks, pal. Right now, I need that."

THE HANGAR

"Saddle up, John. We've got a lead."

I jumped from my chair. "What...?"

"From Acadiana Regional Airport. Iberia S.O. got a 911 call about a strange noise coming from inside a supposed-to-be-empty hangar. We're on our way. I'll tell you more on the way."

In five minutes we were in a unit, blue lights flashing, siren screaming, Sunday morning church traffic parting before us. Brett turned around in the passenger seat to pass on to me what he was picking up on the radio from Iberia S.O.

"Dispatch had her wits about her this morning. While the deputy on duty tried to locate the airport manager to get a key to the hangar door, she called St. Mary S.O. and reported the suspicious circumstances. They passed the word to us in Lafayette. The Dixie Flyboys, a group of private plane owners who meet at the airport every Sunday morning to drink coffee, reminisce about when they had been flyers in the service, check out the weather, and, if favorable, take to the air in private planes for a spin over the area, sighted a scrap of cloth hanging out of a broken skylight in one of the hangars nobody uses much anymore —not since the U.S. Navy turned the facility over to the parish at the end of the cold war. A pile of junk lay scattered out on the tarmac below the skylight. The Dixie Flyboys went to investigate. Getting close, they heard a faint noise from inside the hangar, banging maybe. They tried to get inside, but the sliding door wouldn't budge. Did a voice answer their calls? They weren't sure. A weak response, if there was one."

My breath came in shallow pants. I could feel sweat down my back. My rational mind tried to tell me Medley couldn't be stuck in an airport hangar, but reason couldn't compete with the exhilaration of hope. We turned off Highway 90 at Coteau and bounced over a couple of two-lane blacktop roads through the cane fields until we came to the entrance of the Acadiana Regional Airport.

"We don't have a key, Brett? How are we going to get into a hangar?"

"Look behind you. We've got the force."

I could see a vehicle following way too close for comfort, half eighteen-wheeler, half tank, with LAFAYETTE SHERIFF'S MOBILE COMMAND emblazoned inside-out on the front. If we had made a sudden stop, that behemoth would've creamed us good. But then I knew we wouldn't stop for anything. The deputy at the wheel of our unit could have driven the Indy 500.

We hardly slowed to turn onto the tarmac. I saw a collection of cars in front of the control tower and about a dozen men around a large metal hut to the right.

"That looks like the hangar. Pull up there," Brett commanded our driver. Mobile Command followed behind us. Two burly Lafayette deputies wearing combat boots jumped down from the vehicle and yelled at the cluster of civilians gathered around the front. "Clear the area, clear the area."

The deputies waved our unit to a position twenty feet back from the hangar door. I jumped out and ran to the deputies, who ordered me to stand back.

First they attacked the door with crowbars.

"Hurry up, dammit!" I screamed.

"I hear someone," one of the deputies said to another. Brett had to physically restrain me.

"What is that noise? Is that a rooster crowing?" another

asked.

The crowbars weren't doing the job. "Go for it!" Brett ordered.

The deputies pulled a hook and chain from Mobile Command and fixed it onto the hangar door, waived the big vehicle into position, and activated a motor that could have pulled an anchor from the ocean floor. With a grinding shriek, the door pulled from its hinges and smashed to the ground.

Brett and I ran inside together. Medley lay on the hangar floor, not a foot from the track of the door. Naked, bloody. She raised her head and stared. Alive! I fell down and took her face in my hands.

"Are you OK? Medley, are you OK?"

"Mostly." The word creaked from a raw, hoarse throat.

Brett brought a blanket from Mobile Command, covered her, and was on the radio calling for an ambulance.

I cradled Medley in my arms. "Can I hold you? Is anything broken?"

"Hold me. Hold me."

We were both crying.

And she was mumbling something I finally made out. "Stop! Stop! Save the rooster!"

"What? The rooster?"

What the hell was she talking about? I saw one of the deputies had picked up some kind of big cage with a rooster inside and was about to fling it into the back of his unit.

Medley struggled to sit up, and fell back. "Save him!" she cried with the last of her strength, and passed out. I called to the deputy to put the cage down.

Brett took in the scene and helped. "Maybe it's evidence, or something. We'll be careful with the bird, for whatever reason. Tell her that."

She couldn't hear me.

I rode in the ambulance to the hospital, Brett in the unit right behind. The doctor in the emergency room let me stay with Medley for a few minutes. She was awake now, but didn't want to talk, just wanted to hold my hand. He asked me to leave and pulled the curtains closed for his examination. Nurses came in and out; a lab tech left with vials and packages. Brett sat down at my side.

"I'm posting security, John, and of course I want to talk to her as soon as possible. We figure her assailant, probably that Ma-Loo guy, got off with the cattle shipment, but the operation is still ongoing somewhere around here. Marcus is with DEA right now."

"Cattle shipment? DEA?" I asked. "Drugs? What the hell is going on?"

"Yeah. Cocaine. So what's the surprise about that? Isn't it always? We'll fill you in soon but right now just worry about Medley. We have the rest of this under control."

The doctor poked his head out now and then—telling me good news. No permanent physical injuries, he reported. Hunger, dehydration, exhaustion.

"What about the blood?" I asked. My voice cracked.

"Just contusions. She banged up her hands pretty good trying to budge the metal door. She twisted her ankle, but the x-ray shows no break." Then he put on his 'giving-the-family-bad news' face. "I can tell you she's been through an ordeal."

What the hell did that mean? My mind raced to the possible horrors.

"Can I see her?"

"We're setting up IVs and have a little more to do to clean her up. We need a few more minutes. I'll probably give her a mild sedative so she can get some rest. She's whipped down. Long conversations will have to wait until this afternoon or evening, but you can be at her side. She's asking for you and for someone named Buddy."

"Buddy's her little boy. I can get him here in a half hour

whenever you say it's OK." I would take Emile Petain up on his offer to help where he could.

"Probably best to let her rest first, and look a bit more presentable." He turned to Brett. "Officer, interrogation must wait."

* * *

I sat with Medley while she slept away the afternoon. Emile Petain brought Buddy and Gram for a visit around five. God, she was glad to see them. Brett and Marcus checked in, taking a break from processing evidence from the hangar, and they wanted to talk to Medley as soon as possible. Finally, around seven, after she'd given them some information in bits and pieces, they set up to take a formal statement. From the top.

"I don't know where he came from, maybe out of one of the lab rooms, but he just appeared in the hospital hallway and grabbed my arm. He pulled me out some door to where he had parked, pushed me into the passenger seat of the truck and locked the door."

"And it was Ma-Loo?" Brett asked.

"Yeah. Tattoos and all."

"The green truck?"

"Right. The one I'd been seeing. He told me to shut up and sit still. The shutting up part was easy; I couldn't have choked out a single word. But sitting still? Not possible. I grabbed the door handle to steady my shakes. He screamed at me to get my hand off the door, said if I tried to jump out he'd just let me go. I'd mash into the concrete, and he'd go back and get Buddy instead. He said he needed one of us to get safe conduct out of the country. He preferred me, he said. A kid was just as good for a shield, but he'd enjoy my company." She shuddered. "He grinned at me with those crooked teeth and reached across the seat, brushing my chest. I got a good look at that nest of snakes under his shirt cuff."

"Could you see where you were being taken?"

"I don't know the area around here. At first I was just stunned, disoriented, but when I pulled myself together we were on a four-lane highway. We drove about a half hour. My guess is we were going south. We turned off, and after a bit I saw a sign that said *Acadiana Regional Airport.* I'd never been there before. We turned onto a broad concrete area at the end of which sat a wide-bodied airplane. A ramp led from the ground up to the belly of the plane. On the ground, next to the ramp, a dozen men scurried around a bunch of cows being offloaded from a livestock trailer pulled up alongside. He turned his truck away from the activity at the rear of the strip and headed toward a large Quonset hut on the left, drove through a wide-open sliding door in the building and stopped his truck inside. As soon as he cut the motor, I heard a tremendous din of cackling coming from stacks and stacks of metal cages. Inside each separate cage, a single rooster strutted, scratched, and squawked. Stenciled on a board at the end of each cage, BAYOU BIRDS."

I interrupted. "Brett, that's Senator St. Germain's business."

"Right. Lots to tell you about that, John. This whole thing is St. Germain's operation. But let's stick with Medley for now." He turned back to her. "When you got inside the hangar—that's what that Quonset hut was used for when we had an airbase—what happened?"

"He dragged me out of the truck and frog-marched me across to an interior door on the other side of the building. He opened the door, shoved me through, slammed it and turned a key in the lock. It was dark in there. 'Shut up and be still,' he said through the door. Again. He must have told me that a dozen times. When my eyes got used to the darkness, I figured out I was probably in an office, with a desk, a chair, and cardboard boxes stacked against the wall, some shelves on the side. There was a phone but no dial tone, and the light switch I found didn't work. No electricity, I guess. There was a bathroom off one end. The plumbing worked." She paused.

"You're doing great, Medley." I squeezed her hand.

She smiled.

"After a while I heard voices in the main part of the building. I called out for help—the hell with orders to keep quiet. No one answered. I picked out his voice giving commands in Spanish, recognized a word or two, but not enough to know what was going on. *Vacas, adios, si, si.* Now that I think about it, he had a bit of a Spanish, or Mexican, accent. Then I heard someone say in clear English, 'The cattle are all stowed aboard. The product is off the plane and outside ready for pick up, but we'd better get it inside. There's a mother of a storm brewing out there.' Scraping noises became louder.

"After more time passed, the cackling of the roosters died down. Was that good news or bad? I had no idea."

Her voice was faint now. Brett leaned forward to hear better.

"He came back. Just him, not the rest of them."

"You're still talking about the one called Ma-Loo, right?" Brett asked.

I had noticed that Medley didn't use his name. Unspeakable.

"Yes."

"And then?" Brett prodded.

"He unlocked the office door, grabbed my arm, and dragged me back into the big area where he'd left his truck. And. . ."

Medley closed her eyes and swallowed hard. She squeezed my hand.

Brett spoke softly. "I'm really sorry to have to ask you to tell us, Medley, but he's committed crimes. I need to know what they are."

I held my breath until she answered Brett.

"He didn't rape me," she whispered. "But..."

I held her hand tighter.

"You were naked when we found you. How did you lose your clothes?" Brett asked.

"He took them off me. Tore them off, really. But this time I got them back after..."

"After what?"

Medley squeezed her eyes shut and didn't speak.

Brett looked in my direction and circled his hand to indicate she needed to keep talking. I leaned over the bed and put my head on her chest, my arms on either side of her face.

"Medley, just keep your eyes closed and pretend there's no one here. Tell us what he did to you."

She whispered her response. "He felt me everywhere. Then he masturbated and ejaculated all over me."

She opened her eyes for a moment. I didn't realize I was crying until I felt the gentle touch of her lips kissing tears from my face.

"And then?" Brett's voice was very soft, calming.

"He threw my clothes back at me and locked me in the office. I heard the truck start up and the hanger door open and then close."

Medley reached toward the Styrofoam tumbler on the side table. I held it for her to sip from the straw.

"It must have been late at night then. Out in the big room, the roosters in those cages quieted down. I got used to the dark in the office and tried hard to figure some way to get out of there. The only opening in that room was the door to the big area. Not even a window in the bathroom part. I looked for tools to try to take the door off its hinges. I tried hitting it with anything I could find. And of course I did plenty of screaming."

Brett tried for a little humor. "I guess you put your clothes back on."

"Yeah, I missed a step. You bet." Medley smiled in appreciation of the break.

"Did you sleep?" Brett asked.

"Maybe, some. I don't know. I did pull apart some of the cardboard boxes and try to make a clean pallet to lie on. But when it was dead quiet, I kept hearing scratching that sounded like rats."

I gave her another hug.

"I found a couple of MREs in a drawer in the desk. Maybe they used the place for the National Guard. At least I wouldn't starve to death—not today anyway.

"In what was probably morning, he came back. I say it was morning because the roosters were crowing again. No truck this time." She closed her eyes. "He did it again."

"Masturbated and ejaculated on you?" Brett asked.

"Yes. And again. And again later." She paused. "The last time he didn't give me back my clothes. He tore them into shreds and stuffed them in a little satchel he had. He locked me in the office again, and I heard some more voices. I screamed at them to get me out, but no one answered. From the sounds I figured they were moving out the rooster cages. 'Leave that one,' I heard him say. That's the rooster cage I didn't want you to get rid of. I wanted you to see the sign on the cage, and anyway, that rooster kept me company for another whole day, and night."

"We have him. Marcus took him home to his father; he keeps birds. Then what?"

"During the day I'd seen light coming through cracks around the sliding door and through a skylight up high in the office, so after he left this time, and I heard what was probably the airplane taking off, I thought maybe he was gone for good. I couldn't be sure. He'd said something about 'my Mexican vacation.' But I felt better. As bad as this might be, I told myself, I would live. At least for a while. Many times I hadn't thought that. Gram always said life itself is a blessing."

"That's my girl," I said.

"He hadn't locked me in the office this time but left me in the big room. I worked on the sliding door but got nowhere. I went into the office and tried to figure out how I could get up to the skylight. I was mad at myself when I realized I'd torn up cardboard boxes for a 'bed', but I found some more cartons stacked in the corner. I had the idea to build a pyramid to freedom. I pulled the office desk over and placed it underneath the skylight and went to work. I put together a construction tall enough to reach the skylight and strong enough to hold my weight. Then I took the metal tool I'd used to work on the door, climbed up to the skylight one more time and broke out the plastic. I stuck my head out, but that was all—the opening was too small for me to get through. Cut myself up trying. I held onto the ledge below the skylight, dropped my head, and wept. And then I fell coming down and twisted my ankle." She gave a sardonic smile. "Kind of the last straw."

She spoke more smoothly now. Maybe the worst part was over, I thought.

"On to Plan B. If I couldn't get out of the hole, maybe I could get something else out of it, so I went scavenging for more supplies. I found stuff. Up and down the construction I went, my ankle killing me now, dragging up anything I thought would fit through the opening. I found a couple of pieces of wood, some more cardboard trash, pulled drawers out of the desk, relieved the office shelves of a dead flashlight and coil of rope. I found a rag on one of the shelves, a tin of some kind of grease, wrote HELP on the cloth, and hung it outside the skylight. Maybe someone would notice the flag and a pile of junk that hadn't been out there on the ground before—if, of course, anybody came by on the weekend.

"Every few hours, day and night, I got out of the office and banged on the metal door. Surely someone would come near this building and hear the noise, I thought. My pal, the rooster, helped all he could. When I banged, he woke up and crowed. Poor fellow, he had a lot of crap in his cage by now, but I just couldn't deal with that. I gave him more water in an empty MRE tin. His food was getting low;

I hoped it wouldn't run out. I was getting fond of the bird. Remember that Tom Hanks movie when he had no one and started to talk to a soccer ball? Or was it a coconut?"

Medley had some spirit back.

"And then I heard the commotion of y'all at the door." She clutched my hand. "There you were."

EASTER SUNDAY

Medley raised her chin to savor the sweet scents of Louisiana spring. Sweet olive fragrance wafted through the air. The night before we had had a short rain, and now resurrection fern stood erect on the branches over her head. Azaleas had exploded in color along the sides of the yard. I had worked hard taming the backyard, trying to impose order and symmetry—which of course nature abhors—on ten years of tropical growth. Her appreciation of my work warmed my heart.

From her perch on a lawn chair on the patio at the back of my house, Medley watched me checking out the preparations for our Easter guests. The dark smudges beneath her eyes had vanished, but the glow on her cheeks had yet to reappear. She seemed quieter, occasionally staring at some far-off object I didn't see.

"I'm so glad you cleaned the backyard first, John. Who cares about what the world can see out front? I love it back here. This is Eden."

"Eden? Not! Every time I hear that lesson from Genesis I think Adam and Eve were fortunate they didn't have to cope with South Louisiana critters and crops. Longfellow called it a forest primeval, and that's more like it. If Eden had been in south Louisiana, that first couple would have quickly put on clothes and shoes without waiting to taste the apple."

Medley smiled. That's all. I continued.

"I've tamed most of the area back here, but I still have a lot of work to do around the edges. Poison ivy and a few slithering fellows in the underbrush wonder why someone is disturbing the paradise they've had to themselves for twenty years. At least the mosquitoes are still in winter sleep."

I made a mental note to ask Gram to keep a close eye on Buddy that afternoon. The little rascal now got into everything.

I swung two sacks of crawfish onto a metal table and set out a butane tank near a boiling pot. Easter Sunday is high season for a mudbug boil. I opened another yard chair and sat down at Medley's side, close.

"Feeling OK?" I asked.

"Of course. I wish you'd let me help you with all this."

"Don't you dare lift a finger. It's only been a week..."

"I'm fine." Medley snapped.

No, she wasn't fine.

"There's really nothing for you to do. Kaniesha and Possum had the idea and they're in full charge of the preparations. Kaniesha saw to the invitations. Possum set out a barrel of ice for drinks and put up those tables and chairs. They'll both be here early to meet the guests."

"I should fix something for Gram to call Sunday dinner. She has a way to go to get used to eating crawfish. Me too, actually."

I took her hand in mine. "Don't you go fixing anything. There'll be no shortage of dishes you can eat. Everyone is bringing something."

"So people are bringing more food?"

"You bet. Food and drink. No chicken, however. We don't want that rooster over there to get nervous we might put him in a pot!"

She leaned across the little space between us and kissed me. "I think the real danger he faces is taking him back to Marcus's father's flock. I still can't believe Marcus's father fights roosters."

"Sure does. He even asked me if I wanted him to help

me set up a *palenque* in the cane field over there beyond those azaleas."

"At least we wouldn't see the blood beyond the scarlet flowers!" Her hand snapped up to cover her mouth. "I can't believe I said that."

She laughed. The lovely rippling sound I had been waiting a week to hear bubbled up and danced out into the air. My Medley was on the mend.

"I hear Tony and his wife signed on for a couple salads, Brett and that Lafayette girlfriend will be sure we have beer, and Emile says he made bread pudding—a treat you haven't enjoyed as yet. He makes it with Lejeune's French bread. Marcus will be sure his brood has hot dogs and whatever else children enjoy, and that's just the beginning. Stay in a comfortable spot and prepare to have a feast and watch everyone celebrate your safety."

"I can't celebrate that Ma-Loo got away, and I bet Marcus can't either."

"No, I'm sure not. But what bothers Marcus the most is thinking he put Snap-Dog back on the street for nothing. He'd persuaded the DA to spring Snap from Angola to have him blow the whistle on Ma-Loo, and Ma-Loo blew it on himself. But Marcus, bless him, was willing to swallow a pig to find and free you, Medley, and I'll be forever grateful."

Medley was quiet. I could tell she had something on her mind. I understood her well enough now to know I didn't need to ask what was bothering her. She'd tell me when she was ready. And she did.

"What did you think of Father Cooper's homily this morning, John?"

"I liked it. His message is always about God's love, with a few references to scholarly writing that makes me think and some humorous stories to make me laugh. How about you? Do you like him?"

"I do." She chose her words carefully. "Maybe I could

make a separate appointment to talk to him, unless you'd be OK with me bringing up theological stuff at our pre-marriage sessions."

Anxiety pricked my heart, and a shadow passed over the sun at the very same moment.

"What's troubling you?" I asked.

"That business about atonement."

"Atonement? Like Jesus atoning for our sins?"

"Yes. Father Cooper had a lot to say about that this morning, how we didn't need to be anxious and feel guilty because all that has been done for us. As he talked, I couldn't stop thinking about what happened to me."

Where was she going with this? Was this the 'why do bad things happen to good people' question? It couldn't be that she thought she was somehow at fault for what happened to her. Preposterous, but I'd heard that rape victims sometimes feel that way. I kept my counsel and waited for her to talk it through—if she wanted.

"Before last weekend, I'd been feeling pretty guilty about messing up my life by marrying Jack. Maybe I wasn't really worthy of the blessings coming to me. Buddy, you, another lease on life. But when I lay there on that cold floor, damn close to madness, I got to thinking I was getting my just desserts. Maybe God was..."

Wow!

"No, Medley. There's no way you deserved that ordeal."

"I'm trying to understand. I liked what Father Cooper was saying, kind of felt a weight coming off my shoulders."

I grabbed on to that thought. "What he said made you feel better?"

"Yes."

Relief. Relief because she was saying she felt better and relief because we had someone who could probably do a lot better job of helping her than I could.

"Both, Medley."

"Both, what?"

"Your question was whether you should talk to Father Cooper alone or with me. I say both. You're working through some intensely personal stuff. For that, you need a one-on-one with our priest; at least I think he's *our* priest. But how we both feel about our prior marriages needs to be part of our joint session as well. How about that for a plan?"

She smiled and nodded her head. "That will be my plan. I'll call Father Cooper in the morning."

What I didn't tell her was that I'd been talking to Father Cooper about my own problem—making sure I was done with guilt about what happened to my Mom. Just this afternoon I thought about some special planting of chi-chi camellias up on the Pecan Street corner, right where she died. If I could do that...

An hour later a dozen cars stacked up in the extension of Pecan Street and the back yard buzzed with the conversation of our friends. And music. Brett's girlfriend played the accordion!

I managed to corner Brett to ask some questions.

"Maybe you shouldn't talk about it yet, but if you can, I'd like to know what happened with Senator St. Germain? Did you nail him?"

"You bet we did. The Feds took him into custody on Wednesday afternoon. I don't know the extent of the evidence they have, but right after you left in the ambulance with Medley, an armada of black four-wheel-drive vehicles with FBI stenciled on the side doors descended on the hangar. A dozen agents unloaded equipment for a full-scale CSI study. Remember the agent who came by Lafayette S.O. with the Baton Rouge newspaper—the copy with the picture of cattle being loaded up at the airport? He was front and center in the group. The Feds found trace evidence aplenty in the hangar. We were damn lucky the threatened storm caused Ma-Loo and his crew to move the 'product' inside. Along with Medley's statement, the Feds had enough p.c. for a search warrant of the senator's horse farm. His computer was a gold mine of incriminating data about his operation."

"Where's the senator now?"

"In the Lafayette jail. I understand tomorrow morning his lawyers will be trying for a bond reduction, but the Feds say they have that covered. St. Germain's definitely a flight risk."

"Feds? So he won't be in our court?"

"That's right. You won't have him to defend."

That made me laugh. "You think he'd have a simple PDO handle his defense? Not even for a traffic ticket. I can't wait to see who does represent him for heavy drug charges. Someone will make some big bucks."

Marcus drifted over when he saw us talking. No black T-shirt today, no handcuffs hanging from his belt. He had on his Sunday shirt and slacks. He came with his cute young wife and three little blond boys, the youngest one about the age of Buddy. So Marcus had been a blond when he had hair on his head. Brett gave him a high five.

"We did a good job, Marcus, but I'm sorry once again a big one got away."

Marcus shook his head with a correction. "Not really. Of course I regret we didn't get Ma-Loo after what happened to Medley, but the senator's the big catch here. He had the money and connections to run the operation. I thought I'd really screwed up springing Snap to get his testimony to give us Ma-Loo and then have Ma-Loo escape the country, but the DEA thinks we can use Snap's testimony in the case against the senator. Wouldn't it be great if that piece-of-shit Snap-Dog would be the one to nail the senator's ass in court?"

Brett gave Marcus another high five. "Sweet!"

I chimed in. "I think Possum would give away tickets for the show."

"The DEA is confident the senator will be put away for

a long time. But we do have other regrets. Even if we were able to tie the attack on HaNome to Ma-Loo's operation, the deaths of the boys in Lake Charles and Alexandria are hanging out there unsolved. We'll never know the truth about them, and I regret that."

Brett ran a hand over his face, the hand that wasn't holding a beer. "No, Marcus. Teresa hasn't given up digging into those cases. Ma-Loo couldn't have dreamed up all by himself the idea of using undocumented kids as couriers. Teresa thinks we have a signature *modus operandi*. From now on, anytime she picks up a report of the death of an unidentified kid, she'll dig into it like a dog after a bone until she figures out if the kid was a courier."

Right. After the next kid is dead. So sad. The undocumented are disposable.

"Hey, there's Theresa now."

But she didn't come over to us. When she heard the accordion, she and her husband began a two-step. They dipped and turned, all the while her husband wore his big white Geno Delafosse cowboy hat.

ADA Tony drifted my way, but hung back until he could corner me alone. He was alone also.

"Maria's not with you, Tony? I hope she's doing OK." I had heard Maria had another miscarriage.

"Just OK, John. This is a tough time for her."

"I'm sorry. Please give her my best." What's there to say at times like that?

"I will. I wanted to come this afternoon to tell you I had a long, sad conversation with Mrs. Duncan on Friday to tell her I would have to dismiss the charge against Danny for the murder of Jerome Davis. Ma-Loo was probably the killer of her nephew, but there was little chance we'd bring him to justice. We were now certain Danny Howard knew nothing about it."

"And you told Reg you were dropping the charge, I guess."

"Yes. We still have the death of Clyde Carline to deal with. Mr. Strait himself is going to have to work with the Carline family about that one. They're chastened after the senator's arrest, of course, and they know the death penalty is legally off the table, but they want a long sentence. I think eventually you and I can negotiate a plea."

"With Reg, Tony. Negotiate with Reg. You know I'm out of this case."

"Yeah, I know. Technically. But what about a deal for manslaughter with Judge Johnson to sentence?"

"No comment. But I haven't forgotten Danny Howard. I'm still working on counseling for him, and I'm seeing to it that Mr. and Mrs. Chastant visit often. They're talking about selling their house and relocating to some place where no one knows the story. Bill says he'll open a small business repairing cars. Maybe when Danny gets out— although that may be a while since there's reduced parole eligibility for crimes of violence—Danny can work with him. Danny could be out while he's still a young man. Several prisons have vocational programs through community colleges."

One of the last guests to arrive, Judge Mari Johnson came in singing "Amazing Grace," and wearing one very large pair of blue jeans.

"Hot political news, gang. District Attorney Gerald Strait is going to qualify for the legislative seat that will be vacated by the expected resignation of our esteemed public servant, Senator Robert McAdam St. Germain."

ACKNOWLEDGEMENTS

The author acknowledges with gratitude the counsel of Ann Dobie, Diane Moore, Vickie Sullivan, Stephanie Judice, and her more than daughter-in-law Margaret Simon, accomplished writers all, who patiently guided the development of the writing abilities of someone from another field. Without their encouragement, this work would have vanished long ago.

ABOUT THE AUTHOR

Anne L. Simon was born in the East, educated at Wellesley, Yale and Louisiana State University Law Schools, and moved to South Louisiana fifty years ago. She practiced law with her husband, raised a family, and became the first female judge in the area. Now retired, she travels, enjoys family near and far, takes long walks with her dog Petey, and writes stories based on experiences in her adopted home.

Made in the USA
San Bernardino, CA
30 March 2015